New Pleasures

Jessalyn awoke to find the delicate hint of freshly blooming heather in the air and a pair of pale yellow, pearl-encrusted slippers with matching patterns on the pillow beside her. She squeezed her eyes shut, then opened them again. The shoes and the bouquet of white heather remained. The heather was fresh. Droplets of dew still clung to the tiny blossoms. She reached out and caught one, transferring it to her lips where she tasted it with the tip of her tongue. The water was cool to the touch—as cool as the circlet of seed pearls decorating the top of her shoes. She traced a pattern of pearls on the nearest shoe with her finger, then repeated the procedure on the other one. This was no dream. The shoes and the pearls were real.

As was the pair of cream silk stockings draped across the top of the dresser and the silk petticoat lying across the reclining chair along with a matching corset. Both were daintily embroidered with seed pearls even smaller than those on the shoes. The dress was exquisite, but the shoes . . . Unable to resist the urge, Jessalyn slipped the shoes onto her feet. They fit perfectly.

Jessalyn blinked back tears. She was a highland laird. She knew there was no shame in going without fine clothes and shoes. But deep in her heart, she had always been ashamed of being seen with dirty feet. Somehow the English Earl of Derrowford had understood . . .

Prologue

The clan was done for. The MacInnes lay flat on his back, his massive hands folded over the hilt of his claymore. He was draped in his finest plaid, covered with boughs of holly and stretched out on the board in preparation for his journey to his final resting place in the kirkyard. The mournful wail of the outlawed pipes playing "MacAonghais's Lament" echoed through the cold mist of the glen, announcing the sad tidings. The old laird was dead and the Ancient Gentlemen of the Clan—Auld Tam, Alisdair and Dougal—staggered beneath his weight as they hoisted the board bearing the MacInnes's body off the funeral bier.

The once mighty Cian MacInnes's numbers had fallen so low there weren't enough warriors left to carry their laird to his final resting place. The MacInnes had left six sons and hundreds of kinsmen lying dead on the battlefield and now the warriors of Clan MacInnes (or Clan *MacAonghais* as the clan was known in Gaelic), the hereditary bowmen of the MacKinnon, were gone. Clan MacInnes's unswerving loyalty to their laird and his unswerving loyalty to the MacKinnon laird, and to Scotland's rightful king, had cost them dearly. There were now no husbands for the MacInnes women, no fathers for their children and no kinsmen left to marry and father more children. And the MacKinnon, who lay rotting in prison, could not come to the aid of his allies. There was no food in the glen that could be bought at any price and no Scottish guineas with which to buy it. And the herds of fine highland cattle had fallen victim to the Sassenach army or to the traitorous clans who had chosen to fight with the English. Clan MacInnes had been stripped bare of all its wealth and turned off all its land except the land surrounding Castle MacAonghais. The ancient castle, hereditary home of the MacInnes clan for as long as anyone could remember, was all that was left. A summer of rebellion had cost the clan everything.

One summer of rebellion and an endless autumn of retribution.

The remnants of the once powerful clan stood barefoot and shivering in the cold mist as the old men lifted the MacInnes onto their shoulders. Two boys who had not yet reached their tenth summers and one battle-scarred warrior who'd lived through fifty-two of them proudly drew themselves up to their full heights as they piped the traditional *coronach*, the funeral dirge for the dead. The pitiful procession followed. The old laird was being carried to the kirkyard and every one of his remaining clansmen and women knew that come spring, he'd have plenty of company. Unless someone did something drastic soon, future gatherings of the Clan MacInnes would be comprised of ghosts.

Chapter One

Fort Augustus
near Kilchumin, Scotland
1716

There was no doubt about it. He hated Scotland with every fiber of his being. Far from filling him with a sense of majesty and awe, the soft lavender and deep purple hues of twilight that sparkled off the deep shimmering Loch Ness and surrounded the glen for as far as the eye could see made Neil Claremont, the seventh earl of Derrowford, want to puke.

Major Lord Claremont, as Neil had come to be known since joining His Majesty's Royal Corps of Engineers, stood alone atop Fort Augustus's unfinished battlements as he had every evening during the past four months, watching as the sun sank below the hills and crags of the highlands. Neil used the spectacular Scottish gloaming as his personal barometer, a measurement of his ever-decreasing tolerance for the fresh air and sparkling mountain lochs and burns. And every evening his distaste for the wide-open moors and distant highlands grew stronger. He hated Loch Ness and the moors and glens surrounding it. He hated the gorse and the late-blooming heather covering the moors and the barely passable tracks and trails

that masqueraded as roads in this godforsaken country.
He despised the villages and the small thatch-roofed
crofters' huts dotting the landscape, but most of all Neil
Claremont despised the highlands and the clans that pop-
ulated those impenetrable hills. Those proud, savage highlanders and their stubborn refusal to bow to the will of
a stronger military force were the reason Neil spent his
evenings standing on the battlements of a fortress instead
of bent over his plans and drawings in the comfortable
study of his London townhouse.

"You make a fine target for highland savages, Major.
Standing up there in your pretty red uniform all alone
like that."

Neil turned from his vantage point on the wall and spotted Sergeant Marsden standing on the scaffolding below
him, well out of range of rocks and arrows or the occa-
sional firearms. Neil shrugged. The moors were treeless, the
view unobstructed for as far as the eye could see. "I think
I'm safe," Neil replied. "I don't see any highland savages.
At least not outside the walls." He glanced pointedly at the
barefooted laundresses and whores inside the fort, most of
whom were wearing some sort of drab-colored woven tartan that proclaimed their allegiance to their Highland clans.

Marsden grinned. "Surely you don't begrudge your
poor soldiers female companionship."

"Not at all," Neil told him. "Not as long as you pay
your female companions enough to keep them from slit-
ting our throats at night." There was no need to tell the
sergeant that even though he didn't partake of the bounty
the Scotswomen offered each night, he felt enough pity
for them and their desperate plight to drop a few guineas
in the washtubs for the women to find and claim whenever his tour of the wall-in-progress took him near the
laundry area.

"Ah, that ain't too hard, Major. Seeing as how all it
costs is some bread and ale. And at that rate, we can
save back enough from our daily rations to pay for two
or three whores a night."

Neil gritted his teeth as he cast another glance at the barefooted, tangle-haired, unwashed women roaming the compound. "Imagine what you could get with an entire loaf," he muttered.

Marsden grinned again. "You could buy the whole bloomin' lot of them for that much bread. Just like the Strand back home. But this . . ." The sergeant looked up at his commanding officer, then at the sky as he waved his arms as if to encompass the whole of Scotland. "This ain't a bit like London, is it, Major? Ain't never seen or breathed air as fresh as this in London. Not a dung heap or a tenement in sight."

"Unless you look behind you," Neil commented wryly, his attention focused on the dung heap and the open latrines at the rear of the compound. As proud as he was of Fort Augustus's construction, Neil was ever aware that the unfinished fortress could very easily be considered as much an insult and a blight on the pristine countryside as the uninvited soldiers garrisoned there. Although he appreciated the fact that he'd been appointed to General Wade's staff in order to assist in the building of roads and forts in the Scottish Highlands, Neil's interest was centered around the actual construction, not the motives for it. The inevitable subjugation of the clans that would result from his talent for building gave him no satisfaction. He was an architect and an engineer, not a soldier, and he hated the fact that his presence in Scotland meant that more men, women and children would suffer the ravages of insufferable pride and unbearable poverty. In many ways, Neil likened the highlanders, who scratched a living from barren, rocky soil much too poor to farm, to the mudlarks who scavenged salvageable articles from along the quayside and the bottom of the Thames at low tide. He despised the way the mudlarks were forced to eke out an existence from the city's refuse and the way they lived in unrelieved squalor and poverty. But unlike many of his wealthy, aristocratic counterparts, Neil refused to make sport of the unfortunate youngsters by running them down with his horses in order to relieve their earthly suffering. There was no honor in terrorizing and murdering or maiming the weak and destitute—for sport or for any other reason.

Wretched, unrelenting poverty. Scotland, like London, was full of it. Neil shuddered, unable to take his gaze off the women milling about the muddy parade ground. There was no escaping it. He took a deep breath and thought about London and the hundreds of drawings he had labored over. The plans he'd made for modernizing and improving the city. In London, Neil knew what to do, how to plan, where to begin. . . .

He expelled a breath in a frustrated sigh. London was a city. A city where segments of the population lived under wretched conditions. But here . . . Here nearly everyone outside Edinburgh went shoeless and starved. And because he had honored his grandfather's request and accepted a commission in the army, Neil was trapped in a place he didn't want to be. His duty to king and country and the current Highland rebellion prevented him from continuing his study of architecture with Sir Christopher Wren. The fact that he had been assigned to General Wade's staff and engaged in the massive construction of forts and roads which led into the interior of Scotland should have been enough to satisfy his need to build a better world, but Neil didn't want to build in a land he intended never to see again.

He wanted to rebuild his home. He wanted to rebuild London. He wanted to pursue his dream of creating a new London full of grand buildings and cathedrals to rival his mentor's. He wanted to build parks and squares and neat little rows of houses on small plots of land that would replace the filthy slums of the poor. Neil was very much aware that as long as he remained in Scotland, as long as he stood on the unfinished battlements of Fort Augustus, his wonderful plans for a newer and better London would continue to gather dust in the study of his townhouse.

He turned and gazed at the local women who went barefoot, and thought of the London dressmakers and the monthly allowance he spent to keep his mistress in silks and satins. Deborah constantly complained of having nothing to wear, while these Scotswomen who truly lacked suitable clothing wore their ragged plaids as if they were ermine.

Every time he looked at the women in the compound, Neil despaired of Deborah's future, despaired of returning to London in time to prevent her from finding another protector, or worse, of being forced out of her comfortable house and onto the streets. He'd tried to provide for her, leaving ample money with his solicitor to satisfy her every whim while he was stuck in the wilds of Caledonia, but Deborah understood little of finances. She had already gone through her late husband's fortune and Neil had to make sure that she didn't go through the part of his fortune he'd allotted to her upkeep. Deborah was a spendthrift accustomed to being petted and pampered, accustomed to having Neil spoil her. And should his solicitor be forced to tighten the purse strings to keep Deborah from overspending, Neil knew his mistress well enough to know she would be in the market for a more generous protector. And what if her new gentleman turned out to be abusive or as much of a spendthrift as she was? How could he protect her from that?

Stuck in Scotland and dependent on the judgment and honesty of his solicitor, how long would he be able to keep Deborah from finding herself in the same predicament these women were in? Deborah didn't realize it, but there was a world of difference between the life of a well-kept mistress and a desperate whore, and the difference was money. Money slipped through Deborah's soft, white, carefully manicured hands like water while her Scottish counterparts at Fort Augustus sold their bodies and their futures for bits of bread and ale—for the scraps left from the plates of their enemies. Even from this distance, Neil could see that several of the women were breeding his countrymen's bastards and that knowledge made him angry and sad. Soon there would be more mouths to feed for women who could barely feed themselves.

Neil raked his fingers through his hair in frustration. Sometimes it seemed the whole of Scotland had been created as an affront to his sensibilities. He turned and climbed down the scaffolding to join the sergeant in their nightly inspection of the construction site. Work on the outer wall was progressing at a rapid pace but one section contained a gap wide enough for a single column of men to slip through, while the section of wall behind the latrines remained low enough for men with rope or ladders to breach. Although there had been no sign of the enemy, Neil was uneasy with the situation. He didn't begrudge his men their female companionship or the poor women a way to earn a living, but neither did he trust them. Although he pitied them, Neil could not afford to let his guard down. He made it a habit not to mix with the local women and because he didn't, Neil couldn't be certain that the women inside the garrison were allies, or if the women who entered the fort each day were even the same ones allowed entrance the previous day or the day before that. They seemed amiable enough—mostly down-on-their-luck women intent on selling their wares to the only men around who were able to pay, but Neil knew that appearances were not always what they seemed. History was littered with the remains of forts that had fallen prey to treachery from within, but Neil couldn't convince his commanding officer, Major General Sir Charles Oliver, that prostitutes and laundresses were not stupid, nor were they deaf, dumb, or blind. Sir Charles had allowed the group of Scottish women free rein inside Fort Augustus and he refused to consider the fact that the group of them could pose a threat to the fort's security. But Neil knew better. The gap in the wall provided easy entry from the moor. And the highlanders were desperate.

Instead of continuing his ruthless pursuit of the high-land clans, instead of building forts to aid in the destruction and suppression of the clans and their chiefs, King George should have ended the rebellion by bartering peace. The Old Pretender's army and their supporters had been crushed, their food stores depleted, their crops burned and the livestock slaughtered. The clans were already starving and winter was still several months away. There was no point in pursuing the highlanders, of running them to ground, of destroying them. Not when George could buy the loyalty of the whole of the Scottish highlands with a few wagons of bread and cheese and ale.

"What do you think, sir?" Marsden asked as Neil completed his inspection. "Sir?"

Caught woolgathering, Neil glanced at the sergeant. "Pardon?"

"I asked what you thought, sir."

"I think this country is too bloody poor to be beautiful. I think I'm sick of watching starving women and children bartering their bodies for food."

The sergeant looked down at the ground and awkwardly shifted his weight from one foot to the other. "I meant about the wall, sir. I asked what you thought about the progress we're making on the wall."

"Oh, that." Neil flushed in embarrassment. "I think we should post two more sentries in the gap and add another two men to the patrol of the low wall."

Marsden groaned. "Tonight?"

"Of course tonight," Neil said.

"But, Major, tonight's the celebration."

"What celebration?"

"The celebration Sir Charles ordered to celebrate the completion of the outer wall."

"The outer wall isn't complete," Neil reminded the sergeant. "It has a gap in it measuring four feet across and we haven't received a shipment of stone from Edinburgh in over a fortnight."

"I know, sir, but Sir Charles scheduled the celebration weeks ago."

"But I told him we were slightly behind schedule." Neil ground his teeth together. "I reported the progress on the wall to him at the staff meeting this morning. He didn't mention a celebration. Bloody hell! The wall has a four-foot gap in it. That's no reason to celebrate."

"Don't matter none to Sir Charles whether the wall's finished or not. His schedule's what's important. What's on his schedule is what he reports to General Wade. And his schedule says the wall's finished."

"He lies to General Wade in his progress reports then orders a celebration for the men without informing me?" Neil was appalled.

Marsden nodded. "He ordered extra casks of wine and ale from Edinburgh weeks ago. It came on the last supply train and Sir Charles has had it hidden away in the storeroom ever since. He ordered that it not be touched until the celebration." Although he made a valiant effort, Sergeant Marsden couldn't keep from showing his excitement. "This will be a real party, sir. With food and drink and music. Sir Charles has invited everyone at Fort Augustus to attend and some of the women have even brought vats of mead."

Neil arched his eyebrow at the idea of Scotswomen so poor they bartered their bodies for food bringing vats of precious mead to an English celebration. "What about the sentries?"

"Won't be any sentries tonight."

"Christ!" The fine hairs on the back of Neil's neck stood up in alarm. "Hasn't that fool ever heard of the Trojan horse? Hasn't he read his classics? Doesn't he know to be wary of Greeks bearing gifts?"

Sergeant Marsden scratched his head. "That I can't answer, sir. I don't know if Sir Charles knows those Greeks or anything at all about that breed of horseflesh. I can't say that I've heard of them Trojans either."

"I'm not talking about real horses. I'm talking about a big wooden one with Greek soldiers hiding inside."

"Our sentries ain't reported sight of any soldiers. Greeks or otherwise."

Neil reached up and massaged the fine hairs on the back of his neck and the dull ache beneath them. "I meant the fabled ones, the ones in the stories . . ."

"What stories?"

"The Greek ones," Neil replied. "The classic Greek myths and legends that that fool Charles Oliver obviously knows nothing about. Of course he's never read the classics," Neil continued, talking more to himself than to the bewildered sergeant as he pictured the scrawny, pimpled youth his commanding officer had been during their school days. "Spotty Oliver could barely read English. He isn't bright enough to study the classics. He isn't bright enough to study at all. That's why his father bought him a commission in the army. The only thing Spotty's ever excelled in is drinking and fashion. He's a major general in His Majesty's army," Neil complained, "and the imbecile can barely sit a horse! He doesn't know anything about military strategy. He doesn't know enough about the army or warfare to keep the female enemy outside his garrison or when to keep male sentries posted on the inside but he knows how to order wine and ale and he knows how to throw a hell of a party." Neil ended his diatribe against his commanding officer and turned his attention back to the sergeant. "Is Sir Charles still conferring with the stone cutters from Edinburgh?"

"No, sir. Sir Charles dismissed the masons' guild over an hour ago."

"Good," Neil pronounced. "I need to talk to him immediately and it's best I do so while he's alone."

"That won't be possible, Major," Sergeant Marsden told him. "Sir Charles retired to his private quarters and left orders that he not be disturbed."

Neil cast a glance toward the officers' quarters, then over at the prostitutes roaming the garrison. Spotty Oliver enjoyed a reputation as a fastidious dresser and an inveterate snob. While the women inside Fort Augustus didn't appear to be his commanding officer's type, Neil realized that in time of war, even Spotty Oliver was forced to make a few adjustments in his level of personal comforts. He turned to Sergeant Marsden and arched an eyebrow in question.

Sergeant Marsden shook his head and grinned. "Not quite, sir. You see, General Oliver is conferring with his tailor."

"What?" Neil couldn't believe his ears.

"Last I saw him, sir, Sir Charles was trying on new uniforms for the celebration tonight."

Chapter Two

They kept staring at her. Those Gentlemen of the Clan who had once made up her father's privy council. At first she thought she was mistaken, thought that the events of the last few days had made her overly sensitive, but Jessalyn MacInnes could no longer dismiss the strange looks coming from the group of ancient warriors gathered together at one end of the great hall. There were three of them left—Auld Tam, Alisdair and Dougal. The same three who had struggled to hoist her father's body onto their shoulders earlier in the day. Jessalyn bit her bottom lip and wrinkled her brow as she stole another glance at them. They were definitely watching her. She couldn't blame them. Her father had been dead for over a day and all of her kin—especially the ancient warriors—had a right to know what to expect from their new laird. Auld Tam, Alisdair and Dougal had fought alongside her father. She was a woman. The Gentlemen of the Clan probably thought she was too young, too inexperienced, too *female* to be the MacInnes. And in her heart, she secretly agreed with them. She didn't begin to know how to be the MacInnes.

Jessalyn pulled her threadbare shawl around her shoulders, straightened her spine, and tugged discreetly at her skirt, hoping to magically lengthen it enough to cover her bare feet. Not that there was anything disgraceful about bare feet. Every woman and child in the clan was barefooted because there weren't any shoes, nor a cobbler or a store of leather with which to make them. Her father had spent the last of his guineas on boots and weapons and victuals in preparation for the battle with the Sassenachs. And the leather that hadn't been used for boots and targes had been confiscated by German George's troops when they raided the village. As the daughter of the MacInnes, Jessalyn had willingly sacrificed shoes for her own feet so that her clansmen could be properly outfitted for battle. She didn't mind going barefooted, but she was the MacInnes now and she didn't think it seemly for the chieftain of Clan MacInnes to shiver with cold. Her father had never shivered. And neither would she. Concentrating on the task, Jessalyn wrinkled her brow and bit her bottom lip in a monumental effort to keep her toes from curling against the stinging cold seeping up through the stone floor. There was no room in her life for womanly weaknesses now. She couldn't weep and wail like her kinswomen. She couldn't tear at her hair and cry until her eyes were red and swollen and her throat was raw from her tears. She couldn't mourn her father the way she longed to do. She had to be strong. She had to become what her people thought she was. She had to prove herself worthy of the honor and the responsibility she'd inherited. She had to become the MacInnes. And in order to do that, she had to do what generations of new lairds had done upon the death of the old lairds. She had to put aside her grief and in a show of strength and continuity, call a meeting of the clan council and formulate a plan for survival.

Jessalyn rose from her seat and prepared to leave.

Andrew MacCurran, the MacInnes clan's storyteller, paused in the middle of recounting one of the auld laird's grand and victorious battles against the Campbells and

stared at Jessalyn. "Have I upset you, milady? Or dis-
pleased you in any way with the retelling of this tale?"

The members of the clan who had gathered around
the fireplace to listen to Andrew's stories turned to look
at her and Jessalyn remembered that standing in the midst
of a story had been her father's way of showing his disappointment in or displeasure with the tale. "No," she
hastened to reassure Andrew. "I was just going to retrieve my small writing desk from the solar. Please continue the story. I'll be right back."

But Andrew couldn't continue his tale. He cast a covert
glance toward the Ancient Gentlemen of the Clan. If the
laird left the room she might unwittingly learn of the
plans everyone had gone out of their way to keep secret.
If Lady Jessalyn left, her kinswomen would follow and
if anyone slipped and spoke out of turn, then Andrew
would have failed in the mission the Ancients had given
him—that of keeping Lady Jessalyn distracted. But Lady
Jessalyn was unaware of his problem, and in order to
keep her that way, Andrew pointed to his eight-year-old
granddaughter, Hannah, and said, "go fetch our laird's
small writing desk from the women's solar."

Jessalyn stared at the nub on the end of Andrew's arm
as he pointed to Hannah. Although his other wounds had
healed, Andrew was forever reminded of the losses Clan
MacInnes had suffered in the last rebellion. He had lost
his right hand trying to protect Harry, his firstborn son,
from a Sassenach sword. The loss was threefold. His son
had died on the battlefield and been buried clasping his
father's hand to his breast. Hannah had lost her father
and Ellen, her husband and Andrew MacCurran, the master swordsman, who had spent his life crafting claymores,
forging them from iron and steel and wielding them
against the enemy, had taken the place of the bard killed
in battle and now earned his keep as storyteller.

"Before the end of the story?" Hannah groaned. "Why
can't Jessie go get it herself?"

Hannah's mother, Ellen, gasped. "Because Lady Jes-

salyn is our new laird, that's why. And it's not for the
laird to run and fetch for herself when there are plenty
of others here to do it for her."

"The story . . ." Hannah insisted.

"Go," Ellen hissed. "Do as you're told."

Hannah wrinkled her forehead and glanced over at
Jessalyn instead. "But Grandpa is telling us a story about
how the auld laird saved us. And everyone says that
Jessie . . ."

"Wheesht, child!" Ellen interrupted, ordering her
daughter to be quiet.

But it was as if the lid on Pandora's box had been
knocked ajar. The thought was out and it hung over the
men and women gathered around the fireplace like a nox-
ious odor.

"What has you so troubled, little one? What is it everyone says?" Jessalyn knelt in front of the little girl and
smoothed away the worry lines on Hannah's forehead.

"Lady Jessalyn, she's just a bairn. She doesn't
know . . ." Hannah's mother began.

Jessalyn glanced over at Ellen. "I disagree. I think she
dares to tell the truth because she hasn't learned to dis-
semble yet." She turned to the little girl. "Now, Hannah,
please don't be afraid to tell me what everyone is saying about me."

"They're saying that our clan's in trouble and now
that the auld laird is dead, you must learn how to take
his place."

"That's true." Jessalyn nodded.

"Well, if you're the new laird, it seems to me that
you should not want to write letters, but should want to
stay and listen to Grandpa's story."

"And why is that?" Jessalyn bit her bottom lip to keep
from showing her amusement.

"Because it's important and Grandpa hasn't finished."
Hannah reached out and grabbed hold of Jessie's hand,
squeezing it hard. "Because you're the new laird and you
must listen and learn. Don't you want to hear the story's

end? Don't you want to find out how the auld laird managed to save our clan?"

That was exactly what she wanted to know. "Yes,"
Jessalyn told her. "Very much. That's why I was going
to get my writing desk. I thought I would make notes
while your grandpa spoke and write down a grand plan
to restore Clan MacInnes to its former greatness."

Hannah grinned. "Then if Grandpa won't mind waiting a minute or two, I'll run fetch your writing desk."

An hour or so later, with Jessalyn safely occupied with
the copying of her plan of action some distance away,
Auld Tam, Alisdair and Dougal huddled together near the
door leading out to the old bailey and formulated a plan
of their own.

"The lass dinna look so well," Auld Tam announced
without preliminaries to the others.

"She's takin' Callum's passing hard," Alisdair agreed.

Dougal nodded. "I'm afeard she willna bear up under
the weight."

Unable to stomach the blasphemy, Auld Tam thinned
his lips and narrowed his gaze at Dougal. "I said she
dinna look well, Dougal," Tam repeated. "I dinna say she
wouldna bear up. She's the MacInnes. She'll bear up or
die trying. I promise ye that."

"I know she's the MacInnes," Dougal said. "She's Callum MacInnes's daughter through and through. That's
what I'm afeard of," Dougal added. "Did ye not look at
her, mon? The lass is no bigger than a minute and as
pale as white heather."

Tam peeked over his shoulder and glanced at the lass
in question.

Bent over her writing desk, Jessie MacInnes sat surrounded by the women and children of the clan. She was
dressed in a black shift topped off by a *tonag*, a small
square of MacInnes tartan folded and worn as a shawl.
And although a small fire burned low in the massive
hearth, the damp smoky peat radiated little heat. Still,
Tam noticed Jessie had arranged the members of her

household so that the children and the infirm could take
advantage of the fire's meager warmth. He grinned, sucking air through the yawning gaps between his four remaining teeth, then reached under his bonnet and
scratched his balding pate. They had done the right thing
in accepting Jessalyn as the MacInnes. There was no
doubt about it. She was doing auld Callum proud by taking notice of the needs of her people and putting their
comforts before her own. But then, wee Jessie had always done her father proud, had always thought of her
clan first and herself last. Which was why he and Alisdair and Dougal conspired well out of her range of hearing.

The auld MacInnes had been loyal to a fault and his
loyalty to the Stewart cause had cost him dearly, but no
one could ever accuse Callum MacInnes of being a fool.
He had known what he was about when he chose to support the king across the water's rightful claim to the
throne of Scotland. He had recognized the English en-
croachment onto Scottish lands and understood the threat
to the highland way of life. Callum MacInnes hadn't
fought for James Stewart as much as for an autonomous
Scotland. And Callum had known from the beginning
that the chances of winning were slim. The auld laird
had watched his sons and kinsmen die on the battlefield
and knowing he had brought them to that end had filled
him with sadness and fired him with a greater determination to insure the survival of his line. And insuring the
survival of the line meant taking care of Jessalyn because she was the only one of his seven children left.

Now Callum was gone and it was up to the Ancient
Gentlemen of the Clan to look out for Jessalyn—even if
they had to do it in secret. It was their duty. The auld
MacInnes had ordered it from his deathbed.

"Then we're agreed," Alisdair said. "We'll do as the
auld laird commanded."

"Agreed." The three ancient warriors clasped hands.
"So, how do we go about it?"

Auld Tam straightened his bonnet, drew himself up to his full height, then silently edged his way out the door. Alisdair and Dougal followed close behind him. "We do what we've always done," he replied, once they were safely outside the castle. "We go a-raiding."

Dougal grinned, a sparkle twinkling in his one good eye. "And where are we going raiding?"

Auld Tam nearly cackled with glee as he announced his plans to his co-conspirators. "We're going around the loch and down the glen to the village of Kilchumin."

Alisdair wheezed in reaction. "The Sassenachs are building their fort at Kilchumin."

"Aye." Tam nodded. "What better place to find a healthy, handsome husband for our new laird?"

Alisdair snorted. "Any place other than Kilchumin. The whole of Scotland other than Kilchumin. Why, even an alliance with the Campbells would be better for us and for the lass than a match with one of German George's redcoats."

"I'll not be allying the lass with *Campbells*." Dougal spat the hated name. "I'll not send our innocent Jessie into that nest of traitorous vipers! Have you forgotten Glencoe?" It was no secret that the MacInnes had once been loyal to and under the protection of the powerful Campbells, but the massacre at Glencoe had split the clans and now Clan MacInnes and the Campbells were bitter foes. The MacKinnon had taken the disenfranchised MacInneses in and it was to him that they currently owed their allegiance.

"But you'll wed her and bed her to a Sassenach!" Alisdair protested. "At least the Campbells are highlanders. At least they're Scots."

"Bah!" Auld Tam exclaimed. "Traitorous murdering Scots are worse than the English. Scots who spit on their own honor, then kill their countrymen and side with the Sassenachs can never be trusted. The Campbells are allied with German George today, but tomorrow who knows . . ." Auld Tam shrugged his shoulders. "Better to take a Sassenach and turn him into a good highlander, than to try to make an alliance with the Campbells or their kind. Besides, it's what the auld laird wanted."

Alisdair shook his head. "I dinna hear Callum say such a thing!"

"Ye dinna hear it," Tam told him, "because that's the way the auld laird wanted it. He knew ye'd be against it and he dinna have the time or the breath to argue. He sent ye and Dougal to call the clan from hiding and to fetch the priest because the alliance had already been arranged, the abduction planned and the husband chosen."

"How long have ye known of this plan?" Alisdair demanded.

"The auld laird confided his wishes to me on the eve before he breathed his last," Tam explained. "Despite our loyalty to the 'king over the water,' Callum maintained contact with his allies—including his Whig allies—even while he was in hiding, even unto the eve of his death. Callum dinna trust our highland Whigs, but he trusted the marquess of Chisenden."

"The marquess of Chisenden?" Dougal breathed the name in a tone of what could only be described as reverence. Everyone in the highlands knew of the English king-maker's wealth and reputation. Although Chisenden was reputed to have little liking or respect for the lowland Scottish aristocrats, he had a surprising tolerance and regard for highlanders.

"Aye," Tam affirmed.

"Callum trusted Chisenden?"

"Aye," Tam repeated. "Because before he was the marquess of Chisenden, he was the earl of Derrowford and the earl of Derrowford was Callum's relation by marriage. Chisenden's first wife was the youngest sister of Callum's father."

Alisdair scratched his beard. "I'd forgotten."

"Well, our Helen Rose has been dead many long years now. I was a lad when she died and Callum was still a bairn." Tam said. "But the marquess of Chisenden was quite taken by our bonny lass. Loved her dearly he did and when she succumbed to the childbed sickness Chisenden was prostrate with grief. And when the bairn died . . . Well, the family wasn't sure Chisenden, or Derrowford, as he was known then, would survive his tragic loss. But he did survive and because he was a belted earl he was expected to do his duty once again. The marquess had no choice but to remarry and although I've heard the second marchioness is a fine woman, the marriage was arranged. There was no grand passion between them."

"Our kinswoman is dead. And the blood ties that bound us to her family by marriage died with her," Alisdair said. "So what does the English marquess of Chisenden have to do with our new laird?"

"Do ye not ken?" Dougal demanded his friend and companion. "The marquess of Chisenden is an important man at the English court. He's a Whig and a friend to the Hanoverian usurper. He'll make a right good ally and once we're allied with Chisenden, the forfeitures and retributions against the MacInneses will end."

"I know that," Alisdair commented sourly. "But I dinna hold with profiting from an alliance that means selling our wee Jessalyn into wedlock with an old Sassenach marquess."

"Not Chisenden," Auld Tam interrupted. "Chisenden is still married to his marchioness."

"Then who?" Alisdair asked.

"The grandson," Dougal replied. "The marquess of Chisenden has a grandson. A marriageable grandson and he's here in Scotland. At Kilchumin to be exact." Dougal couldn't keep the excitement out of his voice or the sparkle from his rheumy eyes.

Alisdair raised an eyebrow at Tam.

Tam acknowledged Alisdair's unspoken question with a brisk nod. "Aye. The new earl of Derrowford."

"The new earl of Derrowford? Why I heard that he's the one . . ."

"Aye," Auld Tam said, a hint of pride in his voice. "He's presently engaged in the construction of Fort Augustus and the fine wall going up around it. Word has it that our earl is a pure genius when it comes to building. He would have had the wall finished by now, if it wasna for the delayed shipment of stone out of Edinburgh." Tam scratched at the spot under his bonnet once again, then winked. " 'Tis fortunate we are that the stone dinna make it. A completed wall would have made our little raid much more difficult."

Alisdair snorted in disbelief. "What are we gonna do? Walk all the way to Kilchumin? Just the three of us? Afore we knock on the doors and beg polite admittance?"

"Bah!" Dougal spat in disgust. "We'll not be walking. We'll be riding."

"On what?" Alisdair had every right to be skeptical. Clan MacInnes hadn't owned a horse since the latest doomed Uprising.

"On those." Auld Tam pointed over Alisdair's left shoulder as the sound of muffled hooves penetrated the quiet outside the castle.

Alisdair and Dougal turned in unison and discovered Tam's two unmarried daughters, Magda and Flora, riding into view astride two shaggy ponies.

"Ye only brought two horses," Tam admonished, slapping his bonnet against his thigh in disgust. "Have ye forgotten everything I taught ye about raidin'? What's Alisdair going to ride?"

"We brought *six* horses," Magda announced. "In addition to the ones we're riding."

With the wind abruptly taken out of his sails, Auld Tam, along with Alisdair and Dougal, watched in amazement as she tugged on a rope and pulled three ponies, Munros from the look of them, into line behind her. "We've forgotten nothing, old man." She nodded toward her sister who also held a string of three ponies. "Alisdair can have his pick of these."

"Have any trouble?" Auld Tam asked, suddenly enormously pleased with his female progeny.

Magda shook her head as she removed a tartan woven in the Munro colors from around her shoulders. "With Munros? Och! I'd always heard the Munros paid more attention to their whisky than to their herds or to their women. Now, I know it's true."

"There's nothing wrong with men paying attention to their whisky," Alisdair said.

"Och! Indeed there is not when the men are paying more attention to the *making* of it than to the drinking of it!" Magda shuddered.

"No one waylaid us," Flora informed them. "Or questioned our right to be on Munro lands. We captured most of their herd."

Tam laughed and poked Dougal in the side with his elbow. "See, I told you we should strike the Munros instead of the Sutherlands! The Munros always lose livestock, while the earl of Sutherland is quite fierce in his stewardship of his lands and property." He turned his attention to his eldest daughter. "If ye managed to steal eight horses from the Munros without any trouble, what happened to the boy I sent along with ye?"

"He chose a pony for himself and is taking the roundabout way with the cattle," Flora replied.

"Cattle?" Dougal raised his brow.

"Aye," Magda pronounced. "A cow, a calf and a bullock. I sent Ian ahead with them, but he's taking the dangerous route and he'll be covering the tracks to keep the Munros from following—should they bestir themselves and decide to follow."

"Heaven help the lad if he's caught driving livestock through that corner of Sutherland land." Dougal quickly made the sign of the cross.

"He's a clever lad. He won't be caught," Magda said.

Alisdair rubbed his palms together in anticipation. "Then ye'll be roasting veal on the morrow."

Flora shook her head. "Nay."

"What do you mean nay?" Alisdair demanded.

"He's too young to put on a spit," Flora explained. "But we'll have milk and cream and butter to mix with our oatcakes. Besides, we'll be tending to our bridegrooms on the morrow."

"Bridegrooms?" Auld Tam glared meaningfully at his daughters. "Ye mean bridegroom. One bridegroom for our new laird."

"No," Magda corrected. "We mean bridegrooms. One for our laird, one for Flora and one for me. That's why we brought the extra horses."

"You expect us to stop and choose a couple of likely Sassenachs to be husbands to you while we're in the midst of slipping through the gap in the wall and spiriting away our Jessie's intended? Do ye take us for fools?" Alisdair shouted.

"I take ye for highland warriors," Magda retorted. "I was taught that one highlander was worth the whole of the Sassenach army. Our doomed Uprising notwithstanding, ye've another chance to prove it. Ye may be scrawny and ancient, but you're highlanders and there's three of ye. We've helped ye with the planning and the stealing of the horses and we've taken care of a few necessary and helpful details. So, while ye abduct Jessie's man, Flora and I will choose our own."

Auld Tam had to bite his tongue to keep from roaring in frustration. "That's enough nonsense. Get down off those horses and let us be on our way."

"No," Magda and Flora answered defiantly.

"We stole these ponies. They're ours. They'll not be heading off to Kilchumin without us." Magda gathered her pony's rein and nudged him in the ribs. She turned him toward Fort Augustus and urged him forward.

Tam reached out and quickly grabbed a fistful of mane belonging to the pony Flora was riding to keep his younger daughter from following her sister's lead. "These ponies belong to our new laird," he reminded his daughters. "I sent you to steal them for her so we could use them in this, our most important of missions."

"You mean your most *secret* of missions." Flora glared at her father. "I wonder what Jessalyn will have to say about you bringing her a bridegroom without her knowledge and while she's in mourning for her papa."

Auld Tam studied the hard-packed dirt at his feet before shifting his weight from one leg to the other. "I'm following the auld laird's command by serving his heir in the way that he saw fit. I don't see what Jessie could find wrong with that. And I know ye love Jessie too much to hurt her. Ye wouldn't dare run blathering to her."

"Yer right." Magda grinned. "We won't run blathering as long as we're with you." She smiled triumphantly at her sister, then turned to her father and waited patiently for his capitulation.

"We've no time for ye to choose husbands!" Tam protested. "You've got a full score and eight years and a full score and six years behind ye already and you've not taken the time to choose husbands."

"What was there to choose from?" Magda demanded. "Munros?"

"Our auld laird had six sons," Dougal replied.

"Aye," Alisdair agreed. "Five of them courted ye. What about Connor and Harry and Jamie and Allen and Charlie and Craig? They were all good men. Kinsmen."

"Aye they were. And they wanted to marry us, but they failed to do it afore they went to war and then they dinna come back. Besides, what does it matter who courted us?" Flora asked, tears shimmering in her soft brown eyes. "They're dead. Like all the other good young Scotsmen we might have married, like all our kinsmen."

"But the men in Kilchumin are *English*."

"So what?" Magda asked. "They're young and strong and breathing."

"And if a Sassenach is good enough to be husband

to the MacInnes, then two more will do quite nicely for us," Flora added with a stubborn tilt of her chin.

Auld Tam threw out his hands in exasperation. "All right," he announced. "But don't be saying I didn't warn ye. Two lowborn Sassenach soldiers aren't at all the same as an English earl who comes from a well-favored Whig family."

"We'll take our chances," Flora stated. "For we have no intentions of dying old maids."

Chapter Three

Neil lay on his back staring up at the rough wooden beams crisscrossing the ceiling of his quarters, loudly cursing his own smug arrogance and his ungoverned tongue. In a burst of furious energy, he rolled to his side and attempted to get to his feet, but found he couldn't. The iron manacles clamped on his wrists and anchored around the iron bedstead prevented it. He unbuttoned his red wool coat, shrugged it off his shoulders and managed to get it halfway down one arm, before he realized his coat wouldn't go over the manacles either. He was trussed up like a Christmas goose while the gap in the wall called his name. And he had no one to blame for his predicament but himself. He had deliberately baited Spotty Oliver, deliberately tested his commanding officer's authority, while the four-foot gap in the outer wall sang to him the way sirens sang to sailors at sea, luring them into uncharted territory. The need to resume his duties—to continue to patrol the wall he'd laboriously constructed—bit at him like fleas in a mattress but he'd been too angry to use logic to show that idiotic, overblown, pock-marked, preening fop of a commanding officer the error of his ways. And as a result, Neil now found himself chained to his bed like an animal.

He sighed, then let out a steady stream of vile curses. He should have handled things differently. He shouldn't have barged into his commanding officer's quarters like a bull in a china shop. He should have accepted Spotty's invitation to the celebration, then bowed out as quickly as possible and gone about the business of inspecting the wall as he did every evening with Sir Charles Oliver none the wiser. But he'd botched it because he'd never been able to suffer fools in silence—especially arrogant fools like Spotty Oliver—and he hadn't been able to keep his damned mouth shut or his unwelcome opinions to himself.

"Relax, old man, and indulge yourself," Spotty had said. "Celebrate the long and difficult completion of the fruit of your labor."

"The fruit of my labor isn't complete," Neil said through clenched teeth. "The outer wall is breachable, leaving the fort vulnerable to attack. I see no reason to draw attention to the fact by hosting a celebration."

"Nonsense. I've sent my report to General Wade and informed him that the outer wall has been completed." Spotty stared into a polished silver mirror as he fiddled with a length of gold braid attached to the shoulder of his uniform jacket. "Surely that's just cause to tap the kegs and celebrate."

"Your report was premature, Charles."

"Sir." Spotty corrected, nonchalantly straightening his gold braid and brushing invisible lint from the jacket's carefully tailored seams.

"What?"

"Sir. Your report was premature, *sir*. You may outrank me in society, Claremont, but here in His Majesty's army I am your superior officer."

"Derrowford," Neil told him. "In or out of His Majesty's army, I am the earl of Derrowford and you are merely Sir Charles Oliver. As long as I am in the army, you are, in fact, my commanding officer, but I must be honest and admit that I've yet to find you superior. A superior officer would understand that securing a contract for stone from the mason's guild in Edinburgh in order to overcome a delay in the construction schedule is more important than consulting with one's tailor. And a superior officer would know that having a four-foot gap in the outer wall of one of the first of His Majesty's Scottish perimeter forts is no bloody reason to celebrate!"

"You are insolent, sir!" Spotty's neck and ears turned a bright shade of red and his voice shook with barely suppressed rage. "And your insolence and insubordination compel me to punish you. You shall not attend the celebration or be allowed to consort with the men, have congress with the females, or partake of the libations."

Neil clamped his mouth shut to keep from grinning. If Spotty thought preventing him from attending a celebration he didn't want to attend was a just punishment for insubordination, Neil wasn't going to enlighten him. "Is that all?"

"Sir," Spotty practically spat the word.

Neil didn't bother to hide his contempt. "Is that all, *sir*?"

"No, that is not all." Spotty Oliver was hopping mad. "Derrowford, not only are you barred from attending the celebration, but you are confined to your quarters until further notice."

"I don't think so," Neil replied.

"What?"

"I refuse to be confined to my quarters while the outer perimeter of this fort goes unpatrolled and unprotected."

"You can't refuse. You will return to your quarters of your own volition or I'll have you shackled and escorted to the stockade," Oliver commanded.

"There is no stockade," Neil reminded him with a scornful look. "My orders were to construct the fortifications and to provide barracks and latrines for the troops. The stockade is further down on my list of priorities."

"I am commander of the post. Your job is to build it!" Spotty shouted.

"I'll start work on the stockade as soon as I complete the outer wall," Neil assured him. "And once it's finished you may confine me to it. Until then, I suggest you set me to the task of patrolling the wall."

"H-h-how dare you, sir?" Spotty sputtered. "Does your insolence know no bounds, Derrowford?"

Neil smiled. "Apparently not." He hadn't thought it was possible for Spotty Oliver to get angrier or to turn redder, but Neil soon realized he had been wrong. Major General Sir Charles Oliver was a fool, but he was a vain and powerful fool—the most dangerous of fools—and one who could only be pushed so far.

"Marsden! Stanhope! Guards!" Spotty bellowed. "Escort Major Claremont to his quarters at once and see that he stays there. Shackle him to his cot if necessary!"

It had been necessary. Neil didn't take confinement well—especially enforced confinement. He tossed and turned on his cot as far as the length of chain attached to his wrist would allow and listened to the familiar rumbling voices of Sergeant Marsden and Corporal Stanhope deep into their cups just outside the door to his quarters. All around him the barracks buzzed with the sounds of his fellow officers drinking and carousing. Neil strained to make out the details of Marsden and Stanhope's conversation and was stunned when their quiet debate abruptly ended.

The fine hairs on the back of his neck stood on end as the sound of two heavy dull thumps penetrated the walls of his quarters. "Sergeant! Corporal!" Neil shouted. "Are you there? What's happening to you? Are you all right?" He barely managed to get the questions out before the door to his room crashed open and swung back on its thick leather hinges.

"Nothing's happening to them, laddie. Nothing that a few hours' shut-eye won't fix."

"Who the devil are you?" Neil demanded as the big

ruddy-faced old man, wearing threadbare plaid, stepped through the doorway.

The highlander grinned, showing the dark gaps surrounding his remaining four teeth. "A few months ago, I would ha been yer fiercest enemy, but now, I guess ye can say I'm yer staunchest defender."

"How did you get in?" Neil had to ask, even though he already knew the answer.

"I came through the hole in the wall. Nice of ye to leave it open for us, yer lordship." He studied Neil for a moment, awaiting his reaction. "Ye are Neil Claremont, seventh earl of Derrowford, are ye not?"

"I am." Neil uttered a string of vicious curses and tugged at the shackles clamped around the leg of the iron cot. "What do you plan to do?"

The highlander moved further into the room. "First, I mean to free ye from yer bonds and then I mean to escort ye to a wedding."

"A wedding!" Neil scoffed, pulling harder on his chains. "I'm not going to a wedding."

"I beg to differ, yer lordship, because I'm here to see that you do."

"Who sent you?"

"That's neither here nor there," the highlander replied.

Neil shook his head then tried again. "All right, whose wedding am I attending?"

"Yours, yer lordship," the older man replied earnestly as he pulled a battle axe from beneath the folds of his plaid.

"You're mad!"

"Not at all, yer lordship." The old man stared down at Neil for a moment. "But I am in a bit of a hurry and although I hate to admit it, my aim isna what it once was. And since I'm quite sure you'll be needin' all yer limbs, maybe it's best ye don't watch." With that, the highlander raised the axe.

But Neil didn't heed the warning. He met the highlander's gaze, then watched the axe's rapid descent in a

determined effort to look his murderer in the eyes until
his last moment on earth. And he succeeded—right up
until the moment the old man turned the axe and tapped
him on the temple with the flat of it.

"Stubborn," the old man commented as he hacked
through the shackles on Neil's wrists. "Stubborn and
brave. I like that in amon."

Jessalyn noticed their absence right away. They'd whispered amongst themselves and cast glances her way all
evening and the moment her attention was diverted Auld
Tam, Dougal and Alisdair had stealthily crept out of the
keep. And it hadn't escaped her notice that Tam's two
daughters, Magda and Flora, and young Ian MacCurran
had been missing since her father's funeral either. The
kinsmen might be trying to keep secrets from her, but
Ian had been spotted heading toward Sutherland lands.
She might not have been able to hear what the Ancient
Gentlemen of the Clan were planning, but Jessalyn knew
it involved raiding one of their nearest neighbors. And
while Jessalyn didn't believe in stealing, she saw no
harm in relieving the Sutherlands of the livestock they'd
claimed after the Sassenach soldiers had scattered what
they hadn't slaughtered of the MacInnes's herds and
flocks. As far as Jessalyn was concerned, that wasn't
stealing, it was reclaiming. She didn't object to the raid,
she objected to being kept in ignorance and left behind.
She was laird of the clan and the laird didn't sit idly by
while her clan went raiding without her knowledge. And
as soon as Andrew finished his extremely long-winded
story, she meant to correct their oversight and follow
them.

She calculated the time that had passed since she'd
last seen Auld Tam and his two companions. They had
an hour's head start on her. Maybe more. But she could
catch up to them. They were older and slower. And she
knew a shortcut to the Sutherland border. Jessalyn shifted
uncomfortably in her chair, then caught Andrew's gaze

and deliberately set her writing desk aside. She spared him further embarrassment by remaining seated, but she sent Andrew a message just the same—one that brooked no argument. His gory descriptions of murder and mayhem visited upon rival clans by her father had long since shifted from the realm of fact into fantasy and beyond. The story had lasted long enough and now, it was time for him to acquiesce to his laird's wishes and bring the epic tale to an end.

Jessalyn cupped her hand around the flame to shield the candle from the drafts as she traveled swiftly through the maze of passages beneath the main floor of the keep. Like most old castles, Castle MacAonghais contained numerous hidden rooms and an elaborate network of corridors and stairs, some barred by iron doors known as *yetts*, designed to mislead and confuse the enemy. Most of the below-stairs passages led to the old dungeons, the cellars and the lower latrines. Others led to stone walls, but Jessalyn followed the one tunnel she knew led beyond the castle walls and directly onto Sutherland land. Her ancestor had had it built many years before so that he might meet and court the youngest Sutherland daughter and had later used the passage as a quick means of kidnapping her from her father's land and claiming her as his bride. The door leading to the corridor and the secret room off it were locked and only the lord and lady of the keep had keys. Jessalyn tugged two silver chains from beneath the bodice of her dress. A silver key dangled from each chain. She pulled the chains over her head and used the keys to unlock the two locks in the thick iron latticework of the *yett*. Gripping the keys in her fist, Jessalyn pushed the door open and slipped inside the corridor, carefully locking the door behind her. At the end of the corridor were two more locked doors, both made of thick, heavy oak. The one on the left led to the outside and the one on the right led into the Laird's Trysting

Room. Although the privy council knew of the passage's existence, no one outside the laird's immediate family was ever allowed entrance and no one outside the laird's immediate family knew which corridor led to it or where it ended. In times of peace, the Trysting Room was used as the laird's very private chamber; in times of war, it became a sanctuary from enemies and traitors. Jessalyn learned of the passage shortly after the death of her mother. Her father had handed over her mother's keys, pointing out the unusual silver key and the secret passageway and the room hidden behind its locked door. He hadn't shown her the room, nor had she asked to see it. Her father's grief had been too raw, the memories too dear and the Laird's Trysting Room too private a place to share. He had given her a key and shown her the way and that was enough. For years she'd worn the key on a silver chain around her neck. Now she wore two chains—one thick and one thin— and both keys. Her mother's and her father's.

Jessalyn unlocked the door on the left and stepped into the passageway that led to a cavern hidden in the hills separating her land from the Sutherland's. She was careful, once again, to lock the last door behind her before she replaced the keys around her neck, secreting them beneath the worn fabric of her bodice. She extinguished her candle and hid it in a niche carved high into the wall and made her way through the last passage and into the cave in the dark. The entrance to the cave was covered by a dense thicket that had kept it hidden from view for over a hundred years. Jessalyn traced the outline the keys made on the soft fabric of her dress. It seemed fitting somehow that the keys were together. She inherited one upon her mother's death and the other exactly seven years later. Seven years. Seven children. Her family was reunited now. Her parents and six brothers were together in death. She had been the only girl. The different one. The loner. The outsider. Now, she was the survivor. The only one left. She had gone from being the MacInnes's only daughter to being the MacInnes and tonight she must gain the respect of her clan by becoming the leader they needed. Auld Tam, Alisdair and Dougal had tried to protect her by organizing a raid against the rival Sutherland clan without her knowledge, but Jessalyn couldn't allow herself to be coddled and protected by the elders of her clan. She increased her pace, picking her way in the dark until she reached the mouth of the cave. She pushed her way through the brush and raced down the hills, across the cattle path and onto Sutherland land.

Jessalyn reached the Sutherland land in good time, but to her surprise, her small group of clansmen were nowhere to be found. She searched for some sign of the MacInnes Ancient Gentlemen, but there was none. Jessalyn had been so certain she knew where her kinsmen were heading, but she was mistaken. There was no doubt that the old men had taken it upon themselves to go raiding, but where? The Munros and the Sutherlands were the MacInnes's closest neighbors, but the MacInneses rarely raided the Munros, because the Munros didn't have much to raid. A few shaggy ponies that the MacInneses didn't bother to steal because they couldn't feed them. The only other thing of value that the Munros possessed was the recipe for and the ability to make the best whisky in the highlands. But as long as the Munros were willing to share their whisky with their neighbors, there was no reason to raid them and as far as Jessalyn could tell, the MacInnes men were amply supplied with Munro whisky. That left the Sutherland. Unless . . . Jessalyn glanced toward the southern horizon and caught a glimpse of shimmering waters where Loch Ness curved into MacInnes land. Around and just beyond that narrow strip of land lay Kilchumin. Jessalyn shook her head as if to dismiss the ridiculous notion. Impossible. Surely three old men on foot wouldn't chance it. But her kinsmen weren't where she expected them to be. Although

Jessalyn thought it more likely that her clansmen would go to drink with the Munros rather than raid them, Auld Tam, Dougal and Alisdair might have decided differently. The Munros were easy targets for experienced warriors, but the MacInnes Ancient Gentlemen were also old and tired. Perhaps, they no longer wanted or needed a challenge. Either way, she'd made a mistake. She'd been so convinced that her clan meant to raid the Sutherland that she'd forgotten all about the Munros.

If members of her clan had gone raiding the Munros, she would have to find and join them in the battle, but first she needed a horse. Casting her gaze toward the Mighty Sutherland's cavernous stable, Jessalyn realized she knew exactly where to find one.

A quarter of an hour later, she carefully guided her "borrowed" mount along a treacherous rock-strewn path commonly known as the dangerous route because the path skirted the Munro boundary, cut across a corner of the Sutherland's domain and led deep into MacInnes lands. In the old days, Clan MacInnes had posted armed lookouts all along the path to deter raiding neighbors and unwanted visitors, but now the route was left unguarded. The MacInneses had nothing left to steal and the Munros didn't bother to protect what they had. Only the Sutherlands were wealthy enough to raid and the Mighty Sutherland saw no need to guard a barely passable cattle trail that separated his lands from his neighbors. Which of his neighbors could summon the manpower or the courage to raid him?

Jessalyn heaved a deep sigh and bit her bottom lip. *She* had dared to raid the Sutherland of some of his finest horseflesh and perhaps her kinsmen had dared as well. She rounded the bend in the track and came face-to-face with another rider. Her breath seemed to catch in her throat and her heart began a frantic tattoo against her ribs until she recognized the horseman as one of her missing kinsmen.

Young Ian MacCurran sat astride a highland pony

bearing the Munro marks. He had one fist firmly anchored in the pony's mane and he kept the end of a length of sturdy rope wrapped around his other fist. Another length of rope was tethered around Ian's waist and tied at the end of the two ropes were a freshened milk cow and a young bullock. A calf stood, untethered, alongside the mother.

Young Ian's face whitened as he recognized her, then reddened in embarrassment with the knowledge that his new laird had overtaken him and caught him taking a pony, a bullock, a cow and a calf from Munro lands. He wasn't ashamed of taking the animals, but he was deeply ashamed of being caught at it. If his laird had been a Munro or a Sutherland, he'd be dead.

Jessalyn felt a rush of compassion for young Ian when she saw the chagrin on his face. She wanted to put her arms around him and reassure him. She wanted to show him how much she appreciated his courage, but she knew that doing so would cause him more humiliation. Ian would not want his laird treating him like a child. He had participated in a raid with the Ancient Gentlemen of the Clan and as far as the MacInneses were concerned, that made him a man. Jessalyn must therefore do her best to treat him like one.

She smiled at him as she reined her horse in close to his, then nodded at the cow and calf. "You've done well for yourself. Your father will be pleased. Now tell me where the others are and be on your way with these before the Munros discover they're gone."

Young Ian opened his mouth to reply, but no words came out.

"Ian MacCurran, your laird wants to know where her kinsmen have gone and you must answer." Jessalyn told him. "Are the gentlemen still raiding the Munro stock?"

Ian gave a quick shake of his head. "Auld Tam and the other gentlemen dinna raid the Munros."

Jessalyn raised her brow at that. "You're riding a Munro pony, driving Munro livestock."

Ian grinned suddenly, no longer a young warrior on the cusp of manhood, but a proud ten-year-old boy. "Magda, Flora and I raided the Munros," he announced. "We captured nine ponies, a cow, a calf and this fine young bull."

Magda and Flora had been her best friends from childhood. So they were in on the conspiracy as well. Jessalyn hid her surprise and her sense of betrayal. "Where are Magda and Flora?" she asked. "And where are the other ponies?"

"Magda and Flora rode ahead to deliver them to the Ancient Gentlemen."

Jessalyn frowned. "I came across Sutherland lands and I saw no sign of them."

"That's because they dinna go that way," Ian told her. "They went south."

Jessalyn turned toward the south and caught sight of a glimmer of moonlight dancing off the waters of Loch Ness. "But there's nothing south of here except the loch and Kilchumin." As soon as she said the name, she knew without a doubt where her kinsmen had gone. The English fort at Kilchumin. She turned to Young Ian for confirmation. "Tell me they didn't."

"Aye," Ian confirmed. "They did."

Jessalyn swallowed her horrified gasp and automatically tightened her grip on her mount. A deep foreboding and an undeniable sense of urgency filled her. Her kinfolk, three old men and two young women, were on their way to raid a British fortress. Jessalyn pointed her horse toward the south and nudged him forward. "Go back to Glenaonghais," she instructed Ian. "Take the livestock and go. Stay out of sight. I'm going after them."

"I'll go with ye."

"No," Jessalyn answered. "Go back to the village."

"Ye'll never catch 'em," Ian shouted as Jessalyn rode away.

"Maybe not," Jessalyn agreed beneath her breath as

she pushed her mount into a canter. "But I've got to try." She sighed. Her clansmen had obviously lost the good sense they once possessed. They were raiding the British once again and if she couldn't stop madness, the only thing left for her to do was to join them in it.

Chapter Four

She rode hard, covering the moor at a furious pace in her desperate attempt to overtake her kinsmen before they engaged the British in an act of supreme folly, but Jessalyn knew she'd never make it to Kilchumin in time. She glanced up at the sky. The moon had risen and the darkness that protected the raiders had receded.

"It's not much farther." Jessalyn sagged in the saddle and patted her tired horse on the neck, crooning encouragement, urging him forward. She gazed into the night, then blew out the breath she hadn't realized she was holding as she recognized the approaching raiding party silhouetted in the moonlight. The raid was over and her clansmen were returning. Jessalyn reined her horse to a halt, then closed her eyes and uttered a heartfelt prayer of thanks that her kin were safe—at least for the moment. She straightened in the saddle, tightened her grip on the reins and gritted her teeth, preparing herself to intervene if needed, bracing for the sight of scarlet uniforms and the inevitable sound of gunfire and the metallic clang of swords sparking off one another. But there was no sign of pursuit. Fort Augustus was quiet. Unusually so. The only sounds Jessalyn heard were the muffled sounds of mounted riders, the soft burr of Scotsmen in conversation and the throaty grunts and groans of weary travelers.

Weary travelers with captives. She couldn't believe her eyes at first, so Jessalyn stood in the irons and leaned forward to get a better look. She clenched her jaw and bit back a groan of her own. A rumor had been circulating since the end of the Uprising and the beginning of the construction of Fort Augustus that the British planned to imprison Jacobites at Fort Augustus. They hoped to set an example to the other clans by keeping highland lairds and chieftains incarcerated in a fort built on land that had once belonged to them. Jessalyn had heard her father and the Ancient Gentlemen rage at the arrogance and the injustice of it. Learning that Auld Tam, Dougal and Alisdair had planned and carried out a secret raid to free unfortunate highlanders held at Fort Augustus didn't surprise her. It infuriated her. Not that Jessalyn didn't feel compassion for her fellow highlanders, but she needed the Ancient Gentlemen. Clan MacInnes needed them. Now she understood. Auld Tam, Alisdair and Dougal had gone behind her back, planned and executed this secret raid because they knew she would never allow them to risk their lives in such a foolhardy adventure.

But there at the head of the raiding party was Auld Tam riding one pony and holding the reins of another who carried a blanket-wrapped bundle tied facedown across its back. Tam was followed closely by Alisdair, Magda, Dougal and Flora. While Alisdair and Dougal were empty-handed, the women were not. Magda and Flora each led ponies with blanket-wrapped bundles tied across their backs. Jessalyn's eyes hadn't deceived her. Her kinfolk had raided the British fort and rescued captive highland warriors.

Jessalyn sighed and rode forward to meet them.

Auld Tam moved ahead of his companions and reined his horse in close to hers as soon as he recognized the woman seated atop the big grey gelding as Jessalyn.

"Good evening, wee Jessie." Tam's spirits were soaring as he signaled his companions and waited for them to pull abreast of him. He doffed his bonnet. "I see ye got wind of our secret and sought us out."

"Aye." Jessalyn's one word answer was clipped and terse as she tried to hang onto her anger and lost. "We must talk."

"Not here, Jessie." Tam took one look at the anger etched on Jessalyn's face and feigned a worried glance over his shoulder. "We maun keep moving lest the Sassenachs give chase."

"Da, you know the Sassenachs won't . . ." Magda corrected.

"Wheesht, child!" Tam silenced her. "Our raid was successful, but that willna prevent the Sassenachs from giving chase. We willna be safe until we reach the village. Keep moving."

"But, Da!"

Jessalyn raised a skeptical eyebrow as she glanced from father to daughter and back again.

"Ye heard yer da," Dougal admonished. "Keep moving."

"Well, Jessie?" Tam asked, a hopeful note in his tone as he nudged his pony forward and waited for Jessalyn to do the same. "Do we cross swords now? Or will it keep?"

"It'll keep." She clipped out the words. "Until we get home." She turned her horse and followed as Tam led the rest of the raiding party across the moor toward the almost invisible cattle track that led to the village of Glenaonghais.

But it didn't keep for long. The raiding party had barely ridden into the old bailey of Castle MacAonghais as dawn broke before Jessalyn confronted Tam. The anger that had been simmering throughout the long night rose to the boiling point and Jessalyn paid little heed to the fact that the bailey was alive with the kinsmen and women beginning their work days. "Tam MacInnes!

Have you lost your mind? What have you done?" Jessalyn's mount shifted his weight and nervously pawed at the ground as she waved her arm to include Tam and his co-conspirators.

"The same thing you've been doing if your fine horseflesh is anything to go by," Tam replied.

"*I* did not raid an English fort," Jessalyn reminded him.

"Aye," Tam agreed. "You raided and made an enemy of the Sutherland."

Ignoring Tam's comment and the crowd gathering in the bailey to witness the confrontation between the laird and her ancient gentleman, Jessalyn focused her attention on the raiding party. Turning, she fixed her gaze on Tam's daughters. "Magda! Flora! I canna believe ye joined your father in this madness!"

"Twasn't madness, Jessie," Magda protested.

"The five of you raided an English fort to rescue men from other clans! Who've you got there? MacMillans? Gordons? Stewarts? Ye could have been killed!" Jessalyn's voice quivered with barely controlled anger and more than a little fright.

"We were safer than *you* were raiding the Sutherland," Flora replied, eyeing Jessalyn's mount. "We were in no danger."

"No danger?" Jessalyn glanced at the faces of Auld Tam, Dougal, Alisdair, Magda and Flora—her loved ones and her kin. All the kin she had left. She shuddered in reaction. "Of course there was danger. Fort Augustus is crawling with Sassenach soldiers. What if ye'd been captured? What if they had given chase? I could have lost ye."

"Ye dinna lose us," Flora said. "We're here, Jessie, safe and sound."

"But for how long?" Jessalyn demanded. "What if they're tracking us? What if they follow us back here?"

"They won't," Magda interrupted. "We did what we

set out to do. We slipped in and out of the fort with no one the wiser."

"Did ye take us fer fools, Jessie? We've been raidin' since before ye were born. We made a plan and we followed it," Auld Tam added, cackling with glee. "And we were victorious."

Jessalyn wrinkled her brow as she glared at Auld Tam. "How can you claim victory? I don't see any livestock or flour or oats. I don't see any sugar or molasses or Spanish blankets or carts filled with supplies."

"We got what we went after," Tam replied, smiling broadly as he glanced at the men slung over the backs of the ponies. "That's victory enough."

"Highland captives?" Jessalyn found it impossible to keep the note of disbelief out of her voice when it took every ounce of her control to keep from shouting. "You risked your necks to rescue highland lairds we canna feed? What did you plan to do? Keep them as hostages until their clansmen can ransom them?"

"Nay, lassie." Dougal jumped into the fray to defend Auld Tam and to try to smooth Jessie's ruffled feathers. "We dinna bring hostages. We brought *husbands.*"

"Husbands? Whose husbands?" Jessalyn demanded.

"Yours," Dougal replied.

Caught unawares by Dougal's matter-of-fact pronouncement, Jessalyn's breath seemed to leave in a rush. Her chest tightened as she reeled back in the saddle and nearly fell off her mount. "Mine?"

Auld Tam swung off his pony with a swiftness and dexterity that belied his size and his sixty years and rushed forward to catch Jessalyn before she lost her seat. He dropped the rope he held and reached up to help her dismount. "Easy, lass."

Jessalyn ignored his outstretched arms and slid to the ground without assistance. As her feet hit the turf, she regained her breath and her composure. She stood her ground and looked Auld Tam in the eyes. "I've no need of a husband." Jessalyn glanced over at the captives. "Much less three. Let them go."

Auld Tam shook his head. "I'm sorry, lass, but that I canna do."

"Even if your laird commands it?" Jessalyn asked.

"Even so." Tam shifted his weight from one leg to the other and stared down at his feet.

"You captured three men without my knowledge in the hope that I would wed one of them. But I cannot feed the mouths we've got. So, let them go, Tam. I dinna want a husband."

"We do," Magda interrupted. "Only one is for you, Jessie. The other two are for Flora and me. We didn't just capture a husband for you. We captured husbands for ourselves as well."

"Oh." Jessalyn knew she should be disappointed in her kinfolk, but when she looked at Magda and Flora, at the excitement and the hope gleaming in their eyes, she couldn't be disappointed in them. Jessalyn watched as the young women waited with bated breath to see what their new laird would do. She inhaled deeply, then looked Auld Tam in the eye and made her decision. "Since our highland tradition allows for abduction of a spouse, Magda and Flora can keep the men they chose as husbands if the men agree to wed. But, Tam, I want you to release the man you captured for me," Jessalyn ordered.

Tam reached under his bonnet and scratched his bald pate. "I've told ye before, that I canna do, wee Jessie."

"Why not?"

"Because I gave my oath to your father as he lay dying. I promised him I would see ye well wed and I maun keep my vow."

"I'm in mourning. My father's barely been laid to rest, Tam. There's plenty of time for me to acquire a suitable husband of my own choosing—at a later date. And you've plenty of years left. There's plenty of time for you to see me wed," Jessalyn insisted.

"Nay, lass," Tam said. "You dinna understand. I dinna

promise to live long enough to see you suitably wed. I promised Callum I would see you *immediately* wed to one particular mon. This mon." Tam reached for the rope he'd dropped earlier and pulled the pony forward. He unsheathed his dirk and sliced through the leather thong he'd used to secure the man's hands and feet, then flipped the blanket off the captive. "This mon is to be yer husband. Yer father arranged it."

She expected to see the plaid of a highland chieftain, but the first thing she noticed was the fact that he wore boots. Expensive, highly polished black leather boots. Jessalyn recoiled, automatically taking a step backward. Her father might as well have arranged her marriage to a wild kelpie because the next thing she noticed was the scarlet coat of the uniform of King George's troops.

"This man's a Sassenach. My father would never arrange this."

"Och, Jessie, he did. And, lass, ye know that that's the way of the world. Ye know it's the way alliances are made."

"That's not the way Callum MacInnes made alliances." Jessalyn shook her head in denial. "My father would never propose a marriage between his heir and his enemy—especially when that enemy is a common Sassenach soldier."

"Aye," Tam affirmed. "He would not. Under normal circumstances. But these are not normal circumstances, lass, and as laird of the clan, Callum did what he had to do to protect his heir and his kinfolk. He spent his last breath making the arrangements for yer wedding."

Although she wanted to continue to deny it, Jessalyn knew Auld Tam spoke the truth. She knew her father had breathed his last breath immediately after entrusting his favorite courier with a bundle of important papers. What she didn't understand was why he hadn't seen fit to entrust her to a fellow Scotsman—Highlander or lowlander. Jessalyn was sure that either would have been a better choice for her. "I would have been better off with someone from a neighboring clan. Why didn't he choose one of those?"

"From which of our neighbors would you have had him choose? From the clans who supported the cause and are starving and forfeit like ourselves? Or from the clans who turned traitor and rallied around the English king?" Tam demanded.

Jessalyn frowned.

"Now, you're thinking like a highland laird. Now you understand Callum's reasoning."

"Nay," Jessalyn protested. "I dinna understand why the Laird of Clan MacInnes chose a murdering Sassenach soldier over his fellow countrymen."

"Dinna fret so." Tam reached out and traced the frown lines on Jessalyn's forehead with the tip of his callused index finger. "Tisn't so hard to understand. Callum thought 'twas better to capture an honorable enemy and turn him into a loyal Scot than to wed his only daughter to a mon and a clan who might be worse off than ourselves or to send her into a nest of murdering, traitorous vipers." Tam winked at her. "Besides, this is no common Sassenach soldier." He took Jessalyn by the hand and led her around the head of the pony so she could get a look at her husband-to-be. "This is his lordship, Neil Claremont, the seventh earl of Derrowford, grandson of the marquess of Chisenden and a soldier in German George's Royal Engineers. He's the mon responsible for building the roads to Fort Augustus and the fort itself."

Jessalyn gasped. "Chisenden?" Everyone in Scotland knew of the power the marquess of Chisenden wielded. Jessalyn's voice and her expression mirrored her awe and her dismay as she stared in fascination at the earl and frantically pondered her next move. "We can't keep the marquess of Chisenden's grandson here. Chisenden is sure to want him back. We could ransom him, but to do that we'd have to send a ransom request to the marquess and the marquess might decide to attack us and recapture his grandson rather than part with his gold."

"Jessie," Tam interrupted. "There's no need to fret. I have the marriage documents." He patted his shirt front. "All properly signed and sealed by yer father and by yer betrothed."

"I'm not fretting about the marriage documents." Jessalyn lifted her gaze from the earl to Tam. "I'm fretting because we've got the marquess of Chisenden's grandson hanging upside down and trussed up like a fattened goose. We've got to release him." Jessalyn announced. "At once!"

"But, Jessie . . ."

"Now."

Tam shrugged his shoulders, then lifted the earl of Derrowford's feet and heaved him up and over the side of the pony. He didn't have far to fall, but Derrowford landed hard. Auld Tam winced as the earl hit the ground with a thud.

"Tam!"

"Ye wanted him released."

"Not like that!" Jessalyn hurried around to the other side of the pony and automatically dropped to her knees, carefully cradling the earl's head in her lap. She looked down and was awestruck by the sight of his masculine beauty. There was no other word to describe him. The seventh earl of Derrowford was a beautiful man. Even upside-down he had the face of an angel; a bruised and battered fallen angel, but an angel all the same. Jessalyn canted her head to one side and studied the earl's magnificent face scant inches from the pony's sharp hooves. Fresh blood oozed from a cut on his left cheekbone, trickled down his temple and into his thick dark hair.

Unable to curb the impulse, Jessalyn brushed her knuckles across his chin, noting the slight cleft in it and the prickly feel of whiskers in need of a shave. She reached out and gently swiped at the blood on his temple with the hem of her skirt, then looked up and pinned Tam with an accusing gaze. "He's bleeding."

Tam raised both hands in a sign of surrender. "Don't look at me like that, lass." He pointed to blood on the pony's belly. "He was bleedin' afore I heaved him off his horse."

"What did you do to him before you helped him to the ground?" she asked. "You must have done something. I canna believe a big, handsome man like him came willingly."

"He dinna." Auld Tam grinned. "He might have been chained to his cot like an animal, but he dinna cower in fear or shame when he saw me."

"Chained?" Jessalyn was outraged.

"Aye," Tam said, scratching his chin. "He defied his fool of a commanding officer and was chained to his bed for his trouble. He dinna come willingly, but I tapped him on the other side of his head." Tam pointed to the opposite side of the earl's forehead where a slight bump and a bruise had formed. "With the flat of my ax," he added hastily after seeing the look Jessalyn gave him. "I maun have left marks on his wrists when I cut him free, but I dinna raise blood on his braw face. I wanted him to look his best for ye." Auld Tam shrugged his shoulders. "A stone maun have bounced up and hit him during the journey, but he dinna cry out. Aye, I ken he'll make a fine Scotsman, lass. A worthy mate for the laird of Clan MacInnes."

Chapter Five

Neil opened his eyes and blinked. He stared up at the provocative underside of a pair of pouty pink lips so close to his that he could see their fine texture, almost taste their soft inviting warmth. His head was cradled in her lap and one side of his face was pressed against two firm breasts. He breathed in her scent, identifying it as an enticing mix of warm woman and wildflowers. He knew that if he moved slightly and turned his face in the other direction, he'd discover an even more enticing, more intimate scent of her. But he stayed where he was and watched, in mute fascination, as the rosy tip of a tongue slipped between those luscious pink lips and moistened them. His body tightened at the sight and he groaned in reaction. It wasn't the first time he had awakened to find himself in such a position, gazing at such a splendid sight and he fervently prayed it wouldn't be the last, but the insistent pounding in his head and the dull ache in his right shoulder left some room for doubt. He groaned again; this time in pain, and flinched as she brushed his hair off his brow. "No," he protested.

She ignored him and brushed at his forehead once again.

Neil squeezed his eyes shut, gritted his teeth and

sucked in a breath, then raised his arm to halt her less than tender ministrations. "No, Deborah. Stop! I'd like to oblige you, but I'm afraid this isn't the time."

She snatched her hand back as if he'd burned her.

Realizing he'd hurt her feelings, Neil reached up to catch hold of her wrist, missed, and tangled his fingers in her hair instead. He gently tugged at the silken strands entwined around his fingers, pulling her down closer to him until he brushed her mouth with his and discovered her lips were pressed firmly together. "Come on, love, don't be like that," he murmured seductively. "You know I find you endlessly desirable, my sweet, but my head is killing me! I seem to have had too much of whatever it was we were drinking last night." He managed a crooked smile, then licked at the seam of her lips.

She gave a startled gasp at the intimacy of that gesture and he took advantage of the opportunity and slipped his tongue inside her mouth.

Despite the painful pounding in his head and the sudden, insistent throbbing in his groin, Neil knew he'd made a mistake. She tasted of sweetness and innocence and although he used his tongue to tease and tantalize, to lead her through the intricate steps of the mating dance, she didn't follow his lead. She willingly accepted his kiss, but she didn't kiss back. She didn't know how. It was quite apparent that the woman he held in his arms had never had anyone kiss her the way he was kissing her. Neil ended the kiss, abruptly releasing her as he opened his fist and stared at the strands of hair curling around his fingers. They were a dark reddish color, not coppery red and not brown, but something in between. They certainly weren't blond and they didn't belong to his mistress. "Who are you?" he demanded, pushing back out of her lap so he could see the rest of her face. "Because you sure as hell aren't Deborah."

"Who's Deborah?" she countered in a soft, musical voice.

"My mistress."

His head hit the ground with another hard thump as the lady shoved him out of her lap and scrambled to her feet.

"Wheesht, lad!" The big burly highlander who had barged into his quarters stepped into Neil's line of vision and kicked him in the ankle. "Dinna be talkin' about your mistress in the presence of your lady wife."

"My what?" Neil jackknived into sitting position, then pushed himself to his feet.

"Yer lady wife," the highlander repeated. "Do ye not ken?"

"There's obviously been some mistake." Neil swayed on his feet, then shook his head as if to clear it, groaning slightly as the insistent hammering continued. "I have no lady wife. _I_ am not married."

"Of course yer not married—yet." The highlander chuckled at the notion, then shrugged his shoulders at the young woman standing by his side, tightly gripping her skirts in one fist. "I maun have tapped him a bit harder on the pate than I thought."

"You tap pretty hard, old man. I remember that. And I remember everything else." It was a lie. Neil remembered bits of the previous evening, but he seemed to be missing the most important parts of it. But, of course, there was no need to let the highlander to know that. "I remember _you_." He threw the old highlander a dirty look. "And there's no way I would ever forget _her_." He smiled at the girl.

She didn't return his smile. She turned away from him as a becoming blush colored her flawless cheekbones. She frowned at the highlander, then let go of her skirts. "He dinna know anything about this either. Did he, Tam? That's why you captured him," she accused.

"Nay, Jessie," Tam protested. "I told him I was there to bring him to his weddin' and I abducted him because that's the MacInnes way. We would have abducted him even if ye'd known him forever and even if he'd spent years courtin' ye and bringin' ye gifts and posies. It's tradition."

Neil impatiently raked his hand through his hair while the old man and the young woman exchanged words in their incomprehensible language, then froze as he caught sight of the blood on his fingers, the iron manacles encircling his wrists and the iron rings still dangling from them. His memory of the previous night returned in a rush. He stalked over to the old man and roared, "Where the *bloody hell* am I? What have you done with my men? And what do you intend to do with me?" He fired the questions at the old highlander but the girl he'd kissed so passionately stepped forward to answer him.

Jessalyn didn't flinch as the earl of Derrowford towered over her. She inhaled slowly, allowing him to express his anger and his concern over his men and his own future, before calmly confronting him. "You're deep in the highlands. In a village far removed from Fort Augustus." Jessalyn told herself that the small lie would protect her kin from the earl and his compatriots' wrath and offered a silent plea for forgiveness to the heavens. She ruthlessly dismissed the notion that she didn't want the earl of Derrowford to learn that the fort he was building and his mistress lay just a few hours away around the loch. Once she decided whether or not he could be trusted, she would tell him the truth. Until then, Jessalyn vowed to confess her sin at morning mass. "I do not know how many men you had in your command." Jessalyn placed her hand on his sleeve of his scarlet coat. "But my gentlemen have assured me that the raid on your fort was bloodless and that your men were unharmed."

"Where are they?" he demanded.

"Here, sir," Marsden answered. "And I think they've got Stanhope as well."

The muffled voice came from behind him. Neil turned toward the sound and discovered he was surrounded by highlanders. In addition to the old man and the young woman before him, two older men and two red-haired young women were seated atop shaggy, short-legged highland ponies. Each young woman led a pony with a tartan-wrapped bundle tied across the back. Thirty or so villagers, old men, women and children, barefooted and dressed in threadbare clothing formed a circle around them. Neil narrowed his gaze at the tartans that concealed his men, then faced the young woman before him. "Are those my men?"

"Yes."

"What do you plan to do with them?"

"I have no plans for them," Jessalyn answered truthfully. "But they've been chosen as husbands by two of my kinswomen. Magda and Flora," she indicated the two flame-haired women on the horses, "plan to wed them. If they have no other lawful wives. And if they agree to it. If they choose to stay, they'll be wed as soon as possible. If they choose not to wed, they'll be released on the moors. In the meantime, I give you my word that they'll be well cared for." She nodded toward her kinswomen as they nudged their ponies into action.

Neil watched as Magda and Flora led Marsden and Stanhope away, then turned his attention back to the woman before him. He stared at her lips, at the way her white teeth worried her perfectly shaped lower lip and wondered if the entrancing sparkle of moisture he saw on her lower lip was one he'd left behind when he'd kissed her. "What of me?" he demanded. "Do you have any plans for me?"

"I didn't," Jessalyn replied cryptically. "But I canna say the same for my father."

"What does *that* mean?"

"It means she plans to wed ye," Tam interrupted.

"I see," Neil replied in a deceptively calm voice. "And what gave you the right to plan my wedding? What gave you the right to kidnap me from my bed, haul me deep into the highlands and threaten me with marriage?" He pinned Jessalyn with his sharp gaze.

Refusing to be protected by Tam or intimidated by the condescension in the earl's voice or his penetrating stare, Jessalyn answered for herself. "You did."

Neil raised an eyebrow at that. She reminded him of someone, but he knew he'd never seen her before. For having seen her—and having kissed her, he knew beyond a doubt that he would never have forgotten. "Really? Pray, tell me how the devil *I* managed to do that since I've never laid eyes upon you before."

"You agreed to my father's arrangement. You signed the marriage papers."

"I don't know your father," Neil stated. "I didn't negotiate with him and I didn't agree to wed his daughter or sign marriage papers to that effect."

"Auld Tam says you did," Jessalyn informed him, nodding toward Tam.

Neil glared at the old man. "Pardon me for pointing out the obvious, but he's a kidnapper. I don't think I'll put much faith in what *he* says."

The highlanders gasped in one collective breath, then moved closer, surrounding him, closing the circle and Neil heard the deadly whisper of metal leaving leather as a half a dozen dirks were freed from their sheaths and pointed in his direction. Neil barely had time to register that fact before the young woman stepped between him and her knife-wielding clansmen. "If you were anyone but the earl of Derrowford, grandson of the marquess of Chisenden, and the husband my father chose for me, you'd be dead now," she warned him. "As it is, you'd do well to learn that if you call a highlander a liar, he has every right to cut out your tongue."

Neil placed his hands on her shoulders and gently moved her to the side. He stared at the villagers, challenging them. "Produce the proper marriage papers or cut out my tongue. But be done with it because I'm not a man who takes kindly to threats or who hides behind a woman's skirts."

"Wheesht!" Jessalyn hissed. "Are you daft? Don't you know better than to challenge them?"

"That's right, lad. Be careful how you tread," Dougal agreed, resting his hand on the hilt of his dagger, casting a wary glance at the warriors left in the clan, gauging their reaction.

Neil smiled, then leaned close to her. He smelled the flowery scent of her hair, saw the movement of the soft silky strands as his warm breath brushed her ear. "I don't think I have to worry about losing my tongue," he confided in a very audible whisper. "If I am, as you say, the man your father chose to be your husband, I'll have need of it. For repeating my vows before a priest and for other more enjoyable things."

Auld Tam laughed, breaking the tension. "Aye. Put away yer dirks. The lad is right. We'll not be relievin' him of his life or his tongue and he'll most certainly have need of both. The lad isna daft. He's verra crafty. Crafty as a fox and spoilin' fer a fight. He thinks he's been wronged and he thinks he can defeat a handful of old men, women and children. He's mistaken aboot that. But it doesna matter because I have the signed and sealed marriage papers right here. I can prove we've done him no injury." Tam pulled a folded sheet of vellum from inside his shirt and presented it to the earl.

Neil stared at the scarlet seal. The document had been carefully opened and the wax seal remained intact. His stomach tightened as he unfolded the document. He glanced at the date and quickly scanned the pages. The old highlander had spoken the truth. The marriage agreement Neil held in his hand was valid. He'd never met Callum MacInnes and knew he'd never negotiated with him, but the signature at the bottom of the last page of the document belonged to him. The seal that had made the impression in the wax was the crest of the earl of Derrowford and it hadn't been off his finger or out of his possession since he'd inherited the title.

"Do ye deny that the papers bear your seal and were signed by your hand?" Auld Tam asked.

Neil shook his head. "No. These documents do bear my seal and my signature." He looked at Tam. "It seems I owe you an apology for calling you a liar, old man."

"Aye," Tam agreed, knowing that those few curt words were the only apology the young earl intended to offer.

On hearing his apology, the villagers surrounding the earl sheathed their weapons and stepped back, allowing him more freedom. Jessalyn exhaled slowly, releasing the breath she hadn't realized she'd been holding. But her relief was premature.

"It seems I owe you an apology as well, Miss MacInnes." The earl's voice was rife with sarcasm. "I've come to you with nothing but the clothes on my back. Had I known that you have been my betrothed these past four months and that we were to be so abruptly wed, I would have come with ring in hand."

"Four months! That canna be! My father has only been dead two days." Jessalyn glimpsed the tightly controlled anger in his face and recognized the insulting tone of his voice when he spoke, but his anger paled in comparison to her shock at learning that her betrothal to this English lord had not been arranged while her father lay on his deathbed, but a full four months earlier. Callum MacInnes had bargained her to his enemies just a few months after returning from defeat on the battlefield. He had kept the secret until he lay dying and had deliberately bound Auld Tam, Dougal, and Alisdair with a deathbed promise to carry out his plan by abducting the groom.

Neil thrust the parchment under her nose and pointed to the first page. "Can you read?"

"Of course," she snapped.

"Check the date," he demanded, raking her from head to toe with his cold stare. "I don't think the fact that I was charged with constructing Fort Augustus and betrothed to a highland minx at the same time is a bloody coincidence! Do you? We've been betrothed from the moment I arrived in this godforsaken country. And according to this," his voice vibrated with anger as he turned his attention back to the marriage contract, "we're to be married as soon as I set foot on MacInnes land."

She turned to Tam for confirmation.

"Aye, lass." Tam waved his hand and sent one of the children scurrying into the castle. "Father Moray is expecting ye in the chapel."

Jessalyn took a deep breath. "I do not know whether the signing of this marriage contract four months ago and your arrival in Scotland was a coincidence, my lord, nor do I care," she answered in her haughtiest tone. "Unlike you, I was not given a choice of whether or not to affix my signature to the contract. My concern begins with whether or not you intend to honor it."

Neil stared at the proud young woman standing before him, challenging him, demanding an answer. "I didn't negotiate the contract and I don't recall signing it, so I see no reason to use it to bind us together for the rest of our lives. I release you from this bargain." Neil turned the marriage contract sideways and gripped it in the middle, preparing to rip it in half.

"You canna release her." Tam told him. "And it willna do ye any good to destroy that copy. 'Twas the laird's copy, but there's another. It's in safekeeping with a trusted ally—in London."

"In London?" Neil and Jessalyn spoke in unison.

"Aye," Tam answered. "With someone who is close to his lordship."

That revelation struck Neil like a blow to the heart. He narrowed his gaze at the old highlander. "How close?"

"Verra close."

Neil knew from the painful knot in his gut that he'd been betrayed by the man he loved and trusted more than any other. His grandfather. The marquess of Chisenden. He didn't know why Chisenden had chosen

this particular clan, but Neil didn't doubt that his grandfather, for whatever reasons, had decided to make an alliance with the Scots and had negotiated a settlement
with the MacInnes woman's father. His grandfather had
tricked him. Sold him into marriage. Neil squeezed his
eyes shut as he recalled the pile of papers Chisenden
had sent to be signed just hours before he departed for
Scotland. Routine paperwork, his grandfather had assured him, going so far as to apologize for bothering
him with incidental business details regarding the care
of Derrowford House and the estate when he knew Neil
was eager to spend his final evening in London in the
company of his mistress. The wily old fox knew his
grandson trusted him implicitly, knew Neil was so eager
to spend the evening with Deborah that he wouldn't
bother to do more than scan the first document. Apparently, his grandfather had buried two copies of this
damned marriage agreement in that stack of paperwork.
"Grandfather."

"Chisenden," Jessalyn breathed.

"Yes, Chisenden," Neil forced the name through
clenched teeth. "That conniving gentleman created this
untenable situation in order to force me to do what I've
repeatedly refused to do in the past. Marry and produce
an heir. It appears, Miss MacInnes, that my grandfather,
the king-maker, the all-powerful marquess of Chisenden
sees you as prime breeding stock for the next generation of Claremonts." Neil whirled around to face the old
highlander. "I suppose he knew about my abduction."

"Of course," Tam said. "He knows our ways. He
knows that the MacInneses have always abducted brides
for the lairds of the clan."

Neil raised an eyebrow at that.

"Since our new laird is a woman, it stands to reason
the marquess knew we'd abduct a husband for her," Tam
replied logically.

"Of course, it does." Neil responded in a voice laced
with irony. "It makes perfect sense. And my grandfather

must be enjoying this little farce. I can just see him sitting in his study reading my letters telling him how much I despise the poverty of this place and the stubbornness of its highlanders. Aware of my tastes and preferences, knowing how very much I detest the sight of beautiful barefooted women dressed in rags. Oh yes, Grandfather must be doubled over with laughter at the certain knowledge that he tricked me into agreeing to marry one."

Jessalyn frowned. He made the prospect of honoring his marriage agreement to her sound as appealing as contracting the plague. "I was ignorant of my father's plans for me, but he gave his oath and I'm bound by the terms of the contract that bears his signature."

"So am I." He turned to face her. "I may have been tricked into it, but I gave my word and I'll stand by it. And according to this," he waved the marriage contract around, then cast a critical gaze in her direction, "I agreed to marry you as soon as I set foot on MacInnes land, so I suggest you garb yourself in a manner befitting a lady and the wife of a peer of the realm."

The angry words he flung at her stung. Jessalyn scrunched her toes against the hard-packed dirt of the bailey and fought the urge to look down to see if her feet were dirty. She drew herself up to her full height, straightened her spine and lifted her chin as high as she could without staring up at the sky. Hot tears of shame burned her eyelids and she ruthlessly blinked them back, just as she ruthlessly ignored the hollow ache inside her heart at learning her father had betrayed her so completely. A highlander, any highlander, would understand the sacrifice she had made in forfeiting shoes so that her clansmen would have boots to wear into battle. A highlander would be proud to know she placed the welfare of the clan above her own. A highlander would be proud to have the daughter of Callum MacInnes and the new laird of Clan MacInnes to wife. But the Sassenach earl her father had chosen felt nothing but contempt for her because she was barefooted. It was quite apparent to Jessalyn that her husband-to-be preferred his mistress over the laird of Clan MacInnes. Quite apparent that he preferred a woman with shoes.

"I don't need to marry an earl to gain a title and become a lady, *my lord*," Jessalyn announced. "I was *born* a lady."

"Then act like one." Neil lashed out, knowing that he was being unreasonable, knowing that his anger should be directed at his grandfather and at himself rather than the girl. But he couldn't seem to curb his frustration and rein in his damnable temper. "I have no intentions of standing before a priest and exchanging marriage vows with a bare-legged, barefooted wild highland miss."

"Then *we* have a problem, my lord," Jessalyn announced. "Because I'm the laird of Clan MacInnes and I refuse to stand before God and my dearly beloved confessor and insult them both by exchanging marriage vows with a rude Sassenach earl who's wearing the scarlet uniform of German George's murdering army!"

"You abducted me from a military encampment," Neil retorted. "I came with nothing but the clothes on my back. I have nothing else *to* wear except this scarlet uniform."

"Exactly!"

"Christ!" Neil felt like a fool as he stared down at the dozens of pairs of dirty bare feet surrounding him. "Doesn't anyone in this hellish place own a proper pair of shoes?"

He saw the answer to his question when he looked up and found himself gazing into her angry eyes. But she was too proud to admit it. Neil almost smiled as he recognized the glint of stubborn pride in her eyes as well as the anger. Her eyes were dark blue, he realized, dark blue surrounded by flecks of gold and they were really quite remarkable—even when she was furious. Especially when she was furious.

"This is tradition," she insisted. "It's the highland

way." She wasn't lying. Going barefooted was customary in warm weather, but Clan MacInnes hadn't made a
year around habit of it. Until the rebellion had cost them
everything, including shoe leather, the laird and his family had always worn fine clothes and shoes. "We can't
all be Sassenach earls and have wealthy grandfathers
who buy us army commissions so we can wear bright
red uniforms and expensive black leather knee boots,
now can we?" Her tone was every bit as biting as his
had been. "Some of us are blessed with highland an-
cestors who taught us better than to judge people by the
condition of their tartans or the shoes they wear." She
glared up at him. "Or don't wear."

They squared off, standing toe-to-toe like two gladi-
ators in the center of the old bailey. Neither of them
willing to give an inch in what promised to turn into an
insurmountable battle of pride.

"Lady Jessalyn."

Jessalyn turned at the sound of her name and saw
her confessor making his way across the courtyard. "Yes,
Father?"

"The women and children have labored all morning
preparing the meal for your wedding celebration. Are
you going to disappoint them? Or ask them to continue
to ignore the pangs of hunger churning in their bellies
while you argue with your betrothed?" Father Moray
asked in the soft, chiding tone of voice Jessalyn had
known and obeyed since childhood.

"I don't mean to disappoint the women and the children, Father," Jessalyn explained. "But neither can I exchange solemn vows with a man in a Sassenach uniform."

"And I refuse to marry a woman too stubborn to wear
a pair of shoes!"

Father Moray allowed himself a tiny smile. "Though
it wasn't of your own doing, the two of you have been
given a rare opportunity to bridge generations of abuse,
distrust and misunderstanding to build a better world for
our children. I will not believe that you," he pinned Jes-

salyn with a glance, "will allow selfish and stubborn pride to jeopardize the future of the clan. And," he turned his attention to the earl, "I don't think you're so filled with English arrogance that you cannot see your betrothed's true nature. I believe you'll both agree that a compromise is in order."

Jessalyn nodded in silent agreement as her betrothed voiced his suspicion, "What kind of compromise?"

"The marriage kind." Father Moray replied. "The kind that allows for a bit of give and take." The priest nodded toward the Ancient Gentlemen of the Clan. "Do your duty, lads. Take him inside the castle and when he's properly attired for his wedding, bring his boots to me."

Chapter Six

When it came to marriage, he should have known better than to trust a priest. Especially a *highland* priest! No highlander had ever had an Englishman's best interests at heart and Father Moray was no exception. What did priests know of marriage? Except how to re-cite the Mass? *They* took a vow of celibacy in order to avoid the fate he was facing. That was why Neil found himself shivering beside his bride at the altar in the freezing chapel of Castle MacAonghais barefooted and bare-legged and wrapped in a tattered scrap of MacInnes tartan that didn't reach his knees and barely covered his ass.

He stole a glance at his bride. She didn't seem pleased at the prospect of marrying him and becoming the count-ess of Derrowford. In fact, she looked downright un-happy standing beside him in her white chemise and too-short skirts and his shiny black leather boots. The length of tartan that had covered her bodice was wrapped around his waist and the boots crafted by the finest boot-maker in London were covering her small feet. The toes of his boots were the only parts he could see, but he was a tall man and she was tiny in comparison. Boots that reached his knees must ride even higher on her. Neil felt his mouth go dry and he fought to swallow the lump in his throat as he imagined the comfortable black leather shafts of his boots gloving her pale, slim thighs.

A low uneasy rumbling filled the chapel. Neil became aware of it as his petite bride forcefully elbowed him in the ribs. "Your heart's in mortal danger."

"What?" For a moment, he wondered if she'd read his mind, but the sharp insistent jab of her elbow in his ribs convinced him otherwise.

Neil glared down at his bride. His ribs already ached from hours of bouncing against the side of a horse. He didn't need the additional discomfort.

She glared back at him. "If you don't answer Father Moray, you'll be sporting a gaping hole in your chest where your cruel Sassenach heart used to be. Because if you shame me here in front of my clan after all the trouble they've gone to to arrange this wedding for us, I'll cut it out myself."

Shocked by the vehemence of her fierce whisper, Neil turned to the priest to see what Father Moray had done to upset the prickly highland beauty. He concentrated on the words the priest was saying and was astounded to make sense of them.

"Neil Edward James Louis Claremont, seventh earl of Derrowford, fourteenth Viscount Claremont, nineteenth Baron Ashford doest thou stand before God and this assemblage and take Lady Jessalyn Helen Rose MacInnes, rightful laird of Clan MacInnes, as thy lawfully wedded wife?"

Neil had never fancied himself a coward, but every instinct for self-preservation that he'd ever possessed was urging him to make a break for the chapel door. He could almost smell his own fear and feel the color leeching from his face as he fought to come up with some graceful way to make his exit. He was too young for marriage. Too rich. Too arrogant. Too bloody Sassenach. And much too jaded for an innocent highland maid like her. He took a deep breath, then opened his mouth to speak as he struggled to find the proper words to make these

Scots understand that although he was a man of his word, he'd made a mistake when he'd put his signature on the bottom of that marriage contract. "Aye."

Father Moray gave a nod of approval as the strong Scottish affirmative echoed through the chapel. "Lady Jessalyn Helen Rose MacInnes, laird of Clan MacInnes, doest thou stand before God and this assemblage of kin and take Neil Edward James Louis Claremont, seventh earl of Derrowford, fourteenth Viscount Claremont, nineteenth Baron Ashford as thy lawfully wedded husband?"

"I will," she answered softly, in perfectly accented English.

Father Moray turned to Neil. "Now you exchange tokens. You must give her something, lad. Something to show that you honor the bonds of marriage."

Neil stared at the priest. He'd already parted with his boots, his uniform and his freedom. What more could he give? He glanced down at the signet ring on the third finger of his left hand. It was emblazoned with the crest of the earl of Derrowford.

"No, my son," the priest laid a hand on his arm. "This token must be something for your bride, something that willna' have to be returned to your keeping."

He had nothing of value, nothing that could be used as a marriage token except . . . Remembering the heavy fur pouch belted around his waist, Neil placed a hand on the sporran that held the contents of the purse he had relinquished along with his scarlet tunic. He leaned toward the priest and whispered, "Is coin an acceptable token?"

"Aye." Father Moray grinned. "Most acceptable and most welcome. Give it to your bride," he whispered back.

Neil bent his head and untied the pouch. He removed it from his belt and held it out to Jessalyn.

Father Moray shook his head. "Empty it, lad. Let the clan see what you're giving her."

Neil stuck the sporran in his belt as he took Jessalyn's hands, turned them palm up and cupped her fingers. When he finished, he removed the pouch from his belt, opened it and poured the contents into her hands.

Jessalyn gasped as the heavy gold sovereigns and crowns, Scottish thistle dollars and silver guineas filled her hands to overflowing and clattered against the stone floor of the chapel. She had never seen so much English gold and silver in her life! And now her new husband was giving it to her. Presenting a small fortune in gold and silver coins to her to show that he accepted the terms of the marriage. Her eyes stung from the pressure of unshed tears as she raised her face to look at him.

Derrowford met her gaze. A half-smile shaped his lips and an emotion she couldn't name flickered through the depths of his eyes. She stared at him, captivated by the sight. They were green, she realized. His eyes were the crisp verdant green of larch needles in the spring and Jessalyn marveled at the fact that she hadn't noticed them before.

"You must give him something in return, child," Father Moray reminded her. "Something to show your intent to honor the marriage contract."

Jessalyn pulled her gaze away from Derrowford's and turned to the priest. She chewed her bottom lip as the good father repeated his request. She had already given Derrowford her tartan and her clan. She had nothing else to give. Certainly nothing to match the wondrous gift of life-saving gold and silver coin he had given to her. She had none of the things a bride traditionally brought to her groom. All she had was a crumbling castle, the clothes on her back and her kinsmen. Her father had sold all of her family's fine fabrics and household furnishings, the paintings, tapestries and silver and pewter plate that they'd hidden from the English invaders to buy food last winter. There had been no crops or cattle after the summer Uprising. She'd pawned everything else and sent what jewelry she had to Edinburgh to be sold in order to buy her father a final resting place in the Presbyterian kirkyard. There was nothing left except the brass seal that belonged to the laird of the clan and the silver keys to the Laird's Trysting Room—the keys she wore on silver chains that hung around her neck. The keys. She would give him the silver key her father had worn. But she couldn't give him anything while she held the gold cupped in her hands. She glanced around, seeking a solution, and Auld Tam came to her aid.

"I'll keep it safe for ye." Tam smiled broadly and held out his bonnet so Jessalyn could deposit the money inside it.

She dropped the coins into Tam's woolen cap, then reached up and freed the two silver chains from their resting place beneath her shift. A small silver key hung on each chain. Turning to Derrowford, Jessalyn pulled the thicker of the necklaces over her head. She closed her eyes and gripped the chain tightly in her fist for a moment. He caught a tiny glimpse of the sorrow that crossed her face as she opened her fist and held the necklace out to him. He made no effort to take it out of her hand. Instead, he bent his knees and leaned forward so that she could put in around his neck.

He thought she might refuse. But she surprised him by slipping the necklace over his head and by carefully dropping it beneath his garments, so that it rested against his heart instead of his shirt. He felt the soft featherlike brush of her fingers against the hair of his chest, then the warmth of the silver as the key settled into place. Neil allowed himself to smile at the thought of its previous resting place—lying nestled between her breasts, absorbing the scent of her perfume and the heat from her body. He had the urge to touch her—to lift her chin and look her in the eye and repeat all the promises he'd just repeated to the priest and to her clan. But this time, he wanted to mean them.

"Thank you for giving this to me," he said, softly, too softly for the rest of the clan to hear. "I can see how much you treasure it."

She looked at him and Neil was struck by the unexpectedly hopeful expression in her dark blue eyes. He opened his mouth to speak, to assure her that her trust in him wouldn't be misplaced, but Father Moray interrupted.

"You've exchanged vows and tokens," the priest announced, "before God and kin and by the laws of the Holy Church in Rome and the laws of Scotland, I declare you to be husband and wife. Congratulations, lad, and welcome to the family!" Father Moray clapped him on the back. "My stomach is rumbling and the marriage feast awaits!"

To call the breakfast following the ceremony a marriage feast was a gross exaggeration. It barely qualified as a meal and as far as Neil could tell, nobody except a clan of starving Scottish highlanders would dare term it a feast. Although the members of clan MacInnes greeted the boiled oat porridge sweetened with wild honey and fresh milk and cream with oohs and aahs and great sighs of pleasure, Neil didn't share their excitement. Porridge was the only dish served. There were no hen's eggs or sausages, no rabbit, no venison, no mutton or fish. Only porridge, and even the honey and cream couldn't disguise the slightly burnt flavor of the oats. But the clan didn't seem to notice. Everyone ate with gusto, hunched over their bowls, with their arms curved around their dishes as if to protect them from marauders. Everyone, that is, except his bride—the laird of the clan.

She sat upon the bench with her back as straight as an arrow and with one hand resting in her lap. She made no effort to protect her meal. In fact, she'd started out with a full bowl, but had divided it among her kinswomen, giving them the lion's share of her breakfast, leaving only a small portion for herself. Neil watched in amazement as his bride discreetly scraped the side of her bowl, spooning a tiny bit of gruel into her mouth before closing her eyes and sighing in pleasure. He cast a guilty glance down at his own bowl. It was full. With the exception of one spoonful, the hearty helping of oats and the dripping piece of honeycomb the serving woman had placed in his bowl remained where she'd left it. He'd de-spised porridge as a child and the spoonful he'd just con-sumed to quell the empty rumbling in his belly hadn't changed his opinion of the mush. He found it every bit as disgusting as an adult as he had as a child, perhaps more so. But he appeared to be the only one who did. The rapturous expression on his bride's face told him that she savored her dish of boiled oats the way he sa-vored expensive brandy and leisurely explorations of the female body. He clamped his lips together as she scraped her bowl clean, reluctantly pushed it aside, then licked a minuscule pearl of honey from her lips with the tip of her tongue.

Plunging his spoon in his bowl, Neil crushed the honeycomb, and stirred the sweet liquid into the oatmeal. He waited until his bride was deep in conversation with the child seated on her left before he carefully bumped her elbow and slid his dish in front of her.

Jessalyn turned and looked at him in surprise. "Aren't you hungry?"

Neil ignored her question. "I don't know how things are done in Scotland," he told her, "but this is supposed to be our wedding breakfast and in England I believe it's customary for the bride and groom to share the meal by dining from the same dish."

Jessalyn cast a mortified glance at her empty dish as a rush of color stained her cheeks bright pink. "I didn't realize . . ."

"How could you?" He favored her with a devastating smile that showed his even white teeth and two perfectly matched dimples. "Unless you've another husband in En-gland you've failed to mention."

He was teasing her. Jessalyn stared at him for a mo-ment as the realization sank in. A small smile played about the corner of her mouth as she answered him, "That's entirely possible. I've been betrothed to you for the past four months and everyone I know failed to men-tion it. Since my father apparently wanted a wealthy son-in-law enough to secure an *English* one, I may well be betrothed to a score of rich Englishmen. Tell me, Lord Derrowford, how many men in England are wealthier and more powerful than you?"

"Two. My grandfather is wealthier and more powerful than I am. And so is the king." He tilted his head to one side and studied her. "But they're both married." He pushed his bowl in front of her and handed her his spoon. "After you, Countess."

Jessalyn glanced at the bowl of porridge. "But what about you? You've barely touched your food and I know you must be hungry."

Neil recognized the concerned expression on her face. She was his wife now—for better or for worse—and although he hated to lie, he would not trample her pride once again by revealing his revulsion for oat porridge. "Not at all. I enjoyed a delightful dinner before being confined to quarters and before your friend over there—" He nodded across the table at Auld Tam. "—arrived to escort me to our wedding."

She hesitated a moment longer before she dipped the spoon into the oatmeal. "If you're certain."

He grinned at her. "I'm quite certain. In truth, I doubt I can eat another bite."

Jessalyn's crestfallen expression resulted in a sudden tightening in his chest. Neil bit back a grimace and sucked in a deep, resigned breath. "I suppose I could manage one more."

The pleasure that seemed to light her face from within was his reward for swallowing the charcoal and honey-flavored mush she spooned into his mouth. He took her spoon from her and dipped it into the bowl. "Your turn," he reminded her.

"Aye." She glanced at him from beneath the cover of her eyelashes and smiled a shy hesitant smile that showed her unfamiliarity with the intimate gesture as they ate from the same bowl and touched their lips and tongues with the same spoon. Neil watched her luscious pink mouth curve upward and felt the warmth of her smile down to his bare toes. Before he quite knew how it had happened he had eaten half of the detested porridge in the bowl and she had eaten the other half.

"It may be a Sass—an *English* tradition, but sharing the wedding breakfast like this is a fine way to start a marriage," Jessalyn announced when they had scraped the bowl clean.

"I believe it's supposed to symbolize the sharing a man and a woman experience during the course of their marriage," Neil explained.

"For better, or worse. For richer, for poorer." Jessalyn grimaced as she stared down at the wooden bowl. "It's a fine tradition, my lord, but I'm afraid there isn't much to share. We're a very poor clan."

Neil nodded toward his wedding gift to his bride. The gold crowns and sovereigns and the silver guineas were scattered across the table top for all the members of Clan MacInnes to see. "Not so poor anymore, my lady. The earldom of Derrowford is very lucrative. I'm a very rich man, and now that you are the countess of Derrowford, you're a very rich woman."

"I'm the laird of Clan MacInnes, my lord Derrowford, and now that you've become my husband, your allegiance is to this clan. I'm afraid you'll find that an English title doesn't mean much to Jacobite highlanders."

"Perhaps not," he agreed, "but my coin seems to have made almost as big an impression as our wedding feast."

She couldn't help but smile. "Aye, my lord, that it did."

He stared at her lips. "Neil."

"Pardon?"

"My given name is Neil," he told her. "As the countess of Derrowford, you're entitled and—" He lowered his voice, then glanced at the members of the clan seated around the table. "—indeed, *encouraged* to use it. Especially when we're alone."

"We're in Scotland, my lord, not London. Here I'm

the MacInnes and you're the MacInnes's husband," she reminded him.

"Neil," he persisted. "The MacInnes's purchased husband, Neil Claremont, earl of Derrowford." He stared at her, forcing her to meet his gaze, refusing to back down.

"Neil," she said, at last.

"And you are?" he asked, as if he hadn't just heard her name when they exchanged vows.

"The MacInnes of Clan MacInnes," she answered. "As my husband, you're entitled to call me that."

He leaned closer to her and whispered, "And . . ."

"Encouraged to remember that my people expect me to fill my father's footsteps and that I must be the MacInnes."

"Naturally," Neil allowed. "When we're in the midst of your clan, you must be the MacInnes. I understand that. But who will you be when we're alone?"

"Myself," she answered.

"Yourself," Neil replied in a flat tone of voice. So they were back to that. While he'd struggled to control his simmering resentment and his anger at his grandfather and himself for a few minutes, she had decided to resume her prickly show of power designed to trample his pride in the dust. "That narrows it down to my enemy, the laird of Clan MacInnes or my enemy, the countess of Derrowford. What the devil do I call you? Countess? Laird?"

"As long as we're in Scotland," she said. "And as long as we're alone, you may call me Jessalyn."

"And if we should leave Scotland?" He asked more out of curiosity than anything else.

She stared at him as if the thought that he might take her away from Scotland had never entered her mind. "Scottish soil or not, I'll still be the MacInnes, though I'll make an effort to play the part of the English countess of Derrowford."

Which meant he'd be lucky if he survived his stay in Scotland or his marriage to the laird of Clan MacInnes.

He'd be lucky if he didn't wake up to find a Scottish dirk at his throat or buried in his flesh. And should he prove foolhardy enough to take his *bride* home to meet his family in England, he would have to constantly watch his back and guard his every move. He'd been married less than an hour and the limitless possibilities for further deceit and betrayal stretched endlessly ahead of him. The grandfather who professed his fondness for him had deceived him, betrayed his trust and tricked him into a betrothal and marriage to a highland beauty who hadn't wanted marriage any more than he did, who had reason to hate him and everything he represented and would undoubtedly stop at nothing to be rid of him. He couldn't expect more than that. In truth, he couldn't expect anything. "I doubt you'll have to worry about being the countess of Derrowford for very long," Neil replied sharply. "Unless it's as the widowed countess of Derrowford."

He lowered his voice to a whisper meant for her ears alone, but his words were laced with sarcasm. "Surely, you realize that should we decide to return to England, I will most likely be arrested on the spot and charged with treason for deserting my post at Fort Augustus. And should Spotty Oliver and his soldiers discover me here married to you, I'm sure to be arrested and returned to England and hanged."

Jessalyn wrinkled her forehead. "I didn't realize . . . I never thought . . ."

He raised an eyebrow at what sounded like a genuine gasp of alarm. "Don't worry," he told her. "My widow will be well provided for. Neither you nor your clan should want for anything."

His pointed barbs seemed to have found a mark because she straightened her shoulders and stiffened her spine as if preparing to do battle. "What are you going to do?" she asked.

"The only thing I can do." Neil took a deep breath, pushed away from the table and stood up. He reached out a hand to her. "Survive for as long as I can. However I can. I've been purchased as stud. And to that end, I'll tell you that we English have another quaint tradition that takes place on the wedding day; it's called a honeymoon and it customarily follows the wedding feast."

She hesitated for a moment, then placed her hand in his larger one and allowed him to pull her to her feet. "We have that custom in Scotland as well," she admitted with a blush. "But we prefer to wait until sundown."

Neil shook his head. "Your clan did call this—" He waved an arm at the remains of their wedding meal. "—a feast. And since our English custom demands that the honeymoon follow the feast I thought we might retire . . ." He lowered his voice until it was nothing more than a seductive whisper, "to wherever it is you *customarily* retire and get down to the business for which I was purchased."

"We're in Scotland," she reminded him. "Scottish laws and Scottish customs take precedence over English ones."

"Nearly all of Scotland is under martial law. All, I suspect, expect this tiny patch of it, but I'm an English soldier. It's my duty to spread English law however I can."

"I don't think . . ." Jessalyn wrinkled her brow again and began to worry her bottom lip with her teeth, truly unsure of her next move for the first time in her life.

"Ssh!" he cautioned, reaching out, in an uncharacteristic gesture, to caress her plump bottom lip with the pad of his thumb. "There's no need for you to think. This is part of the marriage contract. Part of the old and honorable tradition of ensuring the survival of the line."

Chapter Seven

T he grating sounds of thirty or so wooden spoons scraping the bottoms of thirty or so wooden bowls ended abruptly and thirty or so pairs of eyes stared at them as Neil pulled Jessalyn to her feet. He tightened his fingers around her arm as he turned toward the castle.

"Wait!" Jessalyn resisted. "I canna leave like this."

"Why not?" He tensed, narrowing his gaze at her and noticing for the first time the effort it took for her to walk in his boots. He wondered how she had managed to keep up with him when they left the chapel.

"These people are my family. I canna leave the table without thanking them for providing this feast in celebration of my nuptials."

Neil relaxed, loosening his grip on her hand as he acknowledged that he understood her action was dictated by duty and courtesy to her kin, not a bout of maidenly nerves. He waited by her side as Jessalyn thanked her clansmen and women in the Scottish language and repeated it, for his benefit, in English. When Jessalyn finished speaking, Neil glanced at her, before clearing his throat and addressing the group. "Before my bri—" he caught his mistake and corrected it, "*the MacInnes* and I retire to begin our honeymoon, please allow me to join her in thanking you for your extraordinary generosity in preparing this marriage feast. For my part, I would like to thank you for your gentle regard for my person." His sarcasm didn't escape them for a handful of clansmen laughed aloud as Neil rubbed the ugly bruise on the side of his head where Auld Tam had "tapped" him with the flat of his battle ax. His head still pounded like a drum, but these highlanders didn't have to know that. "And your regard for the MacInnes's feelings in arranging to have me fetched to Scotland in time for our wedding ceremony." A few more chuckles filtered through the bailey. He managed a wry smile. "You were all here when I arrived," he said, "so I won't add insult to injury by pretending I was eager to marry, but I give you my word that I will be a proper husband to your laird."

One of the old women in the crowd muttered something in the Scottish tongue and a few of the clansmen and women snickered.

"What did she say?" Neil demanded.

"She said," Jessalyn blushed, "that no man is eager for a wedding. It's the bedding they look forward to."

"Aye," the old woman added in English, "and I've yet to meet one who dinna start blathering promises in order to bed a fine lass like our wee Jessie."

Neil felt the tips of his ears redden. "I'm sure you're quite right, Madam. There is that consideration." He managed a smile for the benefit of the audience and reached for the MacInnes's hand. "And my reward for enduring the ceremony and sealing the marriage bargain."

"Not so fast," Auld Tam stepped into Neil's path. "I know it's yer wedding day, but yer the husband of our new laird now and it's never too early to learn how to carry out yer duty."

"If you'll step aside, I'll get on with the business of doing my *duty*," Neil replied through gritted teeth, "for which I do not require instruction."

"No that *duty*," Tam said. "Yer duty as the laird's husband."

"I was under the impression that that *is* the duty of the laird's husband," Neil reminded the older man. "The primary duty."

"Aye," Tam agreed. "But it's no the only one. Ye've other more important things to attend to."

"Such as?"

"Such as standing up for these braw young men—" He paused for dramatic effect, then swept his arms wide to reveal Sergeants Marsden and Stanhope adoringly attended by Magda and Flora. "—who have consented to marry my fine young lassies and become my sons-in-law."

Jessalyn fought to behave as the MacInnes would behave. She acted like a young woman eager to see her relatives happily wed. Pulling her hand out of Neil's, she rushed forward to embrace Magda and Flora. His boots hampered her progress and she would have fallen on her face if he hadn't anticipated her move and automatically reached out to steady her. "I always hoped you would be my sisters." Mindful of the Englishmen standing close by, Jessalyn spoke in Gaelic. "And I want you to be happy. I remember how we used to dream about our futures when we were young and carefree."

"Aye," Flora smiled at the memories. "We were each going to marry one of your brothers. I was going to marry either Harry or Charlie. And Magda was going to marry Connor. And your father was going to arrange a marriage for you with a rich, handsome lord."

"And we were all going to go to Edinburgh and turn the lords and ladies there green with envy at our happiness and our good fortune," Magda added.

Jessalyn's eyes shimmered with unshed tears at the memory of her six brothers and all the other young kinsmen who had died on the battlefields and all of the lovely dreams for the future that had died with them. "That was a long time ago," she said, at last. "When we could still afford to believe in dreams."

"Aye," Magda agreed. "Our lives have changed almost beyond recognition. Once upon a time ye were the daughter of the MacInnes and the sister of the next MacInnes. Now ye *are* the MacInnes. The past is dead, Jessie, along with our bonny lads and we must go on with life the best we can."

"I did what I had to do—what my father bid me to do—to save the clan and our way of life. I had no choice. You do." Jessalyn stared at Flora, then reached out and clasped Magda's hand. "Are you certain this is what you want?"

"Aye," Flora answered, her gaze unwavering.

"They're good men, Jessie," Magda answered. "Och, they're different from yer brothers and from the fine lord ye've just married. They're simple men, serving in the Sassenach army, not because they hate Scotsmen, but because they hated London and wanted a way out of it. We dinna want to live the rest of our lives as maidens. We want children. Will ye give us yer consent?"

"Yes." Her eyes stung with unshed tears and the word caught in Jessalyn's throat as she studied the Englishmen Magda and Flora had chosen and the Englishman her father had chosen for her. They *were* her *sisters*, she realized. Her sisters of the heart. Jessalyn would never have asked or forced Magda and Flora to accept Englishmen as their husbands. She would never have asked them or commanded them to choose Scotsmen from other clans or from the lowlands as their husbands, even though they knew that marrying and producing children would help the clan survive. She would never have forced them to marry at all. And Magda and Flora had known it. Instead, they had chosen to marry outside the clan, chosen Englishmen as her father had done for her in order to provide a measure of protection for the clan from English retribution. "You have my consent and my blessing. From now on, we'll be the sisters we always planned to be."

"Aye," Flora agreed. "Only now we'll all be wed to Sassenach soldiers."

"Well?" After giving his daughters and Jessalyn time to blather in private, Auld Tam turned to the MacInnes and demanded an answer. "Are ye going to allow the weddings and provide a dowry for the brides?" he asked in English.

"Aye." Jessalyn nodded.

"Not so fast," Neil interrupted.

Jessalyn and Auld Tam both turned to stare at him as if he'd suddenly sprouted horns.

"Lad, yer the husband of the MacInnes," Tam warned him. "Not the MacInnes. Ye have no say in this."

"Oh, but I do," Neil answered Tam, but he pinned his gaze on his bride's face. The wistful expression she'd worn as she conversed with her women stung his pride and prodded him to respond. "I understand that as the MacInnes, my wife is the leader of her family. I don't care to interfere in decisions that are the sole concern of her clan, but in my world I'm as much a leader as she is. And this decision affects more than just Clan MacInnes. I'm responsible for these men. I'm their commanding officer and they would not be in this situation if they hadn't been standing guard over me. I won't—I cannot—allow them to sacrifice their personal happiness by having marriages to your kinswomen thrust upon them simply because they had the misfortune to be outside my door when I was abducted." He continued to stare at his wife, challenging her to see his point. "My lady, if you took the opportunity to put your conscience at ease by asking your women if marrying these men was what they wanted, then grant me that same opportunity. Your women are part of your family and you feel responsible for their welfare. I feel the same way about these men."

"Granted," Jessalyn replied shortly before adding the caveat, "as long as you speak where I can hear you."

Neil lifted an eyebrow in wry comment, but wisely refrained from mentioning that she had spoken to her women in a language he didn't comprehend. "Many thanks for your gracious permission," he said, lifting her hand in a mocking salute and impulsively grazing her knuckles with his lips. She sucked in a breath at the contact and a delicate shudder rippled through her, though he couldn't say whether it came from revulsion or desire. Revulsion, he decided moments later, or maidenly apprehension, for when he let go of her hand, she put as much distance as possible between them and motioned for her women to do the same.

Both men snapped to attention and saluted, then Sergeant Marsden spoke. "Begging your pardon, sir, for failing to protect you from attack and for being out of uniform."

Neil returned the salute then moved to stand before Sergeant Marsden. "There was no attack," he informed him. "My abduction was pre-arranged and very well-planned. General Oliver played into their hands by leaving the gap in the wall unguarded. There wasn't much you could have done to prevent the raid." He shrugged his shoulders, then glanced at the tartan *trews* Marsden and Stanhope were wearing. "As for being out of uniform, forget it. As you can see, I'm slightly out of uniform myself." Neil watched as his subordinate struggled to mask his reaction at finding his commanding officer wearing Scottish attire that bared his legs and feet.

"It leaves little to the imagination, doesn't it, Sergeant? Well, consider yourself lucky. You may have had to give up your uniform trousers for the Scots variety, but at least you're still wearing trousers. I feel a bit like those Greek soldiers I mentioned the other day."

"The ones bearing gifts, sir?"

"Yes," Neil answered, stamping his bare feet against the cold ground. "In addition to being famous for bearing gifts, they were also famous for baring their asses and the rest of the private parts of their anatomy. Fortunately for them, the Greeks didn't live in Scotland. They lived in a much warmer climate and *they* didn't have to worry about freezing anything off."

Marsden relaxed enough to nudge Stanhope in the ribs

and crack a smile at his commanding officer. "I guess we're lucky at that, sir. To have traded trousers for trousers and to have been able to keep our boots."

"Don't speak too soon," Neil warned. "You may lose them yet. I don't think there's a proper pair of shoes or boots—save ours—in the whole village. Mine," he wiggled his bare toes against the hard-packed earth, "have already become a part of my marriage settlement."

"We heard," Stanhope said. "Our good wishes on your nuptials, sir. And to you, too, ma'am," he added, when he realized the woman in the white chemise, short skirts and the black leather boots was the major's bride.

"Thank you, Corporal," Neil replied. "Am I to understand that I should be congratulating or commiserating with you on your upcoming nuptials as well?"

Stanhope nodded as he focused his eyes on the ground and kicked at a loose pebble with the toe of his boot. "Yes, sir."

"And you, Sergeant?" Neil asked.

"I've agreed to marry Miss Flora, sir."

"Miss Flora?" Neil raised an eyebrow. "I would have thought you'd have chosen Miss Magda."

Marsden shook his head. "I wear the trousers in my family. I prefer Miss Flora," he explained. "I can't abide bossy women."

"And you, Stanhope? How do you feel about marrying Miss Magda and living among these highlanders?"

"I think Miss Magda and I will suit each other just fine, Major. I was living among highlanders at Fort Augustus. I figure I might as well make a home here where I'm needed. I wasn't planning to make the army my life—besides, Sergeant Marsden and I can't go back to Fort Augustus without you. If we go back Sir Charles will stripe our backs and have our guts for garters for allowing you to leave your quarters."

"You didn't allow me to leave," Neil pointed out.

Stanhope shook his head. "That won't matter to Sir Charles. After he has his pound of flesh from both of us, we'll be cashiered out of the army without a pension if he doesn't hang us first."

Neil glanced over at Marsden.

Marsden nodded.

The devil of it was that Corporal Stanhope and Sergeant Marsden were right. Neil knew Spotty Oliver wouldn't rest until he had his pound of flesh from all of them. He hadn't known anything about the plans for his abduction or the bride waiting for him, but Spotty Oliver wouldn't see it that way. Spotty would never believe he had been an unwilling participant in his grandfather's scheme. Years of animosity and schoolboy resentments had blinded Spotty Oliver where Neil was concerned. But whether he liked it or not, Spotty needed him. He was the architect and chief engineer of Fort Augustus. He had designed and built it from the ground up. Spotty couldn't finish the fort without him and finishing the fort was the one thing Spotty Oliver had to do in order to stay in General Wade's good graces. His sudden disappearance coming so close on the heels of his bitter argument with his commanding officer was bound to present a problem. Spotty Oliver would believe what he chose to believe and Neil was willing to bet Spotty would believe he had arranged his confinement to quarters for the sole purpose of carrying out an escape designed to make Fort Augustus's commanding officer look like an incompetent fool. And although the MacInnes had assured him that her village was located deep in the highlands, he didn't know for sure. He hoped she'd spoken the truth. He hoped that the village was buried so deep in the highlands it would take months for Spotty Oliver to locate it. Because he knew as sure as the sun would rise on the morrow, Major General Sir Charles Oliver would hunt them down and he wouldn't stop until he had them in his grasp.

Neil took a deep breath, then expelled it in a rush. He didn't particularly like this turn of events, but he didn't have much choice. Unless he acted in his role as their commanding officer and ordered Marsden and Stanhope to go back on the solemn pledges they had given to the MacInnes women, there was nothing he could do to prevent them from following him down the path of so-called wedded bliss. In the meantime, the reason for which he had been abducted and brought to the highlands—his own honeymoon—would have to wait a while longer. He had two more weddings to attend. Neil stared at Marsden and Stanhope, his comrades in arms, his friends, his brothers. "I'm not sure this is the right course for you to take," he said. "In truth, I don't like the idea at all. But you are your own men and you've made your choice. So, for better or for worse, as for as long as we're here, we're in this together."

Chapter Eight

"Gone? What do you mean he's gone?" Major General Sir Charles Oliver buttoned the top button of his scarlet blouse and winced at his reflection in the polished silver shaving mirror as he carefully enunciated each whispered word. He wanted to shout at his idiotic aide-de-camp, but the hellish pounding in his head made processing information very painful and prevented him from giving voice to his ire. "I gave you an order, Lieutenant. I sent for you to fetch Major Claremont. He's currently confined to his quarters."

"He's not there, sir."

"He has to be there," Major Oliver insisted. "He's chained to his cot."

"He *was* chained to his cot, sir, but now he's gone." The aide drew himself to his full height and stood stiffly at attention, preparing himself for the general's reaction as he extended his hand and revealed several lengths of iron chain.

"Bloody hell!" Oliver roared. "Fetch his guards. Find Marsden and Stanhope and have them report to me immediately."

"They're gone, too, sir. I checked their cots and searched the barracks. No one has seen them. Neither

Sergeant Marsden nor Corporal Stanhope was at his post when the morning watch arrived to relieve them."

"Damn him! Claremont's escaped!" Oliver shouted, forgetting his hangover, forgetting everything except the fact that he'd been duped by Neil Claremont, the bloody rich, bloody know-it-all-son-of-a-bitch earl of Derrowford. "And Sergeant Marsden and Corporal Stanhope conspired to aid him. I should have known his argument against the celebration last evening was a ruse. It was a ruse to force me to confine him to quarters so he wouldn't be obliged to attend the celebration, I'm sure of it. Claremont's probably halfway to London by now! Find him! Find them! I want him hanged for his bloody insolence!"

"H-hanged, sir?" The lieutenant sputtered, alarmed by his commanding officer's rage.

"Yes, hanged," Oliver snapped. "H-A-N-G-E-D. It's what the army does to deserters."

"We found several sets of pony tracks coming in single file through the gap in the wall and leading right up to Major Claremont's quarters. I don't think the major escaped," the lieutenant ventured. "I think . . ."

"I don't care what you think!" Oliver snatched the length of chain out of the lieutenant's hand and threw it on the hard-packed floor. "I'm the commander of Fort Augustus. *I* think. *You* follow orders. *My* orders."

"I understand, sir, but I feel it's my duty to report my findings and—"

"You found Major Claremont missing from his quarters," Oliver pointed out. "After I expressly ordered him confined to his quarters until further notice. That is all I need to know."

"But, sir, I don't thi—believe—Major Claremont left his quarters willingly or on his own. I believe he was kidnapped."

"Poppycock!" Oliver laughed. "Kidnapped? Don't be absurd? Who would want to kidnap a mere *major* in His Majesty's Royal Corps of Engineers when the commanding officer, a *major general*, is on the premises? And who would have the audacity to march into an armed British fortress in order to kidnap either one of us?"

"This fortress is incomplete and undermanned and we are building it in extremely hostile territory, sir."

"We're a conquering army, Lieutenant. We were victorious in our efforts. Have you seen any hostiles?" He paused before the open window and surveyed the fort and a group of Scottish whores milking cows.

"No, sir."

"Of course, you haven't." Oliver turned from the window and faced the lieutenant. "That's because there aren't any hostiles. We've subdued them. Men, women and children. Right down to their ruddy highland cows. I find it absurd to think that a column of riders could get through the guards posted around our perimeter."

"There were no perimeter guards last night, sir. There weren't any guards at all," the lieutenant reminded him.

"Why not?"

"You ordered every man on the post to attend the celebration, sir."

"I ordered every man on the post *except the men standing guard* to attend the celebration," Oliver corrected in a voice threaded with hauteur and steel.

"No, sir, you didn't. You issued the order that every man attend the celebration. Major Claremont objected to leaving the wall unguarded. That's why—"

"Major Claremont is absent from his quarters without permission. I ordered him confined to those quarters for insubordination to his superior. And at the moment, I consider Major Claremont a deserter. I want your report for General Wade, Lieutenant, and in that report I expect you to make note of the major's current status. Do you understand?"

The lieutenant clicked his heels together as he snapped to attention and saluted once again. As far as General Oliver was concerned the matter was settled. Major Claremont's fate had been sealed. But as far as the lieutenant was concerned the matter was far from settled. He'd write the report the way General Oliver ordered it written and he would hand it over to the general as ordered, but he would also send copies of it and the complete version of his original report detailing his findings of kidnapping to General Wade. "Yes, sir." He struggled to keep the frustration and contempt for his commanding officer out of his voice as he answered.

"Good." The general smiled. "Dismissed, Lieutenant."

"Yes, sir."

"Oh, and Lieutenant," Oliver waited until the aide was halfway out the door before calling him back. "I expect you to submit your report to me and be ready to ride in one hour. I want Claremont found! One can never be quite certain of where Claremont's passions lie, but I'll wager he's hightailed it back to the comforts of London or directly disobeyed my orders by leaving his quarters and the fort in order to secure the services of the Edinburgh stonemasons. Either way, I'll be leading a column to find Major Claremont and the other two deserters and when they return to London it will be to face court martial and hanging."

The lieutenant nodded. He had less than an hour to write his reports and locate the fastest courier on the post.

"Before God and kin and by the laws of the Holy Church in Rome and the laws of Scotland, I declare you to be husband and wife."

Neil listened as Father Moray concluded the ceremony tying the nuptial knot between Sergeant Marsden and Flora MacInnes. He knew the words of the ceremony by heart and much of the Latin Mass as well after having attended three weddings in one day—including his own. An incredible feat for a man who prided himself on having never attended one in the course of his adult years. Indeed, up until today he had successfully avoided all of the social and societal obligations associated with the word and the institution of marriage. And somewhere on the betting books at White's, his gentleman's club in London, was a list of those of his friends and associates who had wagered on just how old the earl of Derrowford would be before he attended *any* wedding, much less his own. Eight and twenty. He would have to remember to inscribe the date and his age in the betting book once he returned to London. *If* he returned to London. *If* he remained alive long enough to do so. A conspiracy of old men had succeeded where everyone else had failed. They had succeeded in marching him to the altar where he'd tied himself to a stranger and sacrificed his grand dreams for the future.

Neil felt a hand on his sleeve and glanced down to find it belonged to the MacInnes. He had been standing to the right of the grooms and she had been standing to the left of the brides, but now, he realized that the newly married couples had paired off and his bride had quietly appeared at his elbow.

"It's done," she pronounced softly as Sergeant Marsden and Flora and Corporal Stanhope and Magda turned to face the clan before exiting the chapel. She seemed as resigned to the marriages as he was and about as happy, Neil thought as he followed the two couples and the priest, automatically tightening his hand on the MacInnes's arm as she struggled to walk in his boots. "They're married. It's time to for me to bestow dowries on the brides," she said.

As they entered the old bailey, the MacInnes frowned at the coins still lying scattered on the wooden tables. Neil watched her lips moving as she stared at the money. "What are you doing?" he demanded. "Praying it won't disappear?"

"Counting," she answered. "And praying. Praying it will be enough."

"How much more do you require?" he asked, the sharp cutting tone back in his voice. "Because that's all the coin I had on me at the time of my abduction. Since

I was crass enough to give you coin in lieu of a wedding ring, why don't you tell me exactly how much more your wedding ring and my stud services are going to cost me?"

"I wish I knew," she snapped. "Just as I wish I knew how much more it's going to cost me. I didn't purchase you and if I had any choice in the matter I wouldn't touch a ha'penny of your *generous* wedding gift, but I have no other funds. In order to gift Magda and Flora with dowries, I have to use some of the Judas coin you gave me and I'm trying to decide on a fair, but generous, amount for the dowries. They must be equal amounts. I can't risk favoring one sister over the other." She wrinkled her brow and chewed at her bottom lip in a gesture Neil was beginning to recognize as one of uncertainty. "This would have been so much easier if you had simply presented me with a few coins instead of flaunting your excess of riches by drowning me in them. With all this coin lying around for everyone to see, how am I supposed to decide what's fair and generous? If I give them too much I'll be accused of flaunting your wealth and if I give them too little, I'll be accused of being miserly and of not appreciating the sacrifice they've made for the good of the clan." She kept her voice low, but Neil could hear the fury and the frustration in it.

"Sacrifice? What sacrifice are your women making for the good of the clan?"

"My women are marrying *Englishmen*."

"Englishmen your women kidnapped. Englishmen who, by virtue of their loyalty to me, weren't given a choice in the matter. Nobody asked them if they wanted to become husbands to a couple of man-hungry highland wenches."

"*You* asked them," she pointed out. "Not more than an hour ago. And they agreed."

"*They agreed* because I'm their commanding officer," Neil told her. "*They agreed* because they had the misfortune to be standing guard outside my door when your clan came calling. *They agreed* because if they chose to return to Fort Augustus without me, they'd be facing certain punishment and a possible death sentence. *They agreed* because the only choice you gave them was marriage to your women or release on the moors."

"They had a choice!" Jessalyn insisted. "They could have chosen release."

"And how long do you think two unarmed English soldiers would survive? Surrounded by highland clans? On foot and wearing bright red uniforms?" he demanded, maneuvering the MacInnes ever closer to the tables so she could get a better count of her coin. He glanced down at it and realized there must be well over a hundred pounds in gold and sterling lying there. "When you reward your women, remember their husbands. They had less choice in the matter than either of us."

Jessalyn studied the coins for a long time. She hated to admit it, but the earl was right. She hesitated. She'd never seen so much money or had a better reason to share it. She allowed her hand to linger over the tabletop before she selected a sovereign, a crown and a guinea to give to each woman.

"There's no need to be stingy with your reward." A rush of warm air brushed her neck, caressed her cheek and sent shivers down her spine as Neil leaned close and whispered in her ear. "Give them more."

"This money has to see the whole of the clan through the autumn and winter," she said. "If the winter's harsh, I'm afraid I won't have enough."

"You'll have enough," he reminded her. "My name alone guarantees that." Neil placed his hand over hers and steered her hand back to the table. "Remember these women are part of your *clan*." He practically sneered the words. "They're your friends and your family. They risked life and limb to help capture you a wealthy husband. Whether you like it or not, you're a wealthy member of the English aristocracy. Share the wealth, Countess.

Reward your women handsomely for their timely inter-
vention in your life and for their sacrifices for the good
of the clan. You can afford it."

Even his sneers were seductive. Jessalyn was shocked
to discover that his voice and his touch had the power
to affect her even when he wasn't being particularly polite or fair or charming. He was as handsome as the
devil, might in fact, be the devil tempting her. "Can I?"

"Trust me," he whispered once again. "I promise
there's more money where that came from. You're a
wealthy woman now."

Jessalyn quickly added two more sovereigns, crowns
and guineas to each pile. She scooped up one pile of
money and presented it to Magda, then turned and
scooped up the other coins and handed them to Flora.
The money they held in their hands was more money
than either woman had ever seen until that day. Auld
Tam's daughters gasped at Jessalyn's incredible generosity and willingness to share what had been her wedding gift from her husband. And tears shimmered in
Tam's eyes at the way in which his new laird had honored his daughters.

"No man should start married life at a monetary dis-
advantage to his wife or his wife's family," Neil said as
he reached out and selected the same amount Jessalyn
had selected, and handed it to Marsden and to Stanhope.
"This should even things up." He shook hands with both
men, then turned to face his new bride. While the
MacInnes had bestowed a fine dowry on her kinswomen,
he had made certain his men were taken care of. Tech-
nically, the coin belonged to the MacInnes, but Neil
made certain that all the members of the clan understood from whence it came.

He expected to see anger on the MacInnes's face and
was surprised to find a serious, thoughtful look there instead. "It doesna seem possible to become so rich in one
day simply by exchanging vows with a man."

"It's possible," he answered. "And in my world, it's

the method most preferred by fortune hunters, but it only works if you exchange vows with the right man."

She tilted her head to one side and looked at him from beneath her veil of lashes in a move that would have seemed transparently coy on another woman, but was completely natural for her. "Are you the right man?"

"That depends on what you're looking for," he answered, the sharp edge of bitterness and betrayal evident in his voice. "If you're in the market for an alliance with England, access to a fortune, a title and a distinguished name as sire for your children . . ."

"I'd like children," she murmured, dreamily. "At least three or four."

"Then I'm the right man for you, at least temporarily. At least your father and my grandfather thought so. But you should know that I had a life in London before I took up my commission in the army. I have obligations there and plans of my own."

Plans that didn't include her—or her children. He didn't say it, but she heard it in his voice. Well, what of it? She had plans of her own, too. Plans that didn't include a Sassenach husband. "Agreed."

"What?" He looked at her, not trusting what he heard.

She smiled brightly. Too brightly. "An alliance with *England*, access to a fortune, a title and a distinguished name as sire for her children. An absent husband. What more could any woman want? Especially a *bare-legged, barefooted wild highland miss?*"

He would have to be deaf, dumb and blind to miss the fury in her voice and in her manner as she flung his insulting words back at him.

"I was trying to determine your needs," he told her. "Because if you're looking for more than what I was purchased to provide, marriage to me is sure to be a disappointment for you."

"That's rich coming from you! Tell me, my lord Derrowford, what hasn't been a disappointment for me? My father's betrayal? My secret betrothal? My wedding? The

weddings of my kinswomen? Before the Uprising, when
we were a well-to-do clan, there would have been a real
feast following the weddings and wine and ale and
whisky and toasts to our health. After the toasting, there
would have been music and dancing and speeches. We
would have worn gowns sewn with silver favors from
head to toe so the clan members could tear off tiny keep-
sakes of our weddings and our *highland* husbands would
have carried boxes of matching favors to give as well.
We would have examined our wedding gifts for the benefit of the guests, then led the way to our new homes
where the women would present us with salt and housekeeping gifts. Our husbands would carry us over the
thresholds then wait impatiently while the women undressed us and put us to bed, carefully untying all the
knotted ribbons on our nightgowns in preparation . . ."
Her words seemed to die in her throat as an embarrassed
blush spread across her face. She cleared her throat and
recovered her power of speech. "But that kind of wedding wasn't possible for me, so I'll just have to suffer
more disappointment, won't I?"

"Suppose we find out."

Caught off-guard, Jessalyn wasn't sure she'd heard
him correctly. Her breath caught in her throat and her
heart beat a rapid tattoo against her rib cage. "What?"

"It's time we retired."

"I beg your pardon?"

"Marriage to me may prove to be a disappointment
in every other way," he said, "but I've never been a disappointment in the bedchamber." He swung her up in
his arms without warning. "It's time we retire to our
bedchamber in the castle and begin that quaint Scottish
custom you call a honeymoon."

Chapter Nine

"Now?" It was all she could think to say as her breath quickened and her heartbeat increased in response to the promise, the mastery in his voice. The man who had swept her up into his arms was clearly a man to be reckoned with, a man beyond her control and outside her realm of experience. Although she hadn't had any intimate experiences with men, she wasn't completely ignorant of the things that took place behind closed bedchamber doors. She had grown up listening to her kinswomen gossiping amongst themselves, praising or bemoaning their husbands' performances in bed and she had had six brothers and a father who bred and raised highland cattle. She knew men were made differently from women and she had some idea of how they were different. But until this morning, she'd never tasted a man's lips upon her own. And while she understood the necessity of her marriage as a means for saving her clan, Jessalyn was uneasy with the idea that the stranger she'd married now had the right to use her body as he pleased. The loss of control over the one thing that belonged solely to her frightened her. What would he do to her? What could he do? If he chose to beat her, would any of her clansmen come to her rescue? Would they dare to interfere? To come between a man and his legal wife?

Even if she was the MacInnes? She'd heard of such things. Over the years, she'd heard whispered comments about this laird or that laird who beat his wife. Such things occasionally occurred within her own clan. Once, she'd overheard her father cautioning one of his warriors against beating his wife too harshly. She hadn't heard what the wife had done to merit a serious beating. But Jessalyn knew the beating had been severe enough for her father to notice and intervene. What she didn't know was what caused a husband to punish his wife so harshly. She wasn't normally a coward, but what if she unknowingly gave her new husband cause to beat her? Who would caution him? Who would watch over her?

"Perhaps, I should call for help."

She didn't realize she'd spoken her thoughts aloud until Neil answered, "I don't need help." He shifted her weight in his arms and started toward the entrance to Castle MacAonghais. A quick glance showed that the door of the castle was open. The huge oak timbers that had once formed a barrier to the entrance had long since rotted off their iron hinges. There was nothing to bar his way.

"Perhaps we should wait," Jessalyn suggested, the sound of an almost overwhelming virginal panic in her voice. "You've had a long and trying day—"

Bloody hell! Neil fought to keep from grinding his teeth in frustration as he listened to his bride question his skills as a lover and his stamina. Would she never cease insulting his manhood? "I'm fine."

"But you must be tired. And your head must pain you. Auld Tam's ax left a lump the size of a bird's egg on your head."

"You needn't concern yourself, my lady. I may have a slight wound—" *A wound that ached like a bitch.* "But I'm perfectly capable of undressing and bedding my bride without assistance." He looked down at her flushed face, at the rapid pulse beating at the base of her throat. "Are you concerned about my welfare, my lady, or have you had a change of heart? Have you decided against fulfilling the terms of the contract your father signed?"

"Of course not! I know my duty. To my father and my clan." Jessalyn's temper flared. "I'd simply rather not be undressed and bedded tonight."

"Then you shouldn't have stood beside me before God and your clan and promised to love, honor, obey or worship me with your body."

"I never . . ." she sputtered.

"With my body I thee worship," he recited.

She wished he hadn't said that. The worshipping him with her body was the part of the wedding vows that made her unsure of herself, made her doubt her abilities to fulfill her duties to her clan. *And to her husband.* She wiggled in his arms, trying to free herself. "Put me down. This isn't dignified."

"It isn't supposed to be dignified," Neil informed her, tightening his arms around her. "It's supposed to be romantic. It's your wedding day, remember? And the husband of your dreams is carrying you over the threshold."

"I dreamt of a *highland* warrior."

"Then I'm a vast improvement." He grunted as she elbowed him in the chest. "Careful. You don't want me to drop you on your *arse,* now do you?" He whispered the words so that his warm breath caressed her ear and tickled the hair on her neck. "That wouldn't be very dignified either. And it would definitely spoil the fantasy."

"What fantasy?" Jessalyn demanded. "This isn't a fantasy. It's a nightmare."

"Oh, no, my lady, that's where you're mistaken," he said, as he stepped over the threshold and into the darkened interior of the castle. He made his way across the entry and started up the stairs. "Everything that's gone before is the nightmare. This is the fantasy. This is the reward for enduring the nightmare."

"For you perhaps, but not for me." She let out a sigh of relief when she realized he'd successfully negotiated the treacherous stone stairs, then sucked in another shakier breath when she realized he was standing before the door to her father's bedchamber. Desperate, she tried to bargain with him, "If you let go of me, I promise not to scream this castle down around your ears."

"I want you to scream," he replied in a tone of voice that made her skin tingle. "And I intend to do my utmost to assist you. Just wait until we get inside."

"My clansmen will come when I scream."

"Undoubtedly," he murmured. "So will you."

"You don't believe me," she stated flatly.

"I believe you, my lady. I promise you." He pressed her against the wall, using his chest to hold her in place while he fumbled with the door latch.

"Then, you should understand that you leave me no choice." Taking advantage of his momentarily preoccupation with the door, Jessalyn opened her mouth to make good on her threat. But Neil was quicker. Leaning forward, he claimed her lips, capturing her breath, kissing her until her scream of outrage became a soft, mewling sigh. "Have you never kissed a man before?" he asked, seconds before the door swung open, banged against the wall and echoed loudly through the quiet halls as if to announce their arrival.

"Aye," she answered, "this morning."

Neil groaned aloud at her innocence, covering her mouth with his own as he carried her into the room. He laid her atop the coverlet and followed her down onto the bed, shifting the bulk of his weight to his forearms to keep from crushing her into the feather mattresses. When she was settled beneath him, Neil broke contact with her lips long enough to whisper, "*I* kissed you this morning. *You* didn't kiss back. Someone's been remiss in your tutoring."

"Well," she told him in an irate Scottish burr that delighted his senses. "Despite what you Sassenachs think, we're not all rutting savages. I may be ignorant of the ways of kissing, but I can learn."

"I'm at your service," he invited, kissing her again,

paying particular attention to her plump bottom lip. He savored the texture, flicking his tongue over it, touching the roughness of the myriad of tiny abrasions, absorbing the metallic taste of blood as he gently soothed the bite marks her teeth had made. He laved the wounds, licking her lips, teasing her, tempting her to open her mouth and allow him further access.

She yielded to temptation, parting her lips, allowing him to deepen the kiss. He complied, moving his lips on hers, kissing her harder, then softer, then harder once more, testing her response, slipping his tongue past her teeth, exploring the sweet, hot interior of her mouth with practiced finesse. As he leisurely stroked the inside of her mouth in a provocative imitation of the mating dance, Jessalyn followed his lead. She moved her lips on his and kissed him back. Her abundant talent and enthusiasm thrilled him as much as it surprised him and Neil made love to her mouth, teaching her everything he knew about the fine art of kissing.

She proved herself to be an excellent pupil, progressing rapidly, mirroring his actions and inventing a few of her own as she moved from novice to expert in the space of a few heartbeats. The jolt of pure pleasure he felt as she used her newfound talent with her tongue and teeth and mouth to entice him shook him down to his bare toes, threatening to steal his breath away along with his suddenly tenuous control. He was as hard as rock beneath his borrowed plaid, reminding him that it had been over four months since he'd held a woman in his arms. The blood pounded in his head and his arms trembled from the strain of holding himself above her while every nerve in his body urged him to lower himself onto her softness, find the hollow in the vee of her thighs, and press himself against her.

Neil forced himself to slow down. He pulled his mouth away from hers as her soft sigh of surrender registered in his brain, reminding himself that despite her new kissing prowess, she was a virgin. Pushing himself to his knees, Neil looked down at his bride. The MacInnes. His breath caught and his heart seemed to lodge itself in his throat at the sight. Her skirts had ridden up her leg revealing an expanse of bare creamy white thigh. Against her thigh lay a badly frayed length of blue ribbon from the garter of her stocking. It peeked out from the top of his black boot. Stocking? He swallowed. Hard. She had on stockings. She'd been barefooted. He remembered insulting her because of it. Remembered the sight of her curling her toes against the hard-packed earth of the bailey. When had she donned stockings? And where had she gotten them? He took a closer look. They were his. She was wearing his stockings tied with a bit of blue ribbon. His stockings and his boots.

Neil sucked in a breath as the tightening in his loins hit him like a punch to the belly. God's blood! Just looking at her had the power to make him ache. He struggled to tamp down his raging desire. His muscles were taut, his member rigid and insistent, and his control was stretched almost to the breaking point. With her hair fanned out across the pillow, her lips swollen from his kisses, the square of flesh visible above her bodice suffused with color, and the silver chain around her neck gleaming against a vivid pink background, she didn't look like a bride. She didn't look innocent. And she didn't look like the stubborn, willful leader of Clan MacInnes. She looked hungry and wanton and more beautiful than anything he'd ever seen. Neil squeezed his eyes shut in an effort to blot out the image. For the first time in his life, he wanted to put his artistic gift to a better purpose than drawing designs for buildings and cities. He wanted to draw her. He wanted to sketch her image on paper, then paint it. He wanted to fill canvas after canvas. Like da Vinci. Like Titian. He wanted to fill canvases with studies of Jessalyn MacInnes. Opening his tightly clenched fist, Neil skimmed the front of her dress with his fingertips. She shivered in response and her nipples budded beneath his feathery touch. He sucked in another breath. When she looked like this, she was dangerous. Dangerous to his peace of mind. And far more potent than the most expensive brandy ever bottled.

He wanted her. Like this. With her skirts riding up her hip. Wearing his black leather boots. With the tattered piece of blue ribbon lying against her leg. He wanted to bunch her skirts around her waist and lie naked between her thighs. He wanted to touch her. He wanted to taste her. He wanted to bury himself deep within her.

Reaching up, Neil unpinned the brooch holding the length of tartan wrapped across his chest and around his shoulder. He yanked the fabric away from his shirt, pulled the fine lawn over his head and unbuckled the belt holding the folds of his plaid together. The fabric slipped down his abdomen and over his hips where it pooled around his legs.

Jessalyn's eyes widened in surprise as Neil stripped off his plaid and bared his body. She quickly squeezed her eyes shut, but curiosity compelled her to open them again and the force of his male beauty took her breath away. He was long and lean with broad shoulders, narrow hips, and a finely-sculpted chest and abdomen. His muscles were taut and the flesh covering them was several shades darker than hers. Thick dark hair covered the center of his broad chest, tapering into a thin line that snaked down over his navel and into another dense thatch of dark curly hair from which a portion of his body stood proudly erect. The sight of that forbidden part of him affected her as nothing else had ever done. Her flesh grew warm and her body seemed to have a mind of its own. The tips of her breasts became almost painfully tight and she had to press her thighs together to hide the embarrassing moisture that pooled in the center of her. She wanted to touch him—to caress that part of him— to see if he was as hot as she was. Taking a deep breath, Jessalyn licked her suddenly dry lips and reached out . . .

The expression on her face—that of a kitten locating a hidden dish of cream—and the way her pink tongue whisked out to moisten her lips, as if she were already lapping up the treat, was Neil's undoing. He gave up the fight to curb his desire and leaning forward, claimed her mouth once more in a hard, needy kiss. He caressed her breasts through her bodice, stroking the hardened peaks as he ran his palm down the worn fabric of her undergarment. He used his fingers to inch her clothing higher, seeking the pleasures he knew lay beneath the tangle of hair at the juncture of her thighs. Reaching the soft triangle, he slipped his fingers between the plump folds of flesh. She was tight and warm and wet and ready.

And so was he. Gritting his teeth as the powerful force of desire ripped through his veins, Neil wedged his knee between her legs, initiating an onslaught of sensual persuasions—the pressure of his knee, the skillful touch of his fingers and his hungry kisses—to convince Jessalyn to open herself to him. She did so willingly and Neil quickly covered her body with his own. He meant to make love to her. He meant to arouse her further and introduce her to all of the delights lovers can share, but his body betrayed him. He could not blot out the wanton image of her that had burned itself into his brain. He teetered on the brink of self-control, fighting himself, fighting her responses until the sound, the sight, the scent of her combined to push him over the edge. Suddenly, he couldn't wait any longer. He couldn't find the strength to put her pleasure above his own. Groaning with frustration at his utter lack of gentlemanly control, Neil fastened his hands on her hips, flexed his taut muscles and pushed forward, burying himself inside her.

The sharp, tearing pain that followed on the heels of extraordinary pleasure took Jessalyn by surprise. She blinked at the abrupt change, pushing away from him— away from the source of her pain, wrenching her mouth away from his, refusing to be tricked into further pain by his devastating kisses. He tightened his grip on her, pulling her closer, using his greater weight to calm her struggles.

"Easy, easy," he crooned the words in her ear, soothing her as he would an anxious mare.

"Lie still," he whispered, straining to keep her from moving, fighting his overwhelming need to withdraw just far enough away from her to savor the heavenly feel as he thrust back in. Again and again. "The worst is over."

The worst is over. That meant there was more to follow, but she didn't care. She wasn't fool enough to allow him to continue his torture. The pleasure he'd wrought with his kisses and his knowing fingers did not make up for the pain he'd inflicted. It didn't matter that the worst was over. She wanted it completely over. "No," she answered, shoving herself back as far away from him as possible.

"Perdition!" He knew she was in pain and he tried to stop himself. But her squirming continued and his choice was to pull away and let her go—let them both go unsatisfied—or to push forward and find release for himself if not for her. He wanted to do the noble thing, but he did the only thing he could do. Lifting her hips, Neil began to move in and out. Slowly at first, then faster until he roared his release, muffling the words in the pillow beside her as he spilled himself within her and collapsed.

She wasn't sure but she thought he'd yelled her name. Jessalyn touched his shoulder. "My lord Derrowford?"

He didn't answer, but his rapid breathing had slowed to a manageable rate.

Crushed beneath his weight, Jessalyn tried again. "My lord Derrowford? Neil? Is this all? Is it over?"

He gave a deep sigh, tightened his arm around her waist and began to snore.

Achy and inexplicably unsettled by his uninspired handling of what should have been a glorious wedding night, Jessalyn sank her teeth into his shoulder. Satisfied that she'd left her mark on him, she heaved his weight off her and rolled to her side, leaving him to snore facedown upon the bed.

Chapter Ten

Neil awoke the following morning rested and re-freshed, despite the fact that his body was a col-lection of aching muscles and bruised flesh. He rolled from his stomach to his side and stretched, somewhat surprised to find himself alone and naked on top of the bed linens instead of beneath them. As he pulled the cov-ers around his waist and felt the penetrating chill of the damp morning air, he realized that at some point during the night he had wrapped himself in the coverlet in order to stay warm. And as vivid memories of his wedding night returned with a vengeance to plague him, Neil re-alized why.

For the first time in his adult life, he'd disappointed his bed partner. And not just any bed partner, but the one he had sworn to love, honor, cherish, and worship with his body for the rest of his natural life, his lady wife, the MacInnes. The woman who would bear his children. The center of the bed drew his gaze like a magnet and Neil couldn't look away. He was ashamed to admit that he had compounded his transgression by immediately falling into a sound sleep after selfishly taking the MacInnes's virginity. He wanted to believe that he'd been a better lover to her, but there, marring the coverlet was the proof—dark red smears of blood. He hadn't even un-

dressed her. He had claimed her virginity by tumbling
her fully-clothed atop the bed linens like some Covent
Garden doxy. Neil ran his hand over his forehead. The
headache that had plagued him since his meeting with
Auld Tam was gone, but he couldn't say the same for
his recollections of last night. The devil take him, but
the memory of her lying beneath him was still potent
enough to bring his male member fully erect. He glanced
around the sparsely furnished bedchamber, half hoping
to find her, half hoping for the opportunity to make
amends for disappointing her the night before. But he
was alone. His bride had disappeared. Except for the virginal stain marking the coverlet, there was no sign that
the MacInnes had ever shared the bedchamber.

He pushed himself off the bed and stood up. The stone
floor of the chamber was ice cold against the soles of
his feet and Neil shifted his weight from one foot to the
other as he looked around for his boots and his stockings. Both were gone. His bride had apparently taken
them with her when she left—along with the rest of his
clothing. All that remained was a length of neatly folded
tartan and his belt.

More than half an hour later, Neil had abandoned the
notion that he would ever be able to pleat that damned
piece of tartan and belt it around his waist the way those
old highlanders had done the day before. He aborted his
eighth attempt and in a fit of frustration, wound the cloth
around his waist like a length of toweling and knotted
it. He had also abandoned the notion that his wife or any
of the members of her clan would show up with food
or his clothing and now that he was decently, if incor-
rectly, covered, he intended to find both.

He stalked across the room and flung open the door
to find an old woman standing in the doorway—the same
old woman who had taunted him at the wedding feast
about wedding and bedding the MacInnes. She laughed
out loud at the sight of him.

Neil was not amused. "I hope to hell you brought my clothes."

She shook her head.

His stomach rumbled loudly and another possibility occurred to him. "Steak and kidney pie?"

She stared at him blankly.

"You know," he snapped. "Breakfast. Food. Sustenance." And in a measure of his hunger and his desperation he added, "oatmeal."

Her wizened face seemed to light up when he mentioned oatmeal, but she shook her head. "Nay."

"Then, what the devil are you doing here?" he demanded. "Besides laughing at me."

"I came for the proof," she answered.

"Proof of what? The fact that I'm still here? Hungry and except for this scrap of cloth, bare-arsed naked?"

"Nay," she answered once more, walking past him. "I've come for the proof of the bedding." She stopped beside the bed, then flipped back the covers and stared at the near pristine condition of the white linen covering the feather mattress. She shook her head and made a clucking sound with her tongue that sounded suspiciously like she'd decided he wasn't man enough to be married to the MacInnes.

"Not there," Neil stalked over to her, snatched the bed linen out of her hand and flipped it back down into place. "There!" He pointed to the dull red marks on the coverlet. She leaned closer to the bed in order to get a better look and Neil yanked the coverlet off the bed and held it in her face. "I can assure you, madam, that I've fulfilled my obligation and deflowered the MacInnes."

"Oooh, aye," she replied with a coyness that was almost as disconcerting as the speculative way she suddenly began to eye him. "And on top of the covers, too. Instead of right and properlike between them. I dinna know Sassenach men could be so randy."

"Oooh, aye," he mimicked in his best Scots burr. "As

randy as the randiest Scotsman. Late at night and in the morning light."

"Then, wee Jessie is truly fortunate. Wait until the rest of the women see this." She waved the coverlet at him.

Neil groaned. He wasn't so sure "wee Jessie" would consider herself fortunate after last night. Especially when her clanswomen were about to wave the proof under her nose. He knew, of course, that once upon a time it was quite common to see stained bed sheets flapping in the breeze on the morning following a wedding, but the barbaric custom was rarely practiced in London anymore and he'd had no idea that Scottish clans still subscribed to the tradition. "Is that necessary?" he asked.

"Oooh aye," she answered. "Verra important. The clan would be disappointed if we dinna display the proof." Seeing the expression on his face, she added, "They might think that there was sumthin' wrong with our laird or with you. And our wee Jessie wouldna want that."

Neil had to fight to keep from gnashing his teeth. No, of course "wee Jessie" wouldn't want her clan to be disappointed. *She* could be disappointed, but she had too much pride to allow her clan to find fault with the way her husband fulfilled his sexual obligation. "Where is the MacInnes?" he asked.

"She's about the bailey tending to business."

"Will you tell her I wish to see her?"

She shrugged. "I can tell her, but I canna promise she'll come to ye. She's tending to verra important matters."

"As important as tending to her husband?" he asked.

"If ye were my husband, I'd say not. But yer Jessie's husband and she's the . . ."

"MacInnes," Neil finished. "I know." He glanced at the woman. "I was on my way out the door to find her when you arrived. I guess there's no reason I can't continue my mission."

"Ye canna go like that," she said, pointing to his makeshift plaid.

He looked down at the tartan tied about his waist, then turned his attention back to the woman. "Why not?"

"It's na proper."

"Then show me how to fashion it properly."

She blushed red to the roots of her gray hair and backed away from him. "I canna. That's the duty of yer wife. Or yer lover."

"Let's see if I've got this right," he said, pacing the length of the room and back again. "My wife isn't here. And even though I wish to see her, she's tending to important matters and may or may not choose to attend me. My own clothing has disappeared and I cannot go to my wife unless I'm properly dressed in a Scottish garment I have no idea how to fashion. And you, a Scottish woman, presumably my relation by marriage and certainly old enough to be my mother, cannot help me fashion this Scottish clothing because it wouldn't be seemly for you to usurp the role of my wife. Which means I'm expected to sit alone and bare-arsed in my bedchamber on my honeymoon until someone brings me my uniform or my wife comes to dress me."

"Aye."

"Well, bugger that!" he exclaimed. "And bugger propriety! I'm going to find my wife."

Neil's appearance in the old bailey, moments later, created quite a stir among the cottagers. Especially since Auld Davina followed close on his heels, waving the proof of the bedding before her like a nobleman waving his coat of arms. The women of Clan MacInnes who gathered around to see if the bed linens bore the stain of the MacInnes's virginal blood took advantage of the unique opportunity to ooh and aah, not only over the blood-stained coverlet, but over the superbly arranged mass of male flesh and sinew that the tartan wrapped snugly around Jessalyn's Sassenach husband's narrow waist displayed so nicely.

Conferring with the Ancient Gentlemen on the far side of the outer bailey, Jessalyn looked up to see what was causing her kinswomen to gather like clucking hens around earthworms and caught sight of her husband striding across the yard a few steps ahead of Alisdair's wife, Davina. She recognized the fabric Davina held in her hands. It was the woven spread used to cover her father's bed. When she'd last seen it, it had been wrapped around her husband. Now, the spread was in Davina's possession, and her husband was wrapped in the length of tartan he'd worn the day before. But instead of being properly pleated and belted into a plaid, the tartan was wound around his hips like a primitive loincloth. For all that his garment concealed, he might as well have strolled through the outer bailey naked. And she wasn't the only one who had noticed. She narrowed her gaze as Sorcha, the widow of one of her cousins, reached out and brushed Neil's flank as he walked by. He didn't seem to notice, but the rest of her kinswomen had. They couldn't take their eyes off him and any second now, Jessalyn fully expected to have to march across the yard and remind the lot of them that he was *her* husband and that they would do well to keep their eyes in their heads and their hands to themselves. She gasped at her kinswomen's and her husband's audacity and her surprise was enough to draw the three Ancient Gentlemen's undivided attention.

"What the devil is the lad wearin'?" Tam demanded, turning his attention to the earl's improper state of dress. He narrowed his gaze at Jessalyn. "Have ye forgotten yer wifely duty, lass? Dinna ye show yer husband the proper way to wear his plaid?"

Jessalyn shook her head. She hadn't forgotten her wifely duty. She'd ignored it. She'd taken his Sassenach clothes and boots in the hopes that he would remain in his bedchamber. After sharing the marriage bed, she had needed some time and distance from him. "I dinna show him how to wear his plaid because I dinna think he'd be up and about so early." It wasn't the whole truth, but it was as much of the truth as she was willing to admit to three of the co-conspirators who had married her to an

Englishman, then looked at her with censure in their eyes because she'd failed to fulfill her wifely duties. They were Scots warriors, her Ancient Gentlemen. They were supposed to be on her side and they were siding with him. Because they were men.

"What are you doing here?" Angry at the Ancient Gentlemen for siding with Neil when they should have remained loyal to her, Jessalyn asked the question much more sharply than she intended when Neil came to a halt in front of her.

Neil flicked a glance over his shoulder as someone brushed his side. He frowned at the old woman holding the stained coverlet and at the growing crowd who pointed to the linen and whispered amongst themselves in a language he couldn't understand, then turned his attention back to the MacInnes, pinning her with his angry gaze. "I'm apparently heading a parade of kinswomen who've been charged with the duty of displaying the proof that you were a virgin until I bedded you." He reached down and grabbed a corner of the bedding and held it aloft. "The MacInnes entered her marriage bed as pure as a newborn babe." He roared, flapping his end of the coverlet in the air. "She bled all over the coverlet when I took her and she's chaste no longer. Have you seen enough, *ladies*?" He sneered the title. "Or will you require further evidence of my Sassenach savagery?"

The women of the clan scattered like a flock of startled chicks.

Neil let go of the bedding and barred his teeth in grim satisfaction before turning back to face her.

Jessalyn heard the note of self-deprecation in his voice and ignored it. She had to be strong in the face of overwhelming temptation. She couldn't allow herself to be swayed by a pair of clear green eyes or a pair of enticing dimples. "How dare you present yourself before me in such a manner?" She demanded. "And how dare you frighten my women?"

"I dare," Neil managed through gritted teeth, "because

instead of waking up beside a warm and willing wife on the morning after our wedding, I was forced to go begging to the MacInnes for my daily bread."

"And . . ." she hinted broadly, waiting for the apology she felt he owed her after the debacle that was their wedding night.

"And you may bloody well be the MacInnes but I'm your husband and like it or not, there are a few wifely duties I expect you to fulfill!"

"And what wifely duties might those be, my lord?" she asked sweetly, too sweetly. Having Neil remind her of her obligations was not what Jessalyn expected or wanted from him.

"I expect you to warm my bed during the night," he responded. "And I expect you to still be there when I open my eyes and when I arise, I expect to be fed and properly clothed."

"Is that all, my lord?" Sarcasm dripped like honey from her lips.

"No," he said. "That's not all. I expect you to be warm and accommodating if I choose to make love to you every morning."

He succeeded in wiping the smirk off her face and replacing it with a most becoming blush. "I'm cold and hungry and horny—though not necessarily in that order. I spent the better part of an hour trying to fasten this damned rag," he indicated the tartan wrapped around his waist, "and nobody seems to know where my bloody uniform and boots have gone!"

"*I* took your bloody uniform and boots," Jessalyn told him. "Like it or not you're the husband of the MacInnes and you'll dress as we dress. I can't allow you or Sergeant Marsden or Corporal Stanhope to wear your uniforms in the village or on the castle grounds." Recognizing the firm set of his mouth and jaw and the belligerent look in his eyes, she softened her edict with an explanation. "Look around you, my lord. There are women and children here. Until you arrived, the only time most of them had ever seen Englishmen was when they rode in here wearing crimson tunics and trousers just like yours, then proceeded to burn and pillage. They terrorized the women and children, killed our kinsmen and slaughtered or stole our livestock. The sight of your uniforms is enough to bring back their memories of that terrible day."

She didn't say it, but Neil saw the way she shuddered and knew that the sight of his uniform brought back *her* memories of that terrible day.

"The people of Glenaonghais have struggled so hard to survive and to put the memories behind them," Jessalyn continued, "that I dare not risk their peace of mind or your safety by allowing you or your men to wear your uniforms."

"Fair enough." Neil nodded in agreement. As long as he was clothed in a semi-modest fashion and fed on a semi-regular basis, he was willing to concede the battle over the wearing of his uniform. His stomach rumbled loudly and he smiled at her. "Then why don't you show me how to properly fasten this thing—" He swept a hand over his tartan. "—so we can eat breakfast. I'm hungry."

His boyish smile didn't affect his wife the way he hoped. Instead of smiling in return, his bride recoiled as if he'd struck her. "Get one of the men to show you," she ordered. "I cannot."

"Why not?" he demanded. "The old woman who came for the proof of the bedding told me she couldn't do it because my wife had to do it." He eyed her speculatively. "You're my wife."

"I cannot," she repeated, unwilling to explain that she couldn't touch him, couldn't fashion the pleats of his garment over his bare skin. She couldn't perform that intimate task until she felt more like a wife and less like a trollop he'd purchased and bedded for the night.

"I understand why you can't allow me to wear my uniform, but this—" He threw up his hands. "This I don't understand. Isn't helping a husband with his plaid each morning something every good highland wife does?"

"Yes."

"Well?" he urged, "have at it." Moving closer to her, he raised his arms. "The sooner you're done, the sooner we can eat. I'm hungry."

Jessalyn flushed a bright red. She could feel the heat from his body and her fingers itched to touch him. But not here. Not in front of the entire village. Not like this. He hadn't earned the right to solicit her tender, wifely ministrations. She couldn't touch him without remembering how he'd boasted of his prowess in the bed-chamber, without remembering how empty his boasts had turned out to be. Her husband was a huge disappoint-ment as a lover and it angered her to discover that the heat and scent and sheer beauty of the man was almost more than she could resist. And since she couldn't trust herself not to give in to her desire to touch him, she used her anger to keep him at a distance. "You're hungry. I'm hungry. We're all hungry. Look around you once again, my unobservant Lord Derrowford. Do you see any food? Do you see any women preparing a meal to break the fast?" She waved her hand toward the long empty tables still set up in the bailey. "There is no food."

"But yesterday . . . last night . . ." he sputtered. "The wedding feast. The oatmeal."

"That was the last of our food stores," Jessalyn ad-mitted. "The women used everything we had to prepare the feast. We'll be going hungry until we can restock the larder."

Neil glanced around. The women who had been show-ing off the blood-stained coverlet were now preparing to launder it while the old men and boys sat on crudely made stools and benches outside the thatch-roofed huts lining the walls of the bailey and whittled. He sighed. The village bordered a loch and a dense forest. Surely, there were fish in the loch and game in the woods. Surely the men of Clan MacInnes—even old men and young boys—knew how to hunt and fish. Why did the MacInnes allow them to whittle away the daylight hours when there was no food in the village? "Why aren't the men out stalking game?" he demanded. "Why aren't they out hunting and fishing instead of sitting around whittling?"

"You ignorant, arrogant Sassenach! Do you still not ken the damage we've suffered at the hands of greedy soldiers like you?" she demanded. "Those men and boys aren't sitting around whittling. They're fashioning spears so that they might hunt and fish to provide food for the clan."

"Spears?" Neil repeated the word as if he'd never heard it before.

"Yes, *spears*," Jessalyn said. "The English confiscated our weapons and the tools we need to make weapons. All we have left are our dirks."

Neil gave a low whistle of begrudging amazement that his fellow countrymen had managed to do the impossible—disarm a clan of Scottish highlanders. "You mean there isn't a single firearm or sword in the entire village?"

"Of course not." Jessalyn snorted. "We managed to hide a few firearms along with a few claymores and battle axes but firearms dinna work without powder and shot and claymores and battle axes aren't much good for bagging rabbits and small game. That's why we need the spears and the snares."

Neil stared out at the dark sparkling waters of the loch. "The water looks deep. Too deep for trolling with hooks and lines."

"Aye, 'tis very deep," Jessalyn replied. "Before the Uprising, the fishermen of the clan took the boats out every morning and netted our catch, but the soldiers slashed and burned our fishing nets and crippled our boats. All we have are hooks and lines." She shrugged her shoulders. "The English army destroyed nearly everything we owned, including our livelihoods with a thoroughness and a savagery I never imagined possible." Her voice broke. "They shot most of the cattle and sheep and hogs along with the geese and chickens, then bayoneted the rest. They spared us because they wanted us to watch the destruction. They spared us because the army feared a public outcry in London against the slaughter of innocent women and children." She managed an ironic laugh. "Quiet, desperate starvation goes unnoticed."

"I'm sorry," he said, turning to comfort her, to put a hand on her shoulder and pull her close, but she stepped away, out of his reach. He let his hand drop to his side. "Perhaps you should send someone to Edinburgh to purchase supplies . . ."

"I already have," she cut him off. "But our stomachs will remain empty until he returns. Unless we're able to catch enough food for an evening meal."

Neil frowned, remembering the look of rapture in her eyes as she spooned up the charred oatmeal. He briefly recalled the way his hands had spanned her waist and the sharp, jutting angle of her hipbones. She couldn't afford to miss another meal. She was much too thin already. "We might be able to catch a few rabbits or fish," he said, "but hardly enough to feed a whole village. So that leaves us with only one other option."

"What's that?"

"We buy or barter food from somewhere else."

"With the exception of the Sutherland and the Munros, our neighbors don't have enough food to spare and even if they did, we've nothing to offer in return."

"You have coin," he reminded her. "You can pay."

"I'll not pay the Sutherland or the Munros for grain and livestock they stole from us!"

"Then we'll just have to resort to raiding and steal what we need." He waited for Jessalyn to say something and when she didn't, Neil followed the line of her gaze to where her plaid was tied about his waist. He moved the silver key she'd hung around his neck to one side and scratched idly at the hair on his chest, then rolled his broad shoulders, stretched mightily and watched from beneath the cover of his eyelashes as Jessalyn devoured him with her eyes. He smiled and shifted his weight from one foot to the other. The tartan slipped a bit lower and he knew that the jutting prominence of his male member was practically all that kept it from sliding to the ground. He didn't like displaying himself so boldly, but he liked the idea of sleeping alone even less. And he'd stroll through the village naked if that's what it took to make her take notice of him and the bit of paradise he could offer her. After all, it was only fair that she be as aware of him as he was of her.

Jessalyn's breath came in shallow gasps as she focused her gaze on her husband's narrow hips. She forgot about anger. Forgot about hunger and the gnawing in her belly. She forgot about everything except the swath of fabric that kept Neil from finding himself completely exposed. The tartan tied about his waist had dipped dangerously low. And although an evil imp of female curiosity wanted the worn fabric to slide off his hips, down his long legs and onto the ground, Jessalyn held her breath and prayed that it would stay knotted.

"Right, wife?" He repeated, reaching out to touch her arm.

"What?" She snatched her arm and her gaze away from him.

"I said that if our neighbors refuse to sell us the food we need in order to survive until our man returns from Edinburgh with provisions, then we'll follow MacInnes clan tradition."

"What do you know of MacInnes traditions?" she snapped.

"I know more about MacInnes customs than most Sassenachs. Especially the time-honored tradition of taking what you want or need by raiding." He quirked an eyebrow at her. "That's how I came to have the MacInnes as my wife."

"Do you think of me as your wife after only one day and night of marriage?" she asked, softly, searching his green eyes for the truth.

"Aye," Neil replied in his best Scots burr. "As does

the priest who married us and the women who spent an inordinate amount of time examining the proof of the bedding."

"You and they may think it," she answered. "But I don't feel it. You took my virginity, but you failed to live up to your boast and make me feel like a wife."

"On the contrary," Neil retorted. "I think you feel very much like a wife. My failure to live up to my boast and my reputation ensured that." He leaned closer and whispered. "On her wedding night, a bride shouldn't feel frustrated or neglected. Nor should she feel she has to endure the marriage bed. On her wedding night, a bride should feel cherished like a lover or a favorite mistress."

"That's easy for you to say," she muttered beneath her breath. "When you're all words and no action."

"What was that?"

"I said—" She lifted her chin a notch. "—that you failed on all accounts, my lord."

"Aye," he agreed. "I failed you on your wedding night and that's what has you in such a fine temper." He followed her fascinated gaze and rubbed at the mark on his left shoulder.

"I'm not . . ." she protested, casting a guilty glance at the dark purple bruise on his left shoulder—the bruise she'd inflicted when she'd bitten him—repaying him in kind for the pain and frustration she'd suffered.

"Oh, yes, you are," he said. "But, my dear MacInnes, we can remedy that. You're welcome to pleat my tartan and touch me any time and any way you like."

"No, thank you, my lord," she replied sharply. "Once is quite enough."

"You're refusing to do your wifely duty?"

"I've done my duty to my clan," she answered, "by marrying you. That's all I care about."

"What of your duty to provide the clan with an heir?"

She looked surprised.

"The purpose of marriage," Neil reminded her, "is to sanctify the union of a man and a woman and to produce legal offspring to inherit as opposed to bastards who do not. You said you wanted children. Three or four, I believe."

Jessalyn lifted her chin a notch higher. "I'm quite certain I've fulfilled my obligation. You look healthy and I've no doubt that I'm with child."

"Then, I suppose the sight of me dressed—or rather, undressed like this won't bother you." He gave her a rueful frown.

"You don't have to dress in that manner," she protested, glancing down at the haphazard way he'd tied his garment. "Tam or Alisdair or Dougal or any of the other men can help you pleat your tartan. They can show you the proper way to wear it."

Neil grinned at her. "Oh no, Mac," he said. "The pleating of my tartan every morning is your responsibility and I cannot allow you to shirk your wifely duties so easily. I didn't marry Tam or Alisdair or Dougal or any of the other men," he echoed her earlier phrase. "I married you."

Chapter Eleven

"Yer a bold and darin' mon to taunt her that way," Auld Tam said to Neil when Jessalyn turned on her heel and hurried across the bailey and into the castle.

Neil faced the old warrior. "Why not taunt her? The worst that will happen is that the temperature of the top half of my body will match the freezing temperatures of my feet and my nether regions."

"Our winters can get very cold, lad." Tam reached under his bonnet and scratched his pate. "She may look tender and soft, but our wee Jessie can be as tough and as stubborn as her father was."

Neil smiled. "I wouldn't expect otherwise."

Tam raised an eyebrow at that.

"Look at her, man," Neil ordered, nodding his head in Jessalyn's direction, watching as she reached the castle doors. "She's one of the most beautiful women I've ever seen, but she's barely a head taller than the children running around the village and so bloody malnourished that I can almost see through her flesh. There isn't a weak bone in her body. She couldn't have survived this long if she wasn't as tough and tenacious, as fearless and as proud as any Scots warrior you ever placed on a field of battle."

Auld Tam heard the pride in Neil's voice. "Aye, she's a right bonny lass."

"A right bonny lass?" Neil couldn't believe his ears. "As far as I'm concerned, she's the best thing this bloody country has ever produced."

Neil hadn't realized he'd admitted so much of his private thoughts aloud until he turned from his leisurely perusal of the sway of the MacInnes's hips and discovered Dougal, Alisdair, and Auld Tam grinning like fools.

"We feel the same way aboot you and England, lad," Alisdair cackled.

Unable to contain his curiosity, Dougal asked, "How are ye going to get Jessie to do her duty?"

"I'm not," Neil declared. "And neither are you." He gave the three old men a sharp look. "You're not to attempt to persuade her or coerce her or blackmail her into it. You've meddled in her life enough."

"But, laddie . . ." Alisdair began.

"No, buts, Alisdair," Neil said firmly. "You trusted her father enough to accept me as his choice for her. You helped make me her husband and now, you must trust me to do what's best. The MacInnes has done her duty to her father, her clan, her church and to her husband. She has earned the right to vent her spleen and take her time deciding how to go forward with our marriage."

"But you just told her that you wouldn't allow her to shirk her wifely duties," Dougal protested.

"Aye," Neil agreed, "*I* did, but I'm not going to try to break the MacInnes's spirit. When she agrees to do her wifely duty, it must be because she chooses to do so— because she wants to."

Alisdair shook his head. "I dinna understand. If yer not going to force her or shame her or persuade her into doing her duty, how are ye gonna accomplish it?"

"I'm going to tempt her into it," Neil announced, grinning broadly.

The three jaws of the Ancient Gentlemen dropped open simultaneously.

"Yer what?" Dougal sputtered.

"I'm going to tempt her into it and if that means running around the village buck naked and allowing every female in the vicinity to tweak the MacInnes's jealousy by ogling me, then it will be worth it."

"Oh, they'll be ogling ye, laddie, if this mornin's anything to go by." Auld Tam began to chuckle. "Yer playin' with fire."

"Yes, I know," Neil said. "But so is she. I'm English and I know that in many ways, the MacInnes still sees me as the enemy, but I belong to her as much as she belongs to me. Eventually she'll want to claim me. In the meantime, I intend to do everything I can to encourage her."

"But ye said that we mustna attempt to persuade her," Alisdair reminded him.

"That's right," Neil agreed. "I said that the three of you must not do anything to try to persuade her. I didn't say *I* couldn't or wouldn't."

"Bloody Sassenachs," Dougal grumbled to his companions in Gaelic. "Always twistin' words around to suit themselves."

"Now, mon," Auld Tam soothed his friend, "this time, he's right. Unless he begins mistreatin' the lass, we canna meddle in his marriage. We're actin' in Callum's stead and even Callum couldna interfere once the vows were spoken."

He didn't understand the language, but Neil recognized the hostility in Dougal's tone of voice and the glares the older man sent his way. He also understood that Auld Tam had settled into his customary role of intermediary. He placed his hand on Tam's arm and asked for a translation.

"Dougal wants to make certain that yer methods of persuadin' are gentlemanly," Auld Tam said.

Neil met Dougal's gaze and shook his head. "I'm afraid my methods will be more mercenary than gentlemanly." He gave a self-derisive snort. "After last night,

I'm very much aware that the only thing I've done to impress the MacInnes so far is to produce a significant amount of coin as a wedding gift and I intend to capitalize on that." He turned to Tam. "Yesterday, you told me that you'd already sent word of my abduction to the marquess of Chisenden."

"Aye," Auld Tam answered warily.

"And the MacInnes told me she'd sent a man to Edinburgh this morning with money to buy provisions."

"Aye."

"That's unfortunate," Neil said. "Because we'll need to send another to the marquess with a note from me requesting—" He halted his words when he saw the disbelieving looks on the faces of the three older men. "You can read it before I seal it if that suits you." At their nod, Neil continued, "—more supplies than the coins I gave the MacInnes will buy. In addition to flour and sugar and salt and molasses and oats and dried meat and fish, we need cattle and sheep and horses and chickens and geese and fishing boats and nets and . . ." He glanced at the men, silently asking for suggestions.

"A good Scots blacksmith," Alisdair said.

"We'll also need firearms with powder and shot and other weapons for hunting and for defense . . ." Neil added.

"Even the marquess of Chisenden canna send firearms," Alisdair warned. "To do so would violate the king's own edict against arming hostile clans."

"As of yesterday, Clan MacInnes cannot be considered a hostile clan, but an ally of the marquess of Chisenden and therefore, an ally of the crown," Neil reminded them. "And," he lowered his voice until it was barely above a whisper, "you had no way of knowing I'd be confined to my quarters and guarded by Corporal Stanhope and Sergeant Marsden when you planned my abduction, but by freeing me and abducting the others, you've ensured that I'll be wanted for escaping and the corporal and the sergeant will be wanted for helping me.

We'll be condemned and hunted down by the commanding officer at Fort Augustus."

"You couldna escaped," Auld Tam scoffed. "I had to cut you loose."

"But will they be able to tell that you cut me loose and that Sergeant Marsden and Corporal Stanhope did not?" Neil asked.

"Of course they can tell. We dinna bother to hide the pony tracks when we breached the gap in the wall. We only hid them once we reached the moor. Any fool should be able to see the pony tracks and know ye were abducted."

Neil snorted. "Major General Oliver is a fool. But that won't matter, because he's only going to see what he wants to see. And he'll want to see that I escaped."

"Why?" Dougal asked.

"Because he hates me."

The three Ancient Gentlemen sighed in unison. "We dinna know."

"You couldn't have known of the enmity between Spotty Oliver and me," Neil said ruefully. "Even my grandfather doesn't know the full extent of it. But I do. Major General Oliver won't rest until he has me clamped in irons once again or swinging from the nearest gibbet. That's why we must have the firearms. We must be able to defend the castle and the village—from Oliver and from anyone else who will want to take what we have."

Auld Tam reached up under his bonnet and scratched his head in a gesture Neil was beginning to recognize as an indication of Tam's level of agitation.

"Fortunately, I made my distaste of Scotland well known. We should have a few weeks to prepare before Scotty realizes I'm not cozily ensconced in my London townhouse and begins looking to the highlands for other possibilities." Neil rubbed his hands together. "What else will we need?"

The three older men looked at each other.

"If we're all out of ideas," Neil suggested, "why don't we ask the women?"

Alisdair looked up and caught his wife's eye, then motioned for Davina to join the group before he asked her what the women of the clan needed from Edinburgh.

"Spindles and looms," Davina replied, laundry basket resting on her hip as she joined the conversation. "And bolts of cloth and packets of needles and pins and buttons and soap and leather goods and a cobbler."

Neil looked askance at the last suggestion. "I was told that going without shoes is a highland tradition."

"Aye, it 'tis in the summer months," she answered. "But, in truth, like the English, we prefer shoes and stockings durin' the cold winter months."

Neil smiled at the honest reply as he wiggled his bare toes against the dirt. "I'm thrilled to hear it." He lowered his voice to address the small group. "There is something else. The MacInnes must believe that the coin I gave her was used to purchase everything except the personal items I intend to buy for her. She must think her man in Edinburgh is the most skillful bargainer Scotland has ever produced, because I cannot risk hurting her pride. We'll explain the appearance of the personal gifts by convincing the MacInnes that I asked you to send a message to my grandfather requesting that a proper dowry be provided and sent for presentation to my bride. Agreed?"

"You think to buy our wee Jessie's favor with English goods and fancy clothes?" Dougal snorted.

"I mean to court her the way she should have been courted before we were wed," Neil replied. "And all women appreciate fine gowns and jewels."

"Not our Jessie. You'd get further with her if you gave her a crew of stonemasons to repair the castle than you will with clothes and jewels."

"Then I'm in luck." Neil grinned. "Because I happen to be a very good architect. I'm much better at building, repairing and fortifying buildings than I am at wooing.

And procuring a crew of stonemasons to help repair my lady's castle is a feat I should have no trouble accomplishing." He caught sight of the smug looks that passed between the three older men. "Especially since there will be no interference from the three of you or the marquess of Chisenden to prevent the crew of stonemasons and the shipments of stone from showing up—as happened at Fort Augustus."

"Yer willin' to rebuild that crumbling old castle to win Jessie's heart?" Auld Tam asked.

"If that's what it takes," Neil said.

It was almost as if his words catapulted the others into action. "Alisdair, go keep an eye on Jessie," Tam instructed. "And Dougal, send young Ian to catch Ranald before he leaves for Edinburgh."

Neil lifted an eyebrow. "I thought he'd already left."

Auld Tam shrugged his shoulders. "Davina, fetch a pen and parchment and sealing wax from Father Moray so the earl can send a message to his grandfather."

Auld Tam waited until the others had hurried to do his bidding before turning to the younger man. He clamped a hand on Neil's shoulder. "Ye had me worried yesterday, laddie, and doubtin' Callum's choice in allying us with a Sassenach—even one as rich and powerful as the marquess of Chisenden, but today, I'm proud to say he made the right decision."

"What changed your mind about me?"

"Every Sassenach I've ever known has used force to get his way. It would be verra simple fer a strong mon like you to break Jessie's spirit, but ye've shown that yer willin' to humble yerself in order to protect it."

"I may be Sassenach and I may have only known her one day, but my grandfather taught me to recognize a person's strengths as well as their weaknesses. The MacInnes deserves to have a man build a castle for her," Neil knelt down on the ground, picked up a stone and idly began to trace the outline of a small feminine footprint until he'd dug a small groove around it. "Her spirit, her courage, her strength, her compassion and her loyalty to the members of her clan are some of the things I admire most about her."

"When a Sassenach pays tribute to a Scot," Auld Tam said, "he becomes worthy of my friendship and my trust." He reached out a hand to Neil. "And when a mon acknowledges a woman's strengths then he becomes worthy of winning her heart."

Chapter Twelve

The marquess of Chisenden lifted the morning mail from the silver salver on the massive oak desk in his study. He sorted the array of cards and invitations scattered on the tray, stopping when he came to a rolled sheet of parchment. He immediately recognized the seal on the parchment and his hand shook as he broke the wax and unrolled the document. It contained several pages. Chisenden's heart seemed to thud against the walls of his chest in anticipation and he heaved an audible sigh of relief when his grandson's distinctive handwriting seemed to leap off the page at him. He whispered a heart-felt prayer of thanks as he read the note and the long list of instructions Neil had written. His grandson was furious with him. That much was patently clear from his letter. He was furious enough to make demands no other man would dream of making of the king-maker—and justified in making them, supremely confident in the knowledge that these demands would be met. But the boy had done his duty like the gentleman he'd been raised to be. He had assumed responsibility and he had written to inform his grandfather that he had done so.

The marquess smiled, his chest puffed out and fair to

bursting with love for and pride in his only grandchild. "Who brought this message?" He demanded of Kingsley, his butler, who waited patiently just inside the doorway of the study. "When did it arrive?"

"A messenger from Scotland delivered it three-quarters of an hour ago, sir, while you were meeting with the king's secretary."

"Where's the messenger?" Lord Chisenden demanded.

"He's in the kitchen, sir. Shall I send for him?"

The marquess glanced at the clock on the mantel and waved Kingsley's suggestion aside. "No need to pull the man away from his meal. I'll speak to him there."

"Sir?" Kingsley's jaw dropped open as he stood stiffly at attention.

"No need to stand there gaping like a fish on dry land, either, Kingsley. Just because I haven't paid a visit to the kitchens since I was a boy doesn't mean that I am not aware of their purpose or their location. I'm not quite in my dotage and I'm completely capable of finding the kitchens in my own home." The marquess folded the letter and placed it in the pocket of his coat. He brushed a speck of lint from his lapel, tugged at the hem of his waistcoat and strode out the door, calling to Kingsley over his shoulder. "I'll speak to Cook. Have someone ready my coach and send a messenger around to the palace requesting an urgent meeting with His Majesty and the First Lord of the Treasury, Sir Robert Walpole. Fetch Lady Chisenden and my secretary, and ask Mrs. Mingot to assemble the rest of the staff as soon as I return from my meeting with the king. I'll also need to speak with the earl of Derrowford's man of business. Send someone out to find him and tell him that I'll require a meeting with him in my study after I've spoken to the staff."

"Trouble, my lord?" Kingsley asked, a worried frown creasing his forehead.

Chisenden grinned. "Not at all. Quite the opposite.

His Lordship has sent instructions from Scotland and we have a great deal of work to do."

The walls and corridors of the house seemed to vibrate with excitement as the marquess of Chisenden made his way through the richly paneled halls and rooms on his way to the kitchen. Maids curtseyed and footmen and other household servants tugged at their forelocks as the master of the house ventured into territory he hadn't trod in fifty years. The hustle and bustle of the kitchen came to a standstill as the marquess breached the threshold. Kitchen maids and assistants halted in their tracks, practically falling over themselves to pay their respects to the man few of them had ever seen up close. Cook wiped the perspiration from her brow, clutched at her ample bosom, and fumbled for a chair to keep her knees from buckling beneath her as Lord Chisenden entered the cavernous kitchen. "I've come to speak to the man from Scotland."

"H-h-he isn't here." Cook stumbled over her words.

The marquess pointed to the empty bowl on the kitchen table. "Kingsley told me he sent the man to the kitchen to get something to eat."

"He ate two bowls of stew, your lordship, then went out to the stables to bed down," Cook reported.

The marquess frowned at that, his thick, dark brows meeting over the bridge of his nose. "I cannot believe that the staff of Chisenden Place did not offer a man who had traveled hundreds of miles to bring me a message from Scotland a comfortable bed indoors?"

"We offered, my lord, but the young man refused it. He thanked me quite profusely for the meal and couldn't say enough about my stew, but he wouldn't hear of taking the bed we offered. Said he'd rather sleep outdoors than put someone else out of his bed or cause any interruption in the household routine." Cook shrugged her shoulders, the idea of anyone preferring to share quarters with the horses instead of in a warm feather mattress quite beyond her comprehension.

"He's a Scotsman," Chisenden laughed. "He probably didn't like the idea of being surrounded and outnumbered by Sassenachs in an unfamiliar house. But he was tactful. It sounds as if he has the makings of a diplomat. I must find the man and shake his hand." He brushed Cook's hand with his own as he walked past her toward the doorway which led through the scullery and outside. "I've asked Kingsley to have Mrs. Mingot assemble the staff in the ballroom. Once I've spoken to the messenger from Scotland, Lady Chisenden and I will speak to the staff." He nodded toward the pots simmering atop the stove and the pans of pastries set to go into the ovens. "If your duties allow it, I'd like you and your assistants to join us."

"Of course, your lordship," Cook lowered her gaze and bobbed a quick curtsey.

"I rarely have the opportunity to say it," he said. "But I thank you for your loyalty and for the work you do." He turned away before anyone had a chance to respond and hurried out of the kitchen.

"I've come to speak to the Scotsman," Chisenden called to the head groom as he strode through the stables.

"He's up there, yer lordship." The groom pointed toward the loft.

Chisenden nodded an affirmative and walked past the stalls lining both sides of the barn. He didn't stop to exchange greetings with the men or admire the expensive horseflesh they tended so diligently. He didn't pause until he reached the ladder leading up to the hayloft. Glancing up, Lord Chisenden wiped his palms down the sides of his immaculately cut breeches, then grasped the ladder and climbed to the loft.

He found the Scots messenger wrapped in a well-worn length of tartan and curled up atop a pile of sweet-smelling hay. Resisting the urge to nudge the man with the toe of his boot, Lord Chisenden knelt down and placed his hand on the man's shoulder.

The Scot jerked awake at the touch and jumped to his feet ready to fight.

"Easy, lad," Lord Chisenden crooned in a Scottish burr rusty from long years without use. "No one here will harm you." He rose to his full height and found himself staring into the face of the messenger who was little more than a boy in a man's body. As he studied the young man's features, Lord Chisenden realized the Scot had reason to wake up flailing. His eyes were dark blue flecked with gold. The gold-flecked dark blue that was the heritage of members of Clan MacInnes—the gold-flecked dark blue that brought back vivid, aching reminders of Helen Rose. But the resemblance to Helen Rose ended with the color of his eyes. A thin, ugly scar marred his face from the corner of his right eye and across his cheek and chin. Chisenden had seen enough battle scars to recognize the mark. Someone had laid the young man's flesh open with a sword. Since the young man was a Scot, the average Londoner might assume the scar had been the result of a raid on a clan of fellow highlanders, but Lord Chisenden knew better. Scotsmen didn't carry cavalry sabers. The scar on the messenger's face had been made by a blow to the face with the flat of a cavalry saber and the marquess was willing to bet that the man wielding that saber had been an Englishman on horseback. Chisenden extended his hand. "I'm the marquess of Chisenden. You brought a message from my grandson, the earl of Derrowford."

The messenger studied the outstretched hand of the older man for a moment, then shook it. "Ranald Mac-Curran. I don't have the message ye want, sir. I gave it to the mon who answered the door at the house."

"Yes, I know. That man was my butler, Kingsley. He gave it to me and I've read it. But there are a few things in it that I'd like to discuss with you."

Ranald shrugged his shoulders. "I canna help ye there, sir," he said. "His Lordship sealed the letter himself and I dinna open it."

Lord Chisenden smiled. "I know," he said. "The earl of Derrowford's seal was intact. I intend to share some of the information in this letter with you, Ranald, because I want your comments and suggestions on the best way to carry out my grandson's instructions. Living in the highlands as you do and having just traveled across Scotland and England, you have a much better understanding of the situation and the conditions we'll encounter than I."

Ranald drew himself up to his full height at the marquess's words and puffed out his chest. "Aye, yer lordship."

"So," the marquess rubbed his hands together, "tell me, Ranald, how is my grandson? Tell me about his abduction and the wedding. How did they go?"

"He weren't verra happy about bein' abducted, yer lordship, but he was real happy aboot having the chains cut off."

"What chains?"

"The chains around his wrists. Auld Tam said his lordship was chained to the bed in his room at the fort when they abducted him."

Chisenden rubbed at the deep grooves in his forehead. Neil was the second highest ranking officer at Fort Augustus. Only one man at the fort had the power to order him chained to the bed. His commanding officer, Major General Sir Charles Oliver. But Neil and Sir Charles had known each other for years. They'd been at school together as boys. Surely Neil hadn't given Sir Charles cause to confine him to quarters chained to the bed like an animal. Unless . . . Lord Chisenden traced the grooves on his forehead to his right temple and began to massage the knot forming there. He must remember to speak to General Wade about Sir Charles as soon as he finished carrying out his grandson's instructions. "Did he say who chained him?"

"I dunno, sir. I dinna hear but Auld Tam said there were guards posted around his door as well."

"Was anyone hurt during the abduction?" the marquess asked.

"His lordship had a cut on his cheek, most likely caused by a stone thrown up by his pony's hooves and a knot on his head where Auld Tam tapped him with his battle axe, but he wasna' hurt. Nor the men guardin' his door or any of the other men at Fort Augustus."

"Good," the marquess pronounced. "How did my grandson seem when last you saw him?"

"He was angry at Auld Tam and the other Ancient Gentlemen at first, but he calmed down a bit after Auld Tam showed him the marriage contract signed by his own hand."

The marquess frowned, remembering the role he had played in tricking his grandson into signing that document. "He admitted the contract was valid? Did he mention my name? Did he say anything about me?"

"He was verra angry with ye, sir."

"But he agreed to the ceremony without any fuss?"

Ranald grinned. "Nay, sir. There was plenty of fuss with his lordship refusin' to marry a dirty and barefooted highland lass and our Jessalyn refusin' to marry a mon wearing a Sassenach uniform. It was a braw argument. They were both verra stubborn and Father Moray had to make them see the error of their ways. If he hadna, they mightna ha' been churched. But they were and we had a verra fine feast to celebrate the weddin's."

"Weddings?" The marquess was intrigued in spite of himself.

"His lordship's and the two Sassenach guards who married Auld Tam's daughters, Magda and Flora."

"They abducted the guards as well?"

"Aye. Magda and Flora took a fancy to the Sassenach soldiers and persuaded them to exchange vows."

"Were they willing or unwilling?"

"They were verra willin'," Ranald answered. "Only his lordship and our wee Jessie balked."

"Tell me all about it," Lord Chisenden urged. "Everything you can remember."

Ranald did as the marquess asked, sparing no details about the things he'd witnessed or overheard right up until the moment he left Glenaonghais to make the journey to Edinburgh and then on to London.

"You made the trip on horseback in a sennight," the marquess commented when Ranald concluded his recitation of the events of the journey. "Traveling with guards and heavily-laden wagons in the company of cattle and sheep drovers and dogs over the Turnpike road through England and on into Scotland will probably take between a fortnight and a month to reach Glenaonghais."

Ranald shook his head. "Ye shouldna count on us makin' it to Glenaonghais in less than a month, sir. We'll have to stop in Edinburgh to hire the stonemasons. That may take a day or two and we canna take the most direct route from Edinburgh. Such a large and prosperous group of travelers would attract too much attention from the Sassenach—" Ranald cleared his throat, "English soldiers and rogue bandits and clans."

The marquess thought for a moment, carefully considering Ranald's words. "I'll send a man of business ahead to buy enough food and supplies to keep the clan from starving until the main provisions arrive. He can also hire the stonemasons, carpenters and drapers in Edinburgh and pay them well enough to make the journey separately. When you reach Edinburgh, you'll be able to travel through the city without stopping for supplies or go around it to avoid attracting too much attention if you find it necessary." He patted Ranald's shoulder. "Get some rest. You've done a fine job. You've earned it. If you change your mind about wanting a bed to sleep in . . ."

"I won't," Ranald quickly replied. "But thank ye kindly for offerin'."

"So be it," the marquess pronounced. "And if there's

anything you need or want while we're preparing for the journey, you've only to ask."

Ranald nodded in understanding, fully intending to take the marquess up on his generous offer just as soon as he had the opportunity to inspect the horseflesh in His Lordship's fine stables.

Chapter Thirteen

The palace doors opened one by one and the guards silently stepped aside as the marquess of Chisenden made his way to the king's chambers at St. James. Although the marquess of Chisenden had been instrumental in hammering out the Act of Settlement that designated Sophia, Electress of Hanover to succeed Good Queen Anne on the throne and the Act of Union that united England and Scotland, he hadn't foreseen the Electress's death. Sophia had died before Queen Anne so her son, George Ludwig, had succeeded her as Elector of Hanover and upon the death of Queen Anne, as King of England. He might be known as the king-maker, but Chisenden was under no illusion about the king. George spoke little English and took almost no interest in Britain or her people. The running of the country was left in the capable hands of the king's cabinet of ministers—like Chisenden, Sir Robert Walpole and Charles Townsend who made up the Whig government. Although he preferred Hanover to London, the current rebellion in Scotland demanded the king's attention and the royal standard flying high above the palace indicated that the king was in residence in London.

"The king is with his mistress." Sir Robert Walpole, First Lord of the Treasury, greeted Chisenden upon his arrival. "He'll join us shortly." He held out his hand. "You've had word?"

The marquess shook hands with his old friend and colleague. "A messenger arrived from Scotland an hour ago with word of the abduction and the weddings."

"Weddings plural?" Walpole asked, eyebrow raised.

"Yes." Chisenden nodded. "Two men charged with the task of standing guard over my grandson were abducted along with him. They chose to marry the young women who abducted them rather than return to Fort Augustus without the earl."

"They are to be commended for their loyalty to your grandson."

"That's true," Chisenden agreed, "but loyalty to Neil wasn't the only reason Sergeant Marsden and Corporal Stanhope chose to stay in the village and share his fate." The marquess moved closer to Walpole and lowered his voice. "Something is amiss with Oliver."

"How so?"

"Neil confided that his schoolboy rivalry with Oliver has escalated. At the time of his abduction he was confined to his quarters for questioning Oliver's decisions."

Walpole grinned. "He has benefited greatly from your tutelage, Chisenden. I imagine Neil was far from supportive when Oliver failed to secure the stonemasons we conspired to delay—or when Oliver chose to lie to General Wade and host the celebration of the completion of the wall *before* its completion."

"According to his note, Neil's primary complaint against Oliver was that the general was paying more attention to his tailor than to the security of the post. It seems Major General Oliver ended his negotiations with the masons' guild in order to consult with his tailor. He refused to post guards along the perimeter to protect the gap in the wall and when Neil questioned that decision, Oliver answered him by ordering two guards to confine him to his quarters, chain him to his cot and stand watch outside his door."

"Hence the abduction of the two guards by the clan," Walpole said. The First Lord of the Treasury shook his head. "We counted on Sir Charles's arrogance and his ignorance when we recommended him for the post."

"We recommended him because even though he holds the rank of major general, Oliver is essentially ineffective as an officer and a leader. He cares nothing about the construction of the fort or the roads. We chose him because we could control him." Chisenden paused. "Our future is linked with Scotland's and because we've no wish to see the highlands or the clans destroyed, we needed someone who would concentrate on furthering his own personal ambitions instead of subduing the clans. Scotland needs the roads in order to bring prosperity to the highlands and our government needs the forts in order to guard against further highland disturbances. What we don't need is a continuance of the hostilities with Scotland or more dissention against the foreign king here at home. Neil has known Oliver since their school days. He knew what to expect, but I must admit that I didn't countenance Oliver's animosity for him."

"I agree that Oliver has become a concern. He's jealous of Derrowford's wealth and his place in society." Walpole clasped his hands behind his back and began to pace.

"Charles Oliver ordered a fellow officer chained to a cot like an animal."

Walpole heard the underlying fury in Chisenden's voice. "And not just any fellow officer," he finished the marquess's unfinished thought, "but a fellow officer who happened to be the king-maker's grandson. The sole heir of the marquess of Chisenden. What arrogance!" Walpole smiled. "However unpleasant the experience was for the young earl, being chained to his bed has become a blessing in disguise."

"Explain yourself," Chisenden demanded.

Walpole walked over to the French escritoire and removed a sheaf of papers from the top of the stack. "I

received the latest of General Wade's reports yester eve."
He handed the papers to Chisenden to read.

The marquess took a moment to scan the military report Oliver's lieutenant had sent to General Wade.

"As you can see, we were fortunate the abduction occurred when it did and that Tam MacInnes was forced to cut the shackles from Neil's wrists. We can prove the earl of Derrowford and his two guards were taken from the fort against their will."

"Prove it to whom?" Chisenden asked.

"A military court."

"Why must we prove Neil was abducted from the fort? *We* know he was abducted. We arranged it."

"I'm aware of that," Walpole said. "But you and I and General Wade and the king are the only ones who understand why the king requested such an alliance with a Jacobite highland clan. Major General Oliver has no idea we conspired to marry your grandson to the laird of Clan MacInnes. He believes the earl is a deserter and is determined to pursue the matter. He's demanding personal satisfaction."

"God's blood! Spotty Oliver knows Neil would never shirk his duty by deserting the king's army! He knows Neil would never give him that satisfaction. And I'll personally hang his head from the Tower gates if he continues to seek retribution against my grandson!" Chisenden exploded.

"I believe that's what Major General Oliver intends for Neil." The First Lord of the Treasury gave his friend a wry smile and quirked an eyebrow. "Did you say Spotty Oliver?"

"School name," the marquess replied offhandedly. "During his adolescence Major General Sir Charles Oliver was known as much for the spots on his face as for his lack of intelligence."

Walpole laughed aloud. "Tam MacInnes didn't bother to hide his tracks once he gained entry into Fort Augustus. According to the lieutenant's report, any fool could tell that Neil and his two guards were taken from the fort against his will."

"Any fool except the commanding officer of Fort Augustus." Chisenden muttered another oath.

"We chose him," Walpole reminded him.

"The clan is in desperate straits. Neil's requested supplies and stonemasons. If I send them, how long do you think it will be before a lackwit like Oliver realizes that all he has to do to locate Neil is to follow the trail of supplies leaving London and Edinburgh and heading into the highlands?"

"We'll do our best to circulate the information that all the supplies you and Lady Chisenden purchase for the earl is destined for a new home here in London in order to throw him off the scent, but . . ." Sir Robert shrugged his shoulders. "The king and General Wade will know Oliver's intent. Neil will never be charged or tried with desertion or treason and should Oliver capture him, he'll be set free upon arrival in London."

"*If* he reaches London." Chisenden frowned. "What's to stop Oliver from shooting Neil on sight? What's to stop him from trying and hanging Neil in Scotland?"

"We will."

Both men turned to find the king standing in the doorway with his mistress at his elbow. The marquess of Chisenden and the First Lord of the Treasury bowed as their sovereign and his lady entered the room.

"We cannot countenance treasonous acts or allow the young earl to raise arms against us, but we shall order that should he be captured, the earl of Derrowford is to be brought to us," the king pronounced. He stared at Lord Chisenden. "We shall send General Wade on a personal inspection of the fort and we shall let it be known that we wish to make an example of the earl for consorting with our enemies. And you shall provide us with a handsome sum so that we might pay a reward for his live return. No one will dare to harm him then." King George addressed both of them. "Agreed?"

"Agreed," they replied.

"Good." The king smiled. "Now, begin at the start and tell us everything."

"My dear Louis, what is it? Are you ill? Kingsley said you had returned from the palace and that you ordered the staff assembled and my immediate presence." The marchioness of Chisenden entered the ballroom accompanied by the whisper of exquisite silk and Honiton lace and the scent of oak moss and ambergris. The swiftness with which she'd arrived, the worried tone in her voice, and her unprecedented use of his given name in the presence of the household staff gave a good indication of her affection and concern for her husband.

"I'm quite all right, my dear." The marquess said as he moved to stand beside his wife. "I summoned the household because we've had a message from Scotland."

Fearing the worst, the marchioness pressed her palm over her heart. "You've news of the boy? Tell me quickly. Is he . . ."

"Oh, no, my dear." He reached for his wife's hand and gave it a reassuring squeeze. "The boy is fine. In fact, he's better than fine. He's taken a bride."

"I don't believe it!" she exclaimed.

"It's true. A messenger arrived from Scotland this afternoon with the news and a letter from Neil." The marquess turned to address the employees standing stiffly at attention and arranged, according to rank and years of service, into three long, uniform lines that spanned the width of the ballroom. "Lady Chisenden and I have asked you here today to share the wonderful news that our grandson and heir, the earl of Derrowford, has taken a bride. Married in Scotland a sennight ago, Lady Derrowford is the daughter of an old family friend—" He intercepted a speculative glance from his wife and paused momentarily before continuing. "—the late laird of Clan MacInnes, Laird Callum MacInnes. The new countess of Derrowford was known as Lady Jessalyn MacInnes in

Scotland and has recently ascended to her father's position as the hereditary laird of her clan. Most of you know that the earl of Derrowford is in Scotland as part of General Wade's Corps of Royal Engineers. As he's engaged in the construction of badly needed roads and forts, he won't be able to return to London with his bride for a while so he's asked that we send household provisions and a few wedding gifts for his bride." The marquess removed Neil's letter from his waistcoat pocket and began to read the list of provisions. "Enough white flour, rye, sugar, salt, molasses, barley, oats, peas, beans, cheese, salted, dried, and smoked fish, apples, pears, quinces, peaches, dried dates, figs, prunes, raisins, herbs, malt, hops, kegs of beer, ale and wine to feed fifty souls throughout the winter months." He glanced at his housekeeper and Cook. "Mrs. Mingot, you and Cook will be responsible for seeing that the countess of Derrowford's Scottish kitchens are properly stocked. And Mrs. Mingot, the countess will need suitable linens, bolts of fabric and household goods—mattresses and pewter—whatever will be necessary to equip a castle. Spare no expense. His Lordship has granted permission to raid the attics of his London townhouse and Lady Chisenden and I shall do the same. Send someone to the earl's house and enlist his housekeeper's aid. Tell Mrs. Petrie that we wish to start first thing in the morning. We must have everything assembled and ready to leave for Scotland within the sennight."

Mrs. Mingot nodded in understanding. "Very good, sir."

"A nursery, Mrs. Mingot," the marchioness added. "As the earl and countess are newly wedded, we should prepare for an heir and include nursery furnishings."

The marquess recognized the damp sparkle in his wife's eyes and smiled down at her. It was just like Charlotte to think of preparing a nursery. She dearly loved children and had wanted a houseful. But it wasn't to be. Chisenden knew she blamed herself because she had only conceived, had only given birth, one time. He knew that she thought he found her lacking. But nothing was further from the truth. He hadn't loved her when they married. He'd been too grief-stricken and still too deeply in love with Helen Rose to appreciate his good fortune in finding her, but Charlotte had always been an excellent wife. He knew that now. They had suited each other quite well and in the fifty-one years since they'd exchanged vows, he had come to care very deeply for her and to rely on her impeccable judgment. He felt a deep and abiding affection for his second wife and held her in great esteem and had he not known Helen Rose, he might have mistaken his deep affection for Charlotte for love. Charlotte had succeeded where Helen Rose had failed. Both his wives had given him sons, but Charlotte had survived her lying-in and her son had grown to manhood, married and lived long enough to sire Neil. For that, the marquess of Chisenden would be forever grateful. And he would forever be tormented by the knowledge that the memories of his three years with and his love for Helen Rose remained vivid and ever constant. Charlotte deserved better. She deserved to be loved the way he'd loved his Scottish bride. Chisenden sighed and reached out for his wife's hand and gave it a gentle squeeze. "Quite so, my dear. Pray Heaven that we'll live to see another generation of Claremonts in the nursery." He cleared his throat then turned his attention back to his grandson's letter and resumed his reading of the listed items. He issued directives and assigned tasks to the members of the staff according to their specialties and abilities, priding himself on knowing the workings of his household well enough to recognize the strengths and weaknesses of each member of his staff. That ability had served him well over the years. It had helped him become "the king-maker," one of the most powerful men in England. He skimmed over Neil's requests for weapons. He fully intended to send the necessary swords and firearms and ammunition, but Chisenden preferred to keep that information to himself until he apprised the king of his plans. When he reached the end of the letter, he turned to his wife once again. "This is where you come in, my dear," he said. "Neil has asked that you select a wardrobe for his bride with slippers to match every garment. He's asked that you order shoes and slippers in the latest styles and in every color of the rainbow. They can be as plain or as fancy as you choose, but they must be of the highest quality. And," the marquess paused for effect, "you must order a pair for every day of the year." A collective gasp arose from the servants who remained in the ballroom—none of whom had ever owned more than three pairs of shoes at one time. Royalty might exhibit such extravagance, but no one had ever heard of an English earl doing so. "And no two pairs should be alike."

Lady Chisenden raised an eyebrow and gave voice to the thoughts of nearly everyone in the room. "He wants me to order three hundred pairs of ladies shoes?"

"Three hundred and sixty-four to be exact," the marquess confirmed. "And one pair of boots—shiny black leather boots made just like the ones Neil had made in London, only smaller."

"Louis, I don't understand. This extreme display of wealth is so unlike the boy. What can he be thinking?"

The marquess grinned and for a brief moment everyone in the room caught a glimpse of the young man Lady Helen Rose MacInnes and Lady Charlotte Woodson had fallen in love with a half a century earlier. "You've always said a lady can never have too many pairs of shoes."

"I never thought I'd admit it," she said flatly, "but I was wrong. No one can wear three hundred and sixty-five pairs of shoes."

The marquess leaned close to his wife and spoke in a low dulcet tone of voice meant for her ears alone. "The clan must be in desperate straits or Neil would not have requested so many supplies. Clan MacInnes is a Jacobite clan, my dear, and our troops have dealt very harshly with the Stewart sympathizers since the rebellion. You've read Neil's descriptions of the poor women who work as laundresses at Fort Augustus. They're paid and they're starving. Imagine how difficult it must be for the men and women who don't earn English silver or gold. The highlands have been picked clean. The clansmen and women are hungry and probably barefooted as well. In addition to being the countess of Derrowford, Neil's bride is laird of her clan. It doesn't matter to Neil whether or not she wears all the shoes. What matters is that he's able to give them to her."

"Very well," the marchioness declared. "By tomorrow afternoon, I'll have every cobbler in London working around the clock making shoes."

"Then, you'll need this." Chisenden produced another bit of sheepskin from his waistcoat pocket. He held the sheepskin in his left hand, carefully unfolding it to reveal the delicate shape of a woman's foot—a foot small enough to fit in the palm of his hand. He smiled at his wife and their gazes met in a meaningful look. "Her feet are no bigger than yours."

Lady Chisenden beamed, looking far younger than her seventy years. "How convenient! When our grandson brings his bride to visit, I'll be able to borrow shoes from her."

"In that case, I suggest you choose colors and styles to compliment your gowns and the gowns that will make up our new granddaughter's bride clothes."

"Her bride clothes!" Lady Chisenden exclaimed. "What dressmaker shall I use? Mine or the one he uses for Deborah?"

The marquess lifted an eyebrow in query. "Deborah?"

Lady Chisenden frowned. "You needn't repeat the widow Sheridan's given name as if you'd never heard it spoken aloud, Louis, nor pretend you weren't aware of her place in Neil's life."

"Of course, *I've* heard her given name spoken aloud,

my dear. *I* wasn't aware that you had heard it or that, being a lady, you would repeat it," he chided.

"Oh, posh," she replied. "I'm a grown woman, Louis, and although our grandson is ever the gentleman and quite discreet, I'm aware of his arrangement with Deborah Sheridan. I hear she's very extravagant and that Neil is extremely indulgent. I know that she lives in a house he rented for her on Bond Street and that her dressmaker's bills are enormous." She glanced over at her husband.

"You know more about Neil's *amour* than I expected."

"People gossip, Louis. Often within my hearing. And you haven't answered my question."

"What question was that, my dear?"

"Shall I hire my dressmaker to make our new granddaughter's wardrobe or shall I have the dressmaker Neil hired for Deborah do it?"

Chisenden shrugged his shoulders in an elegantly aristocratic gesture. "He didn't specify a dressmaker in his letter so I'm afraid that decision is up to you."

"Nor did he specify his bride's size or coloring," the marchioness grumbled. "How like a man to expect me to order the necessary gowns and undergarments for a woman without sending measurements or an idea of her coloring, so that I might select the most flattering styles and hues."

The marquess leaned closer to his wife and whispered, "He did include a description of her, but he compared her size to that of his mistress. I didn't divulge that information because I was foolishly trying to protect your sensibilities. He wrote, *'The MacInnes is smaller than Deborah in every way. She's shorter in stature and slim of hip and torso. Her legs are slender and shapely and although she's less endowed than Deborah, her bosom is quite firm and nicely rounded. Her hair is long and thick and curly. It's a dark red. Not Titian and not brown, but somewhere in between. Her complexion is fair and her eyes are blue.'"*

"Light or dark blue?" Lady Chisenden asked, more out of curiosity than of any real need to know.

"Dark blue," Lord Chisenden answered. "Dark blue with dots of gold in their depths. The mark of the Mac-Inneses. Lady Jessalyn has the MacInnes eyes."

The marchioness heard the faraway note in her husband's voice, saw the familiar shadow of sadness darken his face and knew that he was thinking of his first wife. And she knew from Neil's description that the new countess of Derrowford most likely bore an uncanny resemblance to the fifty-four-year-old portrait of another countess of Derrowford that hung in the marquess's study. "That tells me what *I* need to know about the gowns and the shoes," she said, softly. "Now tell me what *you* are going to do about the mistress."

Chisenden straightened his back and shoved the tender memories aside and looked askance at his wife once again. "Do? Why should I do anything about her? Neil made arrangements for her upkeep before he departed for Scotland."

"Did he end his liaison with her before he left?"

"Not that I'm aware of," Lord Chisenden admitted.

Lady Chisenden frowned at her husband's naivete. "Surely, you don't believe that Deborah Sheridan will just fade into the background? As soon as she hears that Neil has married, and she's sure to hear, she'll make a fuss. She won't let go of our grandson or his fortune that easily."

"She won't have a choice. I'll send for Neil's man of business. I intend to have the man purchase the house Neil rented for the widow and present the deed to her along with the cash settlement she and Neil agreed upon. That should keep her in the manner to which she's become accustomed until she can find another protector."

"And if she's not interested in finding another protector?"

"She'll have to be interested. Neil has a countess now. He won't be needing a mistress."

His quiet belief that Neil would be as honorable and as faithful as he was one of the things Lady Chisenden loved about her husband. He understood that dishonor and unfaithfulness existed in other families, in other households, but he couldn't conceive of it inhabiting his own. Lord Chisenden seemed confident that Neil's man of business would be able to buy Deborah Sheridan off, but Lady Chisenden wasn't so sure. The widow had a reputation for being a spendthrift and she had worked long and hard to capture Neil's attention and get her hands on part of his fortune. Most men, her husband and grandson included, acted with honor and assumed others did the same, but the marchioness of Chisenden was under no such illusion. She didn't completely trust that Neil's man of business would do the job he'd been hired to do and she sincerely doubted that her grandson's mistress would do the honorable and ladylike thing and quietly relinquish her position. And if that was the case, it wouldn't hurt to pay the widow a friendly call to encourage her cooperation.

She patted her husband's forearm. "You take care of the other details, Louis dear," she told him. "I'll take care of the shoes, the gowns, the household, the nursery." *And the mistress,* she silently added.

Chapter Fourteen

"What have we here?" Neil paused before a door made of thick iron lattice tucked away in one of the many passages hidden deep below the castle. He tried to open the door, but there were two sturdy locks on it and both of them were locked. "Tam, do you know where this door leads?"

"Aye, it leads to the hidden chamber." Tam stood beside him.

"Really?" Neil's face lit up like a child's. "A secret room? I guess we'll find out in a minute. I need to inspect that section of the tunnel, too, but the door is locked. Do you have a key?" He turned to Tam. The two of them had spent the morning salvaging timbers from the abandoned crofters' houses outside the castle grounds, collecting and hauling the charred, but otherwise sound, beams into the outer bailey where they would be used to shore up the weakened walls of the castle once the stonemasons arrived from Edinburgh and began work. It was cold and dark in the tunnels and the air heavy and musty-smelling. Neil was eager to complete his inspection and return to the sunshine above ground. Neil shivered as the sweat-soaked length of tartan knotted around his waist dried in the cool air of the tunnels.

"If it's the room I think it is, ye have the key," Tam

told him, pointing to the key dangling from the end of the silver chain around his neck. "She wore it beneath her bodice with her key until she ga'e it to ye."

Neil fingered the key, then studied the locks on the door. Two locks. Two keys. Were the keys identical? Did the one key open the twin locks? Or did it take both keys to open the door to this particular room in the castle? He pulled the silver chain from around his neck and inserted the key into the lock. Turning it, Neil heard the tumblers click into place. His key opened the first lock. Did it also open the second one? He was about to try it when Tam alerted him.

"Someone's comin'."

Neil instinctively snatched the key from the first lock. He turned and stepped away from the door to face the intruder, then raised his arms and dropped the silver chain over his head and around his neck.

"Mind your kilt, mon," Tam warned, pointing to the knot on Neil's belly that had slipped dangerously low on Neil's hip. "Ye wouldna' be wantin' to gi'e our visitor a show."

Neil listened as the sound of bare feet pattering against stone echoed down the tunnel. The footsteps sounded too light and quick to be a man. He tightened the knot at his waist, securing his tartan. "I only want to give one woman a show. Do you think she's interested?"

"Aye," Tam said. "She mun ha'e followed ye down here. She's been watchin' ye fer weeks. But only when she's sure ye can't see her doin' it."

"Are you certain?" Neil demanded, doubt evident in every word. His plan to make his bride jealous had misfired. After two weeks of marriage, the MacInnes's resistance to him seemed stronger than ever. Other than gaining a much greater appreciation for the toughness of Scottish warriors, he was no better off for having challenged the MacInnes to a battle of wills or for having spent two weeks shirtless, bootless and bare-arsed. The other women in the village might stop work to watch him walk by, but the MacInnes never seemed to notice. She had successfully avoided pleating his kilt in the morning and avoided sharing his bed every night since the wedding. Neil thought it the height of irony that he slept in the laird's bed, especially since it was patently obvious to anyone who cared to look that the laird did not.

"Aye. I'm certain. And she's not the only one," Tam grumbled. "At least one part of yer plan is workin'."

Neil turned to find Sorcha MacInnes coming down the hallway, her hips swaying in invitation as she carried a tallow candle in a dish toward him. He groaned aloud as she approached.

"I saw ye and Tam come down here and I knew the rushes in the torches were old and dry and I knew ye'd need more light," she said when she reached him. "I brought ye one."

Neil recoiled from the stench of the candle made of rancid fat. "That wasn't necessary," he said.

"Och, but it was," she replied. "We canna have the laird's new husband fumblin' around in the dark." She held the dish out to him, cradling it in her hands at breast level, offering it to him along with a unencumbered view of her magnificent bosom.

"Thank you." Neil averted his gaze from the display of creamy flesh as he accepted the candle from her and set it in a niche above their heads directly opposite from the niche that held the rush torches.

"Will the light be enough? Or can I offer ye sumthin' more?" Sorcha clutched at Neil's arm, trailing her fingers down his arm from his elbow to his fingertips, gently caressing the back of his hand with her fingers in an unmistakable gesture.

Neil pulled his hand out of her grasp and stepped away from her. "No, thank you. One is more than enough."

Undeterred by his withdrawal, Sorcha moistened her lips and batting her eyelashes at him, tried another approach. "Those timbers look awfully heavy and ye have been workin' so verra hard today. Ye must be verra strong and powerful. I've never seen a young and handsome Sassenach earl who could heft such heavy beams."

"Ye've never even seen *any* Sassenach earl," Auld Tam pointedly reminded her. "Young or otherwise."

Frowning at his intrusion, Sorcha whirled on Auld Tam. "I dinna ask ye to speak yer mind, so what ye say is of no consequence to me, auld mon."

"I've earned the right to speak my mind whenever I choose," Tam told her.

"This is between the laird's husband and me." Sorcha moved closer to Neil and linked her arm around his. "'Tis none of yer business, old mon."

"When the young widow of one of my kinsmen begins flauntin' herself beneath the laird's husband's nose, the laird's husband becomes my business."

"Why shouldna I flaunt myself around him if he's willin'?" Sorcha demanded. "Jessie's made it verra clear that she doesna want him."

"She wants me." Neil made his meaning very clear as he deliberately disengaged himself from the comely widow's embrace. "She may not show it, but she wants me. Almost as much as I want her." He looked down at Sorcha. "And even if that were not so, I am not in the market for a mistress, nor am I on the market. I am husband to the laird of your clan."

"Ye said yerself that ye were brought here to be a stud."

"For the MacInnes," he said coldly. "And for no one else. I won't be servicing you or any of the other women. As far as you're concerned, I might as well be a gelding. I take my vows seriously. I don't dally with kinswomen, no matter how available they are or how prettily packaged."

Sorcha stared at his bare chest. "'Tis a pity." She made a clucking sound with her tongue. "And a waste, 'cause Jessie's cold—"

"Really?" Neil made the query sound ironic, as if nothing could be further from the truth.

"And verra, verra stubborn. She no be warmin' yer bed or pleatin' yer kilt for ye anytime soon and if ye keep flauntin' *yer prettily packaged* wares like this, ye'll wind up a frozen gelding come winter."

More footsteps echoed down the tunnel—angry, strident footsteps that could only belong to one person. Neil turned his head toward them and his gaze collided with the MacInnes's. The look she sent him was scorching and Neil knew that if looks could kill both he and Sorcha would be needing last rites. Even from this distance he could see that the MacInnes was spoiling for a fight and for the first time since he'd issued his ridiculous challenge, Neil felt a glimmer of hope. His plan *was* working. She was very adept at hiding her feelings, but that spark of jealousy that glowed in the MacInnes's dark blue eyes couldn't be disguised. And the MacInnes's jealousy was just what he needed. "Maybe before." Neil laughed. "But it's not bloody likely now." He reached out, took hold of Sorcha's hand and brought it to his lips, kissing her work-roughened knuckles before releasing it. "You, my dear kinswoman, have been the answer to my prayers." He might be dead by winter, but he wouldn't be a victim of the cold. He'd stake his life on it.

Jessalyn came to a stop in front of the little group. The earl of Derrowford stood with his back to the door leading to the Laird's Trysting Room. Auld Tam was on his right and Sorcha stood facing him. Jessalyn walked to Tam. Her voice was cool and crisp with authority as she spoke. "If you will excuse us, Tam, I'd like to speak to Lord Derrowford and Sorcha alone."

Tam doffed his bonnet and bowed slightly to the laird as he withdrew.

Jessalyn waited until the sound of his footsteps receded before she turned to Sorcha. "The other women are in the courtyard bundling bracken into thatch for the roofs of the cottages. What are you doing down here?"

A head taller than the laird, Sorcha placed her hands on her hips and stared down at Jessalyn, an impudent expression on her face. "I saw His Lordship and Auld Tam come down here and I thought His Lordship might need another candle." She raised her chin and gestured toward the tallow candle. "I brought one."

There was no need for candles in the outer bailey where the other women were working. The sun was shining. In order to supply Neil and Tam with a candle, Sorcha had to leave her task and go into the castle to collect one and take it to them. This was the third time she'd caught her cousin's widow eyeing her husband. Had he encouraged it? Had he arranged to meet her here or had she followed him? Jessalyn glanced from Neil to Sorcha. She had entered the tunnel in time to see him kissing the young widow's hand. She would rather have bitten out her tongue than ask the question or hear the answer, but Jessalyn couldn't help herself. She had to know. "Did His Lordship ask ye to help him?"

Sorcha shook her head so that her thick, curly brown hair tumbled over her shoulders and cascaded down her back. She looked up at the earl from beneath the cover of her eyelashes. "Nay. I just thought—"

Jessalyn cut her off. "*I* think it might be best if you return to your duties in the bailey and help the others."

The impudent expression on Sorcha's face turned mutinous as Jessalyn dismissed her. She opened her mouth to speak, then thought better of it and turned on her heel and walked back down the tunnel toward the outer bailey.

Neil lifted an eyebrow in query. "Would you care to explain?"

Jessalyn shrugged her shoulders.

"Then perhaps I should tell you that I don't think Sorcha cared very much for your suggestion," Neil commented. "She didn't appear to be in any hurry to leave us alone."

"She dinna ha'e to care for like my suggestion," Jessalyn explained. "She had to obey it."

"Or . . ."

"She would be punished."

"By whom?"

"By me," Jessalyn said. "In the highlands, the laird has the power of life and death o'er members of the clan. And it wasna me she dinna want to leave, 'twas you."

Neil pursed his lips. "I see," he said, softly. He was beginning to learn to read the MacInnes's moods a little better. During the past two weeks, he had noticed that her English was very precise and proper when she was in control of her emotions, but her Scottish burr became very pronounced when she was disturbed or upset. "Tell me, Laird MacInnes, would you have punished your kinswoman for disobeying you or for offering to provide me with meager comfort?"

"Trysting with the laird's spouse is punishable by banishment from the clan or by death."

"Trysting? With Sorcha?" Neil lifted his eyebrow in query once again. "Is that what you think I was doing?"

"Yer standin' in front of the door that leads to the Laird's Trysting Room."

"The what?" Neil sputtered, blinking in surprise. "I'm sure I cannot have heard you correctly. Did you say the laird's trysting room?"

"Aye," Jessalyn bit out the word.

"There's a room for trysting hidden away in the depths of the castle?"

"Aye and it belongs to the laird."

"You're the laird," he pointed out. "It's your room. Since I didn't know it existed, how can you accuse me of arranging a tryst in it with your kinswomen?"

"Ye have a key to it," she retorted, pointing to the chain around his neck.

"So do you."

"I've never used my key," she told him.

"Neither have I," he replied. "Except to try the lock."

She gasped. "Ye unlocked the door while Sorcha was here?"

"Jealous?"

"Of Sorcha? Dinna be ridiculous!"

But she was. Neil could see it in the spark of fire in her blue eyes, hear it in her voice. He was tempted to taunt the MacInnes with the knowledge of her jealousy of her kin, but decided against it. He refused to give her a reason to punish Sorcha. In her present prickly mood, there was no telling what that punishment might be. "I tried the first lock," he said. "*Before* your clanswoman arrived. I abandoned my attempt when I heard her footsteps in the tunnel. Are you certain there's a room behind that door or that it's used for that one special purpose?" He stared into her eyes and there was a wealth of meaning behind his question.

Jessalyn ignored the meaning behind his question and concentrated on fact. "It's there. And it was used for that purpose."

"How do you know it's there?" Neil queried. "If you've never seen it."

"My father told me of it. I know who built it and why."

"Then it's a recent construction?"

Jessalyn shook her head. "Nay. My ancestor built it over a hundred years ago so he could meet and court his enemy's daughter in complete secrecy."

"Was he successful?"

"Of course," Jessalyn replied. "That MacInnes tunneled to the edge of his enemy's land, abducted the man's daughter and married her without her father's knowledge or consent."

Neil curled his index finger around his chin and pretended to be deep in thought. "After a hundred years, the existence of the tunnel and the room must be common knowledge . . ."

"Nay. Only the Ancient Gentlemen who make up the

laird's privy council know that a hidden room exists. But it's possible that Flora or Magda or Alisdair's wife, Davina, know of it."

"Is your ancestor's enemy still an enemy of Clan MacInnes or has the enmity between your clans melded into friendship?"

"There will never be a friendship between Clan MacInnes and that murdering clan." Jessalyn's vehement denial brought a smile to Neil's lips.

"Then I needn't worry about you trysting with a former enemy in the secret room."

Jessalyn's mouth feel open. She couldn't believe the earl had the audacity to smile at her after suggesting such a thing. "Certainly not!" she retorted. "I dinna enjoy it wi' ye and I ha'e no interest in breakin' my marriage vows by sharin' my bed wi' any other man or of allowin' him to do that to me again."

Neil frowned and the deep furrows in his forehead marred the perfection of his face. "It's not all bad, you know."

"Not all bad for men, ye mean."

"Or for women when it's done right." He reached out and gently pulled a strand of Jessalyn's reddish-brown hair from the corner of her mouth. He stared into her eyes. "Ah, lass," his imitation Scottish burr was deep and tender. "I dinna do it right the first time and I've done ye a terrible disservice. Did ye not find any pleasure in the act at all?"

Jessalyn shuddered in distaste, then tucked her chin and focused her gaze on her feet. "Why should I?" She blushed at the memory. "'Twas embarrassin' and messy and painful." *And lonely.* She had thought that the act would be one of sharing when the two would become one. But she'd experienced none of the closeness, none of the sharing she'd expected. After the embarrassingly intimate act, she'd felt alone, lonely and ill-used. She'd lain wide awake battling tears of frustration and disappointment as she listened to him sleep.

Neil winced as her innocent words twisted a knot into his belly. He'd promised her a wonderful initiation into the world of lovemaking and boasted of his ability to give her pleasure, but the reality had been a huge disappointment. *He* had been a huge disappointment. Neil moved closer to her. Reaching out, he tilted her chin up with his index finger so he could look into her face and read the expressions mirrored there. "Wasn't there anything you enjoyed about the evening? Other than the money and the wedding feast?" He managed a wry smile at the memory of Jessalyn MacInnes's shining eyes as she stared at the gold and silver coins and the covetous gaze she'd cast at his unwanted bowl of oatmeal.

He watched as the MacInnes gave his question serious thought. "I liked the way ye looked at me when I was lyin' on the bed," she answered shyly.

"Anything else?"

She nodded an affirmative. "I liked the way your skin felt beneath my fingers."

"And?" he encouraged.

"I liked the way ye kissed me." She blushed a bright pink.

He smiled again, and this time, his smile reached his eyes. "That's a starting point," he promised as he leaned over, tangled his fingers in her hair and pulling her close, covered her lips with his own.

Chapter Fifteen

Jessalyn sighed. It hadn't changed. His kiss was as warm and wonderful and welcoming as she remembered from their wedding night. Kissing him was the perfect antidote to being the MacInnes from the moment she opened her eyes in the morning until she closed them late in the night. She couldn't worry about the myriad problems that plagued her when his lips were working their magic on her. She couldn't think. Couldn't form a coherent thought. All she could do was feel. And kissing him made her feel more than she'd ever imagined.

It was impossible to keep her distance. Every instinct she possessed urged her closer and Jessalyn obeyed her instincts. She took a step forward and found herself held firmly against his bare chest. This time, the earl of Derrowford didn't disappoint her. He was grace personified and his timing was perfect. He caught her at the exact moment her legs refused to support her any longer. He deepened his kiss and tightened his embrace around her waist in a fluid motion that sent her senses spiraling. His kiss was everything she'd ever dreamed about, everything she'd ever hoped for in a kiss. It was soft and gentle and tender and sweet and enticing and hungry and hot and wet and deep and persuasive all at once. It coaxed and demanded, asked and expected a like response and

Jessalyn obliged. She parted her lips when he asked entrance into the warm recesses of her mouth. She shivered with delight at the first tentative, exploratory thrust of his tongue against hers. She met his tongue with her own, returning each stroke, practicing everything she had learned in her first lesson in kissing him and began a devastatingly thorough exploration of her own. She pressed her palms against the warm, solid wall of his chest.

Neil bit back a groan of frustration when he felt the MacInnes's hands against his chest. This time, he promised himself, he wasn't going to rush her. This time he was going to be a considerate lover and allow her to set the pace of their lovemaking—even if it killed him. With that thought in mind, he let his arms fall to his sides and abruptly broke contact with her lips.

"No," she murmured, her breath soft and warm against his.

"All right," he managed, sucking in a ragged breath as he raised his hands in a gesture meant to prove to her that he hadn't lost all of his control and that he could still behave like a gentleman in her presence.

Jessalyn felt his labored breathing, felt the rapid rise and fall of his chest beneath her palms and the shudders rippling his muscles as he struggled to regain control. "No," she whispered once again.

Neil rested his forehead against the top of her head for a moment then tried to step back out of her embrace.

But Jessalyn refused to let him go. She wrapped both of her arms around his waist and pulled him to her. She breathed in the masculine scent of him, then closed her eyes and tilted her face up, anticipating the feel of his lips on hers. "Dinna."

Neil exhaled slowly and mentally counted to ten before he could speak. "You placed your hands against me," he said. "I thought you wanted me to stop."

"No." She opened her eyes and stared up at him. "I

dinna mean for ye to stop. I only wanted to touch ye, to feel the hair upon yer chest and the beating of yer heart."

He smiled down at her and reaching around behind his back, he took hold of her hands and guided them back to his chest. He positioned her palms against his chest, covering her hands with his own as he leaned forward and brushed his lips against her brow. "Be my guest," he invited, moving her hands over his chest.

A blush heated her face and Jessalyn pressed herself against their hands and buried her face against his shoulder.

"You said you wanted to touch me."

"I do." Her words were muffled. "But . . ."

"But?"

"I canna do it in the daylight. I canna do it unless yer . . . unless we're . . ." She looked up at him, begging him to understand.

"Making love?" There was a hopeful, optimistic note in his voice.

She shook her head. "Nay."

Neil swallowed his disappointment and tried again. "Unless we're kissing?"

She nodded.

"Then kiss me again, Jessalyn."

Her name sounded like a prayer on his lips and Jessalyn eagerly complied with his gentle command.

She kissed him senseless. Or he kissed her senseless. He couldn't tell which. And it really didn't matter. What mattered was that suddenly kissing didn't seem to be enough for either one of them. He unlaced her bodice and buried his face in the cleft between her breasts before nuzzling aside the edges of her garment and laying claim to one pink-tipped, pear-shaped breast and then the other. He breathed in the heady wildflower and woman scent of her as he laved her breasts, using his mouth and teeth and tongue to tease and tempt her. And he succeeded. The MacInnes writhed in his arms, shamelessly rubbing herself against him, working feverishly at the

knot that held his plaid tied around his waist. He felt the
fabric give and moments later, the tartan slipped down
his thighs and lay pooled on the floor around his feet.
He kissed his way back up her chest, over the pulse that
beat a rapid tattoo in her throat, behind her ear, and across
her cheek to her lips. He kissed her deeply, thoroughly,
cupping a breast with one hand as he slid his other hand
beneath her skirts and up her inner thigh, across the soft
curls of her woman's triangle and down into the warm,
moist valley hidden beneath it.

The MacInnes gasped as he explored her with his fingers. She shuddered, an unmistakable sign of pleasure,
moaned deep in her throat and clamped her thighs together to keep his hand in place. He acknowledged her
request by continuing his intimate caresses. She seemed
unaware of her arousal, her actions or of his state of undress, but Neil was acutely aware of her fingers caressing his naked flesh, acutely aware that while he was
caressing her, she was leisurely tracing patterns of tiny
half-circles on his bare buttock with the fingertips of her
left hand and encircling the base of his male appendage
with his right. He gritted his teeth against the incredible
rush of pleasure he felt as the head of him brushed against
the worn fabric covering her stomach. He jerked at the
contact, feeling a painful, almost overwhelming need to
lay her on a bed and taste every inch of her, then lie beneath her while she did the same to him. Neil marveled
at the fact that his knees continued to support his weight
and wondered how much longer he would be able to re-
tain his tenuous control over the desire racing through
him.

He was perilously close to taking her against the rough
stone wall of the tunnel when there was a room designed
for lovemaking somewhere nearby. He needed to locate
the room while he could still think. Dipping his finger
into the bodice of her dress, Neil carefully coaxed the
silver key she wore on the chain around her neck from
its resting place between her breasts. He eased the neck-

lace over her head and held it up for her to see. "You have a key and I have a key," he whispered. "And a room made for trysting. Shall we put them to use?"

The MacInnes stared up at him. Her blue eyes were wide open and dark with passion. Her lips were plump, swollen from his kisses and the soft skin of her face had been abraded by the stubble on his jaw. Her gaze was focused on the silver key dangling from the chain in his hand. She looked dazed and Neil was inordinately pleased to discover that she was as affected by their passionate kisses as he was. "We've discovered that you still like my kisses," he murmured. "And you appear to enjoy touching me. Why don't we see if you still like the way I look at you when you're lying on the bed?" Praying the Laird's Trysting Room had a bed, Neil gave her a hard, urgent kiss and reluctantly withdrew his fingers from her secret recesses. He grasped her wrist to halt the slow erotic wandering of her right hand, then carefully disengaged himself, slipping out of her arms just long enough to insert her key into the second lock on the heavy iron door. The tumblers rolled into place and Neil swung the door back on its hinges. He swallowed a groan of disappointment as he found himself staring down another dark corridor instead of the room he expected. Reaching up, he grabbed a candle from one of the niches and stepped through the opening into the passageway. He held out his hand to her. "I propose that we locate the whereabouts of this trysting room together." He smiled at her. "How about it, sweetheart?"

The endearment that rolled off his tongue as naturally as the morning mist rolled off the heather captured Jessalyn's attention. She stared up at him, at his green eyes and handsome face and the perfectly shaped lips that kissed her to distraction and called her "sweetheart," at his broad shoulders and bare chest. He held out a hand to her and Jessalyn placed her hand in his and stepped forward, right into a puddle of soft wool. She glanced down at her feet, frowning mightily as the softly flickering glow of the candle illuminated the length of MacInnes tartan that should have been wrapped around his waist.

He was naked. Widening her eyes in surprise at the sight of him unclothed and unashamed in the open door-way of the secret corridor, Jessalyn gasped. When she had watched him undress on their wedding night she hadn't realized that that part of him was too large for her or that allowing him entrance into her secret woman's place would hurt so much. She hadn't known what to expect then, but she did now and as she watched, that male part of him grew larger and more prominent. She averted her gaze in an effort to stop it. Not that she was a coward. She wasn't afraid of suffering further pain in the marriage bed. The pain was of no consequence. If only her dilemma was as simple as that. But it wasn't. What she feared more than the physical pain was further disappointment. Jessalyn was very much afraid that she might lose her heart to him. And how could she love a man she couldn't respect and admire? And how could she respect and admire a man who disappointed her so? Although she wanted to give him another chance, the idea that her handsome, Sassenach husband was a failure as a lover was almost more than she could bear to contemplate. She focused her attention on the pool of light behind his shoulder. Beyond that pool of light, at the end of the tunnel was the door that led to the Laird's Trysting Room. She couldn't allow him to take her to the room her father had held so dear in his memory. She couldn't risk it. Not yet.

"No." She pulled her hand out of his.

Neil frowned as he let go of her hand. "I thought you enjoyed kissing."

"I do."

"And touching."

"I do." She lowered her gaze to the floor. "It's the part that comes after that I dinna like."

"My mistake." Neil inhaled deeply, then exhaled

slowly several times. He struggled to rein in his passion, but he couldn't rein in his tongue. "Forgive me for misinterpreting your level of desire, my dear. But when you untied my kilt and started to caress me, I naturally assumed you enjoyed it enough to want the part that comes after the kissing and the touching."

His sarcastic revelation appalled her. She couldn't have untied his kilt. She would have remembered it. And she couldn't have touched him so intimately. Not when she wanted no part of the mating that came afterwards. Jessalyn squeezed her eyes shut, trying to blot out the truth, but the persistent memory of the pleasure she had felt at discovering the velvety softness of the flesh hidden beneath his kilt plagued her. She chewed at her bottom lip and watched from beneath her eyelashes as the earl set the candle back in its niche, retrieved his tartan from the floor and without making any effort to disguise his state of arousal, leisurely knotted it around his waist. "I dinna," she whispered, sadly. "Not yet."

"Then we've a problem, my dear Laird MacInnes," he said. "Because there's a limit to my patience and my restraint. I'm a man. I'm not made of stone and I cannot—will not—continue the touching and the kissing without the part that comes after."

Jessalyn sighed. Having been thoroughly and cleverly introduced to them, she craved his kisses. And now that he had shown her the magic that could be found at the touch of his fingers, she craved that touch just as much as his kisses. She didn't want to mate with him again, but she didn't want to lose the other pleasures he could offer her either. Perhaps another compromise was in order. She moved closer, angled her face toward his and said, "With the kissin', I could be persuaded to show ye how to pleat yer kilt so ye won't be droppin' it at yer feet again."

Neil ignored the way she tilted her face up for his kiss and the provocative way she puckered her lips in anticipation and glanced down at the tartan tied about his waist. "Why worry with all those bothersome pleats," he asked, "when this way suits me just fine?"

"But . . ."

She looked so frustrated and so crestfallen that Neil almost relented and allowed her to have her way. But to do so might eliminate all hope of ever hearing her agree to make love with him again. Oh, he had no doubt that he could seduce her into it, but he didn't want to seduce her into it. He wanted her to want it—and him—as much as he wanted her. Neil had vowed to let her set the pace of their lovemaking, not to do away with it altogether. He wanted to be patient, but he couldn't allow her to dictate to him on a matter as important as this one—on a matter she knew almost nothing about. "I didn't drop my kilt. You untied it. And the only way I'll be interested in kissing and touching you or having you pleat my kilt for me is if you agree to untie it first and do the part that comes after the kissing and the touching."

She didn't like the idea of his issuing an ultimatum to her. After all, she was the MacInnes and the countess of Derrowford. She was his wife and if she wanted to kiss him and touch him and have him kiss and touch her in return, he should be more than willing to oblige. Standing up with him in church and repeating her vows ought to count for something. "You promised," she accused.

"So did you," he shot back. "To love, honor, obey and worship with your body. And so far, you've failed on all accounts."

She tried again. "I like the kissing."

"So do I," he murmured. "Very much."

"Then ye agree to continue kissing me if I pleat your kilt for ye?"

Neil shook his head. "Not at all."

"I dinna understand."

"You have my terms, Laird MacInnes," he said. "I won't agree to anything less." He deliberately turned his back on her, then pulled the *yett* closed and used both keys to lock it.

Jessalyn lifted her chin a notch. "Verra well," she replied haughtily. "I lived without yer kisses before. I will learn to do so once again."

"If you think you must," he responded, shrugging his shoulders in a nonchalant gesture. He opened his fist and stared at the silver key suspended from its chain, then guided the chain over the MacInnes's head, watching as the key settled into the hollow between her breasts. "I'm free most mornings if you change your mind. You know where to find me. The door will be locked," he reminded her, "but I believe you have a key."

Chapter Sixteen

"Are ye goin' to stand there admirin' yer husband all day or are ye goin' to help us with the thatch?" Magda asked.

The question was followed by the knowing laughter of a dozen or so of her kinswomen. Jessalyn felt a blush flame in her cheeks. She glanced down at her feet, shoving her bundle of thatch over into Magda's arms with a force that rocked her kinswoman back on her heels. "I'm not admiring him," Jessalyn replied. "Because there's nothing to admire."

"Och, yes ye are," Magda answered. "Not that I blame ye, Jessie, 'cause I feel the same way about Artie." She nodded toward the opposite side of the bailey where Neil and Corporal Stanhope were re-thatching the roof of the cottage Magda and her husband planned to occupy.

Jessalyn followed Magda's gaze and found herself transfixed by the view. She stood watching, barely daring to breathe as Neil balanced high above her on the exposed rough wooden beams of the cottage. The late afternoon sun glistened off his body and he shimmered in the afternoon sunlight like a god come down from the heavens. A gust of wind whistled through the glen and Jessalyn caught an enticing whiff of salty man and dried heather as he braced himself against the stiff breeze. Her heart began to pound. She swallowed hard, inhaling the scent of him. It made no sense. She had watched the men in the village thatch cottages all of her life and the sight of their labor had never made her feel breathless and achy or filled her with such a sense of longing and belonging until now.

Jessalyn exhaled slowly and chastised herself for her foolish behavior. She should have bitten off her tongue rather than let her pride goad her into promising him that she could do without his kisses. She didn't want to do without his kisses. She wanted more of them—as many of them as he was willing to give. And she wanted them until she tasted her fill. Jessalyn fingered the silver key on the chain about her neck.

"I'm free most mornings if you change your mind. You know where to find me. The door will be locked. But I believe you have a key."

She couldn't get his words out of her mind. In the hours since he'd uttered them, she had heard them echoed in her brain a thousand times. The idea he'd planted had taken root. She definitely knew where to find him because she'd barely let him out of her sight. She found herself watching him all afternoon, Jessalyn sighed. She thought she was being clever and discreet, watching him when no one else was looking, but now she realized she had been fooling herself. Everyone knew. While she'd been watching her husband, everyone else had been watching her. And still she couldn't seem to keep from looking at him.

She supposed Magda was right. There was much she could admire in him other than his extraordinary good looks and his money. In the weeks since he'd arrived at Glenaonghais, she'd been pleased to discover that he worked hard. Once he fully understood the clan's desperate situation, the English earl of Derrowford had pitched in to help. The idea that an English lord and a soldier in German George's army would join the old men and boys of the clan in the making of the spears and the

traps and snares needed for hunting and fishing and the
fact that he had spent days perfecting their use filled her
with pride. A sennight ago, Neil had successfully snared
two rabbits and a grouse. He'd gone hunting with Tam
and Alisdair near the Sutherland boundary and had been
the only one of the hunters to return with game. The
whole clan had watched as Alisdair deftly taught Neil
how to dress his catch. The two rabbits had gone into
the stew pot along with a handful of barley and a few
turnips and the grouse had been placed on a spit and
roasted. The earl had grinned with the pride of a ten-
year-old boy as he'd presented Davina with his contri-
bution to supper. And when he'd learned from Ian
MacCurran that the Munros had chickens, Neil and Auld
Tam and Andrew and Ian MacCurran had organized a
stealthy raid upon the Munros' hen house, returning with
a dozen fat hens and a fine healthy rooster. It had taken
a day or two for the hens to settle in and begin laying
again, but now the clan had eggs and milk to see them
through until the supplies she had ordered arrived from
Edinburgh. And later when he thought he was alone, Jessalyn had seen Neil wading along the edge of the loch,
washing chicken dung and feathers from his feet and
legs, laughing aloud, proclaiming himself "the mighty
barefooted earl of Chicken Thieves." She smiled at the
memory. 'Twas a rare Sassenach lord who could poke
fun at his situation and himself. When she thought about
it, she realized there were hundreds of ways the earl had
sought to make himself useful. Just yesterday, he and
Sergeant Marsden had gathered stone to rebuild Andrew
MacCurran's forge and the crumbling wall around the
bailey, then repaired the wall of one of the empty cottages so Flora and the sergeant could have a home of
their own. And today, he was helping to re-thatch all the
cottage roofs and she'd heard him promise Davina that
he would begin work on the cleaning and repair of the
castle garderobes. Like the hens he had stolen, the earl
appeared to be settling in quite nicely. He had done his

best to make himself useful and managed to befriend
many of her kinsmen and women. The Ancient Gentlemen liked him and boys Ian's age were amused by his
ignorance of highland ways and awed by his determination to learn them. And she couldn't help but be awed
by his determination as well. Jessalyn might not like to
admit it, but she was certain he was having more success adapting to the highland ways than she would have
had adapting to life in London. In truth, Neil Claremont
was a success at nearly everything. She couldn't even find
fault with him for trying to usurp her role as the MacInnes.
He regarded her kinsmen with respect. He didn't treat
them as enemies or as inferiors, but as individuals. Nor
did he point out the error of their ways in remaining
loyal to a weak Stewart king. Their loyalty seemed to be
one of the things he admired most about them, and when
he became aware that there were a few members of her
clan who would have been happier with a male laird,
Neil didn't attempt to encourage them or try to court
their favor. He made it perfectly clear to every member
of the clan that *she* was the MacInnes and that *he* was
her loyal husband. Except for his lack of prowess in the
bedchamber, she couldn't have asked for a better husband—Sassenach or not. She chided herself for continuing to believe in foolish romantic dreams. She was a
woman grown and the leader of her clan. She had no
reason to be so unhappy and dissatisfied with her father's
choice of husband for her. Jessalyn sighed again. It was
harder to give up on her dreams than she'd imagined. If
only he had proven himself to be less of a braggart and
more of a lover everything would be perfect . . . If only
she knew how to help him . . . If only her prickly pride
hadn't made her deny him . . . If only she could learn to
guard her sharp tongue around him . . .

Neil tied another bundle of thatch into place and
stretched the muscles of his lower back. He had known
how to thatch. He had learned the process while study-
ing architecture under Christopher Wren, but his study

had been all theory and no practice. Using thatch as a roofing material was illegal in London. It had been outlawed during the last part of Queen Elizabeth's reign because the closeness of the buildings in London made the danger of fire sweeping through the city a constant threat. The thatch-roofed buildings that preceded the law were allowed to remain and to be re-thatched but it was against the law to put a thatched roof on a new construction. And the fear of fire sweeping through London had been completely justified. Sixty-odd years after Queen Elizabeth's reign the Great Fire raged through the city and nearly destroyed it. Neil wiped the sweat from his brow with the back of his hand. Straightening to his full height, he braced his body against the gusting wind and surveyed the half-finished roof with a sense of pride and accomplishment. He'd had no idea that thatching was so backbreakingly hard or that the view from the roof could be so satisfying. He looked down at the bailey below and caught sight of the MacInnes.

The wind swirled around her, lifting strands of her reddish brown hair free of its braid and plastering her skirts against her legs, silhouetting her body. Neil inhaled sharply and she looked up at the same moment, almost as if she'd heard him. Her gaze connected with his and Neil noticed that the silver chain she usually wore around her neck sparkled against her bottom lip as she held the key in her right hand and absent-mindedly ran it back and forth across her lips, occasionally flicking it with the tip of her tongue.

Neil felt the impact of that almost imperceptible gesture from fifteen feet away. His heart seemed to slam against his ribs and he shifted his weight from one leg to the other, carefully straddling the ceiling beams to accommodate the sudden swelling in his groin.

He ached to touch her again. He wanted to feel her firm breasts in his hands and taste the texture of her smooth skin against his mouth and tongue. He wanted to hold her in his arms and kiss her again and caress her and show her that their wedding night had been the exception to the rule, that he had a reputation for being an excellent lover and that he would be more than happy to live up to his boasts. If only she'd give him another chance . . .

"Major? Sir?"

Neil turned to find Stanhope had been trying to hand him another bundle of thatch to tie into place. He had no idea how long Stanhope had been waiting for him to cease his erotic musing over the MacInnes.

Stanhope grinned at him. "I'm obliged to you, sir, for helping me thatch the roof. I know you have better things to do with your time. But Magda and I are grateful to you and to your lady for giving us the cottage."

"The MacInnes gave you the cottage," Neil said. "I had nothing to do with it."

"I know, sir, but you're the one who volunteered to fix the roof. And well, Magda's a loyal daughter, sir. She would never complain about living with her father, but she waited a long time to get married and she wanted a house of her own and well, being newlyweds and strangers to one another, we needed some privacy."

Neil was amazed by the other man's conviviality. He'd known Corporal Stanhope for months and until he'd been abducted by Clan MacInnes, he'd never heard Stanhope say more than a couple of words at the time. Now, it seemed nothing would shut him up. "You sound quite pleased with your new married status, Stanhope."

"I am, sir. You can set your mind and your lady's mind at ease on that account, sir. Magda and I suit each other very well. I imagine we can make a very good life here once I learn a trade other than soldiering."

Neil finished tying the bundle of thatch into place and raked his fingers through his hair. "You intend to stay in Scotland?"

"I do, sir." Stanhope said. "Once I'm out of the army. There's nothing for me in London. I've no family or friends left and even if I did, Cheapside is no place for Magda to live."

Neil lifted his eyebrow in surprise. How strange that he had married the laird of Clan MacInnes, without ever seriously considering the possibility of living in Scotland for the rest of his life. "What will you do?"

Corporal Stanhope shrugged his shoulders. "I don't know what trade I'll take up yet, but Magda's used to fresh air and trees and heather and plenty of clean water for drinking and washing. She can't get those things in London. Not on what I'd be able to earn. And she'd die without them." He paused for a moment, then glanced over at his commanding officer. "I know you feel differently, sir. I know you hate Scotland and I know you want to return to London and build those grand mansions and cathedrals you've planned. And that's all right for you. London is a good place to live if you've got money and a title. But I don't have money. And as far as I'm concerned, any kind of life here is better than in London."

Neil accepted another bundle of thatch from Stanhope. "The villages are too far apart for effective commerce, the soil's too thin and rocky to cultivate, food is scarce, the roads practically nonexistent, the summers are too short and the winters are too harsh and the highland clans are too proud and prickly to tolerate King George's rule." He snorted. "Compared to London, Scotland's a veritable paradise."

"It is to me," Stanhope said.

Neil shook his head. "I don't understand how it could be."

Corporal Stanhope shrugged his shoulders. "I guess it depends on what you want out of life. You want to leave your mark on the world by building grand cathedrals and squares, and roads and government monuments for all of London to see and admire. I just want to build a good life for my wife and family."

Stanhope's words echoed through Neil's mind long

after the conversation and the thatching of the cottage roof came to an end. Before he'd been abducted by the members of Clan MacInnes, before he'd married the MacInnes, he had known exactly what he wanted out of life. He'd lived for the day he could bid King George's army and Scotland adieu. He had planned to return to London as swiftly as possible and resume his work with Christopher Wren. There were palaces to build and slums to clear away and the neat little houses he planned to construct. Houses for men like Stanhope who wanted more than shabby rooms in Cheapside. But his life and his plans for the future had been changed through the scheming and interference of his grandfather and a few old Scotsmen. He had married the MacInnes and sent for the bribes that he hoped would entice her back into his bed, but he hadn't really thought beyond the presentation of his gifts and his immediate sexual gratification. Now, he owed it to himself and to the MacInnes to decide if he wanted more than just a marriage and a quick tumble. He had to decide if he wanted to share his life with her. Neil sneaked another glance at his bride—at the way she carried herself and of the way she led by example. He watched as she brushed back a wisp of hair with the back of her hand and left a smudge of dirt across her cheek, watched as she diligently concentrated on gathering and bundling an armload of heather for use as thatch. She was beautiful, he decided. And loyal and proud. He wanted London, but he wanted the MacInnes as well. The question facing him was whether or not he wanted her as much as he wanted his dream, whether he could give up his dreams or make her a part of them. And whether she wanted to share them.

Chapter Seventeen

London

By the time the distinctive coach bearing the blue and silver coat of arms of the marquess of Chisenden rolled to a stop in front of the elegant little townhouse on Bond Street, the employees of some of the most fashionable shops in London were already whispering tales of the marquess and marchioness's extraordinary shopping spree. Although the owners of the shops had been handsomely paid for their discretion, it was impossible to keep quiet about the enormous amounts of cash and merchandise exchanging hands. Word had leaked out and the resident of the house on Bond Street had begun her own shopping spree.

The marchioness of Chisenden heard about it from two excited dressmakers and decided that the time had come to pay her a visit. She exited the coach and walked to the front door unescorted, rang the bell and waited.

"I'm sorry," the butler said as he opened the door, "but the mistress is unavailable."

"She'll be available soon," Lady Chisenden remarked. "But until then, I suppose she's out shopping."

"No, madam." The butler shook his head. "The mistress is at home, but she's not receiving visitors."

"She'll receive me," Lady Chisenden replied, removing her card from her reticule. "I'm the *grandmére* of the gentleman who pays for this dwelling." She stepped past the butler into the entrance hall where she dropped her calling card on the silver tray on the antique table beside the door.

The butler glanced at the calling card. CHARLOTTE, MARCHIONESS OF CHISENDEN. "The mistress has just broken her fast, Lady Chisenden. May I show you into the salon while I apprise her of your arrival?"

Lady Chisenden nodded. "Please inform your mistress that I am here on matters of some importance and that I will await her appearance in the salon within the hour."

"But, my lady, the mistress is engaged in her toilette. She is not presentable."

"Mistresses rarely are."

The butler stared at her open-mouthed.

"Yes, yes. My reputation for speaking my mind is well-earned. Now, run along, my good man, and tell her she needn't dress up. I've no wish to prolong my visit by cooling my heels in the salon any longer than necessary." The marchioness gave a dismissive wave of her hand and sent the butler on his way.

Left alone, Lady Chisenden took the opportunity to survey her surroundings. Although much smaller than the salon at Chisenden Place, the room was furnished with tasteful furniture, carpets and paintings by several of the lesser Italian Renaissance painters. She immediately noted Neil's hand in the arrangement of the furniture. Instead of in the more common and more formal arrangement of furniture situated along the walls of the room, the sofas and chairs were placed in conversational groupings near the fireplace and the windows along with several small tables. Neil used the same arrangement of furniture in his townhouse and advocated the use of it in the houses he designed. He had clearly made himself at home here. Lady Chisenden smiled. Her grandson's man of business had been quite surprised when she'd paid a visit to his offices earlier in the morning. It had taken very little persuading on her part to convince him that her grandson had asked the marquess to break the news of his marriage to his mistress and that she had convinced the marquess that the news would be better delivered by a woman. She agreed that it wasn't the sort of thing a lady normally did, but since her grandson was serving His Majesty in the wilds of Scotland she felt she must do as he asked. Neil's man of business had insisted on accompanying her and she'd agreed as long as he agreed to wait in the coach until her business with the widow was concluded. She smiled. Her visit here would serve two purposes. It would satisfy the burning curiosity she felt about Neil and the widow Sheridan and it would protect Neil, his bride, and his future heirs from any greedy demands the widow might make. Somehow she didn't think she would have as easy a time convincing Deborah Sheridan to give up Neil as she had convincing his man of business to part with the property deed the marquess's solicitor had delivered to him the day before or the cash settlement Neil had arranged for Deborah to have at the end of their liaison.

"My mistress sends her regrets, my lady, but she will be unable to attend you within the hour," the butler announced when he entered the salon moments later.

"Really?" The marchioness raised one of her exquisitely arched eyebrows. "How unfortunate!" She walked to the doorway of the salon, then turned and marched up the stairs.

The butler caught up with her as she reached the room at the end of the hallway. "Madame! You cannot go in there."

The marchioness fixed the servant with her most regal stare, knocked once on the door, then placed her hand on the doorknob, opened the door and stepped over the threshold.

Deborah Sheridan greeted her coldly. "I'm afraid I'm not receiving guests this morning, Lady Chisenden."

"I know," the marchioness replied, "The butler informed me that you were engaged in your toilette."

The widow Sheridan smiled. "I had Fenton say that so you'd leave."

"Then you're a liar," Lady Chisenden remarked. "Are you a coward as well?"

"Sometimes," Deborah replied.

Lady Chisenden lifted an eyebrow.

Deborah gave an elegant shrug. "You might say I'm whatever the occasion calls for."

"This must be a rude occasion," Lady Chisenden studied the perfectly groomed young woman her grandson had taken as his mistress. Although she was slightly disappointed that her grandson had chosen a rather obvious and commonplace sort of beauty, Lady Chisenden wasn't surprised. Dressed in a fine silk morning gown that clung to her body, Deborah Sheridan showed off the look men of all ages seemed to find perpetually intriguing. She had the oval-shaped face and delicate features, the white blonde hair and cornflower blue eyes, curvaceous bosom, flat stomach and rounded hips that were all the rage in fashionable London. The marchioness knew the young woman had been a widow for several years and assumed that she and Neil were much the same age. She had seen the widow from a distance at the opera, the ballet and the theater and upon occasion, at gatherings in the homes of the fashionable members of society but she hadn't realized Deborah Sheridan was so young—barely twenty—despite the lines of discontent bracketing her lips and the cold light in her eyes. "Someone must have neglected to teach you how to curtsey to your betters."

"I have no betters."

Lady Chisenden didn't blink an eye at the insult the younger woman delivered. "Perhaps not when you're flat on your back, but you're on your feet now and in the presence of someone who cannot be flattered by your attention or entranced by your looks." She stared at the widow. "I cannot see what my grandson saw in you."

"I should think that's obvious," Deborah puffed out her bosom and preened like a peahen.

"There's no doubt that you're attractive and equipped with huge udders, but you're vain and selfish and un-educated and coarse and despite your foray into wedded and widowed bliss, terribly immature."

"And you must be incredibly *mature*." The widow Sheridan sneered the word. "Every bit as mature as my last husband."

"Your last husband?" Lady Chisenden remarked. "Not your first?"

"My third," Deborah replied. "I married young."

The marchioness was surprised the widow Sheridan admitted as much. "All old men I suppose."

She shook her head. "Only two of them. My first hus-band was an ignorant farm boy of sixteen. My second, almost as ignorant, was the uncle of the first. My last husband was eighty and a very wealthy cloth merchant in Bristol. He left me a fortune, but of course his son inherited the business and the house, so I moved to Lon-don."

"And became a courtesan," Lady Chisenden said. "Such ambition. I've heard that you stupidly squandered the fortune your cloth merchant husband left you."

"What's a fortune for? If not to be spent?" She shrugged her shoulders once again. "When you're young enough and beautiful enough, you can always find men willing to spend their fortune on you. Your grandson is very rich and very generous." She cast a sideways glance at the marchioness. "Has he told you that we're to be married when he returns from Scotland? Is that why you've decided to pay me a visit? Did he send you to welcome me into the family?"

Lady Chisenden fought to keep from blanching at the idea. "He did not," she informed the widow. "As a mat-ter of fact, I decided to pay you a visit because we're welcoming someone else into the family—the new count-ess of Derrowford. Neil's bride."

"What?" Deborah feigned surprise, clutching at her heart before gracefully sinking onto a pink satin divan.

Lady Chisenden raised her eyebrow at the poorly acted melodrama. "I'm sure it doesn't come as that much of a surprise. You can't have gone shopping without hearing the rumors and according to the rumors, you've definitely been shopping."

"I heard several malicious rumors," the widow replied in a breathy whisper. "I didn't believe them. I knew they had to be untrue."

"Believe me," the marchioness replied, carefully enunciating the words, "the rumors are true. My grandson is married. He sent word of it from Scotland. He no longer has need of this house or of the mistress in it." She smiled a little at her play on words, then reached into her purse and pulled out a sheaf of bills and papers. "I came to deliver the settlement my grandson agreed to pay you at the end of your arrangement. Also enclosed is the deed to this house and all of its contents."

Deborah recovered admirably. "Neil bought me the house. Are you certain he intends to end our arrangement?"

"The marquess and I purchased the house to prevent your creditors from turning you out upon the street or sending you to debtor's prison in the event that you fail to find another generous protector." Lady Chisenden burst the widow's bubble of satisfaction. "I'll present you with the deed and the money when you sign the documents terminating your liaison with the earl of Derrowford."

"Neil had legal documents drawn up?"

The marchioness shook her head. "*I* had the documents drafted to protect the countess of Derrowford according to the earl's instructions. When the papers are signed, the earl's financial obligations to you and your creditors is at an end. You will be held responsible for your personal and household expenses—including your clothing bills and the salaries of the household staff."

"No," Deborah said. "I've only your word that Neil

wants to end our arrangement. I don't believe you and I refuse to sign any papers you've had drawn up."

"Very well," Lady Chisenden agreed. "You requested a cash settlement at the termination of your arrangement with the earl. I have the money and I'm quite prepared to turn it over to you and to assume responsibility for any purchases you made before you learned of the earl's marriage and the change in your status. But your refusal to recognize that the affair is over or to honor your part of the bargain means that earl is no longer obligated to honor his." She opened her purse and began stuffing the papers and the money inside it.

"What about the money? What about my bills? Who's going to pay?"

"I assume they'll be paid from the money allotted for this month's portion of your personal upkeep."

"But Neil's factor doesn't give me that much. I've already spent far more than my monthly allowance."

The marchioness shook her head. "You'll have to discuss that with the earl's man of business. I'm sure he'll be able to work out a schedule and a satisfactory method for you to repay the earl the money you owe him."

"Repay Neil? What are you talking about?" Deborah demanded. "I want the factor to give me an advance on next month's allowance for my personal use and make sure that Neil releases enough money to take care of the bill collectors who'll be banging on the door as soon as they learn of his marriage."

Lady Chisenden was almost aghast at the young woman's greed and her audacity. "You don't seem to understand that money from your monthly allowance will no longer be forthcoming."

"I'm well aware of that," Deborah Sheridan sent the marchioness a withering gaze. "If I don't sign the papers, I'm still his mistress and Neil can make his tight-fisted factor give me more."

"He doesn't wish to give you more."

"I know that. He's always complaining that I'm in-

tent on driving Neil into the poorhouse." She rolled her
eyes. "Honestly, you'd think it was *his* fortune I'm spend-
ing."

"You are no longer the earl of Derrowford's mistress,"
Lady Chisenden reiterated. "As such, the earl no longer
wishes to support you or your expensive way of life. You
won't be getting a monthly allowance from him and his
factor won't be paying your bills—unless he chooses to
do so with his own money. Is the situation clear to you
now? You may accept the earl's decision and his settlement or face your creditors and debtor's prison on your
own."

The widow thought for a moment. "I could sell the
house."

"You don't own the house—or it's contents."

"You said I would."

"Only if you sign the documents."

"I don't want to sign."

"Then the house and its contents belong to the marquess and me," Lady Chisenden told her. "And you may
consider your tenancy at an end."

The widow narrowed her gaze. "What if I'm with
child?"

Lady Chisenden eyed the younger woman's slim figure. "A slight possibility since you assured the earl you
were barren."

"My last husband was eighty," the widow remarked.
"I *was* barren with him, but Neil is considerably more
potent."

Lady Chisenden frowned. "The earl of Derrowford
left London over five months ago, you don't look as if
you're with child, but I'm willing to grant that it may
be possible."

Deborah smiled triumphantly.

"Should you present a child within the time possible
for the earl to have fathered it and should the earl choose
to acknowledge your claim, the child will be taken from
you and a trust fund will be set up to provide for its

care. You will relinquish all rights to it as described in
paragraph six, section one of these documents."

The widow Sheridan glared at Lady Chisenden. "You
and the marquess thought of everything," she said. "Except the fact that Neil did not set me aside before he left
for Scotland. He hasn't seen me face-to-face and he may
yet choose to resume our liaison when he returns."

Lady Chisenden shook her head. "Claremont men are
notoriously monogamous." Noting the widow's blank
look, she hasten to explain. "Claremont men sow their
wild oats before marriage, not after it. Once they repeat
their vows, they remain faithful to them. They do not
consort with harlots or take mistresses. Your relationship
with the earl of Derrowford has already ended."

The widow turned away from the marchioness and sat
down at her writing desk. "Give me the money and the
papers, Lady Chisenden. I'll sign."

Lady Chisenden walked through the doorway. The butler waited outside the door where she'd left him when
she'd barged into the widow's bedchamber. "Ask His
Lordship's man of business to come inside," she said.
"He's waiting in my coach."

"The all powerful wife of the mighty king-maker, the
marquess of Chisenden. You came here knowing you
could best me. You certainly were sure of yourself,
weren't you?" Deborah sneered.

"No," Lady Chisenden replied. "I was sure of you."

"I hear you had a busy day," the marquess of Chisenden
remarked to his wife as they met in the parlor for sherry
before going into dinner.

Lady Chisenden glanced at her husband and caught
sight of the tiny smile hovering around the corners of
his mouth. "No busier than yours I'm sure."

"Not at all, my dear," Lord Chisenden replied, before
handing his wife her glass of wine. "I had another audience with the king to acquaint him with the latest details on the situation in Scotland, dropped in on a special

session of the lords, then retired to my club for a few hours. My day was quite ordinary whereas I heard that you visited the bank, the offices of our solicitor, purchased some real estate on Bond Street, and paid a very early unescorted morning call on the tenant of that newly purchased property."

"You were misinformed, Louis. I visited six dressmakers who agreed to furnish a wardrobe with matching slippers, nine cobblers who agreed to fashion the additional shoes Neil requested and the warehouses of four furniture dealers *before* I made the other calls. And I wasn't unescorted. My maid was with me during the shopping expeditions as were three members of the household staff and both Mrs. Mingot and Mrs. Petrie. I left the two housekeepers to manage the purchases I'd made and paid an unplanned call on Mr. Heaton after I learned that the resident of the house on Bond Street had been doing an alarming amount of shopping herself." Lady Chisenden took a sip of her wine, savoring the fine quality and the distinctive nutty flavor, then smiled at her husband. "So you see, I was never unescorted. Mr. Heaton accompanied me. He waited in the coach until he was needed."

"Why didn't you allow Mr. Heaton to continue to handle things just as he's been doing since Neil left for Scotland?" There was a note of censure in Lord Chisenden's voice.

"I'd heard a good many rumors about the money she spends on clothes and I was afraid Mr. Heaton was being too lenient with her. After all, he is a man and she is a courtesan who's been left to her own devices for several months. I was afraid a mild mannered solicitor like Mr. Heaton would be putty in her hands. And I was—"

"Curious." The marquess grinned. "About her and the house our grandson rented for her."

"Yes, I was."

"And I suppose that since I've never taken a mistress, you decided to take advantage of a last opportunity to get a glimpse of a lifestyle beyond your realm of experience and have a close look at the woman Neil had chosen as his mistress."

Lady Chisenden made a face at her husband. "You know me so well, Louis."

"Much better than you know our solicitor," he retorted. "The man is known for his honesty and his penny-pinching. That's the reason I chose him and the reason I encouraged Neil to use him. He's quite a traditionalist. The poor man must have been astonished when you showed up to conduct business."

"He was a bit surprised," she said. "But I reminded him that I was acting in Neil's best interest and that my husband and my grandson held me in such high regard that they would naturally stand behind my purchase of the property and my method of dealing with the resident of it." She tried to look contrite and failed miserably.

"I see." The marquess pursed his lips. "And immediately afterwards you coerced a strange gentleman into accompanying you in a closed coach to a not quite respectable house on Bond Street in the middle of the morning?" He shook his head and made a clucking sound. "Most unladylike. What of your reputation? Will I have to demand satisfaction from Mr. Heaton to squash the gossip?" he couldn't resist teasing her.

"Posh, gossip! Mr. Heaton isn't a strange gentleman, Louis. He's a solicitor and he's handled our business for twenty-five years. Besides, I asked him to wait in the coach in order to preserve my reputation—and yours."

"Oh?" He lifted his eyebrow in the familiar gesture she adored and had spent years perfecting for herself. "How so?"

"I thought it beneath his dignity and mine for him to bear witness to a cat fight between the marchioness of Chisenden and a trollop."

The marquess threw back his head and roared with laughter. "Need I ask who won?"

"I did, of course," the marchioness replied. "I'm older

and I've more experience, but the little she-cat did manage a few scratches of her own."

"Aside from the fact that she's a greedy little trollop, how do you assess the situation?" he asked. "Will she be satisfied or will we be hearing from her in the future?"

"She isn't the type to be satisfied," his wife admitted. "We'll be hearing from her again when she exhausts her settlement. But she did sign the documents I asked Mr. Heaton to draw up and I think we've quieted her for now."

"Documents?" His ears perked up.

"Of course," Lady Chisenden answered. "Legal documents stating that in exchange for the cash settlement and the deed to the house on Bond Street she agreed to relinquish any and all claims, actual or implied, on the earl or the countess of Derrowford, their property and estates and the property and estates of any and all future heirs."

"I'm impressed," he murmured in a low throaty tone of voice that still sent shivers of anticipation up and down her spine.

"I haven't been married to 'the king-maker' for all these years without learning something about negotiations." Lady Chisenden set her glass of sherry down on the nearest table and cast a speculative glance over at her husband.

He didn't disappoint her. "Then what say we forego a formal dinner and have a midnight supper brought to our rooms after we negotiate our way beneath the bed-linens?"

Chapter Eighteen

Neil took the heavy pail of hot water out of Davina's hand as he dismissed her from the kitchen and bid her a pleasant good-night. He emptied the bucket of boiling water into the wooden tub, then walked over to the hearth and tossed a chunk of peat into the fire. He untied his tartan as he retraced his steps to the tub. He pulled it from around his waist and draped it across the back of a wooden chair before stepping over the rim of the tub and gratefully easing his body down into the warm, soothing bath. He watched with complete satisfaction as wisps of steam rose from the surface of the water and floated up toward the ceiling. It had taken some experimenting, but he had finally discovered the correct ratio of boiling to freezing water to fill a proper tub. Five pails for a warm, comfortable bath, seven pails for a steaming one. And after mucking out and repairing most of the castle's old antiquated garderobes all day, Neil had opted for steaming. "Aahh . . ." He closed his eyes and let out a blissful sigh as the hot water worked its magic on his tired, taut muscles.

"Here, laddie, this'll do more fer yer aches and pains than that."

Groaning at the intrusion, Neil opened one eye and fixed his gaze on Auld Tam. "What are you doing here?"

Tam cast a disparaging glance at the steaming bath-tub, then thrust a small clay cup into Neil's hand.

"I brought ye sumthin' to put hair on yer chest."

Neil eyed the cup with suspicion. "I have hair on my chest, old man. And I'm sure you have better things to do than watch me bathe."

Auld Tam tugged off his bonnet and dropped it on the worktable. He scratched his head then reached over and removed another cup from the shelf by the stove. "Aye," he said. "I've come on an important mission."

"Which is?" Neil interrupted.

"I've come to see why a young handsome mon like yerself is attemptin' to catch his death of cold bathin' in a tub of water in the kitchen instead of cuddlin' in a warm bed wi' his bride."

"Who told you I was bathing in the kitchen?"

"I passed Davina on my way and she told me ye were in here attemptin' to catch yer death."

Neil sighed. "Davina should mind her own business."

"She's grown fond of ye, lad," Tam told him. "And she's worried about ye."

"I've spent the whole day cleaning out and recon-structing this castle's ancient garderobes," Neil reminded him. "And while that certainly isn't the most pleasant of chores, it is a chore entirely worthy of a hot bath instead of a quick wash in the freezing water of the loch."

"Which brings us to my second point," Tam contin-ued. "Ye've been thatchin' roofs, repairin' cottages and outbuildin's, constructin' walls and cleanin' shite houses. If ye keep pushin' yerself at this pace, ye'll wear yer-self out before winter."

"I've no choice, Tam. You abducted me from a mili-tary encampment. You know it's only a matter of time before the army rides into this village looking for me. My time here is limited. I have to push to make the cas-tle habitable by winter. The stonemasons I sent for will be here any day and we're not ready. We simply don't have enough men to do the job."

"An' we'll have one less if ye keep workin' yerself into a frenzy." He grinned at Neil. "I dinna go to the trouble of abductin' ye and arrangin' yer weddin' just to have wee Jessie made a widow afore her husband makes her a proper wife."

Neil frowned, wrinkling his brow in warning, as Tam broached the dangerous topic.

Auld Tam ignored the warning. He shoved the wooden chair out of splashing range of the tub with his foot, then settled his bulk onto it. He pulled a metal flask from the depths of his plaid, removed the cork stopper, filled his cup and drained the contents in one long swallow. "Go on, lad, drink up." Tam wiped his mouth with the back of his hand and refilled his cup.

Neil lifted the dram to his lips and tossed the drink to the back of his throat as Tam had done. But unlike Tam, he immediately succumbed to a fit of coughing as a trail of liquid fire hot enough to steal his breath and bring a rush of tears to his eyes seared its way from his throat to his stomach. "What kind of witches' brew is this?" He managed between gasps.

"Whisky," Tam pronounced with a grin of supreme satisfaction. "Scots whisky. The best whisky in the Highlands. Made from an ancient MacInnes recipe and improved upon by the Munros." He waited until Neil recovered from his fit of coughing, then leaned forward and poured him another dram. "Guaranteed to cure what ails ye."

Neil shook his head. "How? By killing me?"

"By pleasurin' ye," Tam cackled. "Fine Scots whisky is like a maiden's weddin' night. It only pains ye once. The first dram singes ye, but the others are puir bliss. Go on, laddie, see for yerself. Only sip it this time."

Neil gritted his teeth, then took a hesitant sip and discovered Tam had spoken the truth. The liquor flowed across his tongue like heated honey, dissolving the knots in his muscles, warming the pit of his stomach.

He looked up at Tam and his surprise must have shown

on his face because the old man chuckled once again. "Warms ye right up. I keep a flask in me plaid."

"I knew there had to be a trick to wearing a plaid and keeping warm," Neil said wryly.

"Aye. 'Tis our way of keepin' warm when we're out raidin' or warrin' wi' the neighboring clans."

"You're not out raiding or warring tonight, old man."

"Och, that's true," Auld Tam admitted. "But whisky's a guid remedy fer other ailments." He pinned Neil with a sharp look. "Like when yer an auld mon and canna find a wife to warm ye bed fer ye or when yer a young mon who canna satisfy one."

Neil frowned. "I wondered how long it would take for you to get back to that. Sorry old man, but a gentleman doesn't discuss the particulars of his marriage bed with his drinking companions."

"As far as I can see ye dinna have a marriage bed," Auld Tam observed. "Ye have an empty one and it doesna look like yer goin' to be remedyin' the situation any time soon." He paused for a moment before continuing. "Now, if it's instruction ye need . . ."

Neil gave a derisive snort. "It's not a question of having the knowledge, the ability or the desire to satisfy her," he replied, extending his cup for a refill. "It's a question of opportunity."

Auld Tam quirked an eyebrow at that. "Yer married right and proper."

"Aye." The thick Scottish burr was a perfect imitation of Tam's. "We're married right and proper."

"Weel?"

"Weel, I promised my bride a spectacular wedding night and I failed to deliver the goods."

"Ye dinna?"

"I did." Neil cupped his hands in the water. He rinsed his hair and washed his face. He sluiced the water from his face and shook his head, sending droplets of water flying in all directions before he opened his eyes and sent Auld Tam a meaningful glare. "She dinna."

"That explains why she's so out of sorts," Tam said at last. "She's ashamed."

"Ashamed? Of me?" Neil reacted immediately. He shoved his empty cup at Tam, then stood up in the tub so quickly that water surged over the rim and onto the floor. He couldn't believe his ears. He was young and healthy and handsome and a peer of the realm. He was a belted earl with a title and a family dating back to the Conqueror and fortune greater than that of the present king. And *she* was ashamed of him!

"Not of ye, exactly." Tam gave Neil a thorough once over, leisurely refilling both cups with whisky before he handed him his tartan. The lad had every right to be proud—and angry. "Of her husband's performance. And of his place in the clan. She canna respect a mon who willna or canna keep his word. And highlanders dinna brag aboot the things they canna do."

"I wasn't bragging," Neil muttered, rubbing the plaid over his chest and legs, using it as a towel, before knotting it around his waist. "I was trying to reassure her by letting her know that while everything else about her wedding had been disappointing, the wedding night wouldn't be." Neil raked his fingers through his hair, grunting, as he ruthlessly worked his way through the snarls and tangles. "It's a wonder I could perform at all! I had a lump the size of a hen's egg on my forehead thanks to you and your trusty battle axe and a bitch of a headache. I'd been abducted, tied across the back of a horse and bounced across Scotland, thrown to the ground, threatened, stripped of my clothing and coerced into repeating my vows before a clan of hostile witnesses, then expected to perform on demand. I ached in more places than I care to remember and—" He squeezed his eyes shut.

"An' . . ."

"As a lover, I left a lot to be desired." Neil could have bitten out his tongue at his unfortunate choice of words. "I barely managed to consummate the marriage before passing out." He opened his eyes and glared at the old man. "I'd never disappointed a woman in my adult life—until the night it mattered the most." He muttered a nasty curse beneath his breath. "I was hoping that the gifts I ordered from London would make a difference, but they've yet to arrive. I've worked like a slave in the village and on the castle—designing improvements and making the repairs we have the men to make in order to provide her with the comforts other ladies take for granted and in the hope that I might win her favor. I've done everything I can think of to lighten her burden of responsibility and I've waited outside the door to the laird's room every morning for the past sennight hoping she would—" He broke off, reaching for his cup of whisky and downing it in one gulp. "I can't think what more to do except improve on the castle and even then, we're so woefully short of men that when the stonemasons arrive . . ." He stared at the empty whisky cup. "Who did you say made this drink?"

"The Munros. Why?"

"The same Munros we've been raiding?"

"Aye." Tam nodded. "They dinna mind the raidin'. 'Cause they'd rather make whisky than tend the horses or cattle or chickens."

"Do they sell this whisky in Edinburgh or London?"

"Sell the *uisge beatha,* the water of life, to outlanders?" Auld Tam cackled. "Of course not. Only highlanders. But not to us. Years ago, a Munro laird married the daughter of the MacInnes brewer in order to learn the secret of makin' it and before the last Uprising the Munros dinna ask us to pay because our clans were connected." Tam shrugged his shoulders, "Durin' the Uprising the current Munro laird supported the Sassenachs to keep from losin' his land, his barley and his stills. An' since the Uprising, we've had to steal it. Besides, we couldna buy it. We've dinna have coin."

Neil grinned, so happy he could've kissed Auld Tam on his bald head. "That's it! That's the answer!"

"To what?"

"To our survival, Tam. I've ordered enough supplies to support the clan through the winter, and I've got enough money to support it for years to come. But the king is determined to open the highlands and unless the clans can support themselves, they're doomed. But crops and herds take time to establish and it will be years—perhaps decades—before Clan MacInnes can support itself. Unless we have something to sell. Something like this." he refilled his cup and raised it in salute to Tam.

"We canna sell what belongs to the Munros."

"Why not?" Neil asked. "We've been eating what belonged to the Munros."

"Most of the animals we've been takin' from the Munros originally belonged to the MacInneses," Tam said defensively.

"So did the recipe for this whisky." Neil smiled. "We'll buy into the enterprise, pay for permission to sell it and pay the Munros to make it."

"Enough." Tam held up his hand. "Puir Jessie." He clucked his tongue in sympathy. "No wonder she's so out of sorts. 'Tis time ye quit tryin' to impress yer bride by rebuildin' her castle and her holdin's and to start impressin' her with yer skills as a lover."

"How?" Neil demanded. "Tell me how."

"Ye start by meetin' her at the laird's room." Tam reached over and patted the younger man on the shoulder. "And do what comes natural."

"She's not interested."

"She's interested," Tam told him. "But she's afeard of being disappointed again. 'Tis no wonder she willna confide in Magda or Flora for 'tis plain to see that my daughters are satisfied wi' their husbands. So satisfied that in a few months I'll be grandpa to two wee bairns."

Neil looked up in surprise. Was it possible? Had he managed to . . . After only one time? "Could the MacInnes possibly be . . ."

"Nay." Auld Tam seemed to read his mind. "Not yet."

He had failed her twice, but he wasn't going to admit that to Tam. "How can you be so sure?"

"Davina," Tam explained. "Jessie dinna meet ye at the door to the laird's room for the first four mornings of the sennight because her woman's time was upon her."

Neil scowled. "She hasn't met me any morning."

"She tried. For the past three mornin's. But she couldna wait all day. I tried to gi'e her as much time as I could but sumthin's always demandin' the laird's attention and she was gone to attend to her duties by the time ye arrived. I came here tonight because I thought it was time ye knew."

Neil hooked his foot around the footstool beside the hearth, pulled it to him and abruptly dropped to a seat atop it. The air seemed to leave his lungs in a rush and his heart began to pound. "I waited every morning thinking that the MacInnes . . ." he buried his face in his hands and shook his head. "I had no idea . . ."

Auld Tam bumped Neil's shoulder with the edge of the flask. "Weel, now ye know. An' now there's sumthin' more important for ye to do than rebuild a castle. Ye can start by drinkin' a toast to the future of the clan."

Neil picked up his cup and allowed Tam to refill it once more. "To the clan!"

"To the clan!"

Auld Tam drained his cup and grinned as Neil did the same. He stared at the young man for a moment, then reached out and jabbed him in the arm. "When they wed, I ga'e my lassies plenty of time alone wi' their husbands and they rewarded me with guid news. It's time I did the same fer ye and Jessie." He pushed himself to his feet, swaying slightly from the effects of the whisky. "Dinna worry aboot the castle or the stonemasons or buyin' whisky from the Munros. Ye worry about yer wife and yersel'. I'll take care of the other details and I'll make sure ye ha'e the privacy ye need to gi'e Jessie a wee bairn of her own."

•   •   •

She wanted to be happy for them. She *was* happy for them. Magda and Flora were her oldest and dearest friends. Of course she was happy for them. So why couldn't she stop crying? Because, Jessalyn thought, as she ruthlessly scrubbed the tears from her eyes with the backs of her fists, she was afraid. Afraid her envy would show. Afraid she wouldn't be able to share in her friends' joy without the bitter taste of jealousy spoiling it. Because, for the first time in her life, Jessalyn wanted what Magda and Flora had.

She was bombarded by daily images of her husband, images her willful mind insisted on reproducing in vivid detail day after day, night after night until she seemed haunted by them. She pictured him hauling stone and timbers with Auld Tam, fishing in the loch with Ian, patiently holding the basket while Hannah collected eggs from the hens he'd helped steal from the Munros, and standing on the roof of Magda's cottage, his MacInnes tartan blowing in the breeze as he thatched alongside Magda's husband, Artie. But most of all she remembered him leaning against the door that led to the Laird's Trysting Room. She remembered his kisses and the feel of his skillful fingers against her, the way he looked with his kilt on the floor around his ankles and the clear green of his eyes and the way that solitary dimple creased his cheek, as he smiled wickedly and reminded her that he was free most mornings.

Jessalyn slid down the wall. She sat on the cold stone floor with her knees drawn up to her chest and rested her back against the thick iron lattice of the *yett*. She tugged at her skirts, pulling them over her feet in a futile attempt to ward off the damp and the cold seeping through the stone. She squeezed her eyes shut, trying to put aside her vivid memories of her husband—the intoxicating feel of his lips on hers, the mating of her tongue with his, and the overwhelming hint of something more exciting, more intoxicating, just beyond her ken.

The early morning air in the tunnels was frigid, but

she felt hot and feverish and achy as if she'd caught the
ague. Jessalyn sighed. She had made the trip down here
four mornings in a row, had sat on the freezing floor and
waited for him to appear, but she'd been bitterly disappointed, almost as disappointed as she had been when
she'd awakened eight days ago to find her woman's time
upon her. She knew what it meant and she realized that
her frustrating and embarrassing wedding night had been
all for naught. She hadn't been as fortunate as Magda
and Flora. Two days ago, Flora had whispered her exciting news and this morning Magda had done the same.
They were both with child. Jessalyn knew that she was
not. And she couldn't stop crying over it. She was plagued
by feelings of guilt for not rejoicing in her dearest friends'
good fortune. She was ashamed of herself for wanting
what they had and terribly, selfishly afraid that their lives
and their friendships were about to change beyond recognition. The gulf between them that had begun when she
became laird of the clan and widened when the three of
them married was sure to become unbreachable once her
childhood friends became mothers.

Magda and Flora's impending motherhood made the
responsibility of being laird of the clan weigh heavier
on her shoulders. Her wedding money wouldn't last forever and Jessalyn was haunted by the knowledge that her
clan depended on her for food and shelter. Would she be
able to buy enough peat for the fires or blankets for the
beds and food for the stew pots? Could she bear to watch
any more members of her clan suffer? Could she stand
to lose any more of her family to the hunger and cold?
And what of the man she had married? He had promised
her security and wealth beyond her wildest imaginings.
Could she count on him when it really mattered? Or
would he fail her the way he'd done on their wedding
night?

She ought to leave. She ought to get up and go about
her business. She ought to march through the doors of
her father's chamber and demand that her husband reas-

sure her. Demand that he do his duty and kiss her long enough to put an end to the frustration that was driving her mad. Surely then she'd find relief from her unsettling feelings. Before, all she'd had to do was convince him to forget about the other and concentrate on the touches and the kisses she craved. Now, she'd demand that he give her a child and be quick about it. She would tell him that he needn't bother with the part she liked, that all he need do was proceed to the part she hated. She didn't care. She was perfectly willing to sacrifice his touches and his wonderful kisses if it meant that he would get her with child. But how? She'd tried ordering him to do her bidding and he'd ignored her demands. Surely there was some way she could accomplish her task without backing down—without conceding defeat or allowing him to claim victory in their battle of wills . . . If only she could discover it . . . For what good was there in being the laird of the clan if she had no power? What good was being laird of the clan if she couldn't get her handsome Sassenach husband to fulfill his duty? Jessalyn bit at her bottom lip and brushed away another flood of tears. Was she destined to follow in her father's footsteps? Would worry and sacrifice and grief drive her into an early grave? Was that all the laird of the clan had to look forward to? Would there never be anyone to share her burden? Would the aching loneliness never end?

Chapter Nineteen

She was waiting for him. Neil quickened his pace. He could see her in the distance sitting on the floor, her knees drawn up to her chin, her back braced against the iron *yett*. He frowned. He imagined her looking up and smiling at him or running to meet him, welcoming him with hot kisses and open arms, but she didn't look up. Nor give any sign of having heard him. As he drew nearer he saw the moment in her shoulders and recognized the sound echoing hollowly in the passageway. She was crying. His stomach tightened and his heart seemed to catch in his throat. His proud, highland laird was crying as if her heart would break.

He stopped in his tracks, then silently retreated into the shadows, momentarily stunned and unsure. Her tears made him uncomfortable, anxious, willing to do whatever he could to end them. Perhaps because they were unexpected and private. His mistress had cried at the slightest provocation. She'd used her tears or the threat of them to wheedle gifts and favors from him. Neil's conscience ached with the knowledge that he had given the MacInnes far more reason to cry than his mistress had ever had and she hadn't shed a tear. She hadn't cried when she'd discovered that her father's oath had bound her to marry a man she didn't know, a man who wore the uniform of the enemy. She hadn't cried when she repeated the vows that gave him rights to her body and to all her belongings. Nor had she shown any indication of having cried the morning after their wedding when she'd been angry and unsatisfied.

But she was crying now. And the sight of it tore at Neil's heart. He wanted to sweep her up in his arms and hold her. He wanted to cuddle her close and promise her everything would be all right. He wanted to rebuild her castle and take care of her clan. He wanted . . . her. The woman he had come to know and admire. The MacInnes with the flame-kissed hair, fierce pride and the determined glint in her eyes.

He took a deep breath, then stepped out of the shadows and started toward her, whistling a jaunty little tune. Suddenly the MacInnes raised her head and looked in his direction. She turned her face to the side just long enough to scrub the traces of tears from her eyes and cheeks with the heels of her hands, then pushed herself to her feet. She straightened her shoulders, stiffened her back and turned to face him.

"You wanted me, milady?" He said the first thing that came to mind.

She lifted her chin a notch. "No. I didn't."

Neil bit his bottom lip to keep from grinning at the angry glint in her eyes. "My mistake." He shrugged casually. "I could have sworn Tam said . . ." He let his words trail off. "No matter." He stepped back as if to leave. "Please pardon me for intruding."

"Wait!"

He waited.

"As long as you're here," she began, "there is something you might do for me . . ."

"Anything."

As soon as he said he word, Neil knew he meant it with all his heart. He stared at her, fixing his gaze on her face and the incredible blue-gold of her eyes. If she ordered him to perdition he'd go. And if she asked him to stay . . . If she asked him to stay, he'd give her a taste of paradise.

"Give me a bairn."

Her words nearly took his breath away. Neil closed his eyes for a moment and sent a silent prayer of thankfulness heavenward. Paradise. She'd granted him paradise and he meant to do everything in his power to return the favor. "My pleasure, milady."

"Yes, I know." She wrinkled her brow and clutched at the folds of her skirt while she pursed her lips in distaste. "I'm willing to do without the kissing and the touching so that you may find your pleasure and gift me with a child."

"I cannot ask you to make such a sacrifice," Neil replied through clenched teeth.

His softly spoken words of sarcasm were lost on her as she replied, "Yer not askin' me to sacrifice. I'm willin'. Just make it quick and as painless as possible."

She appeared calm and unemotional and completely unaware of the insult she'd given him. But her white knuckles and the return of her thick Scottish burr gave her away. "I would be most happy to give you a child, milady," Neil told her, carefully enunciating each word. "But I cannot be quick about it."

"Why not?" she demanded.

He closed his eyes again and sent another brief prayer skyward—this time asking forgiveness for the lie he was about to tell. "The creation of a child takes time."

"It does not!" Jessalyn scoffed. "Flora and Magda are both wi' child and they married the same day we did."

"I don't mean days or weeks or months," Neil elaborated. "I mean time together. I mean that in order to create a child, a man and woman must be careful to take their time. Rushing through the process usually means the difference between success and failure."

"But Magda and Flora . . ."

Neil pinned her with a knowing look. "Magda and Flora have shared their husbands' beds every night since they wed. They've been intimate with their husbands many times. You and I were briefly intimate only once."

"Oh."

She looked so disheartened that Neil would rather have bitten out his tongue than ask the question. But he asked it anyway. "Do you still want a child, milady?"

She lowered her gaze, bit her bottom lip and looked as if she might succumb to tears once again, but she nodded her head and firmly replied, "Aye."

He walked over to her, reaching out to tilt her chin up so that he could read the expression on her face. "Then I suggest we make the most of our time." Neil caressed the line of her jaw with his thumb then let go of her chin. He removed his key from around his neck, inserted it into the first lock and turned the tumbler. He glanced down at Jessalyn, then extended his hand. "Your key, milady."

Jessalyn tugged the silver chain from beneath her bodice, pulled it over her head and handed it to him.

Neil placed the key in the second lock, turning it until he heard the click as the lock opened. He leaned his shoulder against the heavy iron door and pushed. The *yett* swung open on well-oiled hinges. Neil pulled the two keys from the outside locks and handed them to Jessalyn, then bent at the knees and scooped her into his arms. He carried her over the threshold, turning in the passageway and bending low once more as she leaned forward in the cradle of his arms and shoved the *yett* back into place, then used the keys to lock the door behind them.

Neil stood in the passageway for a moment, allowing his eyes to adjust to the darkness of the second tunnel.

"There are carved niches hidden along the walls," Jessalyn whispered. "And candles. Lift me higher and I'll get one."

Neil shook his head. "Never mind the candle," he said. "I can see well enough." He carried her through the tunnel until he reached the doors at the end. "Which one?" he asked.

"The one on the right," she replied.

Neil turned right, waited while Jessalyn unlocked the locks and retrieved the keys, then pushed open the door. He paused in the doorway long enough for Jessalyn to deposit the keys on the shelf carved into a niche beside the door and to light the oil lamp. She gasped in awe as the lamp cast its glow upon the room. The massive room contained every luxury imaginable—the kinds of luxuries Jessalyn had only dreamed about over the past year.

The Laird's Trysting Room was a Scottish nobleman's idea of a bridal bower fit for a queen. Three walls were hung with a dozen gilt-framed Venetian mirrors in various shapes and sizes, exquisite tapestries and a series of nude drawings that clearly bore the mark of and were signed by da Vinci. Satin cushions were scattered around the floor and the floor itself was covered in a thick woven carpet that matched the deep blue velvet coverings of the huge bed that dominated the room. The room was a marvel of architectural engineering. A stone fireplace, laid with wood and kindling instead of peat, was built into the left wall. It occupied a recessed area between the interior shaft of the latrine and the shaft housing the castle well so that the smoke from the fireplace vented up the center shaft to the roof of the castle. Pinpoints of light from arrow loops along the outer walls dotted the floor and furnishings like stars in the night sky. On the wall to the right, a ladies' dressing table held an incredible array of jewel-studded items—brushes, combs and boxes made to hold brooches and jeweled hairpins, and beautiful glass bottles of perfumes and cosmetics. A silk reclining couch piled high with thick fur rugs sat beside a hand-painted screen and a massive chest rested at the foot of the bed, the top drawer opened to display the fine silks, satins and embroidered linens.

Neil crossed the threshold and carried Jessalyn to the

bed. He leaned forward, placed one knee on the mattress and lay her in the center of the blue velvet coverlet.

Jessalyn stared up at him with a look of distressed panic on her face. "Oh no," she protested. "My feet. They're dir . . . I've been sittin' on the floor. I canna."

He immediately understood her objection. She was shoeless and her feet and legs were probably dirty. His heart seemed to contract in his chest. It had been so long since the MacInnes had been in the midst of such luxury that she was fearful of spoiling it. "Yes, you can," he whispered, leaning forward to bury his face in the curve of her neck. "This *is* the laird's trysting room. You *are* the laird. And we are trysting."

"Aye," she murmured, arching her back, baring her neck to his caresses. "So 'tis. I am. We are."

"Aye." He pressed his lips against the pulse at the base of her throat, then worked his way up her chin to the corner of her mouth, then down along her jaw until he captured her earlobe with his teeth.

Jessalyn's lips parted on a sigh. Seizing the opportunity, Neil caught it, covering her lips with his, kissing her deeply and thoroughly until . . .

She closed her eyes and kissed him back. She used her tongue to tempt and tease him as they played the age-old game of advance and retreat, of give and take, of mutual surrender. She followed his lead until he relinquished control and followed hers. They played the game over and over again, leading each other on a merry chase, deepening their kisses with every stroke of their tongues as they teased and tormented each other with kisses that were so hungry and hot and wet and deep that Neil was finally forced to end them.

His arms shook with the strain as he levered himself off her, rolled to the side and propped himself on one elbow.

Jessalyn opened her eyes. "What's wrong, my lord?"

Neil sucked in a shaky breath. "Nothing's wrong, mi-lady."

"Then why did you stop?"

He smiled at her and his smile was the most beautiful sight she had ever seen. It was warm and tender and incredibly provocative. "I stopped in order that you might grant me permission to continue."

She returned his smile, then reached for him.

Neil shook his head. "I want to hear you say it."

"Permission granted, my lord."

He lifted an eyebrow in query.

"I grant you permission to give me a child."

Neil moved close enough to brush her lips with his own. "There is something else, my *laird*," he murmured in his imitation Scots burr. "You've been given this marvelous secret chamber to use for your pleasure. It would be a shame not to use it for that purpose."

"Can you give me pleasure and a *bairn*?"

"Aye," he answered. "I can give you more pleasure than you ever dreamed possible. If you'll let me. Grant me permission to do that, my lovely laird MacInnes, and I promise you will never regret it."

"Only if you promise not to hurt me."

"I give you my word of honor."

"Permission granted, my lord," she whispered shyly.

"One more thing," he said.

"More permissions, my lord?"

"Aye," he nodded, with a wickedly handsome grin. "You have my permission to satisfy your curiosity. Kiss me. Touch me. Do with me what you will."

"Are ye certain?"

"Verra certain."

She kissed him and her kiss was hot and sweet enough to tempt an angel. But Neil wasn't an angel and he didn't need further temptation. Jessalyn pulled him to her until she could press herself against him. She flattened herself against his chest, feeling the heat of his flesh as she deepened the kiss. The twin points of her breasts pressed into him. Neil groaned. Encouraged by his response Jessalyn allowed her hands to roam over his shoulders, and down his back. Neil groaned again. His tongue mated with hers as he showed her what he wanted. Jessalyn continued her exploration. She moved her hands lower until she reached the soft, well-worn wool covering his buttocks. His muscles bunched and rippled under her hands as Neil held her tightly, half-lifting her off the bed as he ground his hips into hers and rubbed his throbbing erection against her. He pulled his mouth away from hers and began to trail hot wet kisses on her face, her neck, her throat, and over to her ear lobes.

"Aah, Jessalyn," Neil whispered close to her ear, "I want to feel you against me and I want to bury myself inside you." His arms began to shake once again. "I want you so badly."

"And I want you, my lord," Jessalyn whispered back.

Neil pushed himself up on his elbows so he could see the expression on her face. "Are ye certain?"

Jessalyn smiled. "Verra certain."

That was all the encouragement Neil needed. He wrapped an arm around her, lifting her long enough to tug the coverlet and the top sheet from beneath her, then lay her back down on the bed. He sat back on his heels, reached down and untied the laces of her outer corset and stomacher, then the drawstring at the neck of her white muslin chemise. He pushed the chemise down over her shoulders and arms. He opened her outer corset and stomacher and discovered the tiny jeweled handle of her eating dirk sticking out of the brown leather sheath at her waist.

"Setting a new fashion for countesses, milady?" he teased, leaning forward to kiss the spot above the dirk.

Jessalyn closed her eyes and arched her back as he sucked at the fabric covering her navel, then covered it with his mouth and breathed on the wet fabric. The sensation sent delightful shivers up and down her spine.

He pulled the dirk from its small scabbard and held it up for her to see. "Ye've brought a weapon to bed. Did you think to have need of it?"

Jessalyn opened her eyes. "I hope not," she whispered. "I hate the sight of blood."

"So do I, milady." He kissed her chin, then licked at the seam of her lips. "Especially my own."

"Then beware, my lord earl." She opened her lips to allow him further access, then murmured between kisses, "because I shall cut out yer heart if ye disappoint me again."

Neil pushed back long enough to stare into her eyes. "If I disappoint you this time, milady countess," he promised. "I'll cut it out myself."

"Then I'll have no further need of it," Jessalyn said. She took the dirk from him and tossed it on the floor.

Neil shoved her outer corset and stomacher aside so he could feast on the sight of her rounded breasts. "You're beautiful," he breathed.

Jessalyn recognized the look of admiration in Neil's warm green eyes and knew that he meant it.

He leaned forward, cupped one smooth satiny globe in his hand, and touched his lips to the rosy center.

Jessalyn sucked in a breath at the wonderful sensation his tiny kiss evoked. Desire gripped her. Eager for more, Jessalyn tangled her fingers in Neil's thick dark hair and held his head to her breasts. "Again," she ordered.

Neil obliged. He touched and tasted and gently nipped at the hard bud with his teeth. And then, he suckled her and Jessalyn thought she might die of the pleasure as her nerve endings became gloriously alive and sent tiny electrical currents throughout her body, igniting her responses.

"It's your turn," he whispered when she lay writhing beside him. "To find out what a Sassenach turned Scotsman wears beneath his kilt. Undo my plaid. Touch me." He sat up and leaned back on his heels to give her access to the knot at his waist.

Jessalyn lowered her gaze, then reached out and untied the knot that fastened the MacInnes plaid around his narrow hips. Her eyes widened at the sight of him. She had seen him naked before, but not like this, not this close, not kneeling before her on a bed. Jessalyn stared. He was beautiful. His wide shoulders tapered into a narrow waist, into slim hips and strong thighs. His chest was covered with dark curly hair that also tapered down into a long slim line which encircled his navel and pointed to the hard erection jutting from another thatch of dark curls. He was big. He was all male. He was completely aroused. And all hers. Jessalyn understood that he was capable of hurting her again, but he had promised not to. He had promised to give her pleasure and she intended to welcome it with open arms and to give it back in full measure. She placed her palms against his chest, then traced that intriguing arrow of rough hair down to its base. His skin rippled beneath her delicate touch, and he gasped aloud as she gripped him.

The feel of him caught her by surprise. She expected the hardness, but she never expected the exquisitely soft feel of the flesh that encased it. He was hard, yet velvety soft and the contrast intrigued her. She stroked him, experimenting with the feel and the motion of him. Neil quivered with pleasure and came very close to spilling himself in her hand as Jessalyn caressed him without shyness and with what could only be termed an innate talent.

"No more," he muttered, leaning his head against her breast.

"More?" she asked, pumping him slowly and gently.

"No!" Neil reached between them and grabbed hold of her wrist to make her stop the exquisite torture.

"Don't you like it?"

"I love it," he groaned. "But there is a limit to how much I can endure before I spill myself in your hand."

Jessalyn frowned. She was hot and achy and almost delirious with need and as much as she enjoyed the feel of him, spilling himself in her hand was not what she wanted. "Then tell me what comes next," she ordered.

"I'd rather show you." He let go of her wrist, sat back on his heels once again, grabbed her chemise by the hem and whisked it from around her waist, pushing up and over her head. Then he untied the tapes of her skirt and smoothed it over her hips and down her legs. Jessalyn kicked free of it and sighed with relief, welcoming her nakedness. Clothing had suddenly become a hindrance. She wanted to feel him against her skin.

Neil turned his attention back to her breasts. He dipped his head and trailed his tongue along the valley between them. He licked at the tiny beads of perspiration. The scent of her perfume teased his nostrils. It was warm, spicy, and all Jessalyn. He tasted the skin above her rib cage, trailed his tongue over her abdomen, circling her navel before dipping his tongue into the indention. And while Neil tasted her with his tongue, he teased her with his fingers. He skimmed his hands over the sensitive flesh covering her hipbones and outer thighs. He felt his way down her body with his hands, finally locating and tracing the deep grooves at the juncture of her thighs with the pads of his thumbs. Easing his way ever closer, Neil massaged the womanly flesh surrounding her mound, then tangled his fingers in the lush auburn hair covering it.

Jessalyn reached immediately, opening her legs ever so slightly to allow him greater access. She couldn't seem to get close enough to him. Her anticipation rose to a fever pitch. She began to quiver and make little moaning sounds of pleasure as he traced the outer edge of her folds with his finger before gently plunging his finger inside. Jessalyn squirmed, arching her back to bring herself into closer contact with Neil. Neil gritted his teeth. The slick warm feel and the scent of her nearly drove him mad. The swelling in his groin grew until he was rock hard and close to bursting. He couldn't wait any longer. He had to have her. He had to feel himself inside her, feel her surrounding him, feel them joined together the way men and women were meant to be joined.

Neil withdrew his fingers and placed his hands under

Jessalyn's hips, lifting her slightly as he leaned forward and positioned himself to enter her.

"I'm ready," she said, squeezing her eyes closed, bracing herself for the unpleasant part.

"You were," he murmured. "Until you did that."

Jessalyn opened her eyes and stared up at him. "What?"

"Prepared yourself to be sacrificed on the altar of my selfish desire." Neil kissed her on the tip of her nose. "Trust me. I won't be selfish this time. I'll give as much as I take."

She hesitated a moment longer, seeking further reassurance.

"Put your legs around me," he whispered, licking the seam of her lips, enticing her with little kisses that tasted of him and of her before he covered her mouth with his in a caress that left no doubt about the pleasure he had to offer.

When he kissed her like that she couldn't refuse him anything. He lifted her higher and Jessalyn wrapped her legs around his waist as he moved forward in one smooth fluid motion and sheathed himself in her warmth.

Jessalyn cried out as he buried himself in her. He muffled the sound with his mouth and his heart began a rapid tattoo as he recognized it as a sound of surprise and increasing pleasure instead of pain.

"That wasn't so bad, now as it?" He brushed her cheeks with his lips, then her eyelids, and finally, her mouth. He kissed her gently, tenderly, reverently, and held her as if she were precious and fragile.

She shifted her hips experimentally, then moaned as the pleasure began to build once again.

"And it only gets better," he assured her.

"Better than this?" Jessalyn lifted her hips again, and this time Neil understood.

"Much better." He struggled to go slowly, fought to maintain control and his body strained with the effort. Jessalyn tightened her hold on him. She put her arms around his neck and held on as he began to move within her. Gently, slowly at first, then faster.

She followed Neil's lead, matching her movements to his until they developed a rhythm uniquely their own. She kissed him as they moved together—kissed his arms, his shoulders, his neck, his chin, the corner of his mouth. And she trusted him to lead her to that place that seemed just beyond her reach—the place where she became him and he became her—the place where the two of them became one. And then suddenly, she felt him shiver uncontrollably, heard him yell her name, and Jessalyn let herself go with him. The world around her seemed to slip away, there was only Neil and the almost unbearable feeling of pleasure spiraling inside her. Tears filled her eyes and rolled down her face as she clung to him. And in a moment of profound pleasure and heart-stopping wonder, she screamed her release. Neil tightened his arms around her, kissing away the tears as the sound of his name echoed around the room.

Chapter Twenty

Jessalyn opened her eyes, met her husband's incredibly green-eyed gaze and panicked. She rolled off the bed in one smooth motion and headed for the door.

"Whoa . . ." Neil recognized the expression on her face and rolled with her. He caught up with her as she reached the door. He hooked his arm around her waist and pulled her back against his chest. "Easy, love," he whispered, calming her. "You're all right. Everything is all right."

Embarrassed by her loss of control and by the trickle of liquid she felt sliding down her thigh, Jessalyn abruptly turned in his arms. "Ye dinna understand," she blurted. "I've got to go. There's work to do . . ."

"Ssh!" Neil placed two fingers against her lips to stop her flow of words, then bent at the knees and lifted her into his arms. He smiled down at her with an expression on his face that could only be described as tender satisfaction. "If you stay on your feet, you'll lose the seed I planted inside you."

"Oh!" She paled at his words. Her face lost all color and her eyes widened in surprise as she realized that the liquid trickling down her legs contained the seed necessary to create new life. She clamped her thighs together.

"Don't fret about it," he soothed, reaching out to

smooth the worry lines from her brow. "You didn't know . . ."

Jessalyn gave him a sharp glance. "I'm not completely ignorant. I know enough to know that making a baby canna be too hard. Young girls get themselves bred everyday."

Neil winced at her terminology and at the white lie he was about to tell her. "Yes, they do," he agreed. "But you're not fifteen anymore. At your—" He caught himself in time. "At *our* age the making of a baby requires a bit more consideration and a great deal of practice. Besides—" He nodded toward the ceiling. "—nothing you could be doing up there is as important as what you're doing down here with me." Neil carried her across the room and placed her on the bed.

"Do ye know what happened to me?" she asked.

Neil leaned over her and kissed her forehead. "Aye, milady. You screamed out your pleasure and then you fainted." He climbed into bed beside her and pulled the covers back over them.

"I've never fainted before." She frowned.

"You've never experienced the little death before," he told her, pulling her close against him.

"The little death?"

"Yes," Neil answered softly. "I believe the French call what happened to you *le petite mort*. The little death."

"Do they?" she asked. "Are ye sure? I thought the French were romantics . . ."

"That's what they say," he replied. "Why? Don't you believe it?"

Jessalyn gave an unladylike snort. "Not if the best words they can come up with to describe what happened to me is the little death. Highlanders are more romantic. We'd use the right words."

"Oh?" Neil bit the inside of his cheek to keep from laughing aloud at her serious contemplation of the meaning of the phrase. "What words would you use?"

"I would call it 'a glimpse of heaven,' " she announced

in French. "Do ye suppose the French named it the little death because they believe death comes in such a way?"

A lock of her hair lay curled on the slope of her breast. Neil traced it with the tip of his index finger. "I think they were hoping it does," he said. "That might explain why they're always fighting us. They're begging for the little death." He wiggled his eyebrows and leered at her. "As were you, my lady."

Jessalyn buried her face against his chest and blushed.

Neil pushed her hair back from her face. "What say you now, my lady wife? Did I disappoint you? Will we be needing your dirk?"

Jessalyn looked up at him. "Not this time," she told him.

"This time?" Neil latched onto her words. "Are ye implying that there will be another?" He asked in his best Scottish burr.

"That depends, milord."

"Upon what?"

"Upon whether or not ye were successful in getting me with child."

Neil leaned over to brush her cheek with his mouth, then grinned and whispered, "There's no way of knowing that for another month, milady."

"Are ye sure?" Jessalyn shivered as his warm breath tickled the sensitive skin of her cheek and traveled to her ear.

"Verra sure," he growled, gently nipping at her ear lobe.

"I suppose we'll need more practice," she ventured.

"That would be best, milady," he replied, careful to keep the sense of elation he felt from showing in his voice, careful to sound as if he were giving the matter serious consideration.

"If I meet ye here tomorrow morning, can ye do it again?"

He held his breath, almost afraid to ask. "Do what, milady?"

"Give me another glimpse of heaven."

Neil grinned down at her. "Aye, milady, I can do that. In more ways than you can imagine."

"All right," Jessalyn placed her hands against his chest and prepared to sit up. "We'll practice again tomorrow."

"If you'd rather," Neil said as he covered one of her hands with his own and carefully guided it down his chest and over his belly to the part of him that was hard and straining for attention. "But there's no need to put off until tomorrow what we can do today." He wrapped her fingers around him and helped her measure his length.

"I dinna know . . ."

"There's a lot ye dinna know, milady," Neil whispered against her lips. "A lot yer aboot to learn . . ."

When Neil opened his eyes again he discovered the MacInnes sleeping soundly, her head resting upon his shoulder. He had no idea how long he'd been asleep. The oil lamp by the door had burned low and the inside of the trysting room was dark and chilly. The pinpoints of light from the arrow loops and the cracks and crevices along the outer walls of the castle had disappeared. Neil eased Jessalyn's head off his shoulder and onto the pillow. He tucked the covers around her, then slipped out of bed and crept silently toward the hearth.

Striking flint onto the kindling in the fireplace grate, Neil patiently nursed the small flames to life and with the light from the fire as illumination, he began to examine the room in more detail. He noticed the little details that had escaped his attention in the heat of passion—like the fact that the room was clean. Jessalyn's father had been dead for over a month, yet the Trysting Room was free from dust and cobwebs. Jessalyn had known the room existed, but she had told him she'd never been inside it and he had no doubt that she had spoken the truth. She had been as surprised as he was when

they'd entered it and discovered the wealth and the luxuries hidden there. The old laird had given Jessalyn a
key upon her mother's death, but had only relinquished
his key to her as he lay dying. There were two locks on
the *yett* which blocked the passage into the tunnel and
two locks on the door to the room itself. Jessalyn's key
had unlocked one lock and his key had unlocked the
other, so how had Callum MacInnes gained entry to the
room without using the key he had given to Jessalyn?

Even if the old laird had kept the room himself after
his wife died, who had kept it cleaned and readied since
his death? Someone else must have been entrusted with
a set of keys. Either that or there was another way into
the room—a secret door or sally port hidden somewhere.
Neil searched the room. The area around the fireplace
yielded an alcove which housed a well shaft where a pulley system enabled the occupants of the room to draw
water from the well, but no secret door. Neil tested the
ropes. The pulley was well-oiled and quiet and the ropes
were in good repair. Temporarily abandoning his search
for the sally port, he drew several buckets of water from
the well. He filled the clay pots and two large ewers with
water and set the containers as close to the fire as possible. With luck, he would find a bathing tub and be able
to provide the MacInnes with a hot bath and another lesson in lovemaking. If not, he would at least be able to
provide her with warm water with which to wash. Moments later, he located a stone latrine and a brass tub
large enough for two behind the painted screen. A large
pottery bowl full of dried flowers and herbs sat on the
back of the latrine. Neil pinched a few of the dried flower
bulbs between his fingers to release the fragrance, then
dropped the powdered remains into the tub. Admiring the
fine craftsmanship, Neil noticed that one end of the tub
was higher than the other and that the lower end had
been fitted with a tap and positioned above an iron-grated
drain in the floor. He closed the tap, then moved the
screen from in front of the tub and placed it where it

would block the view of the latrine, but allow the heat from the fire to warm the bathing area.

"What *are* ye aboot?"

Neil turned at the sound of her softly spoken words. Jessalyn was staring at him, her blue-gold eyes wide with wonder. "I'm aboot to make it possible for the laird of Clan MacInnes to take a hot bath." He wiggled his eyebrows at her. "With me."

Jessalyn pulled the sheet over her breasts, holding it in place with her arms as she sat up in bed and stared at him. "Are ye now?"

"But of course," he answered. "And as you can see, I've everything you need. I've located a tub—" He patted the brass rim of the tub, then nodded toward the water heating by the fire. "And I'm heating the water."

"What about ye?" she whispered provocatively.

Neil shot her a knowing look. "That, my dear countess, is your responsibility."

Jessalyn lifted her arms and let the sheet fall to her waist. "But of course it is," she mimicked his crisp British accent. "And as you can see, I've everything you need . . ."

His talents were wasted as an engineer, Jessalyn decided as he settled down into the hot water and lifted her into place atop him. He might be a gifted and innovative builder, but his true talent lay in his ability to persuade her to part with her inhibitions as she parted with her clothes. She sighed as he separated her womanly folds with his nimble fingers and guided himself inside her. It didn't seem possible, but in the space of a few hours, Neil Claremont had persuaded her to forget the modest, ladylike tenets of a lifetime and to relish in the passion he taught her. Jessalyn could barely believe it, but here she was—completely naked and sharing a bathtub with a man. She laughed softly as Neil shifted his weight and sent waves of water rippling across her body and over the rim of the tub. She braced her arms against the top of it, using it for balance and leverage, as she teased him.

Neil placed his hands on her slim hips and anchored her firmly against him as he licked droplets of water from her breasts. He groaned his pleasure in her ear and his warm breath made her squirm harder.

"I cannot take much more of your style of torture, milady," he warned as she raised herself up as far as she could before sliding slowly down his shaft and wiggling her bottom against him.

She clucked her tongue in sympathy. "Can you not, milord? Because I'm certain I can take quite a bit more if you're able to give it."

"I'm more than able."

Before she knew quite how he managed it, Neil lifted her off him, turned her so that she faced the opposite direction and knelt behind her. He molded himself to her buttocks and slipped inside her.

Jessalyn gasped as he began to move behind her. In and out. Faster and harder until his final thrust sent water cascading over the edge of the tub and across the floor and they both collapsed against it in an explosion of passion and need.

"I have lived long enough to bring an Englishman to his knees," Jessalyn quipped when Neil disengaged himself and helped her to her feet. She stood ankle deep in bathwater as she turned to face him.

"Your accomplishment wasn't so impressive," he told her. "There isn't a man alive—English or Scottish—who wouldn't gladly fall to his knees for the pleasure of tasting you. But I—" He smiled as he traced his index finger from her bellybutton to the triangle of dark auburn curls between her thighs. "I have made a Scottish laird, the bravest—the fiercest of all warriors—beg for mercy."

"I canna believe it!" she teased. "A Scottish laird begging for mercy? Impossible! Surely you were mistaken."

Neil caressed her with his finger as he pretended to ponder her words more closely. "So I was," he agreed at last. "For I believe the lady in question is a beautiful English countess and she wasn't begging for mercy—" He lowered his voice until his words seemed to rumble in his chest, becoming a husky, seductive growl.

Jessalyn caught her breath in anticipation. "No?"

"No," he replied. "She was begging for more."

"I've heard that about English countesses," she managed, her breath ragged with need.

"What?" he demanded.

"They can never get enough," she pronounced with a sigh as he lavished her aching center with attention. "They always want more."

Jessalyn rolled off her husband's chest and onto her back. "Great Caesar's ghost!" she exclaimed. "There's a looking glass above us!"

"Uh hmm." Neil nuzzled her ear.

They had carried their lovemaking to the bed and as Jessalyn stared up at the underside of the canopy, she blushed at the sight of her bare-breasted reflection staring back at her. "I've never seen such a thing. Have you?"

He laughed.

"You watched while we . . ."

"I peeked," he admitted. "But only occasionally. However enticing the opposite view, I was more enthralled with the real thing."

Jessalyn blushed more deeply and buried her face against his arm.

"Innocent," he murmured, pushing her hair back from her face so that he could see her expressions.

"Not so innocent anymore," she protested.

"Still innocent enough not to know that high-class whore houses in London have looking glasses mounted inside their canopy beds," Neil said.

Jessalyn raised her head and looked at him. "They do?"

"The most expensive and exclusive ones do."

"I still canna believe it," she whispered. "All these riches have been hidden away while we were starving." She looked at Neil. "We could have used some of these things to buy food and clothing . . ."

"Don't!" Neil placed two fingers against her lips. "This is your heritage, milady. To sell it would be sacrilege. Your father preserved it for you and your children."

"But we've been starving . . . Our kin have died from lack of food when there was wealth hidden away."

"Your father starved as well," Neil reminded her. "You cannot blame him for protecting this wealth. He sold everything he dared. If he had tried to sell or pawn any of these masterpieces—" He waved an arm toward the da Vinci and the Rembrandt. "—the Crown would have sent soldiers to ransack the castle. Eventually they would've located this room and confiscated the contents and you would've had nothing."

"Except you." She kissed the pads of his fingers. "The handsome rich English lord my father tricked into marrying me."

He froze. And Jessalyn instantly regretted her words.

Neil stared at his wife's face. He knew what she wanted. He knew that after giving him so much of herself, the MacInnes needed to hear him say the words. He couldn't promise her he would stay in Scotland. And until he knew whether or not Spotty Oliver intended retribution for his disappearance from Fort Augustus, Neil couldn't promise to take her home to London. The best he could offer was the truth. "However it came about, I do not regret our marriage."

She let out the breath she'd been holding and forced a tentative smile.

"I *do* regret that you didn't have the courtship or the wedding you deserved."

She fastened her gaze on him and shrugged her shoulders in a studied gesture of nonchalance. "My father was ill. A long courtship would have been impractical and I couldna afford a big wedding. My clansmen did the best they could wi' what they had and still they were ashamed by their inability to present us with wedding gifts."

"Impractical or not, affordable or not, you deserved better," he told her. "Much better than what you got and I hope—" He caught himself before he gave her reason to build dreams for the future. "I intend to make it up to you."

This time her smile was genuine and the light that shone in her face lit her eyes as well. "You already have."

He lifted a brow in query.

"You've given me a glimpse of heaven, milord." She blushed. "Several glimpses. That more than makes up for a plain wedding."

He shook his head. "I want to give you more."

She opened her arms to him. "Be my guest."

Chapter Twenty-one

The rumbling and the empty ache of his stomach woke him the second time. Neil rolled from the bed and carefully placed another log on the fire. He did his best not to wake her, but Jessalyn stirred as he tugged his plaid from beneath her.

She sat up and yawned. "What is it?"

"My belly." Neil chuckled. "It woke me with its complaining."

"Are ye ill?" The expression on her face mirrored her concern.

"I'm hungry. All this lovemaking with my insatiable Scottish laird—"

"English countess," she interrupted. "Scottish lairds canna be insatiable. Whereas everyone knows it's perfectly acceptable for English countesses to be so."

"Where did you hear such a rumor?" he asked. "For I've known many English countesses, but only one Scottish laird and . . ." He leaned over and smoothed her soft curls away from her face and over her shoulder. "And I prefer the Scottish laird."

"Why?" she asked.

"Because she's insatiable," he teased. "But the lovemaking comes at a price and I must have something substantial to eat if she expects me to continue."

Jessalyn swung her feet over the side of the bed. "I'll get something from the kitchens."

Fearing her trip to the kitchens might yield a hefty bowl of porridge or worse—dry oat cakes, Neil lifted Jessalyn's feet and tucked them beneath the covers. "No," he said. "You stay here where it's warm. I'll go." He finished pulling his length of tartan off the bed and began to wind it around his waist in preparation for his trip upstairs.

"No! No! Not like that!" she protested, frowning at the tartan.

Neil let go of the fabric and threw his hands up in the air. "Then how?" He demanded as the tartan slid down his legs and fell to the floor.

"Grab your plaid and a shirt from that chest." Jessalyn pointed to the chest stacked with linens at the foot of the bed. "And bring me that thick leather belt hanging on the peg beside the washstand and the gold brooch from the dressing table. I've attended to all my other wifely duties—" She cast him a wicked grin. "So I might as well pleat your kilt for you."

Neil gathered up the things she asked for and handed them over. "Are you sure you're ready to do this?"

"Aye," she answered. "Lift your arms." She unfolded one of her father's linen shirts, then stood up on the bed and dropped it over Neil's head and arms.

"You know what they'll think if anyone sees me sneaking into the kitchen," Neil said.

"Aye." Jessalyn looked up and her eyes met his. "They'll think I've come to my senses and decided to lay claim to my husband." She lowered her gaze and began to position the plaid around his waist. "Hold it just like that," she ordered as she snugly buckled the belt into place over the folds.

Neil held it.

"Now," she ordered once again. "Watch closely."

He followed every move of her nimble fingers as she deftly pleated the kilt, then looped the tail of it over his shoulder and pinned it into place with the brooch that had once belonged to her mother.

"You'll need a bigger one," she said when she finished.

"Kilt?" he asked, dismayed by the idea that he might have to wrestle with several additional yards of fabric each morning. Or stand patiently while the MacInnes did.

She laughed. "No, a bigger brooch. This one was made for a woman." She touched the gold pin. "It belonged to my mother but it will have to do until we can have a larger one fashioned for you." She sighed. "I would give you my father's but . . ."

"It should only be worn by the laird. I'm not the MacInnes. You are."

"But you're a man . . ."

"I'm husband to the MacInnes," he said softly. "And I'm honored that you've decided to pleat my kilt for me and that you trust me enough to gift me with your mother's brooch." He smiled at her. "I'll be honored to wear it."

"My kinsmen may think it strange," she warned.

Neil shrugged his shoulders. "I'm an Englishman. They already think I'm strange."

She looked up at him, amazed by his willingness to accept her superior standing within the clan. She had clansmen and highland neighbors who were finding it more difficult to do. Perhaps it was because her kin and most of her neighbors had known her from the time she was a child and had never expected her to succeed her father. She had had six brothers—all of whom had been more suited for the role of laird than she was. But he was an English earl and a soldier. As a soldier, Jessalyn knew he was probably accustomed to taking orders from officers of superior rank, but she also knew that as a natural leader, he was much more comfortable giving them and she thought it highly unlikely that he had ever had to take orders from a woman. She found his behavior even more remarkable now that he knew her so intimately—now that he was in a unique position to recognize her secret fears and the flaws in her character that she struggled to hide.

"You're staring, milady. Is something amiss with my costume?" He glanced down at his kilt.

"No, milord," she said. "You look verra handsome in your Scottish finery." She flicked a speck of dust from the row of ruffles on his shirtfront. "All you need is your sword and your sporran."

"And boots." He wiggled his bare toes. "To keep my feet warm."

"Boots would cover your legs."

"That's what they're for. To cover my legs and keep my feet warm."

She tucked her chin then looked up and gave him a coy smile. "Highlanders don't cover any of their best features. They like to show them off."

"I'm more likely to *freeze* them off in this climate. And you wouldn't want that to happen would you, milady?"

"When winter comes, I'll find a length of tartan and make you a proper pair of trews," she told him. "And give you back your boots so you won't have to worry about freezing during our long, cold Scottish nights." She reached out and took hold of his ruffles, pulling him to her for a long, passionate kiss.

"I don't think I'll have to worry about freezing during the long, cold Scottish nights now that I'll have my wife to keep me warm at night." He brushed her lips with his and as he deepened the kiss the rumbling in his stomach grew louder. "I may starve," he teased. "But I don't think I'll suffer the cold any longer."

Jessalyn blushed. "I forgot."

"So did I," he admitted. "But apparently my empty stomach did not."

"Then be on yer way," she told him. "Raid my kitchen and find food enough to sustain ye when ye return to the pleasure ye find in my bed."

"I like the way ye think, milady," he murmured, mimicking her Scots burr. "And dinna worry, I'll bring back food enough to sustain ye while ye find yer pleasure in *my* bed." He leaned over for one more lingering kiss, then left her standing in bed while he crossed to the door.

"Will ye be gone long, my lord Gallant?"

"Oh no, milady. I'll return with food from the hunt—" He turned and blew her a kiss. "—before you have time to miss me."

Jessalyn giggled as she caught it. "Impossible!" she declared. "I miss you already."

He opened the door.

"Dinna forget the keys," she reminded him, pointing to the niche beside the door. "And dinna forget to lock me in."

"Aye, my lord." Neil saluted her, then retrieved the keys from the niche and stepped into the tunnel. He followed her order and locked the door behind him before looping the chains and the keys over his head.

"There's his lordship now," Flora announced.

The clansmen gathered in the bailey looked up as he strolled across it.

"We were beginning to worry, lad," Auld Tam said as Neil approached. "But now we see there was nothing to worry about. Our wee Jessie has a' way wi' the pleatin' of a plaid."

Neil smiled at the older man. "Aye, Tam, that she does."

"We've company comin'," Tam continued. "Runners from the next glen arrived wi' the news an hour ago. A big, slow-moving caravan with livestock and lots of wagons is headin' our way." He motioned Neil to his side and lowered his voice so no one else would hear. "I suspect your gifts from London are arrivin'."

Knowing Tam had ridden over the day before to meet with the Munros about an alliance, Neil asked. "Any news from the Munro?" Neil asked.

Tam reached up and scratched beneath his bonnet. "He doesna have anything against Jessie, but he says he'll not ally his clan with ours unless we have sumthin' more to bargain with than promises."

Neil nodded. He'd expected no less. "We'll try again when the caravan arrives. How long before they get here?"

Auld Tam shrugged. "Four or five hours—maybe longer."

Neil glanced up at the sky, trying to gauge the hours of sunlight left. "Good." He turned to Tam. "I was on my way to the kitchen. I promised the MacInnes that I would bring back something to eat and I've no wish to be delayed."

Tam gave Neil a playful slap on the shoulder. "Worked up an appetite, have ye lad? Weel, get on wi' ye to the kitchen. Davina will fix ye up proper. I'll let ye know when our company arrives."

Neil entered the kitchen to find Davina preparing a tray of food. She looked up from her work and greeted him. "I saw ye makin' yer way across the bailey and I figured ye and Jessie would be hungry."

"How did you know about the MacInnes?"

"Yer wearin' one of the auld MacInnes's fine lawn shirts." She sliced off a wedge of cheese and placed it on the tray, then she hollowed out two round loaves of bread and filled them with rabbit stew. "And yer kilt's pleated."

He gave her a wry grin. "News travels fast."

She poked him in the middle with the edge of the tray. "Hold this while I get the mugs of ale."

Neil grabbed hold of the tray and held it steady as the old woman drew two mugs of ale from the barrel and plunked them down on the tray. The aroma of the freshly baked bread and the savory rabbit stew made his mouth water and his stomach rumbled once again—this time in anticipation.

"Shall I lay a place for ye here at the table or will Jessie be joinin' ye in the master chamber?"

"Neither."

"Then ye'll be staying in the Laird's Trysting Room."

Neil set the tray down and gave the old woman a sharp glance. "What do you know of the Laird's Trysting Room?"

"Enough to know ye'll be needing these." She reached into her apron pocket, withdrew a handful of small brass bells and set them on the tray.

He stared at the bells. There were six of them. "I don't understand."

Davina smiled. "The auld laird used these to let us know what he needed when he retired to the secret room." She pointed to the bells. "Hang one bell on the water bucket and send it up to us if yer hungry. Hang two bells on the water bucket if yer thirsty and three bells if ye want more firewood. Hang all of 'em on a bucket if ye need all three and we'll send it down to ye."

"Bells." He picked up one of the brass bells and jiggled it to make it ring. "I've never thought of using bells."

"Sir?"

"I'm an architect, Mistress MacInnes."

She gave him a puzzled look.

"That means that I design and build buildings."

"Like the fort I heard ye were building for the English soldiers?"

Neil nodded. "Except that in London, I build houses for wealthy lords and ladies and one of the challenges of designing large houses is finding a means of alerting servants when they're needed. I've tried several different means of meeting the challenge, yet I never thought about using a system of bells." He looked at Davina. "Tell me, Mistress MacInnes, who thought of putting bells on the water buckets?"

"I did, yer lairdship," she said. "But only for the secret room because it was the laird's private place and he trusted me wi' the care of it."

"You know where it is. And because it's the only occupied room in the castle below the kitchen you knew there would be no confusing the meaning of the bells." He smiled. "Very clever. Thank you, Mistress MacInnes, for the meal and for giving me an idea." Neil lifted her work-worn hand and kissed the knuckles.

She smiled. "Yer welcome, yer lairdship."

"Have you more bells, Mistress MacInnes?" Neil asked.

"Of course, yer lairdship."

"Auld Tam has promised to let me know when the caravan arrives. Will you alert me?"

"Aye, yer lairdship."

"Good." He picked up the tray and started toward the door.

"Yer lairdship?"

"Yes?"

"Ye dinna have to carry that heavy tray across the bailey."

"What?" He turned around so quickly he nearly upset the tray.

"Ye dinna have to carry the tray across the bailey," she told him. "There's another way to the laird's room." She crossed the room and opened the door to one of the storage rooms attached to the kitchen. "Behind the barrels." She walked over to a rack of ale barrels and rolled it to the side to reveal an opening into a storage room and a set of stairs leading down. "There's a lock on the inside."

Neil paused. "Only one lock?"

"Aye. The laird always used his key to lock it behind him."

"The other doors to the secret room have two locks," Neil said. "They require both keys."

"Nay they don't." Davina shook her head. "The laird's key opens all of 'em."

"Are you sure?"

"Aye," she replied. "Oft times I was wi' the laird when he used it on this door and the locks on the doors in the tunnels."

Neil glanced down at the larger of the keys hanging around his neck. "Are these the original keys?"

"Aye, yer lairdship. They've been handed down from the auld laird who built the Trysting Room to our wee Jessie."

"The lord who built the Trysting Room may have loved his enemy's daughter," Neil mused, "but he didn't trust her."

Davina frowned.

"The lord's key opens all the locks," he explained. "But the lady's key only opens the locks in the doors to the tunnels and the Trysting Room. If her key was a true mate to his, the castle and all its inhabitants would have been vulnerable to attack. He couldn't take a chance that she might betray him. He couldn't forget that she was the daughter of his enemy, so he deceived her—when all the while he was able to confine her to the tunnels and the Trysting Room with a turn of his key."

"Then he never truly loved her," she said. "Because wi'out trust, true love canna flourish." She looked at Neil. "I hope ye willna make the same mistake as our puir misguided ancestor."

He didn't speak. He simply turned and disappeared through the doorway.

Chapter Twenty-two

"What do you mean you haven't found him?" Major General Sir Charles Oliver demanded of the young lieutenant standing at attention before him.

"I mean we haven't found him, sir. We've searched every village and glen from here to the border lands and Major Claremont and the other two soldiers are nowhere to be found. I don't believe the major went south."

"Of course he went south," General Oliver snapped. "Why would he do otherwise? London is south. During his tour of duty here the major made his disdain for Scotland and all things Scottish quite clear. Take my word for it, Lieutenant, Major Claremont went home to London."

"I disagree, sir. We've spent weeks searching and we've found nothing to indicate the major left the fort of his own accord or that he journeyed to London."

"So we're back to that, are we, Lieutenant? You still expect me to believe that preposterous story that Major Claremont and the two men charged with the task of guarding him were kidnapped." General Oliver stared at the younger officer, daring him to continue.

"We found pony tracks inside the fort the morning after Major Claremont and the others turned up missing, sir. There is a hole in the perimeter wall, and on that night it was left unguarded. All signs point to kidnapping as the most logical explanation, sir."

"Logic? Logic? What does logic have to do with anything? I have it on good authority that Neil Claremont is in London hiding behind his grandfather's powerful cloak. And we must find him. General Wade is coming to inspect the fort and the wall must be complete. I require Claremont's presence."

"Whose authority, sir?" The lieutenant forgot himself long enough to demand an answer. "I should like to speak to the person from whom you've received this information."

"The identity of my informant does not concern you, Lieutenant."

"You charged me with the investigation into Major Claremont's disappearance, sir. If you have information as to his whereabouts it concerns me." The young officer stood his ground, refusing to be intimidated.

"I did not charge you with the duty of *investigating* Neil Claremont's disappearance. I charged you with the duty of *finding* him and returning him for trial! I have friends in London," the general boasted. "I have brother officers who keep me abreast of the events and the gossip in town. And the current gossip in London is that the marchioness of Chisenden has ordered enough household furnishings to equip a palace. It's rumored that she has every seamstress and cobbler in town working on an order for the earl of Derrowford."

"What does that have to do with the major's disappearance?"

Major General Oliver walked over to the young lieutenant and clapped him on the shoulder. "My dear fellow, the reason is quite obvious to those of us who are members of society. Major Claremont left Fort Augustus with only the uniform upon his back. He cannot return to his London abode or to the home of mistress for fear of being captured and arrested for desertion so he's setting up housekeeping somewhere other than his townhouse."

The lieutenant winced at the general's insult. "Surely Major Claremont's servants could deliver his old wardrobe to his new home."

"And risk leading us to them? Besides, Claremont is a rich man—" General Oliver paused to remove a speck of lint caught in the gold-braided frogs on the front of his uniform. He made a moue at the mirror hanging across the room from his desk and adjusted his cuffs in a gesture that had come to be automatic. "While some of us must make do with last season's wardrobe, he can well afford a completely new one."

The lieutenant cleared his throat. "Pardon me for saying so, sir, but Major Claremont doesn't appear to care as much about his wardrobe as you do—else he would not have left it behind. And if, as you say, he has ordered a new one, shouldn't he have every *tailor* in London working on it rather than a battalion of *seamstresses*?"

The general paused, staring at his reflection in the mirror while deep in thought. "The seamstresses are dressing his mistress, of course. He's been away from her for over five months. A new wardrobe will amply reward her for waiting patiently for his return." He turned from the mirror and focused his attention on the lieutenant. "Yes, of course, that's it. That must be it because my sources tell me that the cobblers are crafting ladies' shoes. They're to be delivered as quickly as possible." General Oliver snapped his fingers. "And when the goods are delivered, we'll follow them right to Neil Claremont's front door."

"Delivered where, sir?"

Major General Sir Charles Oliver cast the lieutenant a withering look. "Must I do everything, Lieutenant? Finding out when and where the goods are to be delivered is *your* responsibility. Do that, my dear lieutenant, and you'll discover where Claremont is hiding. Well? What are you waiting for?" He motioned the lieutenant toward the door. "You're dismissed. Go! Do your duty, man! Send someone to London to find out. And keep me informed. I intend to be at the head of the column when we ride up to Claremont's front door."

"Yes, sir!" The lieutenant saluted.

There was no doubt about it. Major General Sir Charles Oliver was an imbecile, the lieutenant decided. A stubborn, vain, arrogant imbecile with an axe to grind. Unfortunately Major Claremont had become his whetstone. The lieutenant gazed at the soldiers milling about the post. They were all good men. Dedicated soldiers and engineers. They deserved a better fate than to be relegated to service under Oliver's command. *He* deserved better. Major Claremont deserved better. Major Claremont. The lieutenant glanced up at the sky. He could understand Major Claremont's frustration with General Oliver and his desire to return to London. But Major Claremont wasn't a deserter. He couldn't have left his quarters without help and he was too honorable to involve other men in his escape. There was no doubt in his mind that Major Claremont had been taken from Fort Augustus by force, kidnapped by enemy clans and transported north, deeper into the highlands. But for what purpose? The general was convinced that the major had deserted the army and returned to London. But Major Claremont was too smart to do the obvious. If he had chosen to leave, he wouldn't have taken the most direct southerly route. The lieutenant sighed. He admired Claremont. He liked and respected him and he disliked following General Oliver's orders. But there was no way around it. He knew he'd have to investigate—but he didn't have to go to London to do it. The general's information had proven too reliable for mere coincidence. There hadn't been any commerce on these roads in months and now a large caravan several miles long and heavily laden with household goods and livestock *was* making its way across the countryside. The sentries had spotted it this morning. Heading north. That's what he'd gone to report. But General Oliver had been too full of his own importance to listen. The lieutenant sighed. In

for a penny, in for a pound. Once again, he had no choice
but to report his findings directly to General Wade in
London. And while he was at it, he might as well gather
a few men and ride over to take a closer look at the caravan. If it contained an inordinate number of pairs of
ladies' shoes, it would be best if he knew about it before General Oliver found out. Even an imbecile like
Major General Sir Charles Oliver was bound to notice it
eventually.

Jessalyn felt the draft as the cold air lifted the hem of
her nightdress and swirled it around her ankles. She
turned to find one of several full-length mirrors lining
the wall had swung open to reveal a ghost. She took several quick involuntary steps backward and screamed as
the ghost moved closer.

"Mac!" Neil practically leaped through the opening in
his haste to reassure her. He set the tray of food on the
nearest surface and hurried toward her.

Jessalyn halted when the back of her knees touched
the edge of the chaise. She could go no further. She
squeezed her eyes shut and struggled to regain control
of her racing heart.

"I didn't mean to frighten you." Neil held out his arms.

She hesitated for a brief moment before she stepped
into the circle of his embrace and pressed her face against
his chest. His heart was racing almost as much as hers.
"The looking glass opened and you were standing in the
shadows. I couldn't see your face but I recognized the
kilt and the shirt and for a moment, I thought you were
a ghost."

"Not a chance." He kissed her forehead and her brow,
then bent and brushed her lips with his own. "I'm very
much alive and—" he paused. "Did you say the looking
glass opened?"

"Aye." Jessalyn nodded toward it.

Neil turned and stared at the chasm in the center of
the wall. A full length mirror in an ornate gold-leafed

frame hung open, the bottom portion of the frame cleverly attached to the mirror to disguise the door hidden
behind it. "I apologize for walking through a mirror and
giving you a fright. I searched for a hidden door while
you were sleeping. But I couldn't find it," he said.
"Davina showed me the secret entrance from the
kitchen—"

"Davina knows how to get here?"

"Yes," Neil told her. "She's the only other person your
father trusted with the knowledge. She's kept the room
habitable since his death."

Jessalyn stepped back out of his embrace and looked
up at him. "Then she must have a key as well."

"No," he said. "Your father left the door behind the
mirror unlocked so Davina would have access to the
room, but you and I are the only ones with keys. Which
reminds me . . ." Neil reached out and gently caressed
her cheek with the palm of his hand. A strand of her
hair was caught on her eyelashes and he carefully pulled
it free. "I have your key."

"I know," she said. "You took it with you when you
left to find food."

"No." He shook his head. "I have *your* key. The laird's
key." He tugged the heavy silver chain from beneath his
shirt and held it out to her.

"Thank you," she said, "but I prefer the smaller one.
I've worn it for years."

"You're the laird. You should have this one," Neil insisted.

"But I gave that one to you as a wedding token."

"I know," he said. "And I cherish it as such, but you
didn't know what you were giving me. It's like the
brooch. You should have kept your father's key and given
me the one that belonged to your mother."

Jessalyn shrugged. "I like the smaller one. And since
it takes both keys to open the doors to this place, what
difference does it make whether you have my father's
key or my mother's?"

"It doesn't take both keys."

"Of course it does," she insisted. "There are two locks on every door except the one concealed in the cave that leads outside the tunnels and onto our enemy's land."

"And the one behind the mirror. Your key opens the door concealed in the cave, but it won't lock or unlock the door behind the mirror. I know because I tried it," he paused. "Your key only opens the locks in the doors leading to this room. But the laird's key will lock and unlock every door in the castle."

Jessalyn looked puzzled. "But that means my father could have come here without my mother. But she . . ."

"Could only come here with him."

"He didn't trust her."

Neil shook his head. "Not necessarily. You inherited these keys from your father who inherited them from the previous laird. Just because the original laird used these keys as a means to safeguard his castle against betrayal by his enemy's daughter doesn't mean that your father did the same thing. Your mother may have known about the difference in them."

"The Laird's Trysting Room was their special place. My mother loved to tell the story about the laird who built a secret room in the castle so he could court his enemy's daughter. How they'd scandalized both clans by breaking with tradition and marrying outside their clans. And my father used to tease my mother about scandalizing the kinswomen in our clan because she broke with tradition by refusing to retire to a lying-in room when we were born. She had insisted that the laird's children be born in the laird's bed. My father always thought that was amusing. He'd laugh and say that every bed in the castle was his bed. And if she insisted that it be a bed he slept in, why had she chosen the big bed in the master's chamber instead of the bed we'd been created in. And my mother would laugh and say it was because it was easier to find. But after my mother died, he could have brought . . ." Jessalyn's knees began to shake and she sank down onto the chaise.

"He didn't."

Jessalyn gave him a disbelieving look. She had learned a great deal about men and their desires since she'd entered this room and she found it hard to believe her father hadn't satisfied those needs during the years after her mother died.

Neil held up his hands as if to surrender. "I'm not saying your father didn't take a lover after your mother died. She had been dead six years before the rebellion and your father was a normal, healthy man. I'm sure he had needs, but according to Davina, your mother was the only woman who ever joined the auld laird in this room."

Jessalyn slowly released the breath she'd been holding. "Then why didn't he tell me the truth about the keys?"

Neil shrugged his shoulders. "He knew you'd be the laird one day and he probably thought you'd use the key and discover the truth about it on your own. He had no way of knowing that you'd give the key to me instead of keeping it for yourself." He offered her his key once again.

Jessalyn's eyes met his and she shook her head. "You're my husband. The laird's key was my wedding gift to you. I want you to keep it."

"You're the MacInnes. You may need it one day."

Her eyes met his and the look that passed between them was the look of man and woman who had shared the joys of the marriage bed. "You're husband to the MacInnes and my *ceann feachd*, the warrior who represents me—who stands in my stead in battle. I see no reason why you can't keep the key to my castle." She took the silver chain from him and slipped it back over his head and waited patiently while he returned the smaller key to her.

"But . . ."

Jessalyn reached up and pressed two fingers against

his lips to stop his words of protest. "You can *lend* it to me if it ever becomes necessary."

Neil bowed his head. "I swear I'll never betray your trust, milady."

Jessalyn's heart began a rapid tattoo, her breath caught in her throat and the sudden rush of tenderness she felt for him made her legs go weak in the knees. *She loved him.* The unexpected realization struck her like a bolt of lightning from the blue sky. She loved the way he made her feel. The way he touched her. The irreverent way he had corrupted her title into an endearment. Mac. A name he had given her. A name no one else would ever dare use. She loved the way he said it. The way it seemed to roll off his tongue in moments of passion. She loved . . . him. Everything that was Neil Claremont. *She loved him.* And for now, her love was enough. "I know."

He was surprised by her firm conviction. "How?"

"Because I . . ." She'd almost declared her love for him. "Because you're strong and kind and good. Because you told me the truth about the laird's key when you could've kept it secret."

"To keep such a secret would be dishonorable."

"You're an Englishman surrounded by highlanders," she reminded him. "To keep such a secret might have been in your best interest. I never would have known and if the clan came under attack you could have used the key to escape and save yourself."

"Escape and save myself? And leave you and your clan vulnerable?" He inhaled deeply, then exhaled a rush of air. "If you think that about me, then you've much to learn about men, milady." Neil threw up his hands in frustration and stalked over to the tray of food.

"On the contrary," she replied.

Raising an eyebrow at her stubbornness, Neil removed a bowl of stew and a wooden spoon from the tray and handed them to her before he served himself. He sat down on a chair, balanced the bowl in his hand and began spooning the contents into his mouth with more regard for easing his hunger than for his manners. "We'll discuss it after we eat."

Her eyes shimmered with love as Jessalyn accepted the bowl of stew and sat down across from him. "There's nothing to discuss, milord." She took a bite of stew. "My mind is firm on it."

"You've misjudged my character."

"Nay, I ha' not." She smiled at him. "Because I think you're the finest mon I've ever met."

Chapter Twenty-three

Davina roused him a few hours before dawn. "Wake up, yer lairdship," she whispered.

Neil opened his eyes. Jessalyn lay sleeping beside him and Davina hovered at his bedside.

"I knocked on the secret door, yer lairdship," the older woman apologized. "But ye dinna stir and Tam sent me to tell ye that the stonemasons and the caravan from the marquess of Chisenden in London have arrived. The bailey is full of wagons and carts loaded with goods."

He shoved the covers aside and got to his feet.

Davina caught a glimpse of his bare, well-muscled thigh and immediately bowed her head and averted her gaze.

Neil touched her on the arm. "It's all right," he said. "I'm dressed."

"Will ye be wakin' Jessie? She's the laird. She'll want to welcome the caravan."

"Not this time." He glanced over at the MacInnes. Her hair was free from its braid and fanned across the pillows. One shapely calf and her bare shoulders lay exposed to the frigid air. Neil leaned over and carefully tucked the blankets around her. He liked the fact that she burrowed next to him while she slept, then kicked off the covers when their bodies generated too much heat.

It made him smile. "Let her sleep," he whispered. "She's had so precious little of it that I don't have the heart to wake her." He brushed his lips across her eyelids, then walked over to Davina.

She studied him, eyeing the wrinkles in his shirt. "From the looks of it, ye've had precious little sleep yerself."

Neil took note of her gaze and attempted to smooth the worst of the creases from his clothing. "I didn't mind missing sleep. It was worth the sacrifice." He flashed Davina a wicked grin. "Besides, I didn't dare take off my plaid because I knew I couldn't pleat it. Fortunately, it wasn't necessary."

Davina blushed to the roots of her gray-streaked hair and started toward the stairs.

Neil followed, his eyes sparkled with devilment. "You blush like a maiden, Mistress MacInnes, but you're a woman grown," he teased. "Surely you appreciate the fact that the most attractive feature of the highlander's plaid is that it's easily adaptable to suit a man's needs."

"Aye," she murmured, "I did appreciate that once, but it's been so long ago, I can scarcely recall it."

"If that's the case, we must speak to the MacInnes when she awakens about one of her Ancient Gentlemen's dereliction of duty."

He hadn't thought it possible, but Davina blushed even redder. "The laird shouldna' be bothered wi' such personal troubles," she said. "Jessie has bigger things to worry about."

"I wouldn't know about that," Neil winked and continued his high-spirited devilment. "I haven't measured myself against yer Ancient Gentleman."

"Oh, go on wi' ye!" Davina swatted him playfully on the arm. "Ye know what I mean."

Neil nodded. "Aye, Mistress MacInnes, that I do. I know I can never hope to measure up to the likes of Alisdair MacInnes. The best that I may hope for is to be a suitable mate for the MacInnes." He offered her his arm.

"So let us go relieve the MacInnes of some of her worries by attending to the unloading of the caravan. I ordered a wardrobe for her—with shoes for every occasion. And I'll need your help to keep her from discovering my surprise too soon."

Hours later Jessalyn awoke to find the delicate hint of freshly blooming heather in the air and a pair of pale yellow, pearl-encrusted slippers with matching patterns on the pillow beside her. She squeezed her eyes shut, then opened them again and blinked several times. Instead of vanishing into the mist of some luxurious dream, the shoes and the bouquet of white heather remained on the pillow beside her. Jessalyn pushed her hair away from her face, sat up in bed and looked around for Neil. He was gone, but he hadn't been gone long. The heather was fresh. Droplets of dew still clung to the tiny blossoms. She reached out and caught one, transferring it to her lips where she tasted it with the tip of her tongue. The droplet of water was cool to the touch—as cool as the circlet of seed pearls decorating the top of the shoes. She traced the pattern of pearls on the nearest shoe with her finger, then repeated the procedure on the other one. This was no dream. The shoes and the pearls were real.

As was the pair of cream silk stockings draped across the top of the dresser and the silk petticoat lying across the reclining chair along with a matching corset. Both of which were daintily embroidered with seed pearls even smaller than those on the shoes. Jessalyn scanned the room, following the trail of underclothing to the painted screen where a golden yellow brocade overskirt and bodice hung from gold clothing hooks. She picked up the shoes and stockings and hugged them to her breast. The dress and the underclothing were exquisite, but the shoes . . . Unable to resist the urge any longer, Jessalyn slipped the shoes onto her feet. They fit perfectly. She wrapped herself in a sheet and scrambled out of bed to admire her beautiful shoes in the mirror and discovered wisps of steam rising from the brass tub in front of the painted screen. Not only had her husband given her a gift of beautiful clothing, but during the time she had slept, he had drained the leftover bathwater from the tub and refilled it.

Jessalyn blinked back tears. He hadn't told her he loved her or made any promises beyond the promise never to betray her trust, but he had given her a pair of shoes. She was a highland laird. She knew there was no shame in going without fine clothes and shoes. But deep in her heart, she had always been ashamed of being seen with dirty feet. Somehow the English earl of Derrowford had understood.

After admiring them one last time in the mirror, Jessalyn removed her new shoes and set them in the place of honor on the center of the dressing table then dropped the sheet and climbed into the hot bath.

The inner bailey was a cacophony of noise and activity. Jessalyn arrived to find it packed with wagons and carts piled high with household goods and furnishings and teeming with livestock. The air was filled with the sounds of lowing cattle, of baaing sheep, the grunts and squeals of pigs, the barking of the drovers' dogs and the squawking of chickens, ducks, and geese. Adding to the din was the excited babble of the members of Clan MacInnes and the laborers unloading the multitude of wagons and carts and the men and women charged with the task of overseeing them. Standing on a large crate in the center of all the confusion, directing traffic and issuing instructions was her husband—Neil Claremont, seventh earl of Derrowford. Jessalyn stared in amazement as Davina supervised the unloading of three carts parked near the kitchens and Neil assigned workmen to carry load after load of furniture and tapestries and carpets into the castle. A miracle had occurred while she slept. Clan MacInnes had become wealthy overnight.

"You there!" Neil shouted at one of the drovers. "Get

those cattle out of here! Take them to the enclosure on the west side of the outer bailey. And you! Ask the women where they want the spinning wheels and the looms set up."

Taking great care to avoid anything that might damage her new dress or her shoes, Jessalyn worked her way to Neil's side and reached up and touched his leg.

"What's all this? Where did it come from?" she asked.

Neil turned at her touch. He saw his wife in the golden yellow gown and nearly tumbled off the edge of the crate in his haste to help her up beside him and get her out of harm's way. "All of this," he said, waving an arm to indicate the chaos in the bailey, "is the bulk of the supplies your man purchased in Edinburgh."

"I sent Ranald to Edinburgh to buy food and goods with the coins you gave me as a wedding gift."

"And I would say that he is a very skilled bargainer."

"Yes, he is," Jessalyn agreed. "But he'd have to be the most skilled bargainer in Scotland to buy all of this." She stared at him. "You were very generous, milord, but you dinna give me that much gold. And I never gave Ranald leave to purchase clothes for me." She glanced down at her new clothes.

"No," Neil agreed. "That's the prerogative of a husband."

She met his gaze once again. "Thank you for the bath and the heather and this . . ." She ran her hand down the front of the yellow dress. "'Tis beautiful."

"You're quite welcome, milady," he said. "The dress is quite fetching."

"Thank you again, milord." She did a small pirouette on the crate and lifted the hem of her skirt and the embroidered petticoat so he could get a better look at the shoes.

"And you look quite fetching in it." He leaned closer and lowered his voice to a husky whisper. "I like the dress, but I prefer you the way you were this morning—

naked and wrapped in my arms. Make no mistake about, milady, you don't need clothes to be beautiful."

There was no mistaking the look of admiration in his eyes either, but Jessalyn wanted answers and she could not allow her handsome husband to dissuade her. "Then perhaps ye might explain yer extraordinary generosity."

"A doting husband need not explain his generosity."

She didn't say anything. She simply stood before him and met his unwavering gaze. Until it wavered . . .

"Your Ancient Gentlemen sent word of my successful abduction and our marriage to the marquess of Chisenden. He knew your father, Mac, and he knew of your clan's desperate straits."

Jessalyn straightened her back and raised herself to her full height. "Clan MacInnes isna' a charity case of the marquess of Chisenden. *I* am not a charity case."

"Of course not," Neil soothed. "You're my wife and Clan MacInnes is family."

"You're grandfather is most generous to members of his family." She couldn't keep her hurt pride out of her voice.

"Yes, he is," Neil agreed. "But *I* made use of a husband's prerogative. I asked my grandparents to order a dowry for you. My grandfather sent the other gifts to celebrate our marriage and to welcome you into the family."

"Dinna shame me in front of my clan. Ye know I canna accept all of this." Jessalyn protested. "It's too much!"

"How can you not?" Neil asked. "It's a dowry from my family."

"My dowry shouldna come from yer family," she whispered. "It should ha' come from mine." She bowed her head and focused her attention on the toes of her shoes.

Neil lifted her chin with the tip of his index finger, forcing her to meet his gaze. "How do you know it didn't?"

"What?"

"My grandfather is a generous man with the members

of his family, but he's never been known for generosity toward his enemies. And a Jacobite Scottish laird, involved in a rebellion against his king and country should have been his enemy. Why would he ally his family to a Jacobite clan? Especially a minor one? Unless he owed the laird of that clan a debt of some kind? And if my grandfather did owe your father or your clan a debt and chose this method of repaying it, then there's no reason for you not to accept these gifts, for in a manner of speaking, your clan has provided your dowry."

Jessalyn looked around her at the members of her clan who had gathered in the bailey. Magda had taken charge of a half a dozen spinning wheels and was busy assigning them to the kinswomen who knew how to spin. Flora and Ellen were directing a man to the cottage that had once belonged to the cobbler. Even Sorcha was helping. She had joined a group of women and some of the smaller children herding the geese and ducks into the enclosure Neil and Henry Marsden had rebuilt several days before. Everywhere she looked her people were laboring— with smiles on their faces. Neil was right. She couldn't disappoint her clan. Charity or not, she couldn't refuse to accept the marquess of Chisenden's largesse. "In that case, I'm honored and pleased to accept the marquess of Chisenden's extravagant wedding gifts."

"That's my MacInnes." Neil draped his arm across her shoulder and pulled her closer to his body. "Come on, there's someone I'd like you to meet."

He jumped down from the packing crate and was reaching up to help her down when Jessalyn heard someone calling her name.

"Jessie! Jessie!"

Neil lowered her from the crate to the ground, but kept a protective arm at her back as Hannah MacCurran ran up to them with a black and white collie pup in her arms.

"Jessie! Jessie, ye've got to come see! Davina told me they were all for ye and there's three—"

"Steady, there!" Neil intercepted Hannah, slowing her when she threatened to run headlong into the MacInnes.

Hannah halted, her eyes widening at the sight of Jessalyn in the yellow gown. "Jessie, ye look like a princess!"

Jessalyn smiled at the praise. "Thank you, Hannah. Now, what is it you wanted me to see?"

"Ye've got to come see the three—"

"Puppies," Neil interrupted. "One of the dogs had puppies during the journey. I believe there are three of them and I promised Hannah pick of the litter if it was all right with you and her mother."

"No." Hannah shook her head. "There's four. But that's not . . ."

Neil bent down to Hannah's level and whispered something in her ear.

"Oh," the child replied. "Sorry, Neil."

"That's all right, Elfin." He ruffled Hannah's reddish gold curls. "Run along now."

Jessalyn raised an eyebrow at Neil.

"I told Hannah I'd bring you over to see the puppies after we tended to business with the stonemasons."

"Stonemasons?"

"Yes, milady," he grinned. "You forget that before I accepted a commission in His Majesty's army, I was an architect. My wedding gift to you, my dear MacInnes, is to repair your crumbling stronghold."

Tears sparkled in Jessalyn's eyes. "I don't know what to say."

"You don't have to say anything except that you'll let me have my way in this. Vincenzio and his workmen are among the best stonemasons in Europe. We were lucky to get them. This isn't charity, Mac, it's a necessity if the clan is going to survive another harsh Scottish winter."

She nodded.

"There's something else," he hesitated, a moment before plunging ahead. "Vincenzio is accustomed to taking his orders from kings and popes not . . ."

"Minor Scottish lairds?"

Neil shook his head. "Women."

Jessalyn frowned. "I'm the MacInnes, but you're the architect and my *ceann feachd*. He'll answer to you and," she whispered, "you'll answer to me."

"Tonight?"

"Every night from now on," she promised.

"With pleasure, milady." He took her by the hand. "We have a rendezvous with Hannah and a litter of collie puppies before the end of the day, so let's go introduce Vincenzio to his first female Scottish laird and give him a tour of the castle."

"Not all of it, I hope."

Neil smiled. "Not all of it," he promised. "The Laird's Trysting Room is our secret."

Chapter Twenty-four

The Laird's Trysting Room wasn't the only well-kept secret at Castle MacAonghais. In the two mornings since the arrival of the marquess of Chisenden's caravan of wedding gifts, Jessalyn had awakened in the huge bed in the master chamber to find a bouquet of heather and a new pair of shoes on the pillow beside her. And the surprises didn't stop there for each new pair of shoes was accompanied by dresses and undergarments made to match. When she questioned her husband, he smiled a mysterious smile, kissed her good morning and hurried out to supervise the work on castle.

Jessalyn had never been happier and life for Clan MacInnes was better than it had been since before the Uprising. Jessalyn hoped her euphoria would continue forever, but by mid-afternoon when Ian MacCurran ushered a young man into the kitchen and over to where she sat helping several of the women churn butter, she knew it was impossible.

"I've come from Glen Craig with a message for the MacInnes," the runner announced.

"I'm the MacInnes," Jessalyn stood up and removed her apron, then held out her hand for the message.

"'Tis na' a written message," he said. "But 'tis one

I'd rather tell ye in private." He cast a meaningful glance toward the women seated at the butter churns.

"Come with me." Jessalyn motioned for Ian to follow, then led the messenger from the kitchen to the room that had been her father's study, sidestepping the sawyers and laborers repairing the interior of the castle along the way. Ian waited beside the door as Jessalyn led the young man into the study. She closed the door behind them, shutting out the sound of workmen and the chance that anyone other than Ian might overhear what was said.

The young man glanced around at the fine furniture and the tapestries and paintings hanging on the walls and at the brass candlesticks and the sweet-smelling beeswax candles. Those candles had come from a chandler in London, but soon the clan would be able to make their own from beeswax gathered from the castle skeps and herbs grown in the castle garden. Jessalyn was filled with a sense of pride and a wealth of thankfulness toward Neil and his grandfather because the runner from Glen Craig was seeing her father's study as it was meant to be seen, not bare as it had been two days ago.

"What is it you have to tell me?" she asked.

"English soldiers are comin' your way," he said without preamble.

Jessalyn paled and she fought to keep her voice from coming out in a most un-lairdlike squeak. "The English are coming here?"

He nodded. "Aye. They followed your caravan from Edinburgh. They should be here by morning." He shrugged. "They could have been here already, but they're searchin' every village and glen along the way."

"For what?" she asked, praying she didn't already know. Praying the English soldiers hadn't discovered the identify of her Ancient Gentlemen and Magda and Flora.

"Englishmen," the young man answered. "They're looking for three Englishmen who disappeared from the fort they're building near Kilchumin."

"Why are they searching the highlands for English-

men?" Jessalyn pretended a calm she didn't feel. "The
English soldiers have been here before. Surely they know
we would never harbor enemy soldiers. Clan MacAonghais fought and died for the king over the water."

"They dinna think we're harboring 'em," he told her.
"The word among the villages is that the English think
one of our highland clans abducted their soldiers and are
holdin' 'em for ransom. And there was a richly laden
caravan headin' into the highlands . . ."

"Right to our front door."

"Aye."

Jessalyn sighed.

"My laird wants to know if it's true."

"Is he offerin' his services should the English attack?"
she demanded.

"He dinna say." He shrugged his shoulders, then asked
again, "are ye holdin' Sassenach soldiers for ransom?"
he asked.

"No," she answered truthfully. "We are not. You may
tell your laird that I am recently wed and that the caravan has brought us wedding gifts and badly needed supplies."

"'Tis good that yer improvin' yer castle." The young
man cast another, more avaricious, glance around the
room. "Now, that yer wealthy again, ye'll want to be
holdin' on to yer belongin's."

"Aye," Jessalyn told him, recognizing his look for
what it was. "You may tell your laird of the wealth you've
seen. And you may also tell him that the MacInnes is no
poor defenseless woman to be preyed upon by her neighbors. My husband is a powerful man and as *ceann feachd*
of the clan, he is well able to defend it. 'Twould be much
better to be his ally than his enemy."

"Aye, milady."

"Our cook will provide you with food and drink to see
you on your way. And please thank your laird for his warning."

"Many thanks, milady," He bowed. "And ye need not

worry about my laird's intent. For while he will be most unhappy to learn that ye've already wed, he'll be quite happy to know yer not unprotected, for in truth, my laird has always fancied ye. He offered fer ye himself some five months past when the auld laird still breathed."

Jessalyn opened the door and instructed Ian to escort the messenger back to the kitchen.

"Oh, milady?" The messenger turned.

"Yes?"

"My laird asks that ye send a runner to Clan Munro."

She nodded. "Consider it done." Jessalyn waited until they were out of sight before closing the door and collapsing onto the nearest chair. Her knees were quaking beneath her petticoat and skirts—not just at the news that Sassenach soldiers were headed for Glenaonghais but also at the news that she'd narrowly escaped a marriage to Laird Grant of Glen Craig for he was fifty if he was a day, balding and pock-marked and had breath that could kill a pair of oxen at a hundred paces. She stared at the back of the door. Her father's second-best bonnet, adorned with two eagle feathers, hung on a peg, apparently overlooked by the women who had tended to his body and packed away his personal belongings. Jessalyn reached up and removed the hat from the peg. She held it to her nose breathing in the scent of her father. Five months ago, a highland chief, Grant of Glen Craig, had offered for her and five months ago, her father had turned him down in favor of a Sassenach soldier she'd never met. Jessalyn pressed her father's bonnet to her heart. "Thank ye, Da," she murmured. "Thank ye for Neil."

"You can imagine my surprise when after twiddling our thumbs in Edinburgh for weeks waiting for word from London that the Masons' Guild had quarried the stone needed to complete the wall at Fort Augustus, we were told to join the caravan headed not for the fort, but to the village of Glenaonghais half a day's journey north,"

Vincenzio remarked to Neil as they inspected the repairs to the eastern wall of the chapel.

The master mason had been born in Florence but he had spent most of his early years in London where his father was master mason to Sir Christopher Wren. Vincenzio had apprenticed under his father and become a master mason himself. Neil had known him for years. They had met in London while he was serving his own apprenticeship under Wren.

"We'll need to reinforce the north wall," Neil pointed to the wall. "The mortar's crumbling along the entire section and I would like to remove a portion of the eastern wall of the chapel and add another stained glass window. Something with lambs and children," he said, glancing at the other scenes depicted in the colored glass. "To illustrate God's love as well as his wrath. And the leading on the near section of the roof will have to be replaced." He turned to Vincenzio and found the mason bent over his notes. "So," Neil continued, "you journeyed to that village before you came here. What did you do there?"

"Where?" Vincenzio asked.

"The village you were sent to before you came here."

Vincenzio looked puzzled. "There was no other village. We were sent to Glen Innes and here we are."

"You must be mistaken. The village you were sent to was only a half a day's journey from Fort Augustus and we're much deeper into the highlands than that." It was Neil's turn to be confused.

Vincenzio laughed. "Oh no, my friend, you are the one who is mistaken. Your village and Glen Innes are one and the same. Fort Augustus is just around that bend and beyond those hills. If the crenellations weren't in danger of crumbling beneath our feet, we could probably see it from the wall walks. Neil? Neil, where are you going?" The master mason stood open-mouthed as his friend cursed and walked away.

Chapter Twenty-five

"When did you plan to tell me?" he demanded. "Or did you plan to make me more of a fool by keeping me in the dark forever?"

Jessalyn started at the fury in her husband's voice. He had stormed into the castle shouting her name, demanding to know where the MacInnes was. She had met him at the threshold to her father's study and Neil had taken hold of her elbow and guided her back inside the room, slamming the door behind him with such force that it shook the frame.

Her heart seemed to tighten in her chest. Had he heard the news already? Had someone told him that his fellow Englishmen were coming for him? She took a deep breath and faced him. "I don't know what yer talkin' aboot!"

"Liar!" Neil barred his teeth in a semblance of a smile. Her Scottish burr gave her away. It thickened her speech in moments of passion and extreme emotion. "You know exactly what I'm talking about!"

Jessalyn recoiled from his harsh epithet as if he had slapped her and bitter tears stung her eyes. "I dinna. Truly, Neil, I dinna."

The red cloud of anger lifted in the split-second that Neil saw the sheen of unshed tears sparkle in her eyes, then descended again with a vengeance when he remembered how she'd tricked him the morning he'd been brought to the village. *You're deep in the highlands. In a village far removed from Fort Augustus.* "Glenaonghais." He heard the word in his mind and repeated it aloud, remembering the way she had said it the one time she'd slipped and called the village by name. *The people of Glenaonghais have struggled so hard to survive and to put the memories behind them that I dare not risk their peace of mind or your safety by allowing you or your men to wear your uniforms.* "That's what I'm talking about. Glenaonghais. Glen Innes to Sassenachs like me who don't speak the Scottish tongue. You remember the village deep in the highlands, far removed from Fort Augustus? It turns out that Glenaonghais is a mere half a day's ride from Fort Augustus. You lied to me, Countess!"

"I dinna know ye then!"

"What about now, Countess?" he demanded. "What about last night? Or the night before? Or the night before that? How many nights would you have shared my pillow before you trusted me enough to tell me that Fort Augustus was so close?"

The tears began to fall in earnest, silently gliding down Jessalyn's cheeks, staining them with a silvery trail. "I don't know."

"Why?" he asked.

"I lied to you," she said. "What difference does it make now why I did it?"

"Why?" he asked once more.

Jessalyn hung her head. "At first, I was afraid that if ye knew how close Fort Augustus was, ye'd escape and bring the army down around our heads. And then I was afraid that ye'd abandon me."

He stared at her so surprised that for a moment he couldn't speak. He let go of her elbow and dropped his hand to his side. "I married you," he said, at last. As if that explained everything. "I stood in a chapel before a priest and made promises to you."

"Aye," Jessalyn agreed. "And then ye told me that they were temporary. That I should know that you had a life in London before you took up your commission in the army. That ye still have obligations there and plans of yer own."

"I told you the truth," he said. "Because I thought you should know from the beginning that even though your clan had abducted me, even though we exchanged wedding vows, I was a major in His Majesty's Army and my stay in Scotland was temporary. Like it or not, I have obligations from my life in London that must be attended to."

"Aye," Jessalyn spat out the word. "Like yer mistress Deborah!"

He was stunned. More stunned than if she'd hit him over the head with Auld Tam's battle axe. "Where did you hear about Deborah?"

"You called me by her name the first time you kissed me!"

"Did I?" He remembered the kiss, but he had completely forgotten the words that accompanied it. It struck him then that the MacInnes was jealous. Cat-eyed green with it. Of Deborah. He caught himself before he grinned in satisfaction. Except for including the terms of settlement they had agreed upon and an approximate size comparison for the seamstress to go by in his letter to his grandfather, he hadn't thought of Deborah at all since his marriage. He had had no reason, nor any inclination to think of her when his mind was filled with thoughts of the MacInnes.

"Aye, ye did! And then ye told everybody there that she was yer mistress!"

"She was." He couldn't argue the point.

"Ye were betrothed to me!"

"At the time, I didn't know I was betrothed." He cast her a sharp gaze. "And neither did you."

"Ye would have!" Jessalyn insisted. "If ye'd tended to yer important papers half as well as ye tended to Deborah."

He did smile then, "If I had tended to my important papers instead of tending to Deborah I wouldn't be married to you."

"That's why I didn't tell ye the truth about Fort Augustus," Jessalyn whispered. "Because I knew ye'd rather be with her in London than here in Scotland with me."

Neil raked his hand through his hair and blew out a breath of air. "That might have been true once before I kissed you," he said softly. "But it hasn't been true since."

"You kissed me the first time we met."

"Aye," he answered in his best Scots burr. "So I did."

"Kiss me now," she ordered.

He obliged by kissing her thoroughly. And when he finished, he stepped back and looked down at her. "I can kiss you and still be angry with you."

"Are ye?"

He nodded. "I'm bloody furious, not because you lied to me, but because you risked your life and the lives of the members of your clan by keeping me here so close to the fort. You should have retreated deeper into the highlands where Spotty Oliver cannot find you."

"What's Spotty Oliver? I dinna understand."

"My commanding officer Major General Sir Charles Oliver will send troops after me and he won't stop until he finds me and he'll destroy anyone who stands in his way. He's the reason Tam had to cut me free. He's the reason Sergeant Marsden and Corporal Stanhope are married to your kinswomen. I cannot risk putting their lives in danger or yours. Because when he finds me—if he finds me, he intends to hang me."

Jessalyn's face lost its color. "Why? What did ye do that was so terrible?"

"I dared to question his authority."

The MacInnes let out a sigh of relief. "Is that all?"

Neil frowned at her. "What happened to the men who questioned your father's authority during times of war?"

"They were punished." She looked down at her feet, unable to meet his gaze.

"How were they punished?" Neil insisted.

"By banishment," she whispered. "Or by death."

"Exactly."

Jessalyn reached for his shirt front and grabbed hold of the ruffles. "You must take Auld Tam and Alisdair and Dougal and Flora and Magda and Marsden and Stanhope and go to the Munros. He may not have supported the king over the water, but Laird Munro won't refuse you passage across his land and into the hills. Please, Neil, go now!"

"Why?"

"A runner from Glen Craig arrived earlier this afternoon. They've spotted English soldiers. They're on their way here—to Glenaonghais. They followed the caravan from Edinburgh."

"What were you planning to do? Hide me in the Laird's Trysting Room?" he asked.

Jessalyn bit her lip in a slight hesitation, then shook her head. "No. I planned to have Tam take you onto Munro land and keep you there."

"And now, you want me to take him instead. What part of your plan has changed?"

"I told you about it," she answered honestly. "Please, milord, you must do it. You know the Ancient Gentlemen and Magda and Flora are the ones who raided Fort Augustus. What would happen to them if General Oliver found out?"

"They'll be arrested at the least, tried and executed at most."

Jessalyn began to shake all over.

Neil took hold of her shoulders in a gentle grip meant to steady her and give her strength. "You take them, Mac. You take the clan and as much of the supplies and livestock as you can and hide in the hills. I'll stay here and face Spotty Oliver."

"It took us nearly two days to unload the bailey and herd the livestock into the enclosures. We don't have enough people or time to gather supplies and drive the livestock into the hills and I won't leave them to be slaughtered by the English. And if you stay, Sergeant Marsden and Corporal Stanhope will stay and if they stay Flora and Magda will stay and I'll not have their blood on my conscience." Jessalyn refused to give in. "After searching every village and glen in the highlands lookin' for ye, he willna show any of us any mercy."

"He'll have what he wants. I'll be waiting for him. Here. Alone." He stared at Jessalyn. "The clan will be saved from retribution if I tell him I escaped from my quarters and discovered Glenaonghais on my own."

"If I do as ye ask, what do ye think I'll find when I return?" Jessalyn asked, her voice quivering with emotion. "My husband hanging from a gibbet in the courtyard of my castle? And what of Sergeant Marsden and Corporal Stanhope? Once he has ye, do ye think that yer General Oliver will allow them to remain here wi' their wives? Do ye think he'll just let us be?"

"He'll have to," Neil insisted. "I'll make it part of the parcel of my surrender."

Jessalyn smiled a sad smile. Neil Claremont, seventh earl of Derrowford, had the heart and the courage and the soul of a highland warrior and she loved him to the last fiber of her being, but at times, she thought in a surge of irritation, he was so thoroughly, arrogantly *English*. "Do ye honestly think a mon like that will honor such a bargain?"

"He'll have no choice. I'm a fellow officer and gentleman. A belted earl and peer of the realm."

"Barefooted and wearing a Scottish plaid. How little ye know about the English army or its gentlemen officers! Honor has nothing to do wi' this. He wants to hang you, Neil. He wants revenge. As far as Spotty Oliver is concerned, you're a traitor."

She was right. Neil knew it. He'd always known it. He had even admitted as much to her on their wedding night, but until he had heard the MacInnes speak the words, he had chosen to ignore the fact that the enmity

Spotty Oliver felt for him might very well cost him his life. Neil let his arms fall to his sides in a gesture of defeat. "What would you have me do?"

"I promised I would send a runner to the Munros to warn them of the English soldiers," she said. "Take Tam and the others and go. You'll have plenty of time to warn them."

"We've been raidin' the Munros on a regular basis. What if the Munro laird decides to turn us over to the English?"

"He won't."

"How can you be so sure?"

Jessalyn smiled. "Because the Munro was married to Dougal's sister."

"We've been stealing from Dougal's in-laws?"

"Aye. In a roundabout sort of way," she said. "We've been stealing back what they stole from us."

Neil laughed. "And we'll all just one big happy family."

"Aye."

They exchanged heated glances and Neil was reminded of the fact that she was sending him to safety and preparing to face a column of English soldiers alone. "Where will you be while I'm safely ensconced in the hills?"

"I'll be here. Glenaonghais is mine and I canna allow the English to destroy it."

He stared down at her beautiful face filled with such determination and foolhardy highland courage. "I'll go with Tam and the others to the Munros, but I'm coming back."

"You mustn't."

"I'm coming back," he repeated. "You may be the MacInnes, but you're my wife and will one day be the mother of my children. I will not leave you unprotected. I won't allow you to face Spotty Oliver alone."

Jessalyn smoothed the front of her gown and straightened to her full height. "The soldiers won't arrive until morning," she said. "Get the others to safety and I'll join you as soon as I can."

Neil shook his head. "I'll be back by dark. Meet me in the Laird's Trysting Room. We'll be safe there for the night and we'll face whatever the morning brings together."

"All right," she agreed.

He leaned down and kissed her. "Until tonight."

"Until tonight," she promised, crossing her fingers and hiding her hands in the folds of her skirt, safely out of Neil's line of vision.

Chapter Twenty-six

"**B**race yerself, laddie," Auld Tam muttered to Neil as the MacInnes party left the relative safety of the brush and crossed a stretch of open ground along the border of MacInnes and Munro lands. "Yer about to come face-to-face with the Munro and he's been sampling the barrels."

Neil looked up as the Munro and seven of his clansmen mounted on sturdy highland ponies entered the clearing. The Munro was recognizable by his beetle brow and his ruddy complexion as well as the brooch he wore pinned to his dark plaid and the eagle feathers stuck at a rakish angle in his bonnet. He was also the oldest man there, older than Tam, though he wore his age very well. Neil narrowed his gaze as the Munro nudged his pony forward and rode in for a closer look. He greeted his kinsman Dougal first, then Tam and Alisdair according to their rank. He nodded to Magda and Flora, dismissing them after one glance and completely ignoring Stanhope and Marsden.

He rode up to Neil, leaned forward in his saddle and bellowed, "I'm Lachlan Munro and yer trespassin' on my land."

Neil recognized a thrown gauntlet when he saw one. "We're on MacInnes land." The Munro's breath was flavored with whisky and his plaid reeked of oak and peat. Neil met the old laird's gaze without flinching. "If anyone is trespassing it's you. You trailed us for over an hour before you doubled back onto your land and decided to show yourself."

Lachlan Munro threw back his head and laughed. "Ye must be the MacInnes's Sassenach husband."

"Neil Claremont," he said. "The MacInnes sent us to warn you that English soldiers are headed for MacInnes and Munro land."

"Weel, Neil Claremont, it appears to me that although he's wearing a kilt, an *English* soldier," he emphasized the word, "is already on my land."

"I'm not your enemy."

"That's fer me to decide, laddie," the Munro said. "And we trailed ye fer *two* hours, but only out of curiosity. Ye maun be here requestin' permission to take yerself and yer companions across my land. I canna think why ye would need so many companions if ye'd come only to present me with another proposition."

"I am here at the request of the MacInnes to ask your permission to escort the Ancient Gentlemen of Clan MacInnes and their families across your land to the hills where they'll be safe."

"Do ye not seek safety fer yerself as well?" The wily old man asked. "From what I hear, yer the mon the English are after."

"For myself, I seek permission to cross your land twice—going and returning. The MacInnes is waiting for me back at Castle MacAonghais."

The Munro nodded. "Then ye've not taken the coward's way and chosen to hide behind yer woman's skirts."

Neil looked the man in the eye. "I cannot say that in other circumstances, I might not choose to hide behind my woman's skirts," he said. "But I'll not be leaving the MacInnes alone to defend her land at the point of an English sword wielded by my enemy."

"Aboot yer first proposition . . ." The Munro paused

for effect. "I gave Tam my answer days ago. But at the time, I dinna know the measure of the man proposin' it. And, of course at the time, yer circumstances hadna changed and ye were a much poorer clan. I understand that they've recently improved."

"Greatly improved," Neil replied.

"Then the MacInnes willna need to raid my herds any longer."

Neil shrugged his shoulders. "I will not speak for the MacInnes on that matter for I understand that raiding is a way of life in the highlands. But I've no doubt that when the MacInnes feels she's recovered her losses, she'll turn her attention elsewhere."

Lachlan chuckled. "I heard the Sutherland experienced a loss when his favorite mount went missing from his stables."

"The Sutherland's mount temporarily escaped the confines of his stable," Neil corrected. "He has since been located and returned."

The Munro turned to Tam and grinned. "The boy has a way wi' words. On the whole, I canna say I approve of Sassenachs. But I approve of Callum's choice of a son-in-law. He has the look aboot him of the other earl of Derrowford."

Neil shot Auld Tam and the other two Ancient Gentlemen a questioning glance. "What other earl of Derrowford?"

"Which one are ye?" Lachlan demanded.

"The current one," Neil answered.

The Munro frowned and Dougal was quick to intercede and ask, "What number are ye, laddie?"

"Seven."

"It must ha' been the sixth one," Alisdair said.

"The sixth earl of Derrowford was my father."

The Munro shook his head and scratched his chest. "How old are ye?"

"Eight and twenty."

"Then it couldna been yer father 'cause Helen Rose was long dead by then. He must have been the fifth one."

"My grandfather was the fifth earl of Derrowford," Neil said. "Who was Helen Rose?"

"MacInnes." The Munro answered.

"MacInnes?" Neil breathed, stunned by the revelation.

"Aye. Didna ye know? Lady Helen Rose MacInnes was the wife of the fifth earl of Derrowford."

He knows our ways. He knows that the MacInneses have always abducted brides for the lairds of the clan. Neil remembered Auld Tam's explanation for the marquess of Chisenden's betrayal shortly after Tam revealed his reason for abducting him from Fort Augustus. And although he barely remembered repeating them at the time, the memory of the words spoken at his wedding to the MacInnes came flooding back. *Neil Edward James Louis Claremont, seventh earl of Derrowford, fourteen Viscount Claremont, nineteenth Baron Ashford, doest thou stand before God and this assemblage and take Lady Jessalyn Helen Rose MacInnes, rightful laird of Clan MacInnes, as thy lawfully wedded wife?* Lady Helen Rose MacInnes. Neil hadn't known who she was, but now he understood the significance of the portrait that hung in the place of honor over the marble fireplace in the study of the marquess of Chisenden's London home. And now he knew why Jessalyn had seemed so familiar. She bore a striking resemblance to the woman in the portrait—especially in the eyes. They shared the same remarkable blue-gold eyes. Lady Helen Rose MacInnes was the reason Chisenden had come to the aid of Clan MacInnes.

"So my grandfather had a family connection to Clan MacInnes." It wasn't a question. Neil looked at the Munro and met his steady gaze.

"Aye," the Munro nodded. "He was a good mon. A Sassenach like ye, but a good mon." He made the sign of the cross. "I dinna know when it happened, but I mourn his passin' with ye, lad and I celebrate the fact that ye've become the new earl of Derrowford."

Neil glanced down at his saddle, then cleared his throat, stalling for time while he sought a tactful way of informing the Munro that his grief at the passing of the fifth earl of Derrowford was premature.

"The auld Earl Derrowford isna dead, Lachlan," Dougal came to Neil's rescue once more.

The Munro turned to his late wife's brother. "Nay?"

Dougal shook his head.

"Then how has the young lad become the seventh earl?" he demanded.

"Because the fifth earl is now the marquess of Chisenden," Tam replied.

Lachlan Munro looked to Neil for confirmation.

Neil nodded, then watched as the marquess's name worked its powerful sorcery on the Scottish laird.

"Praise be to God," the laird murmured.

"Praise be to dead Queen Anne," Tam contradicted. "For she's the one who made him so."

The Munro moved his pony in closer to Neil, then reached over and clapped him on the shoulder. "I'm honored to have ye cross my land, laddie, and more honored to welcome ye into Clan Munro. As long as yer fundin' our joint venture into the makin' and sellin' of the finest Scots whisky in all the highlands, yer welcome to all the clansmen ye need to help rebuild yer castle."

The moon had risen and the stars appeared by the time Jessalyn heard Neil's key turn in the locks of the door to the Laird's Trysting Room. She had watched the play of the light from the arrow loops on the floor as she sat before the fire awaiting his return. She pushed off the fur coverlets she had tucked around her and stood up to greet him as he opened the door.

Neil closed the door behind him as he crossed the threshold then turned and leaned with his back against it and watched the MacInnes approach. She wore a pale blue nightrail made from a fabric so thin he could see the tips of her breasts and the dark pink circles of the aureole surrounding them and a pair of pale blue satin Louis-heeled slippers to match.

"Nice shoes," he said.

Jessalyn lifted the hem of her nightgown and extended her right foot, flexing her ankle to give him a better look. "Thank you," she answered softly. "I found them on my pillow this afternoon along with the matching nightrail." She smiled at Neil. "I keep finding extravagant gifts of beautiful shoes on my pillow. I found a pair on my pillow in the bed in the master chamber this morning and another pair on the pillow in this bed tonight. I suspect my castle is enchanted and that a fairy prince is at work here."

"I wouldn't go quite that far up the nobility ladder." He had seen women who were more beautiful than she was, had courted them and shared their beds, but he had never seen a woman he wanted more than he wanted Jessalyn MacInnes. She was his match. His equal. The part of him he hadn't known was missing until she took him inside her.

Jessalyn came to a stop a few feet away from him. She moistened her dry lips and stood quietly waiting for him to make a move.

Neil folded his arms over his chest, and continued his study of her. He leaned against the door, barely daring to breathe as he waited to see what she would do next.

Suddenly realizing that he was allowing her to be the aggressor, Jessalyn lifted her head and looked him in the eye. She took a deep breath then untied the ribbons at the neck of her gown. She shrugged it off her shoulders. It slipped down her arms and settled briefly at her waist, baring her breasts. Neil fought to maintain control. He narrowed his gaze until he was practically scowling. But Jessalyn wasn't fooled or intimidated by his apparent disregard. She stalked him like a tiger stalking her prey, smiling as a muscle in his jaw began to pulse. She moved closer, then lifted her arms over her head and wriggled her hips. Her nightdress fell to the floor in an expensive pool of sheer fabric.

Neil gave up all thought of maintaining control. He opened his arms in welcome and Jessalyn walked into them—a proud highland laird as naked as the day she was born. The sight of her nearly took his breath away. Neil bent his head to kiss her. Jessalyn met him halfway.

"I apologize for keeping you waiting, milady," he murmured. "But I had trouble escaping the Munro's hospitality."

"Sampling the whisky, no doubt." She licked the seam of his lips and tasted the liquor.

"No doubt," he agreed, running his hands up her ribs before filling them with the weight of her breasts.

"And what did you think?" she asked.

"I think I'd rather be here making love to you than sitting around a smelly peat fire drinking whisky with an equally smelly old man." He nibbled at her lips, then trailed a line of kisses from her mouth down her chin and neck to the tops of her breasts, finally ending his journey by suckling first one and then the other of her perfectly fashioned globes. He slid down the door and dropped to his knees in front of her.

"That's good," she said, sliding her fingers through his thick dark hair, pressing his face against her stomach. "Because I can think of a dozen ways I'd rather have you spend your time than sitting around a smelly peat fire drinking whisky with smelly old men."

"Only a dozen, milady?" he teased. "Surely, I've taught you more than that."

"'Tis possible," she answered. "But it's been so long I seem to have trouble recalling them all."

"Perhaps you need a few more lessons," he suggested.

"And perhaps I'll need even more." She wriggled her eyebrows at him in an imitation of the gesture he always used.

Neil reached behind her and cupped her buttocks, pulling her closer. He dipped his head and teased the tiny

kernel of pleasure hidden beneath the auburn silky curls
of her woman's triangle with the tip of his tongue. "My
lady has become a little saucy. I like that in a woman."

He tasted and teased her until she screamed his name
in pleasurable release. Neil held her close as he got to
his feet. He lifted her up, anchoring her on his hips,
cradling her bottom against him as he pressed her back
against the door. Jessalyn tightened her legs around his
waist and carefully guided him inside her. Neil pressed
his lips against the curve of her neck and sheathed himself in her. She was warm and wet and welcoming and
he was rock hard and consumed with wanting. Theirs
was a perfect fit and Neil stroked her with a passionate
urgency that bespoke his great need of her. She met him
stroke for stroke answering him in kind. Taking as much
as she gave.

They made sweet, passionate love throughout the long
hours of the night. Moving from the door to the reclining couch. From the couch to the bed. From bed to bath
and back again. They made love with a bittersweet sense
of desperation—as if the night was the last they would
share and when at last he collapsed on the pillow beside
her and closed his eyes, Neil knew that he was forever
changed by her touch. She had left her mark on him,
branded his heart and soul with her essence. He knew
with unshakable certainty that even should he live to be
a thousand years old, he would never love anyone or
anything as much as he loved the MacInnes. He opened
his mouth to tell her, but the words came out as a soft
murmur too low for her to hear. He kissed the top of her
head, fanning her hair with his breath. Tomorrow, he
promised, tomorrow he would tell her of his love and
his plans for the future.

But when tomorrow arrived Jessalyn was gone. Neil awoke
to find himself alone in the bed they'd shared. An uneasy
feeling settled in the pit of his stomach as he surveyed the
room. His white linen shirt lay neatly folded on the silk

reclining sofa. His fur-covered sporran rested atop it. A pair of trews made from a length of MacInnes plaid and a smaller length of MacInnes tartan lay folded beside it. His black leather boots stood in front of the sofa. She had laid out a pair of trews for him to wear because she knew she wouldn't be there to pleat his kilt for him. Neil jumped out of bed, dressed as quickly as possible and hurried to the door. It was locked. Neil reached for the Laird's key around his neck. It was gone. In its place was the ladies key he had last seen nestled in the warm cleft between her breasts. The words he'd spoken half in jest the day before had come back to haunt him. *What were you planning to do? Hide me in the Laird's Trysting Room?* Whether she had originally planned to or not, the MacInnes had done just that. She had locked him in the Laird's Trysting Room and gone out to face the English soldiers alone. And there was nothing he could do about it.

Chapter Twenty-seven

"Jessie! Jessie! They're comin'!" Ian MacCurran ran into the bailey screaming for the MacInnes. "I saw them."

Jessalyn met him in front of the newly repaired door to the castle. She was dressed for confrontation in the dark blue dress that matched the pair of dark blue shoes decorated with sapphire-studded gold buckles she had found on her pillow on the second morning following the caravan's arrival. She wore a white lace collar on the bodice and a length of MacInnes plaid draped over the skirt, around her waist and fastened across one shoulder with the clan brooch. The key she usually wore on a silver chain around her neck was around Neil's neck and the key she had given him—the Laird's key—was concealed in a hidden pocket in her skirt. Her hair was plaited into a long braid. Her father's second-best bonnet, marked with a sprig of holly and two eagle feathers, covered her head.

Ian stopped and stared.

"How many?" she asked.

"Lots of 'em," he answered.

"Did ye count them, Ian?" Jessalyn asked.

"I tried," he said. "But there was too many of 'em. And they were marchin' too fast. I had to come tell ye."

"They canna come here again!"

"What are we goin' to do?"

"We maun gi' 'em what they want! We maun tell 'em what they want to know!"

"We maun go. We maun run and hide!" The women who crowded into the bailey were terrified of the coming soldiers and looking to their laird—looking to Jessalyn—for answers.

Jessalyn took a deep breath. "I willna force ye to stay here if ye want to take to the hills and hide. But I want ye to understand that if ye run and hide, ye may not have anythin' to come back to. The English will take what they want and destroy the rest. They willna show any more mercy to an empty village than to a full one. And they willna show us any more mercy if we tell them what they want to know than they will if we keep our silence. When they look at us, they dinna see people with hearts and souls and wishes and dreams, they see savages. They see the enemy." She paused. "The English ha' been here before. We survived then and we'll survive now." She motioned for Davina to come forward.

Davina made her way through the crowd of women to Jessalyn's side. She carried a large basket in the crook of her arm and the women looked on as she set it on the ground before them.

Jessalyn leaned over and removed a dirk from the pile in the basket and held it up for everyone to see. "We've gathered every dirk and knife in the castle. Take one for yourself and one for your daughters, mothers, and sisters. Hide them on your person and use them to defend yourself against any English soldier who tries to violate you or any other woman in this village." She raised the hem of her skirt and stuck the knife in the garter holding her stocking, then shoved the basket forward and waited while the women filed past it and selected their weapons.

"There is one other thing ye should know," Jessalyn said when every woman had taken a knife or dirk from the basket and stood waiting for further instructions. "I'm the laird of this clan and I'll defend ye with my dying breath, but make no mistake about this—I'll kill any man or woman who offers information to the English about my husband or the husbands of Magda and Flora. Understood?"

The women of Clan MacInnes nodded.

"Good. Now, spread the word and go about yer business as usual." Jessalyn waved the women away.

Two hours later, a column of English soldiers marched into Glenaonghais for the second time in as many years. The majority of the men were on foot, but two men were mounted on horseback. Jessalyn assumed the mounted soldiers had led the column to the village, but she couldn't tell which man was in charge or if either of them was Spotty Oliver until one of them spoke.

"Good morning, ladies, I'm Lieutenant Burton of His Majesty's Royal Corps of Engineers at Fort Augustus." He nodded to the women in the bailey. "I'd like to speak to the owner of this castle."

Jessalyn left the safety of the circle of women and stepped forward. "I'm Jessalyn MacAonghais, Laird of Clan MacAonghais. This castle and the village surrounding it have been a part of my family for seven hundred years." She gave her name the Scots pronunciation, knowing that to the English, the names all sounded alike.

If the lieutenant was surprised to find the laird of a highland clan was a woman, he did his best to hide it. "A pleasure, ma'am."

Jessalyn didn't pretend politeness she didn't feel. She went straight to the heart of the matter. "Why are you here, Lieutenant?"

"I'm investigating the disappearance of three of His Majesty's Soldiers."

"You've lost three soldiers and you want us to help you find them?"

"Yes, ma'am." Lieutenant Burton knew his answers

sounded foolish. "We believe the three of them were abducted by a highland clan for purposes of ransom."

"I've lost three *hundred* soldiers." Jessalyn meant to hold her tongue, but the anger and bitterness and outrage she'd been holding in check for years bubbled to the surface and found a target in the unfortunate Lieutenant Burton. "Including a father and six brothers. And I saw scores of others abducted by English soldiers for purposes of execution. My clan was forced to leave our village and hide from marauding bands of men—all wearing red coats like yours, Lieutenant. The lands and the homes my family had occupied for two centuries were confiscated by the victorious English government and awarded to a rival clan. We were turned off it and forced to move here—to a crumbling castle on ancient ancestral homeland—only a half a day's journey around the loch from English army barracks that will one day bring about the end to our way of life. We may be forced to endure your presence, but we will not be forced into helping you in your search."

"Madam, you don't understand," Lieutenant Burton said. "We're searching every village and glen from here to Edinburgh. It is imperative that we locate these men." He leaned forward in the saddle and lowered his voice. "If you know anything about their disappearance, it is in your best interest to tell me."

"In my best interest, Lieutenant?" Jessalyn asked. "How can such a thing be in my best interest? Your army has been here before and on that last occasion, my village and my castle were looted and burned and my women terrorized—some of them violated because our loyalties to your English king were suspect. We were punished for fomenting rebellion. As you can see, we're a clan of women and children and a few old men." She looked the lieutenant in the eyes.

The lieutenant looked around, past the crowd of women, to the workmen repairing the castle. "I can see that despite your claim to be a clan of women, old men and children, there appears to be a great deal of activity going on." He met Jessalyn's gaze. "You seem to be fortifying your castle."

"Winter is coming, lieutenant, we're making repairs to our castle in preparation for the harsh months ahead."

"What with, madam?"

Jessalyn lifted an eyebrow. "With the goods and supplies brought to us from Edinburgh by caravan."

"Which caravan, madam?"

"The heavily laden one whose tracks lead from Edinburgh to our door. There has been only one and there's not so much traffic on the roads that you could have mistaken it. But, of course, you knew that already, Lieutenant, because you followed it."

"There's been no traffic to speak of in the highlands for months, madam. A heavily laden caravan accompanied by livestock and drovers and stonemasons was bound to attract our attention—especially since it arrived so quickly upon the heels of the disappearance of our soldiers. It was quite rich and large," he said. "I cannot help but think that it might have contained a considerable ransom."

"It contained my dowry, Lieutenant. I am recently wed and it has taken months for my dowry to arrive."

"I see," the lieutenant replied. "From where did your dowry originate, madam?"

"From my husband."

"And where did he get it?"

"I do not know the source of my husband's finances."

The lieutenant was rapidly losing patience with the word game she was playing. "Come now, madam, even I am aware that every highland clan knows the origins and the connections of the other highland clans."

"There are many lowland Scots," she said.

"Your husband is a lowlander?"

"My marriage was arranged." Jessalyn chose her words very carefully. "It's quite common for women in my position to be betrothed from birth. I know nothing of my husband's connections or allegiances and I've never met his family."

"But they provided your dowry."

"*He* provided it and a factor in Edinburgh arranged the purchase and the transportation of it because the English army stole the one my family provided."

"Is your husband a Jacobite sympathizer?"

"I do not know."

"You don't know your husband's political leaning?"

"I am a woman, lieutenant. I do not concern myself with politics."

"If not politics, what does concern a female lord of a clan?"

"Staying alive." She stared at the lieutenant. "*I* did not abduct your soldiers, Lieutenant." Jessalyn told him.

"You are lord of a clan, madam, you could order it done without participating in the actual abduction."

"I did not abduct your soldiers, Lieutenant, nor did I order it done and I can assure you that no member of Clan MacAonghais or any other highland clan would dare to do so without sanction from the laird."

Lieutenant Burton studied her closely, then signaled several of his men to step forward. "I have the authority to search these premises."

Several of the children began to cry. Jessalyn caught a movement in the corner of her eye and saw Hannah MacCurran, her pick of the litter held tightly in her arms, move behind her mother's skirts. Hannah's eyes seemed as big as saucers and Jessalyn followed her gaze past the lieutenant's shoulder toward the gatehouse where three more riders—all in bright red English uniforms—were entering the bailey. A man tied at the end of a length of rope struggled to keep his balance and to keep up with them as he ran along behind the horse. Droplets of perspiration popped out on Jessalyn's upper lip and the hair at the back of her neck stood up on end at the sight. She knew the man running behind the horses wasn't Neil. She knew that Neil was safely locked in the Laird's Trysting Room, but she didn't know if it was some other member of her clan. She was frightened and it took every measure of her control to keep from wringing her hands and to quell the knocking of her knees. "And I cannot stop you," she said.

"I could order your castle and village torn apart, your livestock slaughtered and your food stores destroyed. Is that what it will take to gain your cooperation?"

"I cannot give you what I do not have," Jessalyn said.

"Tell me, madam, what will happen to your clan if I command my men to do the things I've just described to you?"

"We will starve," Jessalyn answered matter-of-factly. "As we have done since your last visit."

The lieutenant was taken aback by her words and her unshakable courage. He stared at the highlanders, all of whom bore the signs of recent starvation and felt sick to his stomach at the thoughts of what they'd endured. He softened his approach and tried again—this time hoping to sway her with reason instead of threats. "One of the men abducted from the fort is Major Neil Claremont, seventh earl of Derrowford and grandson of the marquess of Chisenden, one of the most powerful men in England. Surely, you have heard of him?"

"I have heard of such a man," she said. "And if he is as powerful as you say he is, perhaps you should enlist his aid in finding his grandson."

"There have been reports that the caravan we followed originated in London not Edinburgh and that it was sent by the marquess. How do you explain that, madam?"

"I cannot explain it. I have never been to London." She gave the lieutenant a half-smile. "My family isn't welcomed at court, so I have never met the marquess or been privy to the idle gossip that I've heard goes on in court circles. I do not know the source of your inaccurate reports."

Lieutenant Burton almost smiled. The woman standing before him was a worthy sparring opponent. A woman of intelligence and wit and courage and loyalty and beauty. He had no doubt that she knew more than she was telling, but he also knew that prodding her further was useless. The lieutenant turned at the sound of the approaching riders and groaned. "That's my commanding officer, Major General Sir Charles Oliver. Madam, please, if you have any knowledge of the missing soldiers, tell me now."

Jessalyn remained silent.

"We appreciate your cooperation, madam." The lieutenant did an about face as the general rode up beside him. He snapped a salute to the general, then turned back to Jessalyn. "I thank you for your cooperation, madam, and I know that if you see any of these men or hear anything concerning their whereabouts, you'll bring it to my attention."

"Of course, Lieutenant," Jessalyn replied, smiling up at him to give credence to the lie.

"Bullocks!" Major General Sir Charles Oliver shouted.

"I beg your pardon, sir?" The lieutenant turned in his saddle to face his commanding officer.

"I said, 'Bullocks!' You won't get any cooperation out of these savages, Burton. Not without a show of force. That's all they understand. Enough of this nonsense. I want answers." Oliver reached down and grabbed hold of the rope tied to the ring on his saddle. He jerked the rope and pulled the man tied to the other end forward.

Jessalyn bit her bottom lip to keep from gasping in horror when she recognized the bloody and battered man as the driver of one of the carts in the caravan. Davina had pointed him out to her and mentioned the fact that he was a Sutherland who had left the highlands and sought work in Edinburgh. She stared at the commanding officer. Spotty Oliver was dangerous. There was nothing in his eyes except contempt. If he uncovered the key to Neil's hiding place, her husband was doomed. Thinking quickly, Jessalyn waited until the general was deep in conversation with the lieutenant, then surreptitiously slipped her hand into her pocket and carefully looped the chain twice so that it would fit around her wrist instead of her neck.

"We encountered the caravan on its way back to Edinburgh." The general said. "And this barbarous creature, this highland spawn, was good enough to volunteer some information about the people who sent it and its contents."

"The lady explained the caravan and its contents to my satisfaction," Lieutenant Burton said.

"She hasn't explained it to *my* satisfaction!" The general shouted. "I am Major General Sir Charles Oliver, commander of His Majesty's Royal Corps of Engineers at Fort Augustus and I wish to hear what this savage highland wench has to say."

She lifted her chin, straightened her back and shoulders and pulled herself to her full height. "I have given my answers to your lieutenant," she answered when the general turned his attention to her.

Oliver's mouth flattened to a thin disapproving line. He turned to Lieutenant Burton. "Did you ask her about the shoes, lieutenant?"

The lieutenant was silent.

"I asked you a question, lieutenant?"

"No, sir. I did not ask her about the shoes."

The general smiled. "Nice shoes, madam." He looked down at Jessalyn's feet.

A chill went up her spine as he repeated the words Neil had said to her the night before.

"You may have noticed that I'm something of a connoisseur of fine clothing." He adjusted the gold braid on the front of his lapel and wiped away an imaginary speck of dust to draw her attention to the fine tailoring. "Your shoes have the look of a London cobbler about them. And your gown is much too fashionable to have been created in Edinburgh. How did you come to possess such finery?"

Jessalyn didn't answer.

"I asked you a question, madam, and I expect an answer." With deceptively calm voice and an almost imperceptible gesture, he nudged his horse forward and knocked her to the ground, then quickly dismounted. He grabbed Jessalyn by the front of her bodice, lifted her to her feet and backhanded her across the mouth. Hannah MacCurran began to cry and her puppy began to whimper. Jessalyn recognized the sounds as she lay sprawled in the dirt. The general moved to stand over her and the MacInnes women formed a circle around him, separating him from his men. "Step back!" he ordered, drawing his sword and placing the tip of it against Jessalyn's bodice front. "Step back and give me room or I'll gut her."

The women opened their ranks.

Oliver pulled Jessalyn to her knees, then drew his sword down the front of her gown, slicing the fabric. "The next cut will be deeper," he warned. "Now, tell me about the shoes! I want to know where they came from."

"Sir! I protest this treatment of a lady!" The lieutenant started forward.

"Stay where you are, Lieutenant." The general glanced at the junior officer. "I'm interrogating this prisoner."

"She isn't a prisoner, sir."

"We are at war with these savages, lieutenant. She's a prisoner if I say she's a prisoner." He turned to Jessalyn. "Now, let's continue. Where did you get the shoes?" General Oliver took another slice of her bodice and this time a line of red droplets beaded against her bodice, staining the white chemise she wore underneath. "My sources tell me that the caravan contained three cartloads of shoes all ordered by the marchioness of Chisenden for the earl of Derrowford. I'd like to see how Derrowford spends his money. Where are they?"

"She doesna know, sir." The cart driver rushed forward.

Oliver stopped him with the point of his sword. "What's

this? Another Scottish hero? Tell me, what doesn't she know?"

"She dinna know about the shoes," he said. "They were a surprise. She doesna know where they're hidden."

"Where are they?" Oliver asked.

"I dinna know. I was . . ."

"You don't know. She doesn't know. What good are you?" General Oliver plunged his sword into the man's chest, twisted the handle, then withdrew it and wiped the blade on the dead man's trews. He cut the rope that had held the man attached to his saddle, but left his hands tied in front of him. "Oh dear," he mocked. "Another dead Scottish hero. Now, who's next?"

Several women let out screams and the puppy began to wiggle and to bark excitedly. Major General Sir Charles Oliver pointed his sword at Hannah. "Shut that dog up!"

Hannah began to cry harder as the puppy slipped out of her hands and began to run around the general's legs. Oliver lifted his foot to kick the dog, but Jessalyn was quicker. She caught hold of the general's silver spur and pulled, upending him. His sword clattered against the ground as he fell and Jessalyn wasted no time. She scooped the puppy up in her arm, struggling with him for a moment or two before she shoved him into Hannah's arms. "Go!" She ordered pushing Hannah away. "Take this dog back to where you got him! Now!" Hannah ran. Jessalyn reached for the general's sword but was brought up short when Oliver grabbed her by the hair. He wrapped the thick braid around his arm and pulled with all his might.

Jessalyn winced in pain but she refused to cry out. She gripped the sword, holding it with both hands as General Oliver got to his knees and pulled her up with him.

"Drop the sword!" he commanded. "Drop it or I'll give the command and have my soldiers shoot every man, woman and child in this village."

Jessalyn didn't budge. She kept the sword pointed at his heart.

"Present arms!" Oliver ordered and the soldiers in the column drew their muskets. The deadly silence seemed deafening. "You may kill me," he told her. "But you and your clan will die."

"Then we all die," Jessalyn told him.

"Sir! You cannot do this!" Lieutenant Burton dismounted and started toward his commanding officer.

"Why not?"

"Because you'll be slaughtering dozens of innocent people. Even if she knew where Major Claremont is hiding, she wouldn't tell us."

"Not even to save her clan?"

"No."

"Then perhaps she'll do it to save one member of it." Oliver surveyed the crowd of women and picked one at random. "Shoot her," he ordered, pointing to Sorcha.

Jessalyn recognized the fear in Sorcha's eyes and dropped the sword.

"That's more like it," the general purred. "Come little savage, we're going on a little journey." He kept his grip on Jessalyn's hair as he pulled her toward his horse, then bent and retrieved the rope he had used on the Sutherland man and tied it around Jessalyn's wrists.

"Sir, what are you doing?" Burton demanded.

"I'm baiting the trap for Claremont."

"How do you know he'll follow?"

"He bought her three hundred pairs of shoes," Oliver replied. "No man would go to that expense to impress a woman. He would only do that if he cares about her. And for her sake, she'd better hope he does." He turned to Jessalyn's kinswomen. "I'm riding out and I'm taking this Scottish rebel with me. If you know where Claremont is, you'd better find him. It's a long way to London and I'm afraid there might not be a whole lot left of her by the time we arrive." He swung up into his saddle, then issued orders to the soldiers. "Give me two hours' head start, then return to Fort Augustus. Once I ride out, shoot anyone that moves." He pointed to the lieutenant. "And start with him."

Jessalyn was so busy running alongside the horse, trying to stay on her feet that she barely heard the first two shots.

Chapter Twenty-eight

Neil's fists were bloodied from pounding on the doors and the walls and he was hoarse from shouting.

Davina was nearly hysterical. "He's taken her, your lairdship! He's got Jessie!"

"Who?" Neil yelled.

"Major General Sir Charles Oliver!" Davina spat out the name. "He shot the lieutenant and Sorcha and he took our Jessie!"

Neil's heart seemed to catch in his throat. Heaven help him but Spotty Oliver had his wife! "How long ago?"

"Hours!" Davina wailed.

Neil began to pound even harder. "Get me out of here!"

"It's no use, yer lairdship." Davina shouted through the secret door. "I've tried every key on my ring. I can't open the door!"

"Break it down! Find Vincenzio!" he ordered. "Do whatever you have to do, but get me out of this room! And hurry!"

"Aye, yer lairdship!" Davina called through the door. "I'll be back with help."

Davina left the entrance to the Laird's Trysting Room and exited through the kitchen. She nearly tripped over Hannah outside the doorway to the kitchen. Hannah held the puppy cradled in one arm, but clutched at Davina's skirt when she attempted to step past. "Have ye seen Neil?" she asked. "I've searched the whole castle and I canna find him."

"Not now, child."

"But I have to find him!"

"I'm trying to get to him myself," Davina assured her.

"Good," Hannah nodded. " 'Cause Jessie told me to gi' my puppy back to him." She wiped at her nose with the back of her hand.

"Och, child!" Davina bent down and used the hem of her skirt to wipe Hannah's tears and her runny nose. "I dinna think Jessie meant ye couldna ha' the puppy. She just wanted ye to get him away before the general hurt him. Ye can keep the wee doggie."

Hannah beamed. "Are ye sure, Davina?"

"I'm sure. Now, run along and play."

Hannah scrambled to her feet and started across the bailey, then turned back to Davina. "Can I keep this too?" She held up the puppy so Davina could see the sparkle of silver glistening in the afternoon sun. "I know she ga' it to Neil when they got married, but she ga' it to my doggie this mornin'. Neil must na want it anymore. Can I keep it?"

Davina squinted. "What is it child?"

"The laird's key," Hannah said. "Jessie put it on my wee little dog. I think it looks pretty. Dinna ye?"

Davina hurried to the child. "I think it's the prettiest thing I've ever seen," she said. "But ye canna keep it."

"Why not?" Hannah asked.

"Because Neil needs it back."

"But I can keep Lady?" Hannah nuzzled the collie's soft fur.

"Aye."

Hannah considered the situation for a moment, then nodded. "Aye." She pulled the silver chain over the puppy's head and handed it to Davina.

Within minutes Davina was back at the secret door.

She inserted the laird's key into the lock and opened the door.

Neil was pacing the length of the room when the mirror suddenly swung open. He rushed the door. "Thank God!" he breathed.

Davina handed him the key.

He lifted the old woman off her feet and swung her around the room. "You wonderful, wonderful woman. Where did you find it?"

"Hannah had it." Davina related the story of how Jessalyn had endured Oliver's punishment in order to sneak the key around the puppy's neck, how she had shoved the dog into the child's arms and ordered Hannah to take it back where she had gotten it as she followed Neil through the mirror and back up the stairs toward the kitchen.

A thought occurred to Neil as he reached the top stair. He turned around and went back to the Trysting Room. Davina followed. "Davina?"

"Sir?"

"What do you know of the laird who built the tunnels and the Laird's Trysting Room so he could court his enemy's daughter?" Neil asked. "Because the MacInnes said the other tunnel led onto his lands, that the daughter used it to reach the Trysting Room. Whose lands are they? Who was the enemy?"

"The Sutherland." She crossed herself at the mention of his name.

"And a portion of his land lies to the south of us, closer to Fort Augustus?"

"Aye." Davina nodded her head. "Takin' that road will cut an hour or so off the journey to Fort Augustus. But the Sutherland is a Government supporter and our mortal enemy. It's death to any MacInnes caught on his land."

"He's not my enemy," Neil said. "I'm a British soldier, loyal to king and country."

"Yer wearin' MacInnes trews."

Neil glanced down at his trousers. "I don't have time to change. I'll just have to take the chance."

"Ye'll need a horse and I canna bring one down the stairs."

"Don't worry," Neil told her. "I know where I can borrow one." Jessalyn had "borrowed" a horse from the Sutherland's stables. That meant the hidden entrance to the tunnel couldn't be too far from the stables. He leaned forward and kissed Davina on the cheek and guided her to the secret door. "I'll bring her back to you," he promised. "Safe and sound. Go now. I'll lock up behind you."

Davina did as he asked and when she passed through the kitchen and entered the bailey once again, she lost no time in finding Ian MacCurran.

"Go!" she ordered. "Find the Ancient Gentlemen and the Munro and tell them what's happened."

Ian shook his head. "There's no need," he told her. "They're already gatherin'."

"Where?"

"They crossed over our border an hour ago. They should be here any time now."

"Find them," Davina instructed. "And tell them to meet his lairdship on the dangerous route. He'll be there waitin'."

Ian nodded and took off running.

Neil locked the door of the Trysting Room behind him, then hurried down the tunnel. He unlocked the door on the left and stepped into the passageway that led to a cavern hidden in the hills separating the MacInnes's land from the Sutherland's. He was careful, once again, to lock the last door behind him before he placed the heavy silver chain around his neck. He didn't bother with candles, he simply kept his right hand on the wall of the passageway until he reached the entrance to the cave. The wood and iron *yett* was covered by a dense thicket that had kept it hidden from view for over a hundred years. The lock was rusty, but it opened smoothly when he unlocked the door. He slipped through the opening, but this time, he left the outer door unlocked. The brush covered door and the cave within would offer him a safe hideaway should he be discovered. Neil pushed his way through the brush and raced down the hills, across the cattle path and onto Sutherland land.

Neil glanced up at the position of the sun. A half an hour or so had passed since he crept into the Sutherland's stable. To his surprise, the mount Jessalyn had taken was saddled and waiting. Neil didn't worry about the possibility of a trap, he simply mounted the horse and rode out of the stables.

He met the Sutherland as he rode onto the path. A tall, whipcord-lean man with snow-white hair, dark eyes and deep grooves on his forehead, the Sutherland blocked the path, forcing Neil to stop or to go around him. Neil stopped.

"I'm William Sutherland," the other man announced. "And you are the earl of Derrowford."

"I am," Neil answered.

"I admire your fine eye for horseflesh, but you're wearing the clothing and the insignia of the MacInneses. I could have you put to death for trespassing on my land and for stealing my horse." The Sutherland pulled a pistol from his belt.

"You must pardon me if I have no time for pleasantries," Neil said. "I'm in a hurry. You may put me to death for trespassing or for stealing your horse as you wish as long as you do it after I kill Major General Sir Charles Oliver for kidnapping my wife." He nudged his horse and started around the Sutherland.

"You may need this." The Sutherland reversed the pistol and handed it to Neil butt end first. "Careful, lad, it's loaded."

Neil accepted the firearm and stuck it in his belt. "Thank you." He leaned forward in the saddle, urging his horse to move.

"No, lad." The Sutherland placed his hand on Neil's reins. "This way. Follow me. It's faster." He turned his horse off the path toward an open field. "And the others are waiting."

Neil followed. "What others?"

"Munro, Ross, Moray, Grant of Glen Craig, my clansmen and other gentlemen of your acquaintance."

Neil glanced across the field where a small army of two to three hundred Scotsmen waited. "I thought you were enemy to Clan MacInnes."

"I'm an ally to the marquess of Chisenden and all his kin." The Sutherland smiled. "That includes Munro and Moray. Grant of Glen Craig is not kin, but he fancied Lady Jessalyn for himself and swore to protect her. Ross is my ally." He glanced at Neil. "The man Sir Charles killed this morning was one of mine."

"The lieutenant?"

"No, the lieutenant is English and he was only slightly wounded. As was Sorcha MacInnes."

Neil had been in such a hurry to reach Jessalyn that he had forgotten to ask after Sorcha and the lieutenant. "How did they come to be wounded?"

"That cur, General Oliver, ordered his men to shoot anyone who moved. The lieutenant and Sorcha MacInnes tried to prevent the general from abducting the MacInnes. The soldiers shot them. The murdered man was a cart driver from Edinburgh and one of my cousins. General Oliver ran him through with a sword." The Sutherland surveyed the assembly. "I can raise more men in a matter of minutes should you think it necessary, but I was wary of assembling too big of an army. I've no desire to be accused of rebelling against the king."

"That won't be necessary," Neil told him. "I only want Oliver."

"What took ye so long?" Auld Tam demanded as Neil and the Sutherland rode up.

"The MacInnes sought to protect me by locking me in the—" He glanced around, unwilling to give away

MacInnes secrets. "By locking me up. It took some time to recover the key."

The Sutherland grinned. "You're an architect, lad. You know all castles have secret rooms. That's no secret."

"The secret is where they put them," the Munro added.

The Sutherland quickly introduced Neil to the clan chiefs. "The other gentlemen you know."

Neil nodded and shook hands with the men. "A state of war still exists between the Government in London and the supporters of the King Over the Water. Make no mistake. Our ride on Fort Augustus—on the commander of Fort Augustus—may well be seen as treason. I intend to get my wife and to punish the bastard who took her, but I cannot ask you to put your necks at risk. You have wives and families of your own."

"Aye, we do," answered the laird of Clan Ross. "That's why ye dinna have to ask."

"We ride to rescue one of our own," Moray said. "The fact that she is the bride of our ally makes her rescue all the more important."

"If rescuing Jessalyn MacInnes from a cur who makes war on women is treason, I'll gladly swing from the gallows!" came the shout from Grant of Glen Craig.

Neil stared at the man. He was fifty if he was a day. Balding and pock-marked. And, Neil had already discovered, it was best to stay upwind of him whenever he opened his mouth to speak.

"My sentiments, exactly, gentlemen!" he exclaimed. "Now, on to Fort Augustus to get her!"

"He'll kill you," Jessalyn said. "But only if I fail to do it myself."

"He may try. But he won't succeed. Besides, I've already won my battle with Neil Claremont. When he rides into Fort Augustus to come to your rescue, he'll be committing an act of treason. And in front of General Wade." Oliver ground his elbow into Jessalyn's spine. He'd dragged her for the first couple of miles, then hauled her up and across his saddle like a sack of grain where he took great pleasure in torturing her. "That's all I want. I want General Wade and the king to see Claremont for the turncoat he is. I want them to see him side with those Scottish savages. I want them to see him as I see him."

She bit her bottom lip until it bled, but she refused to cry out in pain.

"None of this is coincidence," Oliver continued. "He knew General Wade was coming to inspect the fort. He had to have known. That's why he held up the stonemasons. Claremont's failure to complete the wall on schedule and his disappearance, first to London and then to a squalid Scottish castle in the highlands so he could have you warm his bed, was all a ruse. He staged his own abduction and the delivery of the ransom as a way to divide the fort and to divert the men from their construction work. He wanted to make me seem incompetent and unable to command."

"Neil doesn't have to make you seem incompetent or unable to command," she snapped. "You do that all by yourself."

"Careful how you speak to me." Oliver grabbed hold of her braid and yanked.

"Any fool can open his mouth and issue commands," Jessalyn sneered. "You're good at that. You open your mouth and command people to obey you and when they do not, you punish them or you murder them. You envy Neil Claremont because he is something you can never be. He is a leader. Men follow him because they want to, not because they're commanded to."

"Me? Envy Neil Claremont? I think not. You have it all wrong. He always envied me—hated me, really, since we were schoolboys because I was always more handsome than he."

As far as Jessalyn was concerned it was impossible for anyone to ever be more handsome than Neil Claremont and the fact that Spotty Oliver thought he was or ever had been was laughable. "Was that before or after you were named Spotty Oliver?"

Oliver let go of her braid. Her head fell forward against the side of the horse. General Oliver shifted his weight in the saddle and bumped her jaw with his knee with as much force as he could muster. "Your mouth will be the ruination of you—especially when you use it to speak of things you cannot possibly understand."

"I understand that you could never be more handsome than Neil," she said, "because your soul is too ugly and twisted."

"Claremont has found quite a champion in his little Scottish whore, hasn't he? Where did he find you?" He grabbed hold of her braid once again and tugged at it until he forced her to turn her head to look at him.

Jessalyn realized that even though he professed to be well-informed, Major General Sir Charles Oliver had no idea who she was. He believed she was Neil's whore. "*I* found him," she said. "Here at Fort Augustus."

"Impossible," Oliver scoffed. "I've had every pretty whore at the fort. You weren't one of them. I would have noticed."

"Really, General? You think you would have noticed me? You didn't see the women who worked in the fort everyday. You were stupid and careless, General. And the men under your command knew it because you left your fort vulnerable to attack from within. Unlike you, Neil Claremont looks at the women in the camp and sees us for who we are, not what we are. When he looks at us, he doesn't see highland savages or Scottish whores, he sees women with hearts and souls and brains. He tried to warn you about allowing us to come and go as we pleased, didn't he? He tried to warn you that your precious fort was vulnerable but you disregarded his concerns." Jessalyn had learned the details of the raid and Neil's confinement from Magda and Flora who had learned of it from their husbands. "You left the wall unguarded so you could throw a celebration for all the men you were afraid preferred Major Claremont's command to your own. You tried to bribe your men into being loyal to you because you were afraid of Neil Claremont's influence."

Oliver was livid. "He buys whatever he wants! His commission in the army and the right to build Fort Augustus. Even the whores who mock me because of my face powder."

"And you hate him for it because you know in your heart, he could buy and sell you if he chose to do so."

"I am not for sale," Oliver said. "The question is how much did it cost Claremont to purchase you?"

"You're the fashion connoisseur," Jessalyn retorted. "You tell me. According to you, he gave me a king's ransom in shoes." She smiled when she said the words. "He gave me shoes because I had none. He didn't purchase my body. He didn't have to. I'll gladly give him anything he wants."

"I find it amusing to know that he'll be brought down by shoes. He who cares nothing for fashion was rooted out because he was stupid enough to purchase three hundred pairs of shoes at one time. All I had to do to find him was follow the shoes—right to your door."

"And it seems that you even managed to bungle that," Jessalyn reminded him. "You haven't found him—yet."

"Now, I don't have to. He'll find me because I have you," Oliver gloated. "And after I've defeated him, I'll allow him to live just long enough for him to watch me have my way with you. And then, he'll hang. Slowly and painfully. I'm sure you'll enjoy it as much as I."

Jessalyn ignored his threat to rape her. "I'll enjoy watching you face General Wade," she said. "After you lied and told him the wall was complete. What do you think he'll say when he comes to inspect the fort and finds that four-foot gap?"

Oliver called out to the sentry, ordering him to open the gate as they reached Fort Augustus.

"I see you've posted a sentry since the last time we were here. What? No party tonight in honor of General

Wade?" Jessalyn taunted. "Why not? Haven't you completed the wall yet?"

"What are you talking about?" he demanded.

"Your incompetence," Jessalyn told him. "Neil Claremont didn't desert his post. He was abducted. Sergeant Marsden and Corporal Stanhope were taken with him— by force. But you were too consumed with jealousy and hatred to realize that. You've hounded three loyal soldiers, killed an innocent man, ordered your troops to fire on unarmed women and children, and abducted a member of a highland clan with loyal ties to King George. I'd say you're going to get what you want and what you deserve. I'd say you're going to make quite an impression on General Wade."

"You bitch!" He shoved her off the horse. She hit the ground with a thud that knocked the breath out of her. He didn't wait for her to get to her feet, he simply dragged her across the compound. "Your dilemma is that you'll never quite know whether he came because he cares for you or because he hates me," he remarked as he reined his horse to a stop before dismounting.

"There's no dilemma," she said. "When Neil Claremont comes for me it will be because he cares for me and because he hates you. And I won't mind knowing that because I also know that after you receive your just rewards, Neil Claremont will never give you another thought."

Chapter Twenty-nine

"Open the gate!" Neil demanded. "By order of Major Neil Claremont of His Majesty's Royal Engineers."

"I cannot, sir," the sentry called back.

"Is that you, Private Miller?" Neil asked. "You know me. I built Fort Augustus stone by stone and I will bloody well take it down the same way—starting with the man in the gatehouse. Now, open this bloody gate because I won't ask again."

Neil waited for what seemed like a century until the creaks and groans of the massive wooden gates told him that Private Miller was opening them. Neil rode through at the head of his Scottish force, accompanied by the Ancient Gentlemen of Clan MacInnes, and the earls of Sutherland and Ross. He was followed by the Munro, Moray, and Grant of Glen Craig, their men, and several others who had joined the party on the journey to Fort Augustus.

He scanned the parade ground as he entered the fort and discovered the MacInnes chained to the ring of the hitching post in front of the general's quarters. One end of a pair of iron shackles was fastened to the hitching post and the other end was fastened around her ankle. She stood with all of her slight weight on the other leg and Neil could see that her ivory silk stockings were shredded beyond repair and the shackled ankle was badly swollen.

He smiled. If Spotty Oliver had been expecting a poor downtrodden highland laird, he'd been disappointed. The MacInnes had dressed in the manner befitting a highland laird and the countess of Derrowford in the dark blue dress that matched the pair of dark blue shoes decorated with sapphire-studded gold buckles he had placed on her pillow on the second morning following the caravan's arrival. The bodice of her gown was dirty and stained with blood. It was slashed in several places and Neil could see the dark brown lines and tears marring the front of her chemise. What was left of a white lace collar and a length of MacInnes plaid that had decorated her skirt remained. The plaid had been sliced—as if by a sword— but the clan brooch that pinned it to her shoulder held fast. She wore her hair in a braid that was nearly long enough to reach the ground. Bits of bracken and twigs were embedded among the plaits and several sections of hair had pulled free. Her face was dirty and scraped in a half a dozen places and she had bitten her bottom lip. She looked a mess, but she was alive. And as far as Neil was concerned, she had never looked more beautiful. "I have come for Lady Jessalyn Helen Rose MacInnes, Laird of Clan MacInnes." He nodded to Tam who drew his axe and handed it to him.

Neil dismounted and walked over to Jessalyn. He stuck his hand inside his shirt and pulled out a piece of wool and two eagle feathers. "You lost your bonnet, milady," he said as he handed it to her.

Jessalyn's eyes shimmered with tears. I see you found your key." She touched the key hanging on the silver chain around his neck.

Neil bent his head and brushed her lips with his.

"How touching!" Oliver sneered. "How utterly maudlin! I see you've come for your rebel whore."

The highlanders assembled on the parade ground gasped at the insult and every man one of them drew their dirks and prepared to avenge the slur on the reputation of the MacInnes laird.

A muscle ticked in Neil's jaw as Major General Sir Charles Spotty Oliver crossed the threshold of his quarters and stepped outside. He was dressed in a clean, crisp red uniform with shiny brass buttons and lots of gold braid. His sword hung in a scabbard by his side and he wore a pistol in his belt. His boots were polished to a high sheen and his waistcoat and gloves were sparkling white.

"I have come for my *wife*," Neil corrected. "Lady Jessalyn Helen Rose MacInnes, Laird of Clan MacInnes and *countess of Derrowford*, ally and loyal subject of His Majesty the King."

"Your *wife?*" Oliver sneered. "Is that what they call whores in Scotland?"

Neil lunged for the general but Jessalyn grabbed hold of his plaid and held fast. "No, milord, don't!"

Neil turned to look at her. Her blue-gold eyes were huge and shining with love for him. "Please," she said. "He hasn't hurt me."

"I beg to differ." Neil reached out and touched the cut on the corner of her mouth and traced the dark bruise and the swelling along the line of her jaw. "He hit you."

"It doesn't matter," she urged. "What matters is that he abducted me to get you here. He knew you would ride to my aid. He wanted you to. He wanted you to lead a raid on Fort Augustus so he'd have reason to arrest you."

Spotty Oliver could have the confrontation he wanted once Neil got the MacInnes safely out of Fort Augustus. Neil intended to give the commanding officer ample reason to arrest him—if he survived. Because once Neil was sure the MacInnes was out of danger, he intended to kill Major General Sir Charles Oliver for harming her. "Stick out your foot, milady."

She did.

Neil hefted the axe and chopped through the chain.

"Nice shoes," he said softly, staring down at the badly battered blue shoes.

"I lost one of the buckles," she said with a teary chuckle.

"No matter," he told her. "You've three hundred and sixty-two more pairs at home."

"But I like these," she said.

"Then we'll search the heather until we find the missing buckle. Sorry about the manacle," he said. "But we'll get it off you as soon as we get you home. Can you walk?"

She tried, but her ankle couldn't support her weight. Neil started to lift her into his arms, but Jessalyn protested. "I'm the MacInnes. I willna ha' him see me carried."

Neil's heart seemed to swell in his chest at her courage and her strength. He was terrified at how close he had come to losing her. He placed an arm around her waist, then looked at Oliver. "It's over, General. I have what I came for."

"You're out of uniform, major."

Neil glanced down at his clothes. "I'm no longer in possession of my uniform. I wore what I had."

"By adopting the uniform of the area hostiles and by amassing this army and marching on the property of His Majesty King George accompanied by armed hostiles, I declare that Major Neil Claremont, seventh earl of Derrowford, has committed an act of war and is guilty of treason against king and country!" Oliver announced. "Arrest him!"

A half a dozen English soldiers and an equal number of highlanders drew their arms and stepped forward. Neil stood his ground and addressed the English soldiers. "You've no need of your weapons." He looked at the soldiers and then at the highlanders. "Either of you. I've committed no treason against the king or against England. I intend to offer myself into General Wade's custody. I'll submit a full report concerning the events here at Fort Augustus and will face whatever charges General

Wade or the king chooses to bring against me for riding to my wife's defense against an officer of the Crown. But I did not raise an army. The men you see before you are friends, neighbors, and allies of Clan MacInnes and of the king of England. I came for my wife who was taken from her home by force. I have the right to protect my home and my family. As do these men and all of you." Neil stared at the soldiers. "Look at my wife, gentlemen. Observe her treatment at the hands of the commander of this fort. Any one of you knowing this would have done the same. In the words of Grant of Glen Craig, 'If rescuing Jessalyn MacInnes from a cur who makes war on women is treason, I'll gladly swing from the gallows.'"

"Claremont! You will not report to General Wade! You will not destroy my reputation or my career! Fort Augustus is mine to command. *I* decide what General Wade sees!"

"You already have." The group of highlanders parted to allow the Field Marshal and Commander in Chief of all of His Majesty's Forces, Castles, Forts and Barracks in North Britain to ride into view. "And from what I have witnessed here today, I conclude that Major Claremont has the right to settle these serious grievances by choosing his seconds and meeting you upon a field of honor if he so chooses."

Neil shook his head. "As much as I would like to seek personal satisfaction for my wife and for myself, sir, by killing him on a field of honor, I think that having General Oliver stand trial for his offenses in Edinburgh and in London would better serve our country and the people of Scotland. They should know that the Union Act was enacted to benefit both countries. They should be allowed to see that English justice belongs to Englishmen and Scotsmen alike."

General Wade nodded in agreement. "So be it." He turned to the guards and pointed to Oliver. "Arrest General Oliver."

Neil leaned toward Jessalyn and whispered in her ear. "Let's go home, my love."

"No!" Oliver pulled his pistol from his belt and fired.

The impact of the shot spun Neil around. A dozen highlanders and soldiers attempted to draw their weapons, but Jessalyn was faster and closer. She pulled the pistol from Neil's belt as he sank to the ground, pointed it at Spotty Oliver and fired.

Major General Sir Charles Oliver dropped like a stone.

The recoil from the weapon knocked her backward, but Jessalyn kept her grip on it as she got to her knees and crawled to her husband's side. Bright red blood poured from a wound high in his right shoulder. "Neil! Neil! Has he killed ye? Don't ye die on me! Not now that I know ye care! I'm the MacInnes of Clan MacInnes and I order ye to open yer eyes and look at me."

He did. He stared into the startling blue-gold of her eyes. Memorizing her every feature. "I love you."

She leaned over and kissed his lips, his cheeks, his nose, his jaw, his eyes. "Oh, my darling husband, I thought I'd lost ye and I love ye so."

He tried to sit up, but Jessalyn pushed him back down. "Mac, my wife, my dearest heart, the love of my life, you must let me up."

She tried to cradle his head in her lap but found she couldn't lift it. She tried again and failed. "Why?" she asked.

"Because you're hurt, my love. You're bleeding."

She met his gaze, then followed it down to where her left arm was covered in blood. Neil's face seemed to fade before her eyes and she struggled to focus.

"Here, lass, let me help you." Strong arms reached out to cradle her. Jessalyn looked up, recognized the Sutherland colors and promptly fainted.

● ● ●

"I shot him through the heart, dinna I?" She closed her eyes against the pain, then opened them and turned to

Neil. The surgeon had finished dressing her wound and was attending to Neil. General Wade and the clan chiefs had crowded into the surgeon's quarters to watch.

Jessalyn lay back on the cot while Auld Tam and the English blacksmith worked to remove the manacle from around her ankle. "I saw him fall," she insisted, the shock making her more talkative than usual. "I know I hit him."

Relieved to find her wound was slight, that the shot from the pistol had passed through the fleshy part of his shoulder as he leaned toward her and glanced off her arm, Neil shook his head. "You hit him, my love, but not in the heart."

"But that's where I aimed," she insisted as if it were impossible for her to miss, "I aimed for his black heart."

She looked so disappointed, Neil had to bite the inside of his cheek to keep from laughing. "You struck him a little lower."

"I killed him, didn't I?"

"No, I'm afraid not." This time Neil couldn't keep a chuckle from escaping. "But he'll wish you had."

"I don't understand," she said. "Where did I hit him?"

Neil leaned over and whispered the answer in her ear. "Oh!"

General Wade gave her a sympathetic smile. "So, you see, my dear Lady Derrowford, you've been avenged."

"Please," she looked up at the men in the room. "Please, ye mustn't tell anyone that my shot did that. Promise me ye won't."

"Why not, my dear?" The Sutherland asked.

"Because I'm the MacInnes and my clan willna have any confidence in my ability to lead them if they know my aim is so poor."

"Quite so, my dear." General Wade murmured in agreement. "Quite so."

The men in the room swore they would keep their silences, but the women in the fort made no such promises. By nightfall, it was rumored that if Major General Sir Charles Oliver survived his wound, his voice would be much higher and he would no longer need to seek the nightly companionship of women.

Chapter Thirty

Three months later

Jessalyn twisted the lace handkerchief into a tight little knot, then unfolded it and twisted it again.

"Relax, my love." Neil placed his hand over hers and wrestled the mangled scrap of lace out of her grasp. "I've never known you to be so nervous. Remember that you're the laird of Clan MacInnes, the woman who brought an English lord to his knees again last night. He's merely a king and a German one at that."

"I'm not nervous about meeting King George," she protested. "I'm worried about meeting your grandparents."

Neil smiled, then lifted her chin with his index finger and turned her to face him. "You've nothing to worry about. They love you already."

"But he's the king-maker and I've heard that in society, your grandmother is equally powerful . . . What other woman could manage to have three hundred and sixty-five pairs of shoes made in only one month?"

"Can this be my fearless MacInnes talking?" He laughed.

"Neil, this is serious! What if I do something wrong? What if my manners aren't good enough for London society? What if I trip on this train and fall on my face or use the wrong fork? What if the king can't understand me? I canna bear the thought of embarrassing yer family."

"Don't worry," he reassured. "Everything will be fine."

Major General Sir Charles Oliver recovered sufficiently from his wounds to be present at his own court martial. He was currently locked in the dungeon at Holyrood House in Edinburgh, awaiting trial for the murder of Gordon Sutherland and the attempted murders of Lieutenant Joseph Burton, Sorcha MacInnes and the earl and countess of Derrowford.

The king had requested an audience with the earl and countess of Derrowford regarding the incident at Fort Augustus immediately following the court martial in Edinburgh and after waiting two months for their wounds to heal, Neil and Jessalyn had made the journey to London. They had arrived in the wee hours of the morning and although Neil's townhouse was a bachelor establishment, they had gone straight there instead of the marquess and marchioness of Chisenden's home to prepare for the afternoon reception.

His grandparents' household was in chaos. The marquess and marchioness were hosting a ball in their honor after the reception and Neil had declined their invitation to stay there. A household preparing for the event of the season was no place to rest. And the MacInnes needed rest. He was worried about her. The truth was that Jessalyn was terrified of meeting his grandparents and of being presented at court. So terrified, he had caught her sobbing in the bath.

Neil gently squeezed her hand. "It's time."

Jessalyn looked up as the Lord Chamberlain announced her. "Lady Jessalyn Helen Rose MacInnes, Laird of Clan MacInnes and seventh countess of Derrowford." She left Neil's side and stepped forward. After carefully making her curtsey to the king, Jessalyn repeated the words she'd been rehearsing for weeks. "Your Majesty, I stand before you as the Scottish laird of Clan MacInnes and ask to pledge my fealty and to swear allegiance to you, my sovereign, in this year of Our Lord, seventeen hundred sixteen."

King George offered her his hand and Jessalyn kissed it.

"Arise, Laird MacInnes, our most loyal and beloved ally," the king announced.

Jessalyn arose, then offered the king another curtsey and carefully backed away. It was over. She had survived.

Jessaalyn heaved a sigh of relief as her husband beamed with pride.

The marchioness of Chisenden crossed the marble floor of the ballroom, dodging dancers as she hurried to where her husband and the First Lord of the Treasury stood talking. The ball celebrating Neil's marriage to Jessalyn was in full swing and Chisenden Place was near to bursting at the seams with the cream of London society. The marchioness had issued five hundred invitations and nearly everyone who had received an invite to the event of the Season was in attendance. Charlotte knew everyone there. She had prepared the guest list herself and she was quite sure that the name of the blond young doxy who had entered the house on the arm of Viscount Hamilton had not been on it.

She walked up to her husband, placed her hand on his sleeve to get his attention, then stood on tiptoe to whisper in his ear.

"What?" He turned to look at his wife. "You're certain it's her?"

"Of course, I'm certain," the marchioness replied. "I've seen her before and I was close enough to recognize her. Kingsley said Viscount Hamilton brought her."

"What impudence!" the marquess declared loud enough to be overheard. "How dare that young pup bring her here!"

Lord Chisenden patted his wife's arm. "Don't worry, my dear, I'll take care of this."

"Too late," Charlotte announced with a sense of dread. "Look."

The marquess turned to the dance floor in time to see the couples forming the squares. "My god, she'll be paired with Neil before we can stop her!"

The marchioness sighed. "I knew she wouldn't give him up so easily."

"Buck up, my dear. It's too late for us to intervene. We'll just have to trust the boy to handle it as quickly and discreetly as possible." He reached down and clasped his wife's hand.

"That bodice is cut too damned low."

"I thought you liked it, milord." Jessalyn curtseyed low in front of her husband as the musicians strummed the first notes of the dance.

"I do." Neil bowed to her, taking advantage of the exquisite view her bodice afforded him. "And so does every other man in this room. That's the problem."

"No one else has paid me the slightest attention," Jessalyn replied. "You're the only one hovering over my bosom."

"And I intend to keep it that way." Neil looked down at his wife and even the brilliance of his smile wasn't enough to disguise the concern in his eyes as he noted the bright spots of color on Jessalyn's cheeks. "Are you quite sure you're feeling all right? You look feverish." He reached out to place his palm against her forehead, and Jessalyn gently nudged it aside.

"Of course, I'm feverish." Jessalyn laughed. "I've been dancing all night."

"And you've been ill," Neil reminded her.

"I was not ill," she protested. "I was recuperating from a bullet wound."

"Just the same . . ." he began.

"And so were you," she cut him off.

"I'm a man," Neil replied.

"And I'm the Mac—"

"Innes of Clan MacInnes," he finished for her. "I know. And if I remember correctly, Laird MacInnes, you promised to rest."

She smiled up at him. "One more dance."

He shook his head.

"Please, Neil . . ."

He stared down at her and the love he saw shining in the depths of her dark blue eyes nearly took his breath away. When Jessalyn looked at him like that he could deny her nothing and both of them knew it. "All right," he agreed, "one last dance and then we retire to our bed-chamber."

"Where I'm sure to get plenty of rest," Jessalyn rolled her eyes at him to let him know she knew exactly why he thought she looked feverish.

"Saucy wench!" Neil laughed. "You keep that up and I guarantee you get nothing but rest."

"Hah!" She moved in close as she followed the steps of the dance, then turned to her next partner and whirled away before her husband could form a suitable retort.

Neil reached for the hand of the next woman in line, automatically bowing to her as required by the dance.

"Hello, my love."

He recognized the sultry voice and dropped her hand as if she'd burned him. "Deborah," he answered curtly. "I don't recall seeing your name on the guest list. What are you doing here?"

"I had to come," she whispered. "Oh, Neil, I've missed you so much and I'm so angry with you for not coming to see me." She moved in as close to him as she dared, then pouted prettily and squeezed a few tears from her eyes.

Neil stepped back and nearly collided with another dancer. "Our association is at an end, Deborah. I'm sure the marchioness made it quite clear that I've no desire to see you again." The marquess had relayed the story of the marchioness's extraordinary visit to Neil's former mistress over drinks at the club earlier in the day.

"I didn't believe her," Deborah told him.

"You should have," Neil replied. "She spoke the truth."

"Why?" Deborah demanded. "Other married men keep mistresses, why should you be any different?" She nearly screamed in frustration. In moments she'd have to change partners and when that happened she knew Neil would have her escorted off the premises. Thinking quickly, she let go of Neil's hand, heaved a dramatic sigh and sank to the floor in a graceful swoon that would do justice to any actress on the London stage. Neil made no effort to catch her as Deborah slid to the floor at his feet and lay amid a puddle of pale blue satin. Several onlookers let out a cry of alarm as the music came to an abrupt halt and the dancers spun to a stop in an effort to keep from trampling her.

"This melodrama is extremely bad form, Deborah," he muttered beneath his breath, loud enough for Deborah's ears but not loud enough to be overheard. "Even for you."

"Neil?" Jessalyn rushed to his side. "What happened? Is she all right?" She started to drop to her knees, but Neil reached for her arm and kept her from attending to the fallen woman. "Neil! Let go. She's . . ."

"She's fine," he answered. "Aren't you, Deborah?"

Jessalyn looked up at her husband, pinning him with her gaze. "Did you say Deborah?"

He nodded.

"Your mistress?" Jessalyn asked.

"My *former* mistress," Neil replied. "Our intimate association ended before I left for Scotland."

"It did not!" Deborah opened her eyes and shot into sitting position.

"Of course it did," Neil told her. "Because I take my marriage vows seriously. Because I love my wife with all my heart and because I would never knowingly do anything to hurt her."

Jessalyn's eyes sparkled with emotion.

"You continued to support me. Even after you married *her*." Deborah practically spat the word.

Jessalyn stared at Deborah, then looked at Neil. "Did you?"

"I'm afraid so," he admitted. "I asked the marquess to handle the details of ending my association with Deborah and to make certain she was well provided for until she settled on a new protector. I gave the note to Ranald when you sent him to Edinburgh."

Jessalyn beamed at her husband. "That's as it should be. I wouldn't want it said that you were miserly to your mistress or allowed her to suffer until she could find a new man." She looked down at Deborah. "My husband has a deep sense of duty that extends to everyone he knows. Now, get up, Madam. You shame yourself by lying on the floor."

Deborah pushed herself to her feet. "How dare you dictate to me!" She glared at Jessalyn. "I'm an Englishwoman while you're nothing but a highland savage!"

"Aye," Jessalyn agreed. "I'll not deny that I'm Scottish by birth or that some might call me a highland savage. But I'm also the *English* countess of Derrowford and I outrank you in society and in my husband's heart. Go home, Madam. You do yourself no good here. Your presence is an insult to me, to my husband, to my family and to the gentleman who brought you."

"But . . ." Deborah protested.

"Cut your losses," Neil advised, turning away from his former mistress and offering his arm to his wife. "My patience and my generosity has ended."

"Come, Deborah, do as the earl says." Viscount Hamilton put an arm around her waist and steered her away off the dance floor. "My deepest apologies, sir. I had no idea . . ." He nodded to Neil. "And to you, milady," he turned to Jessalyn. "Only a misbegotten fool would mistake you for a highland savage."

•   •   •

"Well," Jessalyn sighed as she snuggled close to her husband. "It's been quite a day."

"That it has," Neil agreed. "And I fervently hope never to have another like it."

"It wasn't all bad," Jessalyn reminded him. "I did become a beloved ally to a king. And I did manage to keep from taking my dirk to Deborah."

Neil laughed. "I was quite impressed with your restraint and very grateful that you didn't take your dirk to Deborah or to me—especially in light of what you did to Spotty Oliver."

Jessalyn pushed herself up on her elbow so she could look at him. "Oh, Neil, I don't blame you for Deborah's appearance at the party."

"It might have been avoided if I had spoken with her in private when we arrived in London."

Jessalyn was thoughtful. "I dinna think so."

"Do ye not?" He mimicked her burr.

She shook her head. "To think I was jealous of her once."

"No longer, I hope?" He pulled her closer and planted a kiss on the tip of her nose.

"No," Jessalyn said softly. "Now, I feel sorry for her."

Neil was surprised. "You can't possibly . . ."

"Oh, but I do." Jessalyn was serious.

"Why?"

"Because she lost you, Neil. Because she'll never share your kisses or hold you deep within her. Because I couldna imagine how I could live without them."

Her words embedded themselves deep within his heart and tears of gratitude shimmered in his eyes as he rolled her to her back and began to show her how very much he loved her.

Ten days later Jessalyn stood at the window of the breakfast room over looking the marchioness of Chisenden's formal gardens.

Rebecca Hagan Lee

"You're up very early, my dear. Is your wound bothering you?"

Jessalyn turned to find the marquess of Chisenden standing by her side. He had dark, almost black eyes, thin lips, an aquiline nose and lively dancing eyebrows. He wasn't as classically handsome as Neil, but Jessalyn knew that in his own day, he had left a trail of broken hearts behind him. "No, my lord. It's completely healed."

"What do you think of my lady's garden?" he asked.

"It's beautiful."

"But . . ."

"It's truly beautiful," she answered.

"But not as lovely as the purple and white heather blooming on the hills around Glenaonghais, is it?"

She looked up at him, questions in her eyes.

"We've been on such a whirlwind of soirees and balls and official functions that I'm afraid I haven't had the opportunity to spend as much time getting acquainted with you as I'd like." He smiled. "I suppose Neil is in his studio?"

"Yes," Jessalyn nodded. "He wanted to take advantage of the morning light."

"What's he doing up there?" the marquess asked.

Jessalyn wrinkled her face. "Painting a portrait of me."

"And Charlotte?"

"*Grandmere* is still sleeping," Jessalyn replied, addressing the marchioness in the manner Lady Chisenden preferred.

"Then you won't object to indulging an old man for a moment?"

"Of course not," she said. "I haven't had the opportunity to thank you for my dowry and for all you've done for me and for Clan MacInnes."

"No thanks are necessary," he said, firmly.

"But, sir . . ."

The marquess offered Jessalyn his arm. "Come with me and I'll explain." He led her into his study, ushering her into the room before closing the door behind them. "There," he said, looking up at the mantel.

Jessalyn gasped as she gazed up at the portrait hanging above the massive marble fireplace. It was like looking in a mirror. The woman in the portrait looked enough like her to be her twin. They shared the same eyes and hair and complexion. The same bone structure. It was uncanny.

"She was the first Scottish countess of Derrowford. My wife, Lady Helen Rose MacInnes." He smiled at Jessalyn. "She was your grand-aunt. Your grandfather's youngest sister and your father's aunt. I believe you carry a part of her name."

"Yes," Jessalyn said. "But I didn't realize . . ."

"She's been dead a long time." The marquess sighed. "Fifty-two years ago this past March. She died giving birth to our son. He survived her by a fortnight. I'm sure your father didn't remember her. He was a baby when she died and most of the members of Clan MacInnes had no knowledge of my connection to it. But Callum was Laird so he had been told. He knew." He turned to Jessalyn. "I had been waiting fifty-two years for the opportunity to repay my debt of gratitude to Clan MacInnes for giving me Helen Rose. I was thrilled when Callum wrote and asked me if I could help save his clan and even more thrilled with the prospect of wedding Neil to you. I wanted to be a part of Clan MacInnes again. Everyone else may have forgotten Helen Rose, but I never have." His black eyes shimmered with unshed tears. "I loved her with the full passion of youth and I treasure the memories of our time together even now."

"Did she like it here in London?" Jessalyn asked.

"She was happy when we were together. But I was young and terribly ambitious and often away from home. I think she tried very hard to like London, but she longed for Scotland. I could see it in her eyes, hear it in her voice." He turned back to the portrait. "I should have taken her home. But Scotland was so wild then, much wilder than today and I worried about her . . ." He let his words drift off. "Most of the furniture and the household goods, paintings, candlesticks, tapestries, and dishes I sent to you belonged to Helen Rose. They were her dowry. You thought I was being exceptionally generous, but I was really paying a debt by returning to you what belonged to Helen Rose's family."

"Louis?" The marchioness of Chisenden opened the door to her husband's study. She expected him to be alone and she nearly retreated when she heard him speaking to someone, but his words compelled her to stay and listen even if it meant the pain of hearing aloud just how much he had loved his first wife.

"Having you here is almost like having Helen Rose back again. You have her beauty and her courage and her loyalty and her heart. I've watched you for a week now and sometimes I forget that you're Jessalyn. I expect you to look at me with love and passion in your eyes the way Helen Rose did, but then I remember that I'm an old man now and that you're in love with Neil, that you're Neil's wife and I realize that no matter how much I loved her, it's time—past time—for me to let her go." A sound caught his attention and the marquess glanced over to where the door of his study stood open. He stared at it and caught a glimpse of Charlotte hovering beside it. He focused his attention on her. "I have a wife who looks at me with love and passion in her eyes—even after fifty-one years. And it's time that I let her know that I love her every bit as much as I loved Helen Rose and more. We had a son and we have a grandson and we've built a wonderful life together. And although it took me a while to realize it, I've loved her for fifty-one years." The marquess walked over to his desk and removed a teak box from a drawer and handed it to Jessalyn. "These belonged to Helen Rose," he said. "Take them and wear them in remembrance with the knowledge that someday they'll belong to your daughter."

Jessalyn took the box. "I'll cherish them." She walked over and kissed the old man's cheek.

Outside the study, the marchioness of Chisenden quietly closed the door. A flood of tears cascaded down her face. In the fifty-one years they had been married, he had never hinted that he loved her except in moments of great passion. Today, he'd told her aloud.

Epilogue

"Are you going to leave me now that you're a wealthy woman?" Neil watched as his wife opened the teak box once again and studied the small fortune in jewels his grandfather had given her.

"Of course not." She lay on the sofa in his studio, modeling while he sketched.

"Then what are you thinking?"

"I was thinking about London and wondering how long it will be before I learn to enjoy it." She glanced at the wood and paper model of a cathedral Neil had made.

"Don't learn to enjoy too much of it," he said, "because you won't be seeing it that often."

"I thought you wanted to build palaces and cathedrals and rows of affordable houses for the working people. I thought you loved the idea of rebuilding London."

"I do," he said, quietly. "But I've learned that I can build something so much more important in Scotland."

Jessalyn sat up and looked at him. "What's that?"

"A home and a family and a country and a life with you."

"Oh, Neil . . ." She began to cry. "You hate Scotland."

"I did once," he admitted. "But that was before I married you. London doesn't hold the allure for me that it once did because now my home is in Scotland."

"Are you sure?" she asked. "Because I'm certain that I can learn to like London if I try hard enough."

He smiled. "I'm sure. I resigned my commission in the army, but I agreed to work with General Wade on the completion of Fort Augustus. And once that project's done, I intend to finish this portrait of you and hang it above the bed in the Laird's Trysting Room. Then I intend to concentrate on Castle MacAonghais. I've a lot of work to do if we're to have it ready for the king's visit next summer. I've designed a system of bells to be used to summon the servants that I'd like to try and . . ."

"The king is visiting Castle MacAonghais? Next summer? But I'll be . . ."

"Well recovered, I hope," Neil leaned over and kissed her. "From the birth of our first child."

"You knew?"

"I guessed."

Jessalyn took his face in both her hands and stared into his extraordinary green eyes. "Are you sure this is what you want?"

Neil grinned. "Verra sure," he growled in his Scottish burr. "I love being husband to the MacInnes. I've come to love and treasure the people of Glenaonghais. I've earned my place in the clan and I'm looking forward to helping the highlands grow."

"How do ye intend to do that?"

"Weel," he teased. "We're going to have lots of babies and I'm going to go into business with the Munro."

"The Munro?"

"Aye," he told her. "We're going to bottle and sell the finest whisky in all of Scotland."

"Scotland's a poor country. Who are ye plannin' to sell it to?"

"England and France and the rest of the world." His eyes lit up with excitement at the idea.

"It'll never work," Jessalyn said. "No one but Scots have ever liked the stuff."

"No one outside of Scotland has ever tried it," Neil

replied. "But once they get a taste of that tiniest hint of heather mixed with honey, they'll buy it by the barrels. By the time we have grandchildren, Glenaonghais Scots whisky will have made you a very rich laird."

"Are ye sure?" she teased.

"Verra sure," he said. "Wait and see."

And she did.

AUTHOR'S NOTE

The history of Clan MacInnes or Clan MacAonghais in *A Hint of Heather* is fictional. There was an actual Jacobite Clan MacInnes living near Loch Ness in 1716 and I have made use of its clan motto, badges, lament, traditional holdings and parts of its history to lend authenticity to my Clan MacInnes, but the allegiances and political history of the clan is entirely imaginary.

While I've made every effort to remain true to the actual history of the region by keeping traditionally Whig clans Whig and traditionally Jacobite clans Jacobite, the characters in this story and the allegiances and political histories of these particular clans and the military personnel and accounts of the construction of Fort Augustus are entirely my own invention or have been altered to fit the story.

Rebecca Hagan Lee

Rebecca Hagan Lee has had many different jobs, earning her beads of experience on the necklace of life along the way, but her desire to write was constant. After graduating from college, she set out to make her mark in the world of television journalism but somewhere along the way, she decided she was a small-town girl at heart and settled in a town where the media consisted of a weekly newspaper and an AM radio station.

Seeking a creative outlet, she turned to writing romance and began to write stories far different from those in the world of television news, but not that far removed from the hundreds of episodes of *Daniel Boone* she watched growing up. She decided to create stories where good guys win, bad guys lose, prostitutes have hearts of gold, and the heroes and heroines who fall in love and persevere are richly rewarded with incredibly bright futures and happy endings. In her world, heroines don't die or get killed to make way for the next episode's new love interest. Her heroines get their men and help them become ideal husbands, lovers, friends, and fathers. In her world, Mingo, Jarrod, Nick, Heath, Ben, Adam, Hoss, Little Joe, and Matt Dillon would never have remained single all these years.

Rebecca lives in a small Southern town with her husband, three dogs, one cat, and two horses. She's active in local writing groups and community theater. When she's not seated at the computer writing, she can usually be found among friends and at the stable.

Her next Berkley/Jove romance, *Once a Lady*, is scheduled for release in 2001.

Rebecca enjoys hearing from her readers. You can contact her through her Web site at *www.rhaganlee.com* or by writing to her at: Rebecca Hagan Lee, c/o The Berkley Publishing Group, 375 Hudson Street, New York, New York 10014.

Turn the page for a preview of

A Rogue's Pleasure

Coming in November from Jove Books!

Anthony dozed. When he awoke, it was dark. Still slouched against the seat, he looked across to Phoebe and Lady Tremont. Heads pillowed on each other's shoulder, they appeared to be sleeping soundly.

He shut his eyes and willed himself to drift off. If only his fatigue, his omnipresent ennui, were the sort that slumber could sate. Still, sleep could be a beautiful escape. Sometimes.

Horses—two of them, he thought—thundered toward them. He bolted upright.

"Halt! Prepare to stand and deliver!"

Seconds later, the coach shuddered to a standstill, pitching Phoebe and her mother forward. Anthony threw out an arm to keep them from falling onto the floor.

Lady Tremont shook him off. "Lord Montrose, whatever is going on? Why have we stopped?" She drew back the window curtain and squinted outside.

Anthony reached for his carriage pistol. He unbuttoned his jacket and slipped his pistol into an inside pocket. "Ladies, I believe we are about to be robbed.

The carriage door flung open. Seconds later, they were staring down the butt of a pistol.

A bald head and a set of massive, crooked shoulders

filled the narrow doorway. A black patch covered the intruder's left eye.

"Out ye go, if ye please. Me master, One-Eyed Jack, craves a word wi' ye," the aging cyclops informed them cheerfully, his index finger poised on the trigger of the cocked pistol.

"My fiancée has a delicate constitution." Anthony shot Phoebe a look, warning her to silence. "I will go with you, only permit her to remain here to look after her mother."

The hulk shook his head. " 'Er too." He studied the thankfully unconscious Lady Tremont. "She can stay."

This fellow is more intelligent than he appears. Hovering between outrage and amusement, Anthony disembarked and helped a shaking Phoebe down the carriage steps.

The moon slipped free of a bank of clouds, silhouetting a slight figure in a slouched hat holding Anthony's driver, Masters, at gunpoint. One-Eyed Jack? The second highwayman turned toward them, and Anthony saw that he also wore an eye patch.

Why, One-Eyed Jack was no more than a lad and not a very sturdy one at that. The boy's long legs were encased in snug breeches that might have been painted on. A dark swallow-tailed coat hugged a trim waist and slim hips. Under more congenial circumstances, Anthony might have found himself asking the young man for the name of his tailor.

One-Eye slipped the driver's weapon into his coat pocket. Squaring his narrow shoulders, he sauntered toward them, his own pistol held awkwardly in his gloved hand.

Eyes wide, Phoebe turned to Anthony. "For pity's sake, don't let him ravish me."

One-Eyed Jack halted a few paces in front of them, and Phoebe swayed. Lantern light showed the boy's cheeks to be as smooth as a newborn's. The fragile felon wasn't even old enough to shave. Anthony suppressed a chuckle, confident that Phoebe would survive the adventure with her well-guarded virginity intact.

"Good evening, milord, milady."

"I am One-Eyed Jack, first knight of these roads," the lad informed them in a low, husky voice.

"So I gathered," Anthony replied, amused by the display of adolescent braggadocio.

The aging Goliath unwedged the pistol from the small of Anthony's back and stepped in front of him, proffering a hat.

"Yer purse and be quick about it, guv."

Careful to keep his pistol concealed inside his jacket, Anthony removed his purse. He dropped the small leather satchel into the hat. When the gunman grunted toward the gold pocket watch dangling from his waistcoat, Anthony obligingly parted with it as well.

One-Eyed Jack smiled at Phoebe. Two rows of even, white teeth flashed in the darkness. "Now your turn, milady."

"M-me? But I have no valuables."

Both footpads stared at the beaded reticule dangling from her wrist.

"Oh this?" Her voice trembled. "But this is just pin money."

"In that case, you should have no problem parting with it," the boy sneered.

Sniffling, Phoebe slipped the reticule off and tossed it into the crown of the hat.

The boy aimed a forefinger at her throat. "I'll have that necklace as well."

She turned pleading eyes on Anthony. "Great Grandmama's pearls. I was to wear them at our wedding. All the Tremont brides do."

Anthony's gaze never left the boy's face. "I promise I shall retrieve them for you ere then, my dear. With any luck, you shall have them to wear to this lad's hanging."

He had the satisfaction of seeing the boy's pupil dilate, nearly filling the turquoise iris of his uncovered eye.

Anthony's satisfaction proved short-lived.

One-Eyed Jack stepped up to Anthony. He lowered the pistol barrel over Anthony's trouser front and cocked the hammer.

"Your lady's jewels in exchange for the family jewels. Seems a fair trade to me." He poked the pistol into Anthony's manhood.

Anthony swallowed hard. One-Eyed Jack was soft as new cheese, but he knew how to hit a fellow where it hurt. He'd underestimated the boy, a mistake he'd not make the next time they met.

"Phoebe, do as he says," Anthony ordered in a low, determined voice.

"But . . ."

"I'd suggest you get your lady bird in hand, milord." The boy grinned. "Otherwise you'll be able to do her scant service in the future."

Anthony looked down at the weapon lodged between his legs and silently prayed that One-Eyed Jack didn't have an itchy trigger finger.

"For God's sake, Phoebe, I've had this a damned sight longer than you've had those blasted pearls," he snapped when she still hesitated.

Phoebe reached behind and unfastened the necklace's clasp. She dropped the pearls into One-Eyed Jack's open palm, tears striping her pale cheeks.

One-Eye removed the weapon and stuffed the pearls into his coat pocket. "If 'tis any consolation, milady, these baubles will be put to good use. And," he added with a wicked grin, "I have left your lord his to console you."

"To the carriage, the lot o' ye, and be quick about it." The elder highwayman gave Masters a shove toward the coach.

The driver's knees buckled.

"For the luv of . . ." The hulk turned to Anthony. "Don't just stand there. 'Elp 'im."

Anthony shrugged even as his brain calculated his odds of success. "Can't I'm afraid. Bad back."

Cursing, the highwayman slung Masters's limp arm around his beefy neck and lugged him toward the coach.

Phoebe lost no time in responding to the directive. She picked up her skirts and fled.

One-Eyed Jack's gaze darted between Anthony and the coach.

"W-why are you still standing 'ere?" He gestured to the coach with his pistol. "Go . . . now."

Smiling, Anthony advanced a step. "But I've no wish to end this encounter . . . just yet."

Anthony lunged forward. Locking both arms around the boy's spare torso, he slammed him to the ground. He pinned One Eye's slender wrists above his head and squeezed. The pistol slipped from the highwayman's grasp.

"Let go!"

Even for a stripling, the boy was delicate as a sparrow, not nearly sturdy enough for such rough pursuits. Easily securing the joined wrists with one hand, Anthony pocketed the pistol.

He smiled maliciously into the frightened face, just inches below his own. "Well, my fine lad, alone at last." He clamped his palm over the boy's mouth. "What, nothing to say?"

The taunt seemed to bring his captive to life. His fingers curled into fists, his arms straining to break Anthony's hold.

Laughing, Anthony remarked, "Well, One-Eyed Jack, for a fierce knight of the road, you certainly fight like a girl."

Like a girl.

Anthony stared down at his prisoner, examining the small, flushed face beneath the hat with a critical eye. The features were as finely wrought as those of a Dresden china figurine, the uncovered eye lushly lashed and set beneath a delicately arched brow. Could it be that Jack was really a Jacqueline in disguise? The body beneath his felt soft in all the right places. He uncovered his captive's mouth in order to better examine the softly curving lips.

"Get off me this instant, y-you . . . you big bully!"

Intrigued, Anthony replied, "All in good time, my little highwayman. But first, I think I'll have a closer look at you."